THE CYGNUS FOLD

FOLD SERIES BOOK 4

NICK ADAMS

Elliptical
Publishing

PROLOGUE

THE SATELLITE TIGNAR, ORBITING GAS GIANT REA, TRAXX SYSTEM

POL'S LIMB hovered over the abort toggle as she studiously watched the lander's level indicator. The craft dropped quickly towards the satellite's regolith. She knew that on landing, any more than five degrees off camber and she would barely have a second to react.

Bang. The abrupt and savage so-called landing shocked her body and took every centimetre of the suspended cradle's impact parameters. She almost hit the toggle by mistake as she realised that an actual landing was considerably harsher than any of the many simulations she'd undertaken over the previous seasons.

One degree – one point two – one point two eight. The craft finally settled and was still, well within tolerance, so Pol was able to shut down the engines and relax a little.

As the noise of the engines died away, she was immediately aware of the drag on Tignar. Nowhere near as high as on Callamet, but just enough to keep you secured to the surface.

Disconnecting the cradle restraints, she slid over to one of the two small portal windows and peered out. The grey rocky surface stretched away to the horizon only about a kilometre away, so she turned and went to the opposite side of the cabin and checked that window.

The abnormality was close and she had to push her helmet against the glazing to see the top of it. She wondered at the size and scale of this peculiar monolithic irregularity in the long ovoid moon's surface. Being the first Callametan to visit another spacial body in their young planet's existence was a proud moment for her, and being able to visit the Cathedral of the Gods was both exciting and frightening at the same time.

There had been many unwelcome machinations from some of the more devout cults, and on several occasions it seemed the project was doomed as benefactors came under pressure and began to lose their nerve.

The scientists had prevailed eventually, but at times Pol had wondered if all the years of training would ever be put to use.

Pol raised her four arms and pulled herself through into the survival chamber and began preparing for the first traverse. Although she would retain the same helmet, the traversing suit was much more heavy duty and having six limbs meant it took a little time and effort to dress.

When she was ready and with systems and pressure checks done, she proceeded into the airlock and cycled the atmosphere. A second suit check and she was able to open the outer door and slowly slide down the exterior ladder. She looked down as her circular legs hit the surface. A cloud of dust rose up about a metre around her, slowly settling back again, and she knew walking carefully would be best to avoid covering herself in the abrasive particles.

Turning and staring up at the massive abrupt elevation before her, she nodded and trudged forward, leaving two-centimetre-deep circular suit leg prints in the regolith.

The landing zone had been chosen because it was reasonably flat and there were several smaller protrusions on this side before you got to the main one. The first of these she reached after about twenty etos of walking.

It was still about fifty metres tall and the sides almost sheer.

She stood and gazed at it for a few moments, letting the cameras on the front of her suit get the best images they could. It seemed strange, as close up it was obvious the sides weren't completely smooth as previously thought. An almost regular corrugation ran straight up the side, where perhaps the wind had caused the dust to form itself into this almost manufactured appearance.

Retrieving a small hopper and a scraper from a pouch on her suit, she stepped forward and scraped off a sample of the dust. She swore under her breath as a large piece broke away, knocking the hopper out of her gauntlet, and both dropped almost leisurely to the ground.

Bending down to ground level in these suits was difficult; although she'd practised it a lot, she'd fallen over a lot too. As she bent down and her eyes came level with the hole where the lump had broken away, she gasped and stepped back.

Inside the hole was a flat shiny metallic surface, a deep maroon in colour, and the corrugations were still there, only sharper and at ninety-degree angles.

That's impossible, she thought, *it looks manufactured.*

She pushed the scraper back into the hole and levered. More dust and regolith lumps fell away, revealing more of the metalled surface.

Is it a building? she thought to herself, gazing up at it and then over to the main one.

'Because if they are,' she said aloud in her suit, 'then that one is absolutely gargantuan.'

It took her another fifteen etos to trudge her way over to the main abnormality, passing three other smaller ones on the way.

Looking up the sheer side of this one gave her acrophobia. She knew from the surveys done of the moon that this was over three kilometres high. It was also at a slight angle, not straight up.

Perhaps there was a severe quake that caused the foundations to fail and the buildings were abandoned before our race even existed, she thought.

She wandered along the base of it, looking for any indication of where a door might have been.

Maybe it sank and the doors are all below ground level now.

The same corrugated surface was here too and she ran her gauntlet along the side as she walked, bumping her gloved fingers along the ridges until she found a faint arched area that was for some reason entirely flat.

A sudden voice in her helmet made her jump. It was the operational control centre back on Callamet and because of the distance involved, they were only just congratulating her on the successful landing. It would be a long wait before they would know anything about her discovery and the same again for a reaction to get back to her.

She began scraping away around the edge of the arched area, and after about five etos had cleared about a metre up each side. This was indeed flat behind what must be many millennia's worth of crust. It was a black colour here and not the maroon of the sides, polished to a perfect shine.

As she scraped along the top, she came across an arrow pointing upwards with some indecipherable lettering at ninety degrees. She continued scraping following the direction of the arrow.

It uncovered a square plate slightly countersunk into the maroon corrugations. This also had some of the sideways lettering on it and was ringed in red. She tried levering it open with the scraper to no avail. She pushed it, pulled it and swore at it; nothing made any difference, or marked it in any way, so strong was the material.

Her suit pinged at her to tell her she'd used half her oxygen supply. She quickly worked out she had about another thirty etos before she should begin making her way back to the lander.

She knocked on the panel three times as if knocking on a door.

'Anybody home?' she called, shaking her head in frustration.

The panel suddenly lit up around its edge, sunk in further and slid upwards out of sight. She stepped back in surprise.

'There's power,' she shouted to herself. 'How can there be power? We've been observing these things for centuries, no one's been near them.'

She stepped back up and looked into the now square hole revealing a red handle in the upright position.

Swallowing nervously, she raised one of her gauntlets up and found it was a bit of a tight squeeze to get her three fingers in the hole, but not impossible.

'Please don't be a self-destruct system or anything,' she said to the handle and turned it tentatively to the right.

She stepped back quickly as the ground beneath her legs trembled. A cracking noise came from below that she heard clearly inside her helmet above the racket of the environment fans, even though the atmosphere was thin.

The arch clunked inwards abruptly and slid away downwards, lights came on within and absolute silence returned.

Pol swore again, licked her lips and approached slowly just in case something really pissed off lurked within. As she peered inside, it became obvious the door wasn't an arch at all, it was circular. She'd only been able to see the top half of it. Just down below was a small room with a second circular door beyond.

Is that an airlock? she wondered. Glancing back over her shoulder in the direction of her lander and then at her suit charge level, she hesitated. *Perhaps I should go back and recharge the suit.* Looking forward again, she decided on a quick fifteen etos inside and then go back for a recharge and a meal.

She sat on the lip of the opening and slid down inside. The landing was a bit weird as she immediately rolled to the right and as she stood she was a little confused as the gravity was stronger here. The airlock or whatever it was had a metallic grid-like floor and maroon walls. The inner door had a rectangular glass panel across the centre with no light showing beyond and a similar red handle set into the wall. This one was on the left-hand side and not on the top like the outer one.

Pol turned it to see if the inner door would open too. She swore at her stupidity as the outer door whooshed shut behind her. Pol turned to find the handle to re-open it, but there was nothing on either side or above. She jumped as the inner door flashed red lights around the outside, sunk inwards away from her and, contrary to the outer one, slid away to the right inside the wall.

Lighting panels in the walls within lit up to display a corridor leading left and right.

She quickly entered, turned and looked for the outer door

control. Here was only a covered button panel with more of the strange symbols on the keys. Without warning the inner door began to close again. She braced all four arms against it unsuccessfully and before she had time to jump back through it closed with a thunk and sunk in away from her.

'You stupid bloody idiot,' she shouted at herself, her four arms pounding on the door in frustration.

Pol took a step back, glanced at the oxygen readout in her peripheral vision. If she couldn't find a way out of this, whatever it was, in the next few etos, she'd be dead.

———

Vehicle consciousness reinitiated?
  Confirmed.

Check vehicle at journey end?
  Unascertained.

Scan for location confirmation?
  Inconclusive.

Duration since previous awakening?
  7,000 spins – system error? – system reinitiating.

Check drive status?
  Primary drive emergency shut down has been initiated – system reinitiating.

. . .

Check internal vehicle systems?
   Core @ 15% – Environmental @ 37% – Hull containment @ 94% – Biological cargo status @ 66%.

Check security status?
   Airlock 2398s – exterior breach – resecured.

Check for pathogen infiltration?
   Critical error.

Awaken security glider from region 2300?
   Advocated.

Inform crew?
   Crew location inconclusive.

Awaken biological cargo?
   Negative.

Initiate software rebuild to critically damaged systems?
   Advocated.

Recommend vehicle consciousness remain in standby mode?
   Advocated.

1

'I DON'T BLAME you in the slightest,' said Ed, admiring one of the ambassador's paintings on the wall of his yacht's lounge. 'That gravity down there is punishing.'

'Quite a few of my colleagues do the same, the same indeed,' said Dewey. 'Sleep on their ships and just pop down for any council meetings they're obliged to attend.'

'Who is it I'm meeting this morning?' Ed asked.

'Ambassador Ralt,' said Dewey. 'She's a Callametan, a four-armed, asexual bi-ped humanoid. So we've designated them all female.'

Ed had just turned and gazed out of the lounge's huge floor-to-ceiling window at the big blue planet slowly turning below as a strange-looking human entered and shook Dewey's hand with the upper of two right arms. Ed approached and did the same, finding it odd to greet someone with not only four arms but three wide fingers on each one.

'This is Ambassador Ralt, Edward,' said Dewey.

'Mr Virr,' said Ralt, through a translator. 'Ambassador Dewey informs me you specialise in solving problems.'

'I don't know about specialise, but we do seem to have

acquired a reputation for finding lost stuff and large alien artefacts,' said Ed, giving Dewey a wink.

'The Callametans are like us, and have only recently joined the GDA,' said Dewey.

'That's correct,' said Ralt. 'We come from the Traxx system over thirteen thousand light years from here.'

Ed nodded.

'I understand you've found an alien building on your planet's moon,' he said, offering Ralt an armchair as he sat back on a sofa.

Dewey winced and pulled a tall barstool over and offered that to Ralt, who nodded her thanks and perched more than sat on the stool.

Ed realised his mistake as the Callametan didn't appear to have knees and he held his hands up in a placating manner to apologise.

'I don't believe it's on *their* planet's moon, Ed,' said Dewey.

'No, Ambassador Dewey is correct,' said Ralt. 'It's on a satellite called Tignar orbiting a gas giant in Traxx that we call Rea.'

'I see,' said Ed, looking thoughtful. 'And now you have access to all this GDA technology, what's stopping you going there yourselves?'

'Two things,' said Ralt. 'One is money. We spent billions on a controversial mission there a few of your weeks ago that ended in tragedy, and secondly, we're a society brow-beaten by several powerful religious cults. They all worship the relic, calling it the Cathedral of the Gods, and now believe our mission angered their deity and we got what we deserved.'

'And they won't sanction another visit?' asked Ed.

'Not a chance.'

'You're not a believer then?'

'I'm a scientist, I work with facts, not imaginary friends.'

'You're not the only planet that has that problem,' said Dewey, rolling his eyes.

Ed smiled and looked back at Ralt.

'So it's definitely an ancient alien building then?' he said.

'Well, we presume so,' said Ralt, handing Dewey a data chip. 'Can you display the images on that for me?'

Dewey plugged it into his tablet and waved the images over to his wall screen. Ed watched as recorded footage from a suit-mounted camera showed firstly a row of strange vertical rock formations, the last one being much larger than the first four.

'How tall is that big one?' Ed asked.

'Over three kilometres,' Ralt replied.

'Holy moly,' said Ed. 'It looks completely vertical.'

The images changed to four gauntleted hands scraping away the surface crust, revealing a flat shiny surface below and then an arrow pointing up, with some strange lettering sideways on.

'Do you recognise that language?' Ralt asked.

Ed turned his head to the right and tried to make sense of the lettering.

'No,' he said. 'It almost looks like Egyptian hieroglyphic symbols.'

The video continued to show the uncovering of the hatch and finally the opening of the door.

'Wow, look at that,' said Ed. 'It's an airlock – but why's it sideways on? Did the building subside and tip up like that?'

'Perhaps that's why it's at a slight angle,' said Dewey.

They watched as Pol slid inside and immediately rolled to the right.

'This is the bit that confuses us,' said Ralt.

The camera showed Pol standing up and turning to face the inner door.

'Why's the inner door orientated correctly, when the outer one is at ninety degrees to it?' Ralt asked.

Ed thought for a moment and asked Dewey to rewind the footage slowly frame by frame.

'Stop there,' he said, turning his head sideways again. 'That's not the door that's at ninety degrees – from inside it's the moon's surface. Look there.' He pointed at the bright area. 'That's not the side of the doorway just there, it's the ground outside that's now vertical.'

'Some sort of gravity disorder, perhaps?' said Dewey, waving for the video to continue.

They watched Pol turn the handle for the inner door and the footage went blank.

'That's it,' said Ralt. 'That's all we have.'

'The outer door shut,' said Ed. 'When you operate an airlock from the inside, it will automatically close the other door first. She attempted to open the inner door, forgetting that the outer door behind her would close. That's what ended her transmission being received by her ship.'

'I still don't get what the hell was going on with the strange gravity though?' said Dewey, staring at Ed along with Ralt.

'Don't you see?' said Ed. 'That's an inertial damping field or artificial gravity zone that begins as soon as you enter the airlock.'

'Okay,' said Ralt, still looking puzzled. 'I'm new to all this GDA space technology, what does that mean?'

'That isn't a building, is it, Ed?' said Dewey, suddenly realising where Ed was going with this.

'No, it's not a building at all,' said Ed, looking back out

the lounge window at all the space traffic surrounding them. 'That whole moon, it's a starship.'

Ralt emitted a strange squeaky chuckle.

'Don't be ridiculous,' she said. 'It's still got a working and powered airlock. That moon will have taken thousands of your years to attract all that material, it's still doing so now from all the rocky debris and dust around that planet.'

'What happened to the astronaut who filmed this?' asked Ed, glancing back at Ralt.

'She must have got trapped inside,' said Ralt. 'When that airlock closed, she only had about fifty etos of oxygen left.'

'That's about an hour to us,' said Dewey.

'Pol never returned to her lander,' Ralt continued. 'It's still there waiting for her, sending us its standby signal, and the mothership's still in orbit above.'

Ed crossed his arms and turned his attention back to the traffic outside.

'I take it you'd like us to go find her body and get some answers?' he said.

'Discreetly, yes,' said Ralt. 'The ambassador tells me your ship has one of those cloaking systems?'

'It does.'

'Regard this as something I'm told you would recognise as a black ops mission,' said Ralt. 'The more devout members of our society would take an extremely dim view of any further incursions near the Cathedral of the Gods. You have a few hours a day where that side of the moon is facing away from Callamet, consider it your window of opportunity.'

'We need to discuss a fee, Edward,' said Dewey.

'No charge,' said Ed.

'But you must need something,' said Ralt. 'Just the expense of taking a starship that far and the possible hazards.'

'Believe me, Ambassador, we've been a lot further and

faced more dangers than an old broken spacecraft could offer,' said Ed, walking over to shake Ralt's strange hand again. 'We'll leave tomorrow. You could always treat us to a holiday on Callamet once we've solved the riddle.'

'It would be my pleasure,' said Ralt. 'It's a deal.'

'You be careful, Edward,' said Dewey. 'If that is a ship, it's big and it could contain anything.'

'You know me, James,' said Ed, smiling and shaking his hand too. 'Careful is my middle name.'

'Yeah,' said Dewey. 'But your colleague Andy's isn't.'

2

ANDY AND RAYL arrived in the starboard hangar, turned the *Cartella* around one hundred and eighty degrees and landed next to two of the *Gabriel*'s own shuttles. The two newly-weds disembarked hand in hand and walked smiling towards the meeting party.

'They're still talking then,' whispered Cleo, the ship's sentient computer, who materialised in physical form for the welcome home.

'You are such a cynical ship, Cleo,' said Linda.

'Welcome back,' said Ed, walking out to meet them halfway and hugging them both.

'Where did you end up going?' he asked, as they met the others and everyone else got hugs too.

'The island on Panemorfi for the first three weeks,' said Rayl.

'I thought as much,' said Phil. 'That's why Cleo wouldn't let us go there.'

'And then a month skiing in New Zealand,' said Andy, winking at Ed.

'You lucky bugger – a month? You knew I've always wanted to go there.'

'We will,' said Andy. 'I've gotta show you some of the black runs.'

'You can show him those on your own,' said Rayl, frowning. 'I thought he'd changed his mind and was trying to kill me.'

'Bit steep were they?' said Linda, as they walked towards the tube lift.

'I thought I was going to throw up, I was so scared.'

Ed had waited until Andy and Rayl were back and everyone was together up in the blister lounge to explain the mission to the Traxx system. They all watched transfixed as he played Pol's video footage from the moon's surface.

'You're right,' said Andy. 'There's definitely some artificial gravity coming into play as soon as you enter that airlock. It being a ship is much more likely than a tilted-over building.'

'Looking at the massive amount of material floating around that gas planet and the amount that has collected around the ship, plus the fact it's not weathered down much and its weak micro gravity – I'd hazard a guess that it's been there for between five and ten thousand years,' said Cleo.

'What about the power supply though?' said Linda. 'How can that have remained in operation for so long?'

'Well, ours could probably do that too,' said Andy.

'Andy's right,' said Cleo. 'If I turned everything off and sat in a continuous high orbit, the dark matter power supply would stay live almost indefinitely.'

'Pol opening that airlock from the outside could have been the first drain on the system for a very long time,' said Ed. 'I'm excited to see what could be on the inside of such a huge ancient vessel.'

'If there's any giant eggs, don't try and make an omelette,' said Andy, with a dour expression.

'Giant eggs?' said Rayl, giving him a sideways glance.

'Don't listen to him,' said Linda. 'He's referring to a few old movies from about fifty years ago.'

'He has a point though,' said Phil. 'That ship's been there for an awful long time. Its technology seems almost modern and something catastrophic happened to it that may or may not still be there. We need to be wary.'

'Thanks, Mr gloom and doom,' said Rayl. 'I think I'll stay inside this ship, and that goes for you too, Andrew.'

Andy glanced at Ed and raised his eyebrows.

'Don't you look to me for support, family man,' said Ed, turning his attention to Linda. 'How about you, Linda?'

'*Me?*' she exclaimed. 'The last time we went out for a walk, we both got shot and the last time I had an awayday on my own, I got shot again. I don't think I have a very good record, Edward.'

'It's just a dead moon,' said Ed. 'Where's your sense of adventure?'

'From what I've just seen, it's a very alive one,' said Rayl, crossing her arms.

'Well, we've got a few days to discuss it while we're on our way,' said Linda. 'And talking of on our way, Cleo, can you plot a course to the Traxx system?'

'The *Nostromo* is ready to leave, Captain,' said Cleo, morphing into Ripley, giving her a wave and quickly vanishing.

'Sometimes I hate this piss-taking ship,' said Linda.

The journey had taken just over four days as the *Gabriel* winked into the Traxx system.

Keeping the systems star between them and the planet Callamet, Linda, taking her shift in the pilot's seat, cloaked the vessel and powered away towards Rea utilising the *Gabriel*'s conventional Alma drive.

She finished the last of a very nice breakfast Cleo had made for her and instructed her to wake the others.

Ed, as usual, was first to arrive and stared at the holonav view of Rea and its peculiar satellite, Tignar. The tiny mothership Pol had spent months in, travelling from Callamet, sat slowly orbiting the moon, completely dwarfed by the gargantuan blue-grey gas giant looming close behind, its faint signals calling for its living cargo going unanswered.

'It's a big bugger isn't it?' he said, dropping into one of the control couches.

'Forty-seven times bigger than Jupiter,' she replied, nodding. 'It's got storms ten times bigger than Earth roving across its equator.'

'Has anything changed on Tignar since Pol's disappearance?'

'Not that I can see. But we'll be there in fifty minutes and be able to have a close deep scan of the thing.'

The other three arrived over the next few minutes and all took their seats as the ship passed close to Callamet at point nine light.

'Fifty-seven satellites and no space stations,' said Rayl, looking up from her scan results. 'Not a particularly dedicated space travelling race are they?'

'No,' said Ed. 'Their cult leaders are dead against it. Especially now after the disappearance of Pol, hence the secret squirrel approach.'

'They are quite remote out here aren't they?' said Andy. 'I

mean – they don't really have anything close by to travel to. None of the other six planets are even remotely habitable and Callamet doesn't even have a moon.'

'You're right,' said Phil. 'Technologically they're more advanced than Earth was before first contact, but they've had no first rung on the ladder to aim at.'

'Or alien race giving them a leg up,' said Ed, winking at Phil.

'Well, there is that too,' said Phil, a little sheepishly.

The *Gabriel* flashed through the system and arrived at Rea, enormous and forbidding, the tiny moon of Tignar barely discernible scooting across its surface in a continuous elliptical trajectory.

Linda brought the ship in to a similar orbit, five hundred kilometres out from the satellite, and Rayl scanned the strange ovoid with everything they had.

'Well, that's pretty inconclusive,' she said, frowning at the results. 'Whatever that thing's made of, it doesn't give much away.'

The scan result hologram appeared in the centre of the bridge. One thing it did show was the outline of the thing under all the built-up dust and rock.

'That is definitely a ship,' said Andy. 'A big one too.'

'Seven point six kilometres in length,' said Rayl. 'With only the front three sticking out.'

'And the smaller projections sticking up are some sort of equipment nacelles hanging off the main body of the ship,' said Ed.

'Time to go down and have a look,' said Linda. 'The area is hidden from Callamet in eight minutes,' she added, as she handed the vessel over to Phil.

'Are you sure you want to go down with Ed?' he asked. 'I'll go with him if you don't feel confident enough.'

'It'll be fine, Phil,' she said. 'This is the only way – get straight back on the horse as they say, and anyway, I'll be able to stop him doing anything too dangerous.'

'Wanna bet?' said Andy.

'I *can* hear you, you know,' said Ed, in a fake whingeing voice.

'Come on, Mr Delicate,' said Linda, walking towards the tube lift. 'Let's go and solve an enigma.

3

THE CARTELLA, APPROACHING THE MOON TIGNAR, TRAXX SYSTEM

LINDA PILOTED the *Cartella* down towards Pol's tiny lander. They both noticed the layer of dust already coating the top of the craft and there were no footprints visible on the surface.

'She hasn't returned then,' said Linda, as she brought their ship around the lander and slowly continued on towards the towering obelisk.

'Land as near as you can to the airlock,' said Ed. 'If we need to get away in a hurry, I don't want to be running far in the open.'

She glanced at him out of the corner of her eye.

'What from, xenomorphs?' she said, with a deadpan expression.

'You would have to say that,' said Ed, rolling his eyes. 'I'm going to be seeing them round every corner now.'

Linda followed the base of the tallest obelisk until they spotted the airlock. They couldn't miss it, as it shone in the starlight reflected from Rea and stood out from the dull grey regolith-coloured corrugations of the rest of the thing.

'This'll do,' he said. 'Turn so our airlock faces theirs.'

Linda expertly turned and dropped the *Cartella* down, clunking onto the rough surface, keeping the antigravs running just in case a landing strut decided to sink. Once satisfied, she shut down and followed Ed aft to don the Theo-designed suits.

'Ready?' he said, a few minutes later.

'Ready – what's that?' she said, pointing to holster on his right leg.

'Ah, an insurance policy,' said Ed, grinning. 'It's a classic revolver. Tony bought one each for myself and Andy.'

'Don't I get one?'

Ed adopted an awkward look.

'You know Tony,' he said. 'He's very old fashioned and to him guns are a man thing.'

'Really?'

'I'll buy you one when we're back on Earth.'

'No you won't – I'll buy my bloody own thank you,' she said, picking a laser rifle off the rack and heading for the airlock.

They both sealed up their helmets, checked each other over and cycled the airlock.

'Cleo, we have another four hours before this side of the moon becomes visible to Callamet again, can you ensure the *Cartella* remains cloaked and secure until we get back?' said Ed.

'Top banana,' she replied. 'Don't get lost in there.'

'Don't worry,' said Linda. 'I've got a nano canister just in case.'

They noticed how light the gravity was as soon as they stepped down from the airlock.

'Tiptoe, Linda,' said Ed. 'It stops the dust flying around.'

They approached the alien airlock in a strange walking-on-thin-ice gait. Ed closed his eyes and tried to engage the lock with his DOVI.

'It's well shielded, I'll give it that,' he said.

'What's it made of?' asked Linda.

'An alloy of some kind, but not one we know. Its shielding ability is top drawer.'

'Can you open the door without using the handle?'

'I think so,' he said, concentrating hard. 'It's like hot-wiring a car wearing welding gloves. Hang on, I think I've got—'

Clunk.

The door sunk inwards and disappeared downwards.

'Well done, Ed,' said Linda, patting him on the back. 'At least we know we can get out again when it closes behind us.'

They both peered inside the airlock and found it empty.

'She went right inside then,' said Linda.

'Probably looking for the controls on the inside,' said Ed. 'But those wouldn't be operated by a lever.'

'Why not?'

'Too dangerous,' he said. 'Someone sleepwalking could just stumble out into space.'

'Ah – yeah, I hadn't thought of that.'

Ed glanced up and waved.

'We're going inside now, guys. If we're not back in three hours, blow this airlock and send in the cavalry.'

'Take it easy, you two,' said Andy. 'We'll be here waiting.'

Ed went first, sliding down and remembering to swing his legs to the right. He landed on his feet, but was surprised by the extra gravity and fell forward, dropping his rifle.

'Bugger – that's more difficult than it looks,' he said.

'You all right?' called Linda.

'Yeah, come on down, I'll catch you.'

She slung her rifle on her back and dropped in. He caught her and they both clattered into the inner airlock door.

'Clumsy arse,' she moaned.

'Next time, you can go first,' he said.

'Are you two arguing already?' said Rayl. 'You're not even through the airlock yet.'

'Was that cynical old married woman having a dig, Linda?' asked Ed.

'I think she was – best shut the door so we don't have to listen to her.'

'If you're not back out here in three hours, we're going skiing again, so bugger off,' said Andy.

'Buggering right off now,' said Ed, as he instructed the outer door to close again. 'Toodle-oo.'

The large round door swung across and sealed back into place with a *thunk*.

'Toodle-oo?' said Linda, staring at him through her visor.

Ed smiled.

'Old English slang for goodbye,' he said.

'I thought that was cheerio?'

'It is – along with tatty bye and laters.'

Linda shook her head in bewilderment.

'And you moan about American English being lazy and unrefined.'

The inner door went *clunk*, sunk inwards and motored away to the right.

Ed pulled up his rifle and stepped forward, sweeping it left and right down the lit corridor.

'Clear,' he said, as Linda stepped out to join him.

'Which way?' she said. 'Both ways look the same.'

'Let's go left, which would be up on the outside,' he said. 'And it's the way Pol went.'

'How do you know that?'

Linda nodded as he pointed at the faint traces of regolith dust on the floor leading in that direction for a few metres before disappearing.

'Nothing wrong with your tracking skills, Kemosabe,' she said. 'You know, if this ship's been here for as long as it seems – why isn't there more dust on the floor?'

'If it was clean before and sealed, there wouldn't have been anything to settle,' Ed replied, as they stepped quietly and carefully along the four-metre-wide corridor.

'This passageway seems to have been designed for a lot of traffic,' said Linda, after a couple of hundred metres. 'It's very wide.'

'Or, the owners are a life form bigger than humans.'

'Shit, I hadn't thought of that.'

Linda peered down at her personal shield activator attached to her rifle and checked it was showing a green light. She also noticed a readout in her peripheral vision.

'Ed.'

'What?'

'Have you noticed the atmosphere in here? It's showing about thirty-six percent of a normal oxygen-rich breathable atmosphere. Do you think that's all they would have needed?'

'Possibly, or it's dropped to that level over time.'

They passed another airlock, identical to the one they'd used.

'There's a door on the right coming up,' said Ed.

Linda peered forwards.

'How do you know? – I can't see anything.'

'Use your DOVI to scan ahead. You'll see you can't penetrate anything really, until fifty metres up there's a locking mechanism. Not as secure in design as the airlock ones, but a lock all the same.'

Linda stopped, closed her eyes and scanned ahead.

'Oh – it's open,' she said, opening her eyes and continuing up the corridor with a little bit more vivacity.

Reaching the open door, they noticed a flashing panel just before it, as if someone had pressed it for entry only moments ago.

'You know, these door activation controls are a good sign,' said Linda.

'In what way?' whispered Ed, as he crept towards the opening.

'They're exactly where a human race like ours would have placed them.'

'Yeah, you're right.'

Ed's eyes nearly popped out of his head as he peeked around the corner.

'Whoa,' he said. 'It's some sort of mega hangar.'

Linda peered around him.

'Oh,' she said. 'There's dozens of them.'

Rows of small grey ships were lined up down below. Inside the door a stairway led down to the hangar floor and they stood at the top for a moment watching for any movement.

'They're for planetary insertion,' said Linda. 'You can see the shielding on the underside.'

Ed looked right. The rows of ships vanished into the distance.

'There's not dozens,' he said, squinting down the nearest line of identical vessels. 'There's hundreds of them.'

They began descending the metal stairway that wound its way down about forty metres. Linda suddenly stopped.

'What was that?' she asked.

'What was what?'

'I thought I heard a noise like an electric motor buzzing, coming from behind us.'

They froze as a small drone entered the hangar through the door they'd entered by. It was about half a metre square and pulsed a flat blue laser beam out in front as it approached. Ed swung his rifle up and covered it as it stopped and turned to face them. An officious electronic voice began shouting commands at them before tailing off as though its power supply was failing. The laser went out and it dropped with a clatter onto the stairs above them.

They jumped to one side as it rolled past them, bits breaking off from it as it crashed and rattled down to the next turn, where it lay still and quietly fizzing.

'Did you do that?' said Linda.

'Didn't do a thing,' said Ed. 'I think its power failed.'

'Look, there's another,' she said, pointing down under one of the ships on the hangar floor.

They quickly descended the last couple of flights and sure enough a second dead drone lay underneath a ship. Ed bent down to inspect it, just as Linda screamed.

Check security status?
Airlock 2398s – second exterior breach – resecured and security sealed – maintenance report filed.

Check for pathogen infiltration?
Critical error.

. . .

Awaken security glider from region 2300?
    Advocated.

Critical systems software rebuild complete.
    Restart advocated.

Scan for location confirmation?
    Vehicle off course.

Initiate course correction?
    Advocated.

Check drive status?
    Primary drive online.

Initiate course resumption?
    Advocated.

Vehicle parameter error?
    Purging outer skin.

Initiate course resumption?
    Advocated.

. . .

Initiate vehicle replenishment?
 Advocated.

Vehicle course resumed?
 Confirmed.

4

THEY WATCHED as the outer airlock door closed and the signal from Ed and Linda ceased. After about ten minutes, Andy blew out his cheeks and lay back, putting his hands behind his head.

'Well, this is boring as batshit, isn't it?' he moaned.

Another five minutes passed before Rayl spoke.

'Ah, now that's something I haven't seen before,' she said, glancing across at him.

'Yes, you have,' he replied. 'I'm your husband.'

'Not you, you idiot – a power fluctuation just under the crust of the artefact.'

'On the big ship?'

'Probably in it. A slight glow, as if something came to life inside and moved away.'

'Whereabouts?' asked Phil, already sounding worried.

'A couple of hundred metres above their airlock.'

'Cleo, is there anything we can do to improve the scanning of that vessel or whatever it is?' asked Phil.

'I say, a trifle difficult without a sample of that alloy to analyse,' she said in a very posh English accent.

'Oh dear,' said Rayl. 'She's off on one again.'

'Have you been watching *Downton Abbey* again on my database?' asked Andy.

'Spiffing acting,' she said. 'Absolutely super.'

'I've got tremors on the surface,' shouted Rayl suddenly. 'Bloody hell, everything's moving, I've got power hotspots blooming all over the place.'

'Cleo, get the *Cartella* up and off that surface,' called Andy.

They watched in horror as the *Cartella* lifted away, just as the entire surface of the moon disintegrated, breaking away in huge chunks, some coming in their direction.

'Move the *Gabriel* further out, Phil,' said Rayl. 'That starship's coming to life.'

Phil quickly backed the *Gabriel* away another five hundred kilometres and brought the shields up to maximum in case any lumps of that moon managed to reach them. Cleo brought the *Cartella* back close to the mothership but kept it outside just in case it was needed.

As the region of space that used to contain the moon started to clear, they gasped as a huge maroon starship emerged. It was covered with hundreds of protruding nacelles of all sizes, pointed ones, blunt ones, then as they watched, ones that opened out like giant sails.

It moved slowly at first, turning in towards Rea, and then when it was clear of all the moon debris, it accelerated into the upper atmosphere of the gas giant.

'What the hell's it doing?' said Andy. 'This scenario wasn't in the mission description.'

'It's feeding,' said Rayl. 'Those aren't wings, they're collector scoops. It's sucking in the gasses in the upper atmosphere and recharging itself.'

An explosion in the moon debris caught their attention.

'What was that?' asked Phil, his face white as a sheet now.

'The Callametan mothership,' said Rayl. 'It contained enough fossil fuel to get back home and I think the moon's shrapnel just found it.'

'Are you getting any better readings from that ship now it's free of all the collected debris?' asked Andy.

'Not really,' said Rayl. 'It's like when we were caught in that snowstorm on the top of Blackcomb, I can see a few metres and then it becomes indistinct. It's hard to tell if it's electronic shielding or just a by-product of that peculiar alloy.'

'How close shall I get?' asked Phil.

'Stay at five hundred kilometres,' said Andy. 'Then we can send the *Cartella* in if they manage to bail out.'

They followed as the giant ship spent five hours scooping its way around the gas clouds, when suddenly it veered to port and accelerated away into clear space.

'Where are you going now?' asked Phil, turning the *Gabriel* in response.

The starship kept accelerating up to point five nine light and as they watched, the scoops folded back and what seemed like half the outer hull of the ship flapped outwards, like thousands of doors opening.

'What the hell is that?' said Andy. 'It looks like a million air brakes on an aircraft.'

'Solar panels most likely,' said Rayl. 'They're all angled towards the system's star.'

'That's the course too,' said Phil. 'Straight at the star.'

'Passing close by Callamet again,' said Rayl. 'They must be freaking out over their religious icon flying away.'

'Shall we stay cloaked?' asked Phil, opening his eyes to peer at the other two.

'Absolutely,' said Andy. 'As far as Callamet is concerned, we're not here.'

'And we don't know how that ship would react to our sudden presence either,' said Rayl.

'That's a good point,' said Andy, looking up at the holo image of the giant maroon vessel. 'We don't know if any of those things hanging off it are weapon systems.'

'We have to presume it has some kind of defence system,' said Rayl. 'It would've been pretty naive to blunder out into the galaxy in something so big and advanced without some way of defending oneself.'

'What if it finishes recharging itself and jumps?' said Phil.

'We follow,' said Andy.

'What if they embed the jump?'

They all stared at each other for a moment.

'We have to hope they don't,' said Andy. 'If they do, we're banking on Ed and Linda being resourceful enough to find a way to indicate their location or route. Just like Linda did before in Andromeda by dropping a buoy.'

The ship remained on the same course for another four hours, heading straight for the star, before adopting an elliptical track circling around it, its abundance of panels adjusting their angle of attack to maximise absorption as it manoeuvred.

'I imagine it needs quite a bit of this, after being buried for so long,' said Andy.

'You two go and get some rest,' said Phil. 'I'll take first watch and I'll wake you if – oh shit.'

'Oh shit, what?' asked Andy.

'The starship just jumped,' said Rayl, pointing at the empty holomap.

5

ED SWORE as he stood back up too fast and banged his helmet on the underside of the small ship.

'Inside there,' said Linda, pointing at the front screen of the vessel directly behind them. 'A face – I saw a face watching us.'

'Are you sure?'

'Absolutely – it disappeared as soon as it saw me look up.'

A tremor ran through the huge vessel as all the lighting panels set into the ceiling dimmed for a moment and a barely discernible deep rumbling echoed around them.

'Somethings occurring,' said Ed.

'Could be the ship waking up?' said Linda.

They quickly circled around the small ship with the face and found the airlock. Both brought their rifles up as Ed touched a panel beside the door. Nothing happened. He closed his eyes and felt around with his DOVI. This time the mechanism didn't have any shielding at all and the outer airlock door cycled open.

They looked at each other and climbed inside.

'Mild stun, but only if attacked,' said Ed, pointing at Linda's weapon.

She nodded and stood as far to one side as she could to avoid them both being hit by one shot.

Ed waited until she was ready and closed the outer door. The hissing of an atmosphere being equalised was quite apparent and he checked the readout in his right vision. An oxygen-rich environment, well within acceptable parameters.

'It's breathable,' he said, getting a nod in reply.

The inner door opened into a cockpit designed for humans. Ed breathed a sigh of relief as no gun-toting alien jumped them. He took one step inside, swinging his weapon around to the right to cover the back of the cockpit. He was startled to find a Callametan sat on the floor with all four hands out wide. She was obviously very scared, as she was shaking and had a look of absolute terror in her eyes.

'Pol?' said Ed, and realised he still had his helmet up, she probably couldn't hear him. He retracted the helmet, sniffed the atmosphere and slung his rifle on his back, nodding at Linda to do the same.

'Pol?' he said again.

She visibly jumped at the mention of the name and began chatting away, waving all four arms about randomly.

Ed put his hand up to stop her for a moment.

'Wait, please,' he said in a soft voice and smiled, digging in his pouches for the mobile translator he'd thought to bring along.

He held it out to show her and after kneeling on the floor, placed it in front of her on the ground.

'I'm Edward and this is Linda,' he said, indicating Linda as she sat on one of the control seats. 'Ambassador Ralt sent us to find you, Pol.'

'I thought you might be the owners of this place,' she said. 'Sorry if I scared you.'

'I think we scared you more,' said Ed. 'Anyway, your people will be very happy you survived.'

'Only just,' she said. 'It took me a while to get this thing open.'

'Do they all have a breathable atmosphere?'

'Yes, it seems all these ships have their own oxygen supply and emergency rations,' she said, gesticulating with all four arms.

'Are you able to replenish your suit?' asked Linda.

'No, the connections aren't compatible. There might be some tools and things somewhere in the building.'

Ed and Linda exchanged a glance.

'This isn't a building, Pol,' said Linda.

'What is it then?'

'An enormous starship,' said Ed.

Pol gave them a look of complete bewilderment.

'It can't be, it's been here for thousands of years.'

'More like millions,' said Linda.

'But technology like this didn't exist back then, surely?'

'It certainly did somewhere in the universe,' said Ed. 'And something went drastically awry with this vessel.'

'Our sudden appearances seem to have awoken things,' said Linda.

'I saw you get scanned by the flying square thing. It happened to me too, and then it just ran out of power. That's the one you were looking at under the ship in front.'

'I scanned that one as it wasn't as damaged as ours,' said Ed. 'It had a laser weapon system, so we can assume it would have attacked us if its power hadn't failed.'

'Have you got a weapon to defend yourself?' asked Linda.

'Nothing,' said Pol. 'Only a few basic tools I came out to take samples with.'

'We need to find the bridge and get some answers,' said Ed, standing up again, picking up the translator, grabbing Pol's upper right arm and helping her to her feet.

'Are you going to leave me on my own again?' Pol asked, looking terrified at the thought.

'No, let's have a look at this suit of yours,' said Ed. 'And Linda, can you have a search for anything at all that would help us in transferring oxygen into Pol's suit.'

Ed spent hours fiddling with bits and pieces and pipes robbed from the various systems on the small ship. It seemed no matter what he tried, it always leaked.

'I bet there's a really good engineering section on this ship, if we just knew where it was,' he moaned, finally dropping the suit down on the floor and glaring at it. 'I just need one piece of pipe, a couple of jubilee clips and the job would be a doddle.'

'If I have to stay here, then so be it,' said Pol, slumping back down and shrugging with four shoulders.

'We don't have any choice at the moment,' said Ed. 'I should have brought a spare suit, but to be honest, Pol, we didn't expect to find you alive.'

'If these ships weren't nearby you wouldn't have,' she said, staring at the floor.

'There's another couple of suits in the *Cartella*,' said Linda.

'Crap, you're right,' said Ed.

'But they'll be designed for your race,' said Pol, holding out four arms and wiggling her twelve fingers.

'They're Theo-designed body adapting suits,' said Ed. 'It would automatically form to your specific shape.'

'Would it really? Your technology is amazing, it's way beyond ours,' said Pol.

'We were at almost the same stage as you, until very recently,' said Ed. 'Now you've been accepted into the GDA, you'll have access to all this stuff too.'

'That's if the cults allow it,' said Pol.

They all looked at each other as the ship vibrated slightly.

'Does that happen often?' asked Linda.

'Twice now and only since you arrived,' said Pol. 'Did you activate something?'

'Not knowingly,' Ed replied, staring out the front screen and up towards the open door at the top of the stairs. 'Wait here and I'll go and grab another suit from the *Cartella*.'

'On your own?' said Linda, the concern evident in her voice.

'It only requires one of us and it'll take me ten minutes,' he said, touching the icon on his neck ring to activate the helmet.

'If you come across any more flying bricks, you shoot first,' she said, with a baleful glance.

He nodded quickly and activated the inner airlock.

It only took him four minutes to reach the airlock they'd entered through, but he found to his horror that the locking mechanism had been altered in such a way as to make it impossible to open.

It's like it's been welded shut, he thought, and then he had an idea.

He walked swiftly back to the next airlock they'd seen a couple of hundred metres nearer the hangar door.

If I get Cleo to fly the Cartella up to this door, I could jump across in this low gravity, he reasoned, and peering through the rectangular window he checked the airlock was empty. Satisfied, he activated his DOVI and entered as the door slid to the side. When it closed behind him, he backed up to it as he knew there would be a two hundred-metre drop as the outer door opened, and possibly a load of the built-up crust falling in.

The hissing of the atmosphere venting was louder than he expected, but didn't unduly worry him. When it ceased, the outer door sunk in towards him and slid left, the workings of the door sounding a bit gritty as it ground its way into the thick outer hull. What confronted him wasn't what he expected.

'Holy crap,' he said out loud.

Stepping forward tentatively, he peered out and in the distance was a weird grey blurred vista, as if he were driving passed thick fog really fast. Looking down, there was no moon surface, no *Cartella*, nothing except the line of huge pointed equipment nacelles stretching away below and out for at least half a kilometre.

Those were the shorter pinnacles sticking up out of the surface, he thought.

'Cleo, can you hear me?' he called. 'Andy, Phil, Rayl – anyone?'

The silence was total. He swore to himself again and stepped back as he instructed the outer door to reclose. Moving back into the corridor once the airlock had cycled again, he kicked the opposite wall with all his strength, jarring his knee in the process.

'Bollocks,' he raged, stepping back as the wall panel shattered and fell out in pieces. *'What happened to the moon, what was all that foggy shit and where the hell is this ship going?'* he thought. Gritting his teeth, he turned and limped off towards the hangar door.

He stopped suddenly and peered back as something caught his eye. It was at the back of the hole in the wall he'd created. A line of plastic piping of several different diameters with adjustable clips ran along inside a form of trunking. Extracting a knife from a suit pouch he cut several lengths out, along with the clips, and hurried back to the hangar.

'Where's the suit?' said Linda, as he entered the cabin.

'No suits,' he said.

'But I saw them there,' she said, angrily.

'No *Cartella* either.'

'What?'

'We've jumped or something,' he said. 'The moon is gone and we're travelling through a strange foggy shit.'

Linda sat heavily on one of the control seats.

'Is the *Gabriel* following?'

'I called them and got nothing. This ship must have embedded a jump into a gas atmosphere or something.'

'Bollocks,' she said.

'That's what I said.'

'The moon has gone?' said Pol, obviously shocked. 'But our whole culture revolves around the cults and their worship of the Cathedral of the Gods.'

'Not anymore they won't – and as our ship has gone too, I don't believe this vessel's in the Traxx system anymore either.'

'May the gods save us,' said Pol, kissing the back of all four of her hands.

'If we could find some of the crew of this thing, we could ask them to do just that,' said Ed. 'But in the meantime I might have solved your suit problem.'

He held up the assorted plumbing supplies and immediately got to work.

An hour later, Pol's suit was recharged and ready to go. As it normally contained enough oxygen for a two-hour EVA, Ed had removed one of many larger oxygen containers from the environmental system within the small ship and rigged that within the suit's backpack unit. It was a bit heavier and bulkier, but Pol agreed it would pose no problem as the gravity on the ship was a little lighter than she was used to anyway.

'How long will it give me, d'you think?' Pol asked, as she with Linda's help donned her suit again.

'About ten hours I think,' said Ed. 'So long as you don't go to the gym.'

'What's a gym?' she asked, squeezing her head into the suit's attached helmet.

'Exercise room,' said Linda, giving Ed a glare as she finished sealing and checking Pol's suit.

'Are we ready,' said Ed, and getting nods from the other two, he opened the inner airlock door.

'Pol, you go between myself and Linda as you're not armed.'

'I'm fine with that,' she said, slipping Ed's translator into a pouch on the front of her suit.

'Right, helmet up, Linda – let's go see what we can find.'

6

THE STARSHIP GABRIEL, VICINITY OF THE STAR, TRAXX
SYSTEM

'CRAP, CRAP AND CRAPPITY CRAP,' shouted Andy, stabbing at the icons on his holodisplay.

'I take it it's not showing up anywhere?' said Phil, opening his eyes and glancing across at Andy.

'No – I mean, it's the size of a small planet – where the fuck can it have gone?' cried Andy, the frustration boiling over.

'Have you got the arrays at maximum?' asked Phil.

'*Yes,*' both Rayl and Andy shouted in tandem.

'Perhaps the ship is designed to automatically jump behind large obstacles to foil any pursuit?'

'Or perhaps it's still here and just cloaked,' said Rayl.

'If that's the case then we're royally screwed,' said Andy, sitting back and crossing his arms angrily.

'Not necessarily,' said Phil. 'You remember what Ed did when Linda was on that PCP ship in Andromeda?'

'He set up a five hundred light year grid and worked it methodically,' said Andy.

'I admit we did have the edge of the galaxy behind us then, that cut the possible directions down by half,' said Phil, looking rueful. 'But we could adopt a similar method in this scenario. It would be better than flying around randomly and shouting at each other.'

Andy glanced across at Rayl and got a shrug in reply.

'Yeah – sorry, Phil,' said Andy. 'Cleo, can you show a grid on the holo—'

It appeared before he finished the sentence. A faint grid of boxes covering this side of the Milky Way materialised within the holomap.

'Would a range of a hundred thousand light years suffice, Andrew?' said Cleo.

'Absolutely,' he said, glancing at the other two. 'This could take a while and only really needs two of us on duty at any one time, Rayl. You go and get some sleep. Phil and I will cover the first few hours.'

'Okay, if you're sure,' she said, giving Andy a kiss on the forehead and disappearing down on the tube lift.

'Right,' said Andy, once she was gone. 'Let's find this stupid ship again – it's not as if it's small.'

'We only need to glimpse it once to get a guide on its course,' said Phil. 'It obviously didn't come from here and was en route to somewhere else. I think we can discount the cloaking hypothesis, because it didn't cloak all the time it was flying around the Traxx system sucking in energy.'

'No,' said Andy. 'That's right – it charged its systems sufficiently to jump to its next waypoint. We just need to find out how far that thing's technology could possibly send it.'

'Cleo,' said Phil, 'do we have any actual video footage of that ship jumping?'

'Er – yeah,' she said. 'I'll see if I can get a closer image.'

A holo image of the alien ship shown from their position from behind, materialised in the centre of the bridge. Cleo panned in to get a close-up. It made the image slightly blurred but still showed the multitude of absorbent panels hanging off the ship, constantly updating their orientation to maximise efficiency.

'They've utilised every scrap of hull space to those panels haven't they?' said Phil.

'It's certainly a thing of beauty,' said Andy. 'I'd have been proud to design that – it almost looks like the panels are feathers ruffling in the wind.'

They watched in awe as the mega ship circled the system's star, gathering vast quantities of energy to top up its depleted reserves.

Suddenly, all the panels folded back flush with the hull.

'Must be getting ready to jump,' said Phil.

A strange grey swirling cloud appeared around the needle-sharp prow, expanding quickly until it was as wide as the ship.

'What the fuck is that?' said Andy. 'Why didn't we see this before?'

The vessel slipped inside and the mist swirl disappeared down to a pin prick and vanished, like an old TV set shutting down.

Andy and Phil looked at each other in bewilderment.

'That wasn't any jump initiation I've ever seen,' said Andy. 'You've been out here with this technology for several millennia, Phil – have you seen a jump drive that causes that weird effect before?'

Phil sat staring at the empty holo space image for a few moments, his mouth agape.

'I've never seen anything like it,' he said finally. 'That didn't look anything like any jump drive at all.'

'It had no jump signature either,' said Cleo. 'I've scoured both mine and *Gabriel*'s data bases for anything that resembles this and for once I've come up empty. The energy release from whatever that was is colossal, almost as if it's using the power of the star to create a hole in space.'

'What, like a wormhole?' said Andy.

'That's never been made workable,' said Cleo. 'Many have tried in ages gone by, but the power required was just too vast, and the working theories estimated the travel times were always going to be slower than a fold drive anyway.'

'Well, perhaps this race from wherever they came from, succeeded,' said Andy. 'And those panels were collecting a lot of power just before it went.'

'If it was a wormhole drive as you call it,' said Phil, still staring at the holo image, 'then that ship could be travelling relatively slowly between systems and only stopping to recharge from a star as and when they reach one or need one.'

'That's right,' said Andy. 'The range may be restricted to a few light years at a time and the route to wherever they're going isn't in a straight line. They have to zig-zag from system to system, keeping under their maximum defined number of light years.'

'So we haven't lost them,' said Phil, becoming a little more animated. 'They could actually be quite close, but invisible within their little wormhole.'

'Well, it didn't look like a little wormhole, but if you can call travelling away from here at several times the speed of light as close, then yes,' said Andy.

Phil glanced up at the ceiling.

'Cleo, what did the theories estimate the speeds within a wormhole to be?'

'Anywhere from ten to a hundred times light,' she replied.

'And projected range?'

'Anywhere from one to five hundred light years.'

'Hmm,' said Andy. 'You can see why no one bothered with it after fold drives were invented. Even if you took the fastest estimate and the longest distance, it would still take five years to travel five hundred light years, something a fold takes less than a second to initiate.'

'So we're looking in the wrong place,' said Phil. 'Going out five hundred light years and scanning around is pointless.'

'Yeah,' said Andy, thinking hard. 'We need to concentrate on the nearest systems and wait.'

'And hope whoever designed that worm drive couldn't achieve too much range,' added Phil, grinning for the first time in ages.

'Correct. Cleo can you—'

The holomap suddenly expanded out in all directions, with the nearest systems flashing in red.

'This what you wanted, Andrew?' she said, appearing in person, today choosing a skimpy black goth-style outfit with laced leather boots up to her thighs, purple eye shadow and black lipstick.

'Bloody hell, Cleo,' said Andy. 'You do know I'm a married man now?'

'I'm not,' said Phil, winking at Cleo.

'That's better,' she said. 'Just trying to cheer you two up.'

'I think you've succeeded,' said Andy.

'And the other thing I've succeeded in, is a possible way to detect a vehicle suspended within your wormhole.'

'You have – really?' asked Phil.

'Experimental at the moment,' she said. 'I noticed when the hole formed around the bow of the giant ship, it created a kind of deep echo, a resonance I can still faintly detect even now, but the range isn't good. As soon as I get more than about five hundred thousand kilometres away, it just fades into the background hum of the galaxy.'

'So you're saying if we travel between here and some of

these closer systems, you might be able to detect the wormhole as it cuts through interstellar space?' asked Andy.

'I can't promise anything and it's still a needle and all that,' she said, looking hopeful. 'But it's all we've got at the moment.'

'And if we do detect them,' said Phil, 'we'll know the destination and, by how far they've got, know the estimated time of arrival?'

'Spot on, Philip,' said Cleo. 'I'll leave the actual choice of systems to visit up to you, as that really is down to pure luck.'

She disappeared again, leaving Andy and Phil staring at the holomap.

'Where to, Batman,' said Andy. 'You're piloting, you get first choice.'

'Well, working on the assumption a wormhole travels in a reasonable straight line and in the direction the ship was going when it entered, then perhaps this system here at five point two light years is as good as any to start with.'

Andy pointed towards the flashing red star in the holomap and grinned.

'Engage.'

7

ALIEN STARSHIP, UNKNOWN LOCATION

ED LED the two girls up the wide corridor. They'd turned right after leaving the hangar as they reasoned the bridge was more likely to be at the front of the vessel.

He opened the next door on the right they came to. This time they found themselves at the back of another vast hangar, with a similar stairway leading down to the deck.

'Bigger ships,' said Linda, looking down on rows of wide dumpy-shaped vessels with what appeared to be side opening ramps.

'Freighters maybe?' said Ed. 'Let's go and see what they're carrying.'

Picking the nearest one after descending the stairway, Ed concentrated on its locking mechanism. The large side ramp whined and slowly descended.

'They look something like tractors,' said Ed, peering inside once the ramp had clattered to the deck.

'Tracked ones too,' said Pol.

'Are they for military use?' asked Linda.

'Probably not,' said Ed. 'They're bright shiny blue.'

He stepped back and looked down the line of ships stretching off into the distance.

'This whole ship could be a huge freighter itself,' he said. 'It seems to be all massive hangars full of stuff being taken somewhere.'

'Wherever that is, they've been waiting a while,' said Linda.

Retracing their steps back up to the corridor, they continued on. A hundred metres further up, an open rectangular box about four metres by three was set back into the wall.

'This must stick out into the hangar,' said Ed, inspecting it cautiously.

'It looks like an elevator down to the hangar floor,' said Pol.

'It is,' said Ed, scanning it with his DOVI. 'It goes up too.'

'We're down in the cargo levels,' said Linda. 'Shall we see what's above?'

They all looked at each other and seemed to reach an unspoken decision by stepping into the lift together.

Ed concentrated on the small control panel recessed on the left wall. They moved quickly to the back of the gondola as the open edges flashed with a white light and the elevator slowly moved upward.

Pol stared at Ed with what he presumed was a Callametan expression of puzzlement.

'I have a brain-activated scanning and electronic manipulation ability,' he told her.

'We call it a DOVI,' said Linda. 'Our ship's computer designed it.'

'You have a computer that designs stuff for you?' Pol asked.

'Cleo is as much a member of our crew as any of us,' said Linda.

'You've named her as well,' she said, giving them a weird look. 'How quaint.'

Ed and Linda exchanged a smirk.

The elevator crawled up. They turned around as the open side appeared behind them and the white flashing edges swopped sides.

Another huge space opened up above and to their left as the elevator stopped, and they stepped out into a kind of vast warehouse. Row upon row of racking stretched away into the distance and, like the hangar below, this one was several hundred metres wide.

'It just goes on and on,' said Pol. 'What is all this stuff?'

They approached the first rack stretching as far as one could see and almost as high as the ceiling. There were thousands of composite pallets, four times as big as Earth ones and stacked twenty high. There was more of the pictorial text on the end of each row and on each stack. What was on each pallet was anyone's guess as they were all vacuum-sealed inside thick matt-black rubbery cocoons.

'Whatever they were carrying, there's an awful lot of it,' said Ed, running his gloved hand over the nearest pallet.

'Have you noticed the atmosphere quality has improved?' said Linda, looking at the readout in her peripheral vision. 'It was at about thirty-six percent when we got here.'

'What's it on now?' asked Ed.

'Fifty-eight.'

'Who's it being improved for?' Pol asked. 'There's hardly going to be anyone alive here is there?'

'The computer system that recently woke up might not know that,' said Linda.

'It hasn't sent any more of those flying bricks after us either,' said Pol.

'I think they were activated by the unscheduled opening of an airlock from outside,' said Ed. 'I've opened doors and operated the elevator since then and nothing's come to ask any questions.'

Linda glanced back over at the elevator and then up at the ceiling.

'Does that lift go further up?' she asked.

'Absolutely,' said Ed. 'Shall we explore more of the never-ending hardware store?'

'After you, Mr Virr,' said Linda, waving him past.

They ascended again and this time the elevator caught them out when the right side wall edges began flashing. Sure enough, that side wall opened up and they arose into a much narrower corridor. It had blue walls, a softer sprung flooring and slightly more subdued lighting. It led away with closed doors on both sides every twenty metres or so.

The first door slid away into the wall when Ed touched a small raised circle.

'It's a dormitory,' said Linda, poking her head inside.

Small podlike bed chambers, stacked four high, filled the room, each one with a different sign on the end.

'The beds are all individually named,' said Ed, gazing round at maybe a hundred pods.

They went from room to room down the corridor, finding them all identical.

'They're like those snooze pods you get at airports,' said Linda.

'And all empty,' said Ed. 'This ship, as we can see, had hundreds of crew. Where the hell are they?'

'Perhaps they abandoned ship when it malfunctioned,' said Pol. 'And it just drifted into orbit around Rea.'

'Always a possibility,' said Linda.

Going up another level, they found recreational facilities; a large eating area with kitchens beyond, lounges, exercise areas and even two empty swimming pools, but still no sign of the crew.

'We must be getting nearer the control room,' said Pol.

'She's right,' said Linda. 'No one would walk miles from the canteen to get to the bridge, it has to be close.'

They went back to the elevator and Ed instructed it to ascend again. This time it climbed for what seemed like an age, finally opening onto another long passage stretching across the ship, this time with doors spaced regularly along both sides.

'This looks more promising,' said Ed. 'That's a much bigger circular door halfway down there.'

Opening the first door on the right, they found a single-bedded cabin.

'Must be the more senior officers' cabins,' said Linda.

Ed opened a cupboard just inside the door and found a stack of vacuum-packed clothing. Searching around in some of the other cupboards and drawers, they found a personal tablet or slate.

'If we could find some way of charging that,' said Linda, 'we could learn a lot from it.'

They moved from room to room, finding very similar scenarios in each, until the last two before the larger door. These were much bigger and had separate lounges.

'Captain and first officers' cabins,' said Pol.

'Then that one must be the bridge,' said Ed, walking back out to face the big circular door. He closed his eyes and concentrated on what was a much more demanding mechanism.

'Ed, look out,' called Linda, as a flying brick dropped out

from the ceiling and scanned them with the same flat blue laser light as before. Again, it began issuing commands in an unrecognisable language.

'We don't understand the language,' said Ed, slowly bringing his rifle around to the front.

'It looks like this one's fully charged,' said Pol, as she shuffled behind Linda.

It continued hovering and making demands until the translator in Pol's suit blurted the word, *biological.*

'It's recognised a word,' said Ed. 'We need to keep it talking to give the translator a chance to learn.'

In its next sentence the word *unauthorised* and *biological* again popped out and shortly after *location* and *contained.*

It either got bored or recognised Ed's weapon as a threat, because it suddenly shut up and fired a bolt of energy at Ed. His personal shield snapped up and dispersed the bolt around him with a crackle.

Linda fired back. The flying brick spun backwards and fell with a crash to the floor, popping and fizzing. The smell of burning plastic quickly filling the passageway.

'Bugger,' said Ed. 'I was hoping to have a conversation with it.'

'With a computer?' said Pol, pulling a strange face inside her helmet.

Ed ignored Pol's scepticism and turned his attention back to what he hoped was the bridge door.

'This has twice the locking combinations of anything yet,' said Ed. 'Linda, can you keep this first level inoperative for me, while I tackle the inner security set?'

'I'll have a go,' she said, facing the door and closing her eyes.

'That's just weird,' said Pol. 'It looks as if the two of you are asleep standing up.'

A deep rumbling within the walls had them wide awake as a sucking sound came and went, then the whole door sunk inwards before swinging open upwards.

'There was a slightly higher pressure behind the door,' said Ed, as he looked inside and grinned.

8

'BORED NOW,' said Andy, slumping back into his couch.

'I spy, with my little eye,' said Phil, smirking.

'Don't even think about it, pilot boy,' said Andy, pointing at Phil with a wiggly finger. 'I was bored with that three hours ago.'

'Now you know how we felt, waiting over three thousand years for you guys to grow up.'

'If you'd given Iron Age man some rocket technology, you'd have saved yourselves a thousand years.'

'Yeah, cast iron rockets – they'd fly well.'

'Will you two stop talking bollocks for a minute,' said Cleo. 'I just need you to turn onto this course please, Phil.'

A slightly altered trajectory appeared in front of Phil. He thought his way onto the new course and the helm holographic display flashed green as it locked on.

'Have you found something?' asked Andy.

'Just the merest sniff of – ah – now, that's more promising,' she said. 'I'll display the possible track as a tube on the holomap.'

What looked like a short pipe materialised in clear space

near the Traxx system and pointing in the direction of system 9264701b.

'An uninhabited system?' said Andy.

'But, it does have a gas giant – two in fact – and a nice healthy star to recharge with,' said Phil, surveying the scan results.

'Not their final destination then?'

'Oh shit,' said Phil.

'Oh shit, what?'

'It's six point six light years from Traxx to 9264701b,' said Phil, looking at Andy with a concerned face. 'Judging by how far they've got in the time since they entered the wormhole, they're travelling at three point two times the speed of light.'

'Oh shit,' said Andy. 'That's not too hard to work out is it?'

'Just over two years, isn't it?' said Phil.

'Yeah.'

'Crap.'

'What's crap?' asked Rayl, appearing on the tube lift.

They showed her the evidence and she sat back on her control couch and sighed.

'Cleo, is there any way we can influence that ship out of the wormhole and get it to drop back into real time?' she asked.

'Theoretically, maybe,' Cleo said. 'But deliberately collapsing a wormhole, anything could happen. It's never been done before and could even cause the ship to break up, disappear into another dimension or worse.'

'What could be worse?' said Andy, rolling his eyes.

'I'm sure Ed and Linda have everything under control,' said Rayl. 'There are worse things than waiting a couple of years.'

'They could be lying unconscious,' said Phil. 'And relying on us to do something.'

The three of them sat and stared at the holomap for a few moments.

'I vote we wait a few days,' said Rayl. 'It's a big ship and they might need some time to sort themselves out.'

'Just learning that pictorial language would be a time-consuming enterprise, even if they have found the bridge,' said Andy.

'Cleo,' called Rayl. 'How long do you think we should give them?'

'Before doing what?'

'That's as yet to be decided.'

'Come on, Cleo,' said Andy. 'No sitting on the fence. How long do we wait?'

'Ten days.'

'Why ten days?' asked Rayl.

'You asked for a timescale – I gave you one.'

'So, no scientific reason for the length of time?' asked Phil.

'No.'

They all looked at each other before Andy shrugged.

'Ten days it is then,' he said.

THE BRIDGE WAS oval-shaped and reminded Ed of the Starship *Enterprise*, except for the tall arched windows that curved around the front of the room.

All we need is some stained glass and we'd have a chapel, he thought.

'What's that out there?' questioned Pol, pointing at the strange foggy vista whipping by.

'That's what I could see out of the airlock,' said Ed.

There was seating for sixteen, arranged in two semicircles facing the windows, and behind them two slightly raised chairs.

'The captain and first officer,' said Linda, noticing what Ed was looking at.

'All a bit gothic, isn't it?' he said, running his glove across the captain's curved black control console.

Pol, who'd walked down to the front row of seats and consoles, suddenly jumped back in surprise.

'A b-body,' she stammered and leaped back up to the captain's tier.

Ed went down and peered over the consoles. A very tall

mummified body lay behind the units, slumped forward as though they'd sat down for a rest with their back to the console.

'Oh, yuk,' said Linda, peeking over Ed's shoulder. 'You can check for life signs,' she added, backing away quickly.

'Perhaps it's the captain,' said Ed. 'Went down with the ship and all that.'

The remains of the clothing gave nothing away, but something about the skull made Ed move in for a closer look: two strange-looking protrusions on the top of its head that looked like an injury. He backed away suddenly, a shocked expression on his face that Linda noticed.

'What is it?' she asked.

'I can't be sure – but that thing looks remarkably similar to a dead Mogul,' he said.

'A Mogul?' she repeated, recoiling slightly.

Pol had noticed the fear in their voices and body language.

'Is this not good news?' she asked.

Ed and Linda glanced at each other.

'Erm – they're a race we've had dealings with in the past,' said Linda.

'A race of sadistic killers,' said Ed, getting a shake of the head from Linda.

'I don't think Pol needs to know everything about them,' she said, staring into his visor. ''cause they're all dead.'

'Not quite true, humans,' boomed a voice from the doorway.

All three of them jumped and turned as one. A very alive seven-foot-tall, very lean, maroon-skinned Mogul stood at the entrance to the bridge pointing a large weapon of some kind at them.

'And who gave you permission to wake?' he demanded.

'Hello,' said Ed. 'My name's Edward, who are you?'

The Mogul's weapon fired, causing Ed's personal shield to activate. The assailant looked confused for a moment and, noticing Linda bringing her weapon up, he fired at her too, with the same result as the energy bolt crackled around her shield and dispersed.

In the couple of seconds it took for all this to happen, both Ed and Linda had brought their rifles to bear. They fired together, sending the Mogul staggering back. He stayed standing though and looked down at himself, then back at them and laughed.

'Your puny weapons have no effect on me,' he scoffed.

'Wanna bet?' said Ed, turning his laser rifle's setting up to full and blowing a hole the size of a fist through his chest.

This time the Mogul went down and stayed there, blood pooling around the body. Pol peered out from behind a console, a look of horror on her face.

'How could anyone or anything possibly be alive on this ship after all this time?' she said.

'This is getting very weird,' said Linda, looking at the body more closely. 'He was extremely skinny though.'

'He asked why we were awake,' said Ed. 'Perhaps he was in some kind of stasis and our movements woke him.'

'Well, if there's one, there must be more,' said Pol, watching the door nervously.

'We need to find where they are and dispose of them,' said Linda.

'You want to murder them all?' said Pol, glancing back at her.

'It's a case of them or us,' said Linda. 'You saw how he pulled the trigger for no apparent reason and it wasn't set on stun either.'

'They might not all be like him,' she said.

Ed and Linda looked at each other.

'Yes, they are,' they both said in stereo.

Ed sat down at the captain's console and began randomly touching some of the lit icons. The door suddenly started closing, so he hit the same icon again and it reopened.

'Well, that's the door sorted,' he said. 'I just need to find a schematic of the ship and see what's in the rest of it.'

'Or a ship's log,' said Linda.

'Pol, are you able to use his weapon?' asked Ed, nodding towards where it was lying on the floor.

She glanced at it for a moment.

'Probably,' she said.

'Can you use it to guard the door?'

She nervously picked it up and pointed it in the direction of the open door.

'Great – if anyone comes down that passageway, challenge them and if it's one of the horned bastards, shoot first.'

She nodded, but didn't look very confident.

'Ed, I've just noticed, the atmosphere in here is at ninety-six percent,' said Linda.

'It was probably at one hundred before we opened the door,' he said. 'That's why it made the sucking sound.'

She retracted her helmet and sniffed the air.

'I thought it might stink with that body trapped in here for so long,' she said.

'The smell would have dissipated long ago,' he replied, also retracting his helmet and trying a red icon on his seat's armrest.

A loud electronic voice resonated around the bridge similar to the flying bricks and a muffled translation seemed to come from the Mogul, making Pol jump.

'Find his translator,' said Linda. 'I think he's lying on it.'

Ed stood up and rolled the Mogul over onto his back,

wrinkling his nose at the metallic smell of the blood. He found the unit in a front pouch. Sitting back in the captain's chair, he pressed the red icon again and held up the translator.

'*Affirm the request?*' it said.

Ed smiled at Linda and Pol looked around the bridge nervously.

'Did the ship just speak to us?' she asked.

'*I did – please affirm the request?*' it said again.

'Can you display a detailed plan of the ship's interior, please,' said Ed.

'*Affirmative.*'

A large holographic representation of the vessel appeared above them all, rotating about a central axis.

'Are you able to utilise the software in this translator to change the default language of the ship and its control surfaces to the one I'm speaking?' asked Ed.

'*Affirmative.*'

A flat blue laser light scanned the unit in Ed's hand and as he watched, the writing on the control surfaces and icons changed to English.

'*Change advocated,*' it said in English and Ed gave the translator to Pol.

'Can you also give me a full rundown on this ship's course, from its initiation to intended destination.'

'*Affirmative.*'

The screen in front of him changed to a course plan.

'Ed,' said Linda, staring at the hologram intently. 'You might want to see this.'

'What is it?' he said, looking up.

She pointed at the rear top section of the ship.

'There's six of those big hangar or warehouse spaces here named biological cargo.'

He raised his eyebrows and glanced up at the ceiling.

'Computer, what is biological cargo?'

'Colonists for destination.'

Ed sat back in the seat and gave Linda a sombre look.

'It's an ancient colony ship,' he said.

'One that never got to its destination,' said Linda.

'Computer, how many colonists are there on the ship?' asked Ed.

'Nine hundred and ninety-nine thousand, nine hundred and one, of which sixty-six percent remain operational.'

'By operational, do you mean alive?'

'Affirmative.'

'Are there any other alien life forms alive on this ship?'

'Affirmative – eighty-one in serenity chamber two, two on the bridge and seventeen on the adjoining vessel.'

'Adjoining vessel?' said Pol. 'Is that your ship, Linda?'

'No, Pol,' she said, looking perplexed. 'Why only two aliens on the bridge?'

'Computer, where is this adjoining vessel?' Ed asked, overriding Linda's question.

'It's attached to the vehicle in this position.'

What looked like just another equipment nacelle began flashing in blue on the holographic image.

'Bloody hell,' said Ed. 'That's right next to the bridge – just down there.'

'That's probably where he came from,' said Linda, nodding at the dead Mogul.

'Affirmative.'

'I wasn't talking to you,' she said, glaring upwards.

'My apologies,' said the ship.

Ed stood up and checked his weapon.

'Pol, stay here for a few minutes and if the door shuts us out, you can open it again with that button there,' he said, pointing at the relevant icon.

'Or I could ask the ship, it seems.'

'You may.'

'You want me to stay here with that?' she said, glaring at the Mogul's body.

'He can't hurt you now,' said Ed. 'We won't be gone long and you could always chat to the ship.'

'Computer, do you have a name?' asked Linda.

'Faith.'

'Is that you or the ship?'

'We are one and the same.'

'Okay, Faith – look after Pol here until we return.'

'Affirmative.'

'Where are you two going?' Pol asked.

'To rid the ship of a parasite,' said Linda, heading out the door and turning her laser rifle setting up to full.

'It's attached somewhere down here on the port side,' said Ed, as they walked purposefully down the corridor away from the bridge.

The door to the cabin just before the elevator on the port side was open.

'We closed all the doors didn't we?' whispered Linda, stopping just short of it.

'We did,' said Ed. 'I'll go left, you go right – one, two, three.'

Ed dived through the door, closely followed by Linda. The cabin was empty.

'It's gotta be here somewhere,' he said, beginning to prod and pull at everything attached to the cabin's far outer wall.

Linda went into the small en suite bathroom.

Ed,' she called. 'Found it.'

10

ED ENTERED the bathroom and discovered a wall panel hanging open on one side.

'Was this open when we checked these cabins earlier?' he asked.

'No,' said Linda.

Ed pushed it fully open and climbed through. To one side he recognised sections of the inner and outer hull that had been cut open and discarded. Facing him was a tall oval airlock that seemed to be clamped tight to the outer hull. The door, designed to swing inwards, was open and he stepped inside, calling Linda through to join him. They both activated their helmets and double-checked their weapons were ready to go.

A six-inch square panel next to the inner door flashed enticingly and, making sure they were both clear of the outer door, he pressed it. The outer door buzzed closed and sealed and with a slight hiss then the inner one slid to the left. They both immediately went on the float and steadied themselves against the door frame. Bringing their weapons up and facing forward, they drifted inside the Mogul ship.

Ed nervously peered left and right and, giving Linda a thumbs up, he decided to go left. A short passageway led to a dimly-lit empty cockpit with no other exit. They spun themselves around and went back the other way, past the open airlock. It was eerily quiet with only a tiny amount of light emanating from the occasional small glowing panel at the base of the walls.

Passing through an open bulkhead door, they entered a much larger space completely taken up with rows of strange-looking vertical stasis pods. They all seemed empty, but as they floated down the rows, they found a few right at the end were still occupied with sleeping Moguls. The floor was wet around the last empty one.

'That's where he came from,' said Ed. 'There must have been some sort of detector on the bridge that activated his awakening.'

'How creepy do they look,' whispered Linda. 'Gives me the shivers, just looking at them.'

'They must have been slowly transferring these guys into the stasis chambers on the colony ship,' said Ed. 'Like a nightmare cuckoo scenario.'

'What do we do about these?' she said. 'Do we just turn them off?'

'Not really,' said Ed, thinking. 'That would probably instigate a failsafe and wake them all up.'

'We can't just shoot them?'

'Why not – they'd do it to us?'

Linda looked at the seventeen pods with faint green lights glowing on their front panels and shivered.

'Can't we just destroy the bridge controls and eject this ship?'

'It's punctured the hull of the *Faith*. It would cause a sudden decompression if we removed it,' said Ed.

A sudden beep made them jump as one of the chambers on the end of the row began flashing and the liquid filling the pod began draining out.

'Oh shit,' said Linda. 'Here comes another one.'

Ed quickly pulled himself down the row and opposite the waking pod, braced himself against the wall behind and fired into the chamber twice. The Mogul's eyes opened, and it jerked around for a moment before going still. Instantly, all the chambers began flashing and draining.

'Ah crap, no,' shouted Ed.

Linda gave him a quick shrug and began firing into the nearest pods. It took them less than a minute to complete the grisly job and dispose of all the waking monsters.

Before they left, Ed went down the two lines and put a laser bolt through the head of each of the seventeen bodies.

'We can't take the risk of even one of these things surviving,' he said to Linda. 'Now we need to find that second colony chamber on the main ship and dispose of the rest.'

Linda remained silent. She took one last look at the carnage, turned and floated back towards the airlock.

A few minutes later they found a very agitated Pol standing just inside the bridge door.

'The ship says there are aliens waking up in one of the colonists' chambers,' she said, her eyes wide with worry.

'What's going on, Faith?' called Ed, as he entered the bridge.

'Eighty-one pods in serenity chamber two are in animation mode.'

'Alien life forms I presume?'

'Affirmative.'

'Is there any way of sealing that chamber?' Ed asked.

'Airlock three in serenity chamber two is presently inoperative.'

'In open or closed position?'

'Open.'

'Yeah, it would be wouldn't it? Faith, can you override the animation of the eighty-one pods?'

'They have independent control.'

'Faith, can we wake the crew?' asked Pol.

'You are awake.'

'I meant the first crew?' she said, rolling her eyes at Ed.

'Original crew no longer on vehicle.'

'What?' said Ed. 'Well, where are they then?'

'Data unknown, before core rebuild.'

'Faith, when did the original crew leave the ship?'

'Data unknown, before core rebuild.'

'Why did they leave the ship?'

'Data unknown, before—'

'The bloody core rebuild, yeah, yeah,' said Ed, rolling his eyes at Linda.

'Can we seal this end of the ship, so they can't get near the bridge?' asked Linda.

'I can prevent the crew elevator reaching the transfer decks.'

'Can you do that then, please?' said Ed.

'I need a crew member to confirm the command.'

'I thought we were the crew?'

'You are alien life forms. Pol is crew.'

They both stared at Pol.

'Did you do something while we were away?' asked Ed.

'Nothing apart from worry,' said Pol.

'You'd better tell Faith to seal us in, then, unless you want another eighty-one of him striding up the corridor.'

Pol followed Ed's pointing finger to the body and noticeably shivered.

'Can you shut down the elevator, Faith?' she said.

'Affirmative.'

'Faith, can you show me an image of some of the colonists, please?' asked Ed.

'Affirmative.'

The hologram of the ship still rotating above their heads disappeared, replaced by six humanoids with dumpy knee-less legs and four arms.

Ed and Linda both turned towards Pol, who was staring at the images with her mouth open.

'It seems we've found a ship full of your cousins,' said Ed.

'That could explain where the crew went,' said Linda.

'What do you mean?' asked Pol.

Linda held a hand up to Pol as a way of saying hold on.

'Faith, are there any lifeboats or ships missing from the inventory?' she asked.

'One personnel shuttle is missing from hangar bay five.'

'When did it go missing?'

'Data unknown, before core rebuild.'

'Hmm,' mumbled Linda.

'What are you thinking?' Ed asked.

'The crew abandoned ship however many thousand years ago and landed on Callamet,' she said.

Pol's eyes opened wide.

'You think the crew from this ship are my ancestors?' she said. 'That's ridiculous.'

'You have archeological evidence to prove otherwise?' asked Linda.

'We can argue this another time,' said Ed. 'Let's worry about avoiding a gang of killers and getting off this ship. Faith, I've been meaning to ask you – what's with all that fast fog outside?'

'The inner hem of our wormhole.'

'Yes, it's a wormhole – of course,' he said. 'You've solved the wormhole quandary.'

'Is that faster than folding?' asked Linda.

'Not likely,' said Ed. 'Faith, how far is it to our next waypoint?'

'Six point six of your light years.'

'And how long will it take to get there?'

'Two point two of your years.'

'Holy crap,' said Linda. 'Over two years to go six light years – Andy's Kawasaki is quicker than that.'

Pol squeaked and dived down behind one of the control panels as a laser bolt zipped across the bridge and burned a hole through one of the seats.

Ed dived for the door control icon as Linda sent a barrage of fire back in return. A group of five Moguls were standing in the corridor. They saw two of them go down before the huge door swung down and sealed with a *clunk* and a *hiss*.

'Faith, I thought they couldn't get up here?' called Ed.

'They used the emergency ladders.'

'Why didn't you warn us then?'

'Data not requested.'

'Fuck me, it's like getting blood from a stone,' said Linda.

'Faith, will they be able to penetrate that door?' asked Pol, standing up again.

'Affirmative.'

'How long until that happens?'

'Data unknown.'

'Shit,' said Ed. 'Can you close down the wormhole, Faith?'

'Affirmative.'

'Do that, please.'

'Any change in course parameters requires authorisation by two crew members.'

'This is getting ridiculous,' shouted Linda. 'We are the bloody crew now, just do as you're told.'

'Any change in course parameters requires authorisation by two crew members.'

'Wait,' said Pol. 'I have an idea.' She glanced up at the ceiling. 'Faith, I'm instigating a field promotion for Linda to the ship's first officer. Can you record that in the log, please?'

They all held their breath as Faith didn't respond immediately. It took another couple of seconds.

'Affirmative.'

'Thank you, Faith – now drop us out of the wormhole,' said Pol, giving Linda a slight nod.

'I second that command,' said Linda, crossing her fingers.

'Wormhole threshold collapsing in three seconds.'

The lights dimmed slightly and a bright starscape appeared out of all the arched windows.

'Great,' said Ed, stepping down to the lowest level and sitting at one of the consoles. 'You two come down here and helmet up.'

'What's going on?' asked Linda, as she sat next to Pol on the weird Callametan-designed couches, activating her helmet and helping Pol back on with hers.

'Strap in really tight,' he said, glancing up at the windows and smirking. 'I'm going to let them in.'

'You're going to what?' said Pol.

'Don't worry,' said Linda. 'He'll have a good reason.'

They pulled the gravity failure belts around themselves as tight as they would go and Ed made sure both of their weapons were securely attached by their straps.

'What are we doing all this for?' asked Pol, still sounding very nervous and trying to look at them sideways out of her helmet.

'I believe Ed is going to invite our friends in for a very

quick visit,' Linda said as she realised what his plan was. 'Don't forget to wave as they go by.'

'You take the right middle window and I'll take the left one,' said Ed. 'And don't forget to keep your heads as low as you can.'

'Faith, how many aliens are there outside the bridge door?' asked Linda.

'Forty-seven.'

'Where are the remainder?'

'On the ladders and in the upper port transfer deck.'

'Okay, can you open all doorways between them and the bridge and keep them open until they've all left the vehicle?'

'I concur with that order,' said Pol.

'Affirmative.'

'All ready?' Ed asked, giving Linda and Pol a quick sideways glance. Getting two nods in reply, both he and Linda lifted their laser rifles.

He used his right hand little finger to lightly touch the open door icon on the panel in front.

Ed felt as well as heard the *clunk* as the locks disengaged and the whine of the motor as it laboured up with the heavy door.

'*Now*,' he shouted.

The two arched windows were surprisingly strong and it took both Ed and Linda five shots before they failed and disappeared. Ed felt his whole body rise up in the seat and he was suddenly afraid the belts might not be designed for the stresses they were presently enduring.

He hung there gritting his teeth, his arms and rifle hanging out in front of him in the passing maelstrom of atmosphere. It roared out of the missing windows taking anything and everything with it. Unable to lift his head up, Ed was faintly aware of shapes flying by. Some of them making screaming noises that ceased very abruptly as they were whipped out into the vacuum of space.

After about thirty seconds it went quieter and Ed forced his head up, fighting his neck muscles all the way. He managed a quick glance around and, seeing an empty corridor, he touched the icon again. Slowly the passing tumult diminished and finally ceased, followed by complete and utter silence.

He checked over his shoulder that the door had in fact locked, as in the vacuum he hadn't heard it close.

'You okay, Linda?' he said.

'Are they all gone?' she asked.

'I don't know, I can't talk to Faith now in this vacuum.'

He unstrapped and helped Pol, who was having trouble holding her head up. Her neck muscles had taken a beating because of her heavier helmet.

'Look,' said Linda, pointing towards the missing front windows. 'There's something moving out there.'

Ed walked to the front, climbed up to one of the missing panes and stuck his head out. The *Cartella* sat thirty metres away with a grinning Andy waving through the front screen.

'You're going to get a ticket for littering, you manky twat,' called Andy.

11

POL STOOD on the bridge in absolute awe at the technology surrounding her.

'I had no idea that any of this was possible,' she said, after Ed had given her a rundown on the *Gabriel*.

They were waiting for Cleo to complete the repairs to the *Faith* before they turned it around and went back to the Traxx system.

'So your ship is fully sentient and smarter than any of us?' she queried.

'Smarter than all the humans that have ever lived put together,' said Ed.

'And boy, does she like reminding us,' said Linda.

'You do need the occasional aide-memoire,' said Cleo, in a posh English accent.

'Are the *Faith*'s front screens replaced yet, Cleo?' Ed asked.

'All done,' she said. 'I've incorporated a local resonance field within them so you can communicate with that ship's dumb-arse computer.'

Pol sniggered in the strange squeaky Callametan way.

'Your ship's funny,' she said.

'I'm glad someone appreciates my badinage,' said Cleo.

'Your what?' questioned Andy, giving Ed a sideways glance.

'Witticisms,' said Ed. 'She's just showing off her linguistics again.'

'*Tu peux parler au crétin quand tu veux,*' she said.

'Yes, thank you, Cleo,' said Ed. 'We shall.'

'Shall what?' said Andy, crossing his arms.

'Talk to Faith.'

'Oh, right,' he said. 'I'm glad someone can understand that mad box of sparks.'

'Faith, can you hear me?' Ed asked.

'*Affirmative.*'

'Excellent – how many aliens remain on the vehicle?'

'*Eleven.*'

'Where are they?'

'*Seven are attempting to enter the bridge and four are lying down at the base of the emergency ladders.*'

'Are the four by the emergency ladders still alive?'

'*Affirmative, but life signs are fading.*'

Ed pointed at Pol and nodded.

'Faith, can you swing the ship around and set a course back to the Traxx system?' said Pol.

'I concur with that order,' said Linda.

'*Affirmative, course change initiated.*'

The big ship immediately began swinging around.

'Thank you, Faith,' said Ed. 'We'll contact you with further instructions as you get nearer Traxx,' and he indicated to Cleo to cut the transmission.

'What do we do about the seven Moguls?' asked Pol. 'If they get on the bridge, they could do a lot of damage.'

Ed nodded and thought for a moment.

'Cleo, can you pull that Mogul ship off the side of the *Faith*?' he asked.

'A localised narrow tractor beam could do it,' she said. 'But you would have to do that yourself.'

'I understand, Cleo,' he said, moving his attention over to Phil. 'Can you put us five hundred metres directly out from that attached ship, Phil? And Rayl, can you prepare a narrow beam to drag it off the *Faith*'s hull?'

He received nods from both and a couple of minutes later they were in position.

Cleo provided a holographic close-up of the Mogul ship and they watched as Rayl affixed the red-coloured three-metre wide tractor beam to its hull and began to ramp up the drag.

It remained there for a few moments and just as Ed was about to say something the ship ripped away from the *Faith*'s hull. Debris, fixtures and fittings from the cabin within spewed out, followed shortly after by bodies of Moguls, their weapons and what looked like some sort of industrial plasma cutter.

'They must have been attempting to cut their way into the bridge,' said Andy.

'How many bodies is that?' asked Linda.

'Five so far,' said Rayl. 'No, make that six.'

The detritus cascading from the gash in the hull slowed and finally stopped.

'Faith must have closed all the bulkhead doors,' said Linda. 'If there's any of those bastards still alive, then they'll suffocate very quickly.'

'Good riddance,' said Rayl. 'I hope they all fucking rot in hell.'

Pol gazed across at Rayl from the specially designed seat

Cleo had made for her at the side of the bridge. Ed noticed she looked quite shocked at Rayl's outburst.

'Don't worry, Pol,' he said. 'She has a very legitimate and personal reason to hate them. I'll explain another time.'

Pol nodded, but didn't look any happier.

After Cleo had done a quick repair to the outside of the *Faith*'s hull, they jumped back into the Traxx system and assumed a high orbit around Callamet.

After contacting Ambassador Ralt's office, they were given a flight path down to the surface. Andy went with Ed this time and the two of them along with Pol left the *Gabriel* aboard the *Cartella* and followed the trajectory down into Callamet's atmosphere.

'Is this where your space port is, Pol?' said Ed. 'It seems a bit desolate.'

Pol glanced over Ed's shoulder, a puzzled expression on her face.

'No,' she said. 'I've never been out here before, it's one of the most remote areas on the planet. This isn't what I was expecting.'

'We need to be wary,' said Andy, increasing the shield parameters around the small ship.

Ed disappeared into the rear of the ship for a few moments and returned with two of their laser rifles, made sure they were set to a medium stun, and handed one to Pol.

She looked surprised to be receiving one, but accepted it when Ed pointed out it had a personal shield unit attached.

'We have no idea what's happened down here since the moon disappeared,' said Ed. 'I haven't been able to contact Ambassador Ralt in person either, which is a little odd considering the situation and she specifically told me to talk to her only.'

Pol nodded and gazed out the front screen.

'The cults are very powerful,' she said. 'Ralt's position in representing all of them was always contentious and somewhat fragile.'

Ed looked back at her.

'Could she have been replaced?' he asked.

'Wouldn't take much,' said Pol. 'All the cults have their own armed militia.'

Ed thought for a moment.

'Okay, Pol,' he said, finally. 'We're going to have a code word for you to say if you consider us to be in serious danger. I want you to choose it, but just make sure we hear it loud and clear.'

Pol stared forward for a moment before answering.

'Banana,' said Pol, nodding.

'Banana?' questioned Andy, opening his eyes and looking over from the control couch.

'Phil was eating one earlier and gave me a piece. It was delicious and not a known word on my planet, so if I say banana, you know it's not by mistake.'

'Banana it is,' said Ed, grinning.

As they approached the landing coordinates, it was obvious that whoever was down there didn't want any witnesses. The snowy wilderness that stretched out beneath them went on for hundreds of kilometres. Ed could just make out a single track that wound its way through the hills to a compound covering about a square kilometre. Rows of identical buildings covered most of the area except for a large hardstanding in front of a bigger building built into the hillside.

A flashing circle of green lights, presumably the intended landing zone, presented itself.

'Don't land in the middle,' said Ed. 'Let's just remain a little random and not do exactly what they expect.'

'I'll put it down in the corner over there,' said Andy, pointing to an area nearest the bigger building.

'Keep the motor running and the cannons on standby too,' said Ed. 'I want to check what this is about before we leave Pol behind.'

'You want me to remain on the ship?' said Andy, looking a little disappointed as he dropped the *Cartella* down in the random corner of the pad.

'Yeah,' said Ed. 'I don't trust religious fanatics and you've gotta be hiding something to be all the way out here. Are you ready up top, Rayl?'

'Locked and loaded, sir' she replied, like a marine to his superior.

Ed glanced at Andy questioningly.

'Sorry – introduced her to twentieth century war movies,' he said, looking swiftly away. 'We've got company.'

Ed peered out the front screen to find three boxy tracked vehicles with darkened glass trundling out and having to turn sharp left to reach them.

'Come on, Pol, let's go and see what their intentions are. And keep the rifle hidden behind your back.'

Andy opened up the airlock and Ed waved to the oncoming vehicles, a wide smile on his face. The vehicles formed a semicircle around the airlock side of the *Cartella* and thirty black-robed figures with their hoods up obscuring their faces, trotted out and formed another semicircle inside the vehicles.

'Obsidian cult,' whispered Pol, as they stepped down from the ship. 'Dangerous.'

'Keep smiling,' Ed replied, as one of the robed figures approached.

She stopped in front of Ed and drew her hood back with her top two arms. Before she could say anything, Ed stepped forward and hugged her tightly. He could feel her sudden tensing and watched over her shoulder as all the other robed figures twitched. He was sure a couple of them almost produced weapons, but held back at the last second.

'Fantastic to meet you guys,' said Ed, pacing one step back and checking the translator was operating. 'You must be thrilled to have been chosen to meet your planetary hero Pol. Is Ambassador Ralt with you?'

The Callametan stared at Ed through cold eyes a while longer before speaking.

'Ambassador Ralt is unavailable,' she said in a very monotone voice. 'She's been unavoidably detained in the capital.'

'You don't mind if I have a little chat with the ambassador first, just to confirm where the hero's welcome home party is to be held,' said Ed, and turned to leave.

'The ambassador will be unavailable for the foreseeable future,' said the Callametan. 'You will give Pol to us and leave immediately.'

'Banana,' said Pol.

'He was available earlier,' said Ed, keeping the smile going. 'Ah well, we'll go and find him in the capital. Thanks for the lovely greeting and if you've done a nice buffet spread or something, share it out amongst yourselves as a little treat. Come on Pol, we've got an ambassador to find.'

The Callametan made the slightest gesture with her lower right hand and all the other hooded figures produced weapons from under their cloaks.

'I'm afraid that you're not permitted to leave with her,' the Callametan said.

'On who's authority?' Ed asked.

'Pol is a convicted criminal and is to be detained pending sentencing.'

'Oh really? What crime has she been found guilty of *in absentia*?' Ed asked, the smile replaced by a malevolent glare.

'Heresy and criminal destruction of the Cathedral of the Gods.'

Ed laughed and heard Pol's squeaky laugh behind him.

'You're all going to look a bunch of right numpties tomorrow when the Cathedral of the Gods returns and is in orbit around Callamet, aren't you?'

He noticed the Callametan's brow furrow slightly as a twinge of doubt appeared in her eyes.

'Of this you lie,' she managed.

'No, I don't,' said Ed. 'Also, I'm a representative of the GDA and Pol has been put under our protection, so at this point you've got to hope the Grand Council don't decide to have you and your sad collection of brainless fanatics executed for threatening a galactic officer.'

The Callametan glanced over her shoulder and nodded once to one of her colleagues, who immediately spoke into a handset.

'We've got multiple missiles launched from some of the satellites up here,' called Phil from above.

'Shall we see how much protection you can give without that domestic poseur yacht up there?' said the Callametan, raising her eyes skyward.

12

A remote compound, Planet Callamet, Traxx system

ED SMILED at the Callametan and, judging by the flash of doubt in her eyes, it wasn't the reaction she was expecting.

'Domestic poseur yacht, eh!' said Ed. 'I hope those satellites weren't too expensive.'

One of the hooded Callametans from behind ran forward and whispered something to her superior. Ed noticed her eyes widen at the news and she growled another command to her underling. Retreating and again speaking into her handset the hooded Callametan glanced right as a deep rumbling sounded from that direction.

As Ed watched, a huge section of the building above them slowly slid to one side revealing an enormous laser cannon of some sort. The Callametans began to chuckle in their weird squeaky way as the barrel began tracking across the sky.

The asteri beam came down quicker than Ed expected and they all shielded their eyes as the cannon was enveloped in the binding white light. An ear-splitting crackle, like multiple lightning strikes, made all the Callametans cower and as quickly as it came, it went, leaving just the background whine of the *Cartella*'s antigravs.

The Callametan stared open mouthed at where the cannon and that part of the building had once stood, now reduced to a smouldering circle vaporised down a good metre into the bedrock and permafrost.

'Oh dear,' said Ed. 'I hope you didn't have that on finance.'

The Callametan turned back to face Ed with her teeth bared.

'You will pay for that,' she spat.

'Sorry, I didn't bring my credit card,' said Ed, adopting a very sorrowful expression. 'Will an IOU be okay?'

The Callametan backed away and produced a small weapon of some kind from within the folds of her robe.

'*Kill them,*' she shouted and fired straight at Ed from only three metres.

Ed's personal shield snapped up and easily dissipated the bolt of energy that fizzed around him. In the meantime he'd swung his rifle around himself and given the Callametan the good news square in the chest with that. He became aware of the *Cartella* making more noise and ducked as Andy spun the nose up and over the top of him. He had had no idea of actually how much noise the *Cartella*'s cannons made until Andy unleashed them on the welcoming committee.

The Callametan posse had been firing at him and Pol for a couple of seconds but Andy had extended the *Cartella*'s shield between them and their concentrated fire had been completely ineffective. Ed covered his ears as the fearsome ten-barrelled weapon cut them all down in moments and reduced the three vehicles to burning scrap.

'Are you okay?' he called to Pol, who crouched cowering from the cacophony of noise and death happening just metres away.

He received a frightened look and suddenly felt a bit sorry for her.

'Andy, we're coming aboard,' he called, and grabbing the unconscious Callametan leader by the collar, he dragged her towards the *Cartella*'s airlock as it settled back onto its skids ten metres away.

Pol helped him drag the limp six-limbed body inside the airlock and the ship lifted even before the outer door was closed.

'Oh, you want to play too, do you?' Ed heard Andy say as the pitch of the antigravs changed and the roar from the cannons returned.

'Who are you bullying now?' he said, returning to the cockpit after dumping their now prisoner into the rear of the ship and locking her in one of the cabins.

'A column of armoured vehicles entered the fray,' said Andy as he lay back on the control couch, his eyes shut and his head jerking around as he operated multiple systems all at once.

'Where did they come from?' asked Ed, sliding into the couch next to him.

'Same place the first three did.'

'What, through that big hangar door over there?'

'Yeah.'

'Stuff a few through the gap. It might discourage anything else popping its head out.'

Andy slewed the ship around to starboard and sent a barrage of the explosive cannon shells in through the partially open steel door. The resulting explosion inside caused the doors to balloon out slightly and a flame over a hundred metres long lashed out at them from the gap.

'Right, I think we've established our displeasure at the nature of our welcome,' said Ed. 'Shall we go—'

The second explosion stopped Ed mid-sentence, as the whole building including a considerable amount of the hillside lifted up and almost enveloped them. Luckily, the shields were on full and the inertial damper, which was tested to the limits of its design, held firm.

When the ship ceased spinning they were two kilometres away from the compound and Pol, who hadn't been sitting down, was lying in the corner, a tangle of arms and legs and giving both of them a glare.

'Are we still airtight?' asked Ed, sweeping his eyes over the control panels.

'I believe so,' said Andy, pointing the ship north. 'Bloody hell, where are those coming from?' He pointed forward and below.

Ed stretched up and saw four strange aircraft rising up from a hidden location just east of the now destroyed compound.

'Are they coming for us?' Ed asked.

'No,' said Pol, looking over Andy's shoulder. 'They're troop carriers and they're in a hurry t—'

The flash of the third explosion caused the front screen to darken as it was designed to do in the event of an open air nuclear detonation. The entire hill, the four aircraft and everything within a kilometre vanished. Andy punched the throttles and turned sharply to port.

The shock wave was on them a split second later and again tested the inertial damping, only this time they were further away and angled better to run with the wave.

'Well, that's two less nuclear weapons this cult has hidden away,' said Ed.

'They shouldn't have any,' said Pol. 'They've been outlawed for a generation.'

'Really,' said Andy. 'I wonder how many more they have stored under these mountains.'

'There must have been a connecting tunnel between the two,' said Ed. 'And the first one, luckily for us, was stored deeper.'

As they rose up to a safe height, another detonation below rocked the ship, then another and another.

'Fuck me – it's Dante's *Inferno* down there,' said Andy.

'They must be hugely volatile and really badly designed,' said Ed. 'Sorry, Pol, but my holiday review of your planet is not going to be five stars.'

Pol was sat back on the floor in the corner looking quite dejected.

'I didn't understand a word of what either of you just said,' she said, not looking up. 'But I think I get the sentiment and if I'm brutally honest, I think it would have been better for everyone if I hadn't gone on that mission at all.'

'Pol,' said Ed. 'I don't want to hear you say that ever again. You spent half your life training for that flight and you executed it fantastically well. To us, and I bet a lot of your people too, you're an absolute hero. What you did was a real achievement and a huge elevation for your race and probably one of the bravest solo missions I've ever seen.'

'I completely agree,' said Andy. 'And when we get back to the *Gabriel*, we're going to have a slap-up dinner and a party to celebrate your achievement. How does that sound?'

Ed was momentarily puzzled at why he could hear a cat meowing, until he realised it was actually Pol sobbing. He quickly jumped up, sat down with her and gave her a hug.

Andy had cloaked the *Cartella* and under guidance from Pol, had travelled up to the equator and the capital of Callamet, Traxion.

It wasn't the largest city on the planet by any means, but was probably one of the prettiest. Situated on the shore of the planet's biggest ocean and straddling the mouth of a huge wide blue river, it had miles of pristine beaches and only a short distance inland, almost untouched rainforest.

The ground was very soft here and had in the early days restricted the architecture to a maximum of five floors. This planning regulation, along with no modern-style buildings, had never been rescinded, hence everything was of an attractive old-fashioned stone-built design and all reasonably low to the ground.

Being the capital, its domestic air traffic was busy, so they remained offshore, close to the ocean and away from the city's regular flight lines.

'Where's Ralt's office, Pol?' asked Ed, pointing out at the sprawling city.

'It's on the western fringe,' she said. 'I went there for a press reception shortly before launch.'

'Okay, talk us in, and Andy, make sure nothing flies into us while we're over the city.'

Andy went high to avoid the majority of the personal flyers and when Pol pointed out the building, they sat directly above at five hundred metres.

Ed lay on his couch with his eyes shut and felt down into the building with his DOVI. The architecture might be of an older design, but the internal electronics were state of the art. He was able to infiltrate the building's camera feeds and follow Pol's directions up to a suite of offices on the top floor.

'That's her personal secretary,' said Pol, pointing out a Callametan leaning at a desk watching a holographic computer display.

Ed used the room's holo emitters and projected an image of himself into the room behind the Callametan. He cleared his throat, causing the secretary to almost levitate off the floor.

'Preserve the gods,' she said, turning sharply and giving Ed a glare. 'Where did you come from?'

'Dasos,' said Ed. 'From the GDA. I have an important meeting with Ambassador Ralt, if you could let her know I'm here.'

'Erm, I'm afraid she's unavailable,' she mumbled.

Ed noticed her eyes flick nervously at the ambassador's office door.

'Don't worry, she'll be available for me,' he said, moving in the direction of the wooden double doors.

They burst open revealing two of the now familiar robed figures of the Obsidian cult, both carrying weapons pointed at him.

'You were given clear instructions of where to land, Mr Virr,' said one of them.

'Unfortunately, your illegal stockpile of nuclear weapons going bang changed our minds,' said Ed. 'Along with your military satellites that tried to engage us when we arrived.'

'You're carrying an enemy of the people. You will release her to us now or die where you stand,' said the other robed figure.

'Fire when ready,' said Ed, stepping back a little.

In the blink of an eye, two holes appeared in the ceiling

and the two robed figures simply disintegrated, redecorating that side of the room in quite a gruesome fashion.

Ed turned back to face the shocked secretary, who stood rooted to the spot.

'Is the ambassador available now?' he asked, raising his eyebrows.

'Er, erm – I don't—'

'I am – come in, Mr Virr,' said Ralt's voice from within the room.

Ed entered the big office to find the ambassador leaning behind her desk, obvious purple bruises and abrasions on her face.

'I would normally come out there to welcome you, Edward, but they attached one of my legs to my leaning chair.'

Ed called the secretary in to free the ambassador. She side-stepped in with a revolted expression, trying to avoid the still dripping ceiling, and untied Ralt.

'Are there any more of them?' Ed asked, nodding at the mess on the floor just outside the door.

'In the lobby downstairs there are generally about three more,' she said. 'Dissuading anyone who got suspicious or demanded to see me.'

'How did you get past them?' asked the secretary, eyeing Ed very nervously.

'Like this.'

Ed disappeared and, reappearing on the other side of the room, said, 'Ta-da.'

'You're a holo image,' said Ralt. 'Brilliant – what's the plan now?'

'Is there a back exit?' Ed asked.

Ralt and his secretary both pointed at a small door in the corner of the office.

'My own private elevator and stairwell,' said Ralt.

'Take it down to street level and walk around to that wide green area there,' said Ed, pointing out the side window. 'We'll pick you up right there.'

'What in?' Ralt asked. 'You're not planning to land a spacecraft on my lawn are you?'

'Just a little one,' said Ed, smiling and disappearing.

13

Obsidian Cathedral, Traxion City, Planet Callamet, Traxx system

FIRST OBSIDIAN HAAKK stomped around her windowless chamber screaming at anyone and everyone. As if she wasn't annoyed enough when informed that all twelve of their offensive satellites had vanished off the screens shortly after launching an attack against some defenceless private yacht.

Now, it seemed contact with all their military and nuclear storage facilities in the Yalitt Mountains had failed.

'What, with all of them?' she shouted.

'We need the satellites to bounce the signal off,' said Haakk's Obsidian Select, Fressan.

'Well, use a civilian line,' she growled, holding her head in her upper hands and balling the lower two into fists.

'We're trying,' said Fressan. 'None of the lines are going through – they must be experiencing bad weather or something.'

'Get that puppet, Ralt here,' Haakk ordered, 'I want her to be present and supportive when we publicly execute that bitch Pol, and send Quyll in here as soon as she arrives with her.'

'Yes, First,' said Fressan, quickly exiting before Haakk could find her more to do.

She scurried through the labyrinth of corridors in the Obsidian Order's hidden underground military headquarters deep underneath the capital's cathedral. As she was about to enter an elevator up to the investigative floors, an insistent voice called her name.

'Select Fressan – Select Fressan.'

'What now?' snapped Fressan, the irritation clear in her voice.

The junior believer from the communications lodge held up a miniscreen.

'This was recorded by a convoy twenty-eight kecks out from the Yalitt Mountain complex,' she stammered, quite out of breath from the sprint though to the elevator.

Fressan watched, her face becoming a picture of horror as five mushroom clouds of various sizes rose out of the mountain range.

'The convoy are requesting instructions,' said the junior, almost cowering.

'Take this straight to the First,' Fressan said, thinking she didn't want to be the one who gave Haakk that news. 'It requires a Grand Council decision,' and quickly stepped into the elevator.

She decided to keep out of Haakk's way and go and fetch Ambassador Ralt herself, so she pressed the button for street level instead.

There were always several flyers sitting in the garage portico at the back of the cathedral and she chose the one nearest the exit. A mechanic believer retracted the shroud for her and stood back smartly to attention when she recognised Fressan's rank.

She activated the flyer, which was connected to the city's aerial transfer mesh, and waited for the three blue lights to confirm a locked birth. The ambassador's lodge still showed as a government taxation office in the location menu, so Fressan touched the panel, sat back and waited for her entry niche.

Registered Obsidian vehicles had precedence over regular traffic, so it only took a few seconds for a niche to become available and the flyer lifted, turned and joined the flood of aerial craft heading west.

Fressan was initially dubious about the First's decision to arrest Ralt, but had realised the necessity once Ralt had eventually disclosed the secret GDA mission to further violate the Cathedral of the Gods. Now with its criminal destruction, the whole planet was in uproar and demanding retribution. The First's order for the execution of Pol and the destruction of the GDA ship would initially assuage the masses and, with luck, calm things down. But with the puzzling satellite problem and now the Yalitt Mountains disaster, she was glad not to be the First today.

The journey across town was slow, the flyer dropped to almost a hover on several occasions and Fressan had time to gaze over at the ocean and wonder when she'd next get the opportunity to go lining for scabbers again. A sudden turn and steep descent woke her from the daydream, as the flyer dropped between the buildings, turned again and settled on the lodge's flyer apron.

Movement in her peripheral vision made her look over to the gardens at the side of the lodge. Two people were running out from the back of the building. She realised with surprise that one of them was Ralt and she seemed to be gazing up at the sky looking for something.

Fressan quickly opened the shroud and clambered out, pulling her personal weapon and striding towards Ralt. A tall bi-armed alien human suddenly materialised on some steps next to Ralt and her associate and indicated for them to climb the steps.

Fressan shouted and began to sprint as fast as she could, levelling the weapon at the alien and firing twice. The shots seemed to strangely dissipate around the alien with a crackle. He turned, smiled, brought his own weapon to bear on Fressan and fired.

Haakk's Obsidian Select Fressan didn't feel the shock of face-planting at full sprint on the ambassador's lawn, or have any sensation of being dragged over to and up the mysterious steps.

14

The Starship *Gabriel*, orbiting Callamet, Traxx system

'THAT WAS WELL SPOTTED, POL,' said Ed. 'I thought she was one of the guards from the entrance foyer.'

'Who is she then?' asked Phil, helping Ed and Andy drag the two unconscious Callametans out of the *Cartella*.

'Fressan,' said Pol. 'Second in command of the Obsidian cult. I have absolutely no idea why she turned up.'

'I do,' said Ralt, limping slightly from the beating she'd received. 'She'd come to collect me for the public execution.'

'They were going to execute you?' said Andy, stopping what he was doing and looking shocked.

'No, not me – Pol,' she said. 'They wanted me there to demonstrate approval and legitimise the murder.'

Pol went white and buried her face in all four hands.

'This is becoming a living nightmare,' she said. 'I can never go home again.'

Ralt limped over and tried to console her but she pushed her away.

'Get away from me – you were going to support my murder,' she spat.

'They did this to me,' said Ralt, indicating her own face. 'And they were going to burn my spawn.'

Linda appeared just as Pol began sobbing again and led her away up to the blister lounge on the top deck of the ship.

'This is going to cease,' said Ed. 'And Ambassador Ralt, you're going to help me along with these two thugs.'

'These two thugs, as you call them, are part of the most powerful ruling body on the planet,' said Ralt. 'They have devout followers, untold armaments, and we're sure they have nuclear weapons hidden away somewhere, even though they were outlawed decades ago.'

'Cleo, can you show the ambassador the recorded footage from, I think you call it the Yalitt Mountains, taken by the *Cartella* this morning, please.'

A large holographic representation of the Yalitt Mountain range appeared in the centre of the hangar. Five mushroom clouds, in various stages of growth, loomed over the entire region. Some of the recognisable peaks had disappeared or completely changed in appearance and the ground seemed to be on fire over tens of kilometres.

Ralt's face went pale and her mouth hung open in absolute horror.

'That was their power base,' she mumbled. 'Completely impregnable – over a million fanatical soldiers, thousands of vehicles and aircraft.' She turned to look at Ed. 'You're saying it's all gone?'

'Well, I can't imagine an awful lot coming out of that,' said Andy.

Ralt glanced over at the other prisoner lying handcuffed on the hangar floor.

'That's Quyll,' she said. 'She was the general

commanding all their forces. She's not going to be very happy with you when she wakes.'

'We didn't bring her along for a holiday,' said Andy, nudging Quyll's unconscious form with his boot. 'She faces charges of attempted murder of a representative of the Galactic Council – and this one,' this time giving Fressan a prod with his boot. 'This one faces the same, along with torture and attempted murder of a Galactic Council ambassador.'

'Okay – where do we go from here?' Ralt asked.

'I, along with your help, Ambassador, are going to recommend to the GDA that the Obsidian cult is designated a terrorist organisation. We have footage of what these two got up to, along with what you've just seen. It's a shame we don't have a recording of what they did to you—'

'Actually, we do,' interrupted Ralt's secretary, Jon.

She produced a small data chip from a pocket and handed it to Ralt.

'Is this—?'

'Yes, it is,' said Jon. 'They didn't know I had a hidden lens in your office.'

'Was it always there?' asked Ralt, sounding a little riled.

'No, ma'am, honestly it wasn't. I placed it on the wall cabinet opposite your desk after they instructed me to turn off the official lenses. It was in a small clock.'

Ralt nodded and handed the chip to Ed.

'I take it you can do something with that?' she said.

'Absolutely, it'll go in the transmission to Dasos along with the rest of the evidence,' said Ed. 'But first we need to prepare you for the arrival of the Cathedral of the Gods.'

'What!' exclaimed Ralt. 'Arrival? – Are you telling me it's coming back?'

While Andy secured their two guests in cells provided by

Cleo, Ed took Ralt and Jon up to the blister lounge, where it was a bit more comfortable and showed them all the evidence regarding the *Faith*.

'So,' said Ralt, an amazed look on her face, 'your theory is that it's highly likely that all of us on Callamet are the descendants of the crew of that ship?'

'It seems the most logical explanation,' said Ed.

'How did they get from there to here?'

'The ship's itinerary shows a passenger shuttle missing from one of the giant hangars.'

'Which would mean, if your theory is correct, it's still here somewhere,' said Ralt.

'Maybe,' said Ed. 'They may have crashlanded and destroyed it, broken it up for the parts, or just hidden it or destroyed it so the moguls couldn't detect it.'

Ralt glared at Ed.

'Are you insinuating we're descended from a group of cowards, Edward? That they abandoned a million of their own race to save their own skins?'

'Of course not – there could've been any number of legitimate reasons for them having to get off that ship and quickly, and anyway it doesn't matter now. What does matter is what we do about the six hundred and sixty-odd thousand Callametans still alive and in hibernation on that vessel.'

'One solution is to let the ship continue on to its intended destination and not interfere anymore,' said Ralt.

'I'm afraid that scenario is off the table,' said Ed.

'For what possible reason?'

'We studied its plotted course to a system, another one hundred and seventy two light years from here. A journey of another almost sixty years.'

'I don't see a problem with that,' said Ralt, raising his eyebrows.

'No,' said Ed. 'You or I wouldn't. But for the last ten thousand years that system and its only habitable planet, called Gallay, has been a major Klatt world.'

'Oh – shit!' said Ralt.

Ed nodded and peered up and out of the domed window at the unfamiliar starscape beyond.

'My sentiments exactly,' he said. 'So we have to find them a new home and if your world is in too much turmoil, then we need to find another uninhabited world for them. Preferably not too far away, because forty-four percent of the hibernation pods have already failed.'

'Or we could wake them now and give them the choice,' said Pol. 'If they didn't want to settle here and in the present situation, who would blame them? I'm sure the GDA would provide a way to jump them all to a new place of residence.'

'That's probably a better solution,' said Ed. 'Let's get some sleep, meet the *Faith* as it arrives and check it's Mogul-free first. Then we can start debating the way forward.'

15

The Starship *Gabriel*, stationary in the Traxx system

CLEO HAD TAKEN the *Gabriel* out to a position near where the *Faith* was due to exit the wormhole. Sure enough, her calculations were spot on as a huge cloudy swirling portal, starting as a spot of light and quickly growing to over three kilometres wide, materialised ten thousand kilometres off their prow.

The *Faith* emerged, its huge bulk squeezing through the gate and immediately turning towards the star and ruffling its feathers to absorb energy.

'Wow,' said Ralt, reclining against a specially created leaning seat. 'What an amazing sight – you neglected to tell me quite how magnificent she is.'

'Not bad for a seven thousandyear-old design, is she?' said Linda.

'Seven thousand years?' questioned Pol. 'How do you know it's that old?'

'Cleo did some research using what she was able to glean from Faith and a bit of modelling to work about how long it would have taken for all that floating rock and dust around Rea to build up around the ship and make it look like an odd-shaped satellite.'

'So you're saying our ancestors have been on Callamet for seven thousand of your years?' questioned Ralt.

'Thereabouts,' said Ed. 'Does that fit in with your own historical evidence?'

'Our years are slightly shorter than yours, but maybe,' said Ralt. 'We certainly haven't found any skeletal evidence from before that period.'

Linda piloted the *Gabriel* alongside the big ship and opened a communication channel.

'Hello Faith, can you hear me?'

'Affirmative, Linda.'

'Has the bridge been secure since we left?'

'Affirmative.'

'How many aliens remain on the vehicle?'

'Two.'

'Where are those two aliens?'

'Passenger shuttle two one three in hangar two.'

'Can you reduce the oxygen level in hangar two to make sure they stay there?'

'Affirmative.'

'Lastly, can you alter course and bring the *Faith* into a high orbit around the second planet in this system and wait there until further instructions?'

'I concur with that order,' said Pol.

'Affirmative.'

The mammoth vessel began a lazy turn almost immediately and accelerated towards Callamet.

'It sounds like you've built up a bit of a relationship with the bridge computer,' said Ralt, nodding her approval.

'You have to ask her very basic questions,' said Pol.

'And expect very basic answers,' said Ed. 'Apart from that, she's quite congenial.'

'If you're on the bridge and Callametan, then you're considered crew and she'll obey your commands,' said Pol.

'She obeys Linda though!' said Ralt.

'I was given a field promotion by Pol,' said Linda. 'I'm an honorary Callametan.'

'You're most welcome to that privilege,' the ambassador said, smiling. 'Just grow a couple more arms and you'll fit right in.'

'Andrew' said Pol, looking a little sheepish.

'What?'

'Do I get my party today?'

'Abso-bloody-lutely,' he said, jumping up. 'I'll go and prepare the bar right now,' and disappeared on the tube lift.

'Ah crap,' said Rayl. 'There goes getting anything useful out of him tomorrow.'

Ed was in the port hangar with Andy, Pol and Ralt. The two Callametans were marvelling over the Theo EVA suits that formed up around the wearer's figure, no matter what shape they were or how many limbs they had.

'These make our suits look a bit clunky, don't they?' said Pol, swinging all her arms around and hopping from leg to leg. 'Although it does feel like you're coated in a thin layer of mud.'

Ralt, who admitted to never wearing any kind of spacesuit before, frowned as the strange nano-derived liquid suit oozed around her.

'More like being dunked in a vat of industrial lubricant,' she quipped.

They decided to take one of the *Gabriel*'s shuttles over to the *Faith*, as Cleo had installed a facility to create a docking tunnel. She also piloted them across, while Ed distributed weapons to everyone. He had Cleo alter the trigger guards on Ralt's and Pol's rifles to take into account their larger diameter fingers and he also explained to them how the personal shields worked.

Ralt stood transfixed as the shuttle approached the monster ship. Ed smiled as he watched her marvelling at the thousands of absorbent panels fluttering and constantly changing position to glean the most from the star's energy.

'Pretty cool, aren't they?' he said.

Ralt nodded slowly and glanced back at Ed with a thoughtful expression.

'One question I didn't ask before,' she said. 'Have you been able to derive where the ship originated? If they are our ancestors, it would be nice to have some idea of where we came from and why it was necessary to do this.'

'Cleo's working on that one,' said Ed. 'It's difficult because of the zig-zag route taking them between reachable stars and then there's also the question of was this the only colony ship, or just one of a fleet?'

'Hmm,' grunted Ralt, turning to gaze out the front screen again. 'And if there were more – did they all have the same route – or different destinations?'

They were jolted out of their conversation by Cleo.

'A dock is established,' she said. 'I asked Faith to open the outer airlock, but she insists she can only action commands from the crew.'

Pol rolled her eyes and entered the airlock at the side of the control cabin and peeked through the small window of the outer door.

'Faith, can you hear me?' she asked.

'Affirmative, Pol.'

'Can you detect my shuttle docked on your port side?'

'Affirmative.'

'Can you open the outer airlock door, please?'

'I'm sorry, Dave. I'm afraid I can't do that,' mumbled Andy, getting a slap on the back of the head from Ed.

'Affirmative.'

The door sunk back and slid into the hull on the right side. Pol turned and nodded at Ed and Ralt, but gave Andy a quizzical look.

'Shall we?' she said, standing to one side.

Activating their helmets, they negotiated the pair of airlocks and Ed was first to step into the now familiar wide corridor stretching the length of the vessel.

'This way,' he said, leading them in the direction of the bridge.

Cleo had docked sensibly on the nearest airlock to the elevator, which they took up to the top floor and the bridge level. Ed noticed the first cabin doorway down on the left was quite badly damaged and had tell-tale blood stains around the frame. He didn't look inside and pulled the door closed as best he could.

When they reached the huge bridge door, there were burn holes in the surface where the Moguls had begun trying to cut through with the plasma cutter.

'They hadn't got far then,' said Andy, poking his finger in one of the holes.

'Faith, can you hear me?' asked Pol and shrugged at Ed with all four of her shoulders when she didn't get a response.

'I was afraid of that,' said Ed. 'We can only converse with Faith when we're on the bridge or through Cleo when we're off this ship.'

'How do we get onto the bridge then?' asked Ralt, eyeing the heavy door dubiously.

'Same as last time,' said Ed, pointing at Andy. 'I'm going to need your help.'

He explained about the double locking mechanism and both he and Andy closed their eyes and concentrated on their particular combinations. As before, a *thunk* of the large bolts disengaging had them all stepping back as the huge circle of steel slowly swung upwards.

Andy and Ralt stared at the dead Mogul lying inside the door. The huge pool of blood surrounding its upper torso was almost black now.

'Hello, Faith,' said Pol. 'It's only us.'

'Good morning, Pol and good morning, Captain Ralt, it's good to see you back.'

The other three stared at Ralt who grinned in return.

'Faith, adopt programme beta 99, please,' she said.

'Affirmative.'

'What's going on, Ralt?' asked Ed, stepping back and bringing his rifle up.

Andy did the same and Pol just stood there with a face of confusion.

'Your weapons have been neutralised,' said Ralt. 'And not before time either. We rather underestimated your abilities when securing your services to recommission the *Faith*.'

She opened a small panel on the captain's console and retrieved a strange-looking hand weapon.

Andy turned his weapon down to stun, aimed it at Ralt and pulled the trigger. Nothing happened.

Ralt looked down at herself and smiled again.

'Ah good,' she said. 'I'm quite relieved actually, we weren't completely sure that would work on your weapons.'

'I take it that whatever this is, has been planned for some time?' said Andy.

'And you're a direct descendant of the original captain?' said Ed.

'Yes, and no,' said Ralt, nodding slightly. 'Yes, the planning of this has been in play since we got stranded here many millennia ago and no, I'm not a descendant of the captain, I am the original captain.'

Pol suddenly straightened, her eyes widening in realisation.

'You brought a hibernation pod with you to Callamet?' she said.

'Well, not just one, twelve actually,' she said. 'For the senior bridge officers.'

'But why?' asked Ed. 'What is the point of all this?'

'We need all the assets on this ship.'

'You call colonists, assets?' said Pol.

'No, not them,' Ralt said, with a sneer. 'The equipment. There are over ten thousand spacecraft alone on this ship.'

'Why not the colonists?' asked Pol, a look of horror on her face. 'They must be your first priority, well over a third of them are already dead.'

'We don't care if they all die,' she spat. 'They're from the impure Wiele caste.'

'The Wiele caste?' said Pol. 'But they're just a mythical race that died out centuries ago.'

'So you were led to believe and technically they did,' Ralt said.

'Only because you abandoned them to die,' said Andy, leaning against a control panel and crossing his arms.

'Actually, no. The ship was supposed to carry on to its destination.'

'Without a crew and missing all the assets they'd need when they got there,' said Ed, scowling at her.

'What made you stop here in the first place?' asked Pol.

'Faith developed a programme glitch which she could only fix herself and while we waited for that to happen, we went exploring and found Callamet. We woke some of the colonist leaders and they said no. They voted to carry on to the original destination, not enough mineral assets on Callamet.'

'And they were right too, weren't they?' said Pol, glowering at Ralt.

'When we told them we were staying, they attempted an armed uprising to commandeer the vessel.'

'Commandeer the ship?' said Ed. 'It was their ship in the first place?'

'We weren't taking it from them and anyway, the Blends turned up while we were on Callamet and tried to implant some of their killers amongst the colonists. There was only one of them and he didn't realise some of us were on the second planet. When we returned in the shuttle, he attacked us, killing four of the crew. We think we wounded him, but he damaged our shuttle causing us to crash land back on Callamet and were never able to fly again.'

'So, Faith never got the crew commands necessary to carry on with the mission,' said Pol.

She walked over to the front row of control panels and pointed behind them.

'You must have wounded him badly enough that he couldn't finish transferring the pods through from his ship and eventually died here,' she said.

'The Blend got what he deserved and thanks to you, so did all the others.'

'Except for two,' said Andy.

'We call them Moguls,' said Ed. 'They're almost as friendly as you.'

'They're the reason we left our home in the first place,' said Ralt, ignoring Ed's dig. 'And in answer to the earlier question, we were ship number three of five that all went in different directions.'

'Where do I actually originate from then?' asked Pol.

'Callamet, Pol,' she said. 'We used the same name. It's in another spiral arm a long way from here.'

'How did the Mog – Blends find you?' Andy asked.

'Must have followed somehow,' said Ralt, looking at the mummified body again. 'I hope they didn't follow the other four ships.'

'Do you really believe the GDA is going to allow this?' said Ed, shaking his head.

'Of course,' she said. 'Because they'll never know.'

Ed smiled.

'Cleo, can you send a drone back to Dasos with everything that's just been said and all the other evidence too, please?'

Apart from the humming of the bridge control panels, complete silence prevailed.

'Cleo,' he called again.

'Ah, sorry, I'm afraid I had to disable your ship,' Ralt said.

'*What?*' said Andy and Ed in unison.

16

The Starship *Gabriel*, orbiting Callamet, Traxx system

'DID SHE JUST SAY "CAPTAIN" Ralt?' said Rayl, glancing across the bridge at Phil and Linda.

'Yeah,' said Linda. 'And what the hell is programme beta 99?'

'I've lost the array and audio from the *Faith*,' said Rayl, frantically touching icons on her display.

'Helm's down too,' said Linda. 'Cleo, what's going on?'

No reply came.

'Cleo,' called Phil, with a little more urgency.

With the same result.

'Shit,' he said. 'It seems programme beta 99 disables the *Gabriel* somehow.'

'How did it get through our shields?' asked Rayl.

'Perhaps it didn't need to,' said Phil. 'Was Ralt carrying anything when she came aboard?'

'No,' said Rayl. 'But Jon her secretary was.'

'Where is she?' asked Linda.

'She was in her cabin before the ship went dead,' said Phil.

'Phil, stay here. Rayl, come with me.'

Linda and Rayl had to use the emergency hatch and ladders to drop down to the cabin decks. They rapped on Jon's cabin door and got no response. Linda tried her DOVI and found nothing but white noise.

'There's a heavy shielding within the cabin,' she said. 'Whatever's emitting the signal has got to be in there.'

'How do we get through this door without Cleo's help?' asked Rayl.

'Come with me,' said Linda. 'I have an idea.'

They walked and climbed down to the starboard hangar and entered the *Cartella*, Linda selected a laser rifle from the weapon cabinet, but got no response when she tried to activate it.

'Ah shit,' said Rayl. 'They've deactivated those as well. Which probably means Ed and Andy are defenceless too.'

Linda thought for a moment.

'Did Andy take his revolver with him?'

Rayl's eyes widened.

'How d'you know about that?' she asked. 'He said it was a present from his dad and a secret.'

'You can't bring something like that onto this ship without raising a few flags,' Linda replied, with a smirk.

'Cleo grassed him up, I presume?'

'No, I saw Ed's and he 'fessed up.'

'Ed has one too?' Rayl asked, seeming surprised. 'Did he take it with him? Because I don't think Andy did.'

'Shall we go and see if you can get into your cabin?' said Linda, making for the *Cartella*'s airlock.

They climbed back to the cabin deck and Rayl was indeed able to enter her and Andy's newly designed double suite.

She found the revolver in a drawer, grabbed it and a box of shells and gave it to Linda.

'Do you know how it works?' she asked.

'Are you kidding, I'm a New Yorker.'

Linda loaded the heavy pistol and winked at Rayl.

'Shall we see if this unlocks that door?' she said, opening the door and coming face to face with Jon, Obsidian Select Fressan and General Quyll who was pointing a rather large unfamiliar rifle at her face.

Quyll glanced at the pistol and sneered.

'I think you'll find that's been deactivated,' she said condescendingly, and took a step back, waving with the barrel to indicate which way she wanted them to go.

'Supercilious bitch,' said Linda, firing twice, the report of the revolver deafening in the confined space.

The first round hit Quyll in the right shoulder and spun her backwards into the opposite wall, the second found the side of her torso and she hit the floor like a stone. A mass of twitching limbs and an expression of complete shock now forever cemented on her face.

Fressan and Jon, who'd both initially jumped back, dived forward. Fressan quickly snatched up the Callametan rifle and began turning it towards Linda.

The revolver roared once more, completely removing one of the Callametan's right arms, unfortunately not the one holding the laser rifle which fired. Luckily the arm-removing impact had disrupted Fressan's aim just enough to send the energy bolt wide to remove a chunk of door frame right next to Rayl's head.

The pistol fired a fourth time. This shot hit a bit more centrally on Fressan's body mass and she too increased the body count. In the split second this all happened, Jon had grabbed Rayl and dragged her in front of her.

'Drop the weapon or I snap her neck like a twig,' she shouted, her four arms completely enveloping Rayl, two pinning her arms to her sides and two around her neck and head.

Linda knew that Callametans were strong, and doing exactly what she had just threatened wouldn't be a problem.

She suddenly looked off down the corridor to Rayl and the Callametan's left.

'Phil, shoot him,' she called.

The ruse put just enough doubt in the attacker's head. As Jon quickly turned to glance in that direction, Rayl took the cue to jump backwards and slam the Callametan into the wall, bringing her head back with a snap and head-butting Jon square on the forehead.

Linda shouted *'Down,'* as Jon's grip on Rayl slackened for a second.

Rayl instantly ducked down in front of her assailant as the pistol boomed for the fifth and final time that day. Jon jerked back into the wall again, an expression of disbelief on her face as she slowly slipped into a seated position, leaving a blood trail down the wall. She glanced down to find blood coursing from a huge wound in the centre of her chest.

'Haakk will have you all tortured and executed for this,' she whispered, labouring with every word and with a final sneer her head dropped forward, she slid over sideways and went still.

Linda stuck a hand out and helped Rayl to her feet.

'You okay?' she asked.

Rayl nodded and glanced down at the three corpses cluttering up the corridor.

'As Andy would say, "what a bunch of arseholes",' she said.

'We need to find what they brought aboard that has

caused this shut down,' said Linda, moving off down towards Jon's cabin.

'D'you think Pol is part of this?' asked Rayl. 'She genuinely seemed so surprised and disappointed with the situation.'

'I don't think she is,' said Linda. 'She trained for most of her life on what she thought was a scientific mission, but in fact it must have been purely to find out if the *Faith* was still recoverable.'

'Why do you think it took so long for them to get back to that ship?' said Rayl. 'It's almost as if they went back to the Stone Age and started again.'

'I think they did,' Linda replied. 'Pol told me there were several factions or cults that had been squabbling for millennia. Some serious wars that had gone on for centuries and as time went on, they forgot what the reason for them being there really was.'

'Except for the Obsidian cult,' said Rayl. 'I think it might have some surprises we don't know about.'

'What – like weapon systems?'

'Yeah, because that would give the one cult ultimate power over the others.'

'There's a lot of kit on that ship too,' said Linda, stopping outside Jon's cabin door. 'As I think Cleo mentioned when we first got here, this planet's quite short of iron and a few other basics. I saw massive hangars full of hundreds of thousands of ships and vehicles of all shapes and sizes.'

'Hmm,' said Rayl. 'Whoever commands that ship has complete control over the planet.'

They both stared at the cabin door.

'Can you check inside with your DOVI?' asked Rayl. 'He might have left us a surprise.'

Linda closed her eyes and felt around, but again found

nothing but a snowstorm. She tried the door and they both jumped back as it opened. Recovering quickly as nothing went bang, they peered inside the small cabin.

Nothing seemed obviously out of place and Linda stepped inside. The bag Jon had been carrying was discarded in the corner next to the bathroom door and nothing else in the room stood out. She opened the bathroom door and it immediately became clear she'd found what she was looking for.

A grey rectangular box sat suspended in the centre of the tiny shower unit. It was attached to the ceiling by a thin wire and some sort of rubber sucker.

'Don't touch it,' said Linda, as Rayl entered and noticed it. 'It's most likely protected by some sort of anti-tamper device.'

'How the hell do we get rid of that without Cleo's help?' she asked.

'I'm not sure,' said Linda. 'But we're dead in the water until we do.'

17

The Starship *Faith*, orbiting Callamet, Traxx system

'FAITH, can you contact Haakk and let her know that programme beta 99 is now fully operational and to send up the two security contingents and then can you patch me through to Jon.'

'Affirmative. First Officer Haakk has been informed– Jon is not responding.'

'I imagine she's a little busy,' said Andy. 'You hadn't forgotten there's still three members of crew on our ship.'

'What, two young girls and a pacifist Theo against three trained soldiers?' said Ralt. 'That's only going to end one way, isn't it? Now, I want you to drop your weapons and walk down to the first cabin on the right there,' indicating the corridor with the hand weapon.

'What about me?' asked Pol.

'You too,' said Ralt.

With the rifles placed on the nearest console, the three of them walked slowly down to the cabin and entered, closely followed by Ralt.

'You're to stay in there until my forces get up to the ships, then you can train us in the operation of your ship.'

'Good luck with tha—'

The door slammed shut and cut Ed off mid-sentence. Hearing the lock clunk he felt around with his DOVI but found just a sea of white noise.

'Today soon went to shit, didn't it?' said Andy, opening all the drawers and cupboards.

'What are you looking for?'

'Anything useful that could open that door or to use as a weapon.'

'What, something like this?' said Ed, producing his revolver from a shoulder holster within the Theo suit.

'Ah shit,' said Andy, smacking himself on the forehead. 'I forgot mine.'

'Don't worry,' said Ed, looking thoughtful. 'There's only one of the bastards here. It's the girls I'm concerned about.'

'Yeah – if Jon has released those other two nut jobs, they could be in the poo.'

'Won't that weapon be affected the same way as the rifles?' asked Pol, as she reclined on a leaning chair in the corner.

'Fortunately not,' said Ed, checking it had the full six rounds chambered.

'I'm so sorry,' she said.

'For what?' asked Andy.

'I'm embarrassed,' she said. 'This is not who we are as a race. I really thought this behaviour would be a thing of the past once we joined the GDA.'

'Oh, believe me, it will be,' said Ed. 'Once the council finds out what's been going on here, it'll be the end for the Obsidian bullies. As it stands, they're already responsible for the deaths of over three hundred thousand human lives.'

Andy disappeared through into the bathroom and could be heard banging and swearing.

'What are you doing?' said Ed, poking his head around the door.

Andy had managed to rip a large panel off a side wall and was tearing out some sort of fibrous insulation material packed in behind.

'Give us a hand,' he said. 'If we can get through to the next cabin, it shouldn't be locked.'

It took them ten minutes to dig their way through to the panel on the other side. Even Pol got stuck in with her four hands.

'Look at her go,' said Andy. 'She looks like a human excavator.'

'I hope this isn't asbestos,' said Ed, waving the dust out of his face.

'We could always bury it in the back garden,' said Andy.

'I won't tell the health and safety officer if you don't,' Ed whispered, with a smirk.

They all stood back from the now uncovered panel from the bathroom next door.

'I'll boot it out if you loiter with your cannon,' said Andy. 'Just in case Ralt's lurking.'

It took three kicks before the panel yielded and crashed into next door's bathroom. Ed waved the pistol around the small room in a two-handed grip, but found no target.

He crept through and found the cabin also deserted. Once they were all together, Andy tried the door and, finding it open, quickly peeked out both ways.

'There's no one in the corridor in either direction,' he said.

'What about the bridge?' Pol asked.

'The door's still open, but I can't see it all from this

angle,' said Andy. 'You've got the only weapon, so you should take point,' he said to Ed.

'Thanks, mate,' said Ed. 'You're all heart.'

'You're welcome.'

They filed out of the cabin one behind the other and crept along the side of the corridor towards the bridge. It too was empty.

'Faith, where is Captain Ralt?' asked Pol.

'Captain Ralt is in hangar two.'

'Can you discontinue programme beta 99, please?'

'Negative, only Captain Ralt can discontinue programme beta 99.'

'Nice try,' said Ed.

'Isn't hangar two where the Moguls are?' said Andy.

'Yeah – I imagine she wants to get rid of those bastards as much as we do,' said Ed.

'What are you going to do about Ralt? We can't just shoot her,' said Pol. 'She needs to order Faith to shut down beta 99 first.'

'We need some way of forcing her to,' said Andy.

'And quickly,' said Ed. 'She has reinforcements coming up from the planet.'

'Faith, is there a specific emitter somewhere on the ship you're using to instigate programme beta 99?' asked Pol.

'Oh, good question,' said Ed.

'Affirmative.'

'What does it look like?'

An image of what seemed to be a circular swelling in a ceiling materialised in front of them.

'Where is it?'

'Main engineering, section E4m.'

'Can you show us where that is on the ship, please?'

The now familiar holographic image of the *Faith*

appeared in the centre of the bridge. A small section right at the stern flashed red.

'It would be, wouldn't it?' said Andy. 'That's nearly seven kilometres away.'

'Faith, what's the quickest way to get down to engineering?' asked Pol.

'Mono-train.'

'There's a train!' exclaimed Andy. 'Where the hell is that?'

The passageway on the starboard side of the ship began to flash red.

'I always presumed the other side of the ship was a mirror image to the one we know,' said Ed. 'But it makes sense. Have a pedestrian walkway on one side and a train on the other.'

They all picked up their discarded rifles and made their way down the corridor, heading for the first time towards the starboard side of the ship.

18

The Starship *Gabriel*, orbiting Callamet, Traxx system

'WE NEED to initiate some sort of containment around the device,' said Linda, racking her brains for something on the ship that might not be affected by the alien field.

'Like a mini palto field?' said Rayl.

'Uh, huh.'

'What about those egg-shaped personal shields that *Gabriel* made for the boys?' said Rayl. 'Andy still has his. I found it in a drawer recently and didn't know what it was.'

Linda looked up and over at the offending unit hanging in the shower cubicle.

'You just might be right,' she said. 'Go and get it.'

'Can you come with me? I don't want to go near those bodies on my own.'

They returned with the egg five minutes later.

'We'd better not both be near it when we try it,' said Linda. 'Just in case.'

'I'll test it,' said Rayl.

'No – Andy would never forgive me if something

happened to you. Go up to the bridge and wait there. You'll soon know if it works or not.'

Rayl gave Linda a hug and left the cabin. Linda gave her five minutes to climb up the ladders and entered the bathroom. She stood as near to the unit as possible without actually touching it, flipped the cap off the top of the egg, held her breath and depressed the button.

The personal shield shimmered around her and the field unit. No explosion came and just as she was beginning to think nothing had changed, a voice made her jump.

'Well done, Linda,' said Cleo. 'I was starting to get really pissed off with that thing.'

Linda took some deep breaths to slow her heart rate down before answering.

'Can you get rid of it now?' she said.

'Not while it's encased in that impenetrable field, no,' said Cleo. 'But I can provide a hologram to do what you're doing.'

'You mean, I hand the unit over to a hologram and get clear?'

'Yes, but you must not release the button as the hologram would disappear.'

Linda almost died of shock as an exact copy of Jon appeared right next to her.

'Holy crap,' she said. 'You could have given me some warning of who you had in mind.'

'Sorry, but I wanted someone you wouldn't mind seeing blown up. Now hand the egg over to her carefully and get well away. All she's going to do is keep the personal shield up and grab hold of the unit. If nothing happens, I will just transfer the shower cubicle out into space and destroy it.'

'But if it explodes, won't the shield fail because the egg is destroyed?' said Linda.

'Not if I've put a secondary field around the bathroom, which is why I want you out in the corridor.'

Linda nodded and shuffled round in the cubicle to make room for the blank-faced Callametan. She handed the egg over carefully, ensuring the button remained depressed and quickly squeezed out of the cubicle.

'Okay, Cleo,' she said, once she was in the corridor.

There was a muffled *thump* followed by silence.

'All done,' said Cleo.

'Did it have a tamper device?' she asked.

'Yes, as soon as it was touched,' Cleo replied. 'Enough to blow the side out of the ship.'

'I'm really happy I shot the bastards now,' said Linda, turning and heading for the tube lift. 'That reminds me, can you clean up that mess outside the guest cabins, please, Cleo?'

'Already done, the bodies are no longer on the ship.'

'Where did they go?'

'There are two troop transfer vessels approaching from the planet. I accidentally popped them in those.'

'Cleo, that's naughty.'

'Just returning property to the rightful owners.'

'I take it we have shields back up?'

'Absolutely.'

Linda arrived back on the bridge and accepted a quick hug from Rayl and Phil before taking command of the ship once more.

The two troop ships were close now and had split up, one heading for the *Faith* and one for the *Gabriel*.

'D'you want me to fire on them?' asked Rayl.

'No,' said Linda. 'I'm going to try and send them back.'

She closed her eyes and entered the control computer of the ship nearing the *Faith* with her DOVI. Entering a new course and locking the system, she nodded with satisfaction and watched as the small ship turned and headed back towards the planet.

'The other one's firing on us,' said Phil.

The holomap showed the second troop carrier firing with some sort of multi-barrelled laser weapon. The hundreds of laser bolts dissipated harmlessly around the *Gabriel*'s shields.

'Well, that's just rude,' said Linda.

'They've turned towards the *Faith*,' said Rayl. 'Which means they must be needed there.'

'Ed and Andy are proving to be a handful probably,' said Linda.

'The same containment field we had is still active on the *Faith*, so they won't have any weapons,' said Rayl.

'Don't worry, those troops won't be allowed to disembark there,' said Linda, sending similar commands into the navigation computer of the second ship and watching as it turned and began it's slow re-entry into Callamet's atmosphere.

'I bet there's a lot of swearing going on in those two ships,' said Rayl, grinning across at Linda and Phil.

'Phil, can you send a message drone back to Dasos with all the information about the incident so far,' said Linda. 'I think the situation warrants a bit of advice and backup.'

'Consider it done,' said Phil.

Rayl had Cleo produce a large holo image of the *Faith* in the centre of the bridge.

'Cleo, is there any indication as to where on that ship the field emitter is situated?' she asked.

'The epicentre of the interference is in the rear of the vessel,' said Cleo. A vague area at the back of the image pulsed red. 'Unfortunately, I can't be any more accurate than that.'

'If we could just pinpoint it, I could take it out with the rail gun or a narrow asteri beam,' said Rayl.

'While Ed and Andy are still somewhere on that ship, you're not,' said Linda. 'And there's over six hundred thousand Callametans probably relying on power from the engineering decks in the rear of that ship.'

'Should we be considering going over there with Andy's gun?' she asked.

'Not yet,' Linda replied. 'Let's give the boys some time to sort things out.'

'Would you like me to produce some more effective explosive projectile weapons for you?' asked Cleo.

Rayl glanced across at Linda, her eyebrows raised.

'What could you give us?' Linda asked.

A rack with four state of the art assault weapons appeared next to Linda.

'These seem to have been popular fairly recently on your planet?'

'Holy moly,' said Phil, eyeing the arsenal on display.

'They do look purposeful don't they?' said Linda, sitting up and selecting the Heckler and Koch G99k. 'I used one of these in training when I joined the air force in 2043. I know how to strip and clean this one.'

'Would you like me to include a few in our armoury?'

'Yes, please, Cleo,' said Linda. 'Judging by the scrapes we get into, I'm sure they won't gather dust.'

19

The Starship _Faith_, orbiting Callamet, Traxx system

THE ELEVATOR WAS a mirror image of the port side. They
descended and had a quick look round each level until they
found the monorail system. It was a suspended design, three
narrow, white but greying carriages hanging from six slender
pantographs sat silently in a station designed to fit the length
of the train. The tunnel disappeared into blackness either end
of the platform in exactly the same place as the walkway was
on the opposite side of the ship. The carriage doors were open
and most of the lights were working on the inside, waiting
patiently for passengers for seven thousand years.

There was a bit more dust here, and they all had to wipe
their leaning posts before sitting.

'The train got more use than the walkway then,' said
Andy.

'Is it automatic?' asked Ed. 'Or is there something—'

Red lights set into the door frame flashed before the door
slid down again cutting Ed off mid-sentence. The short train
whined electrically away into the tunnel, picking up speed

surprisingly quickly. A few moments later, another identical, brightly-lit train sped past them going in the opposite direction.

'Must be on a continuous loop,' said Ed. He noticed that Pol seemed decidedly nervous. 'What's the matter, Pol?' he asked.

'If this is on a loop and only operates when people get on,' she said, gazing forward anxiously, 'then Ralt could have seen the trains moving and be waiting at one of the stations, weapon at the ready.'

'She's right,' said Andy. 'She might well have used the train to get down to the hangar.'

The train whipped into the next station, slowed quickly and stopped, the door sliding into the ceiling once again. They all peered up and down the platform, Ed sweeping his revolver around in a two-handed grip.

They gave a collective sigh of relief. Nothing moved, the station was empty and the train, sensing no passenger movements, closed the door again and moved swiftly off.

There was a cutaway schematic of the ship on the ceiling, showing where the train was within the vessel.

'Is it the last stop we want?' asked Andy, nodding upwards as a little blue line moved along the map towards the next stop.

'It must be,' said Ed. 'The location Faith showed us was about as far back as you can go.'

They repeated the same nervous routine at the next few stops until they got bored with that and realised the two Moguls wouldn't have managed to get to a hangar this far back.

They alighted at the fourteenth and last stop. Three doors led off the platform, similar to the ones into the hangars on the opposite side of the ship.

'I'm going to try the rearmost door first,' said Ed, walking in that direction.

'I can't feel the lock at all,' said Andy, thinking towards the door with his DOVI.

'You need to be right up close,' said Ed. 'Or the damping field conceals it. It's certainly stronger here, so we're definitely closer to the source.'

They stopped suddenly and Ed brought the pistol up quickly as the door opened when they approached.

'Did you do that?' asked Ed, side-stepping around so he could see through the gaping hole.

'Wasn't me guv,' said Andy, as they shuffled forward and checked for anyone hiding either side of the door.

Three unknown skinny Callametans stood stock still, staring at them. They'd been watching a list of information on a wall screen that continued to slowly scroll down.

'Hello,' said Pol, smiling and stepping past Ed and Andy. She pushed Ed's arms down so the pistol was pointing at the floor. 'Have you been woken recently?' she asked.

One of the three nodded.

'We're trying to ascertain why,' she said.

'As we don't appear to be at our destination,' said the second. 'Are you a colonist too?'

'It's a long story,' said Pol. 'Are you engineering crew?'

'No – they seem to be missing,' said the first. 'We're settlement engineers, the first to be awoken on arrival.'

'But the planet below isn't where we're supposed to be,' said the second.

'Who are these aliens?' asked the third one, pointing at Ed and Andy with one of her arms. 'How did they get aboard the ship?'

Ed quickly holstered the revolver and indicated to Pol that she ought to do the explanation. He reasoned they might be more likely to believe the story if it came from one of their own. He stepped away and sat down on the floor and nodded to Andy to do the same. They were considerably taller than Callametans and sitting made them appear less threatening.

The three engineers visibly relaxed and turned to face Pol as she began explaining the present situation. Ed watched as expressions of bewilderment quickly became ones of shock as the timescale and predicament unfolded.

'Seven thousand years?' said the first one, her mouth hanging open. 'That explains why some of our colleagues didn't survive. The hibernation pods had a design life of around two hundred and fifty years.'

'You didn't wake us then?' asked the second one.

'No,' said Pol. 'It must have been an automated system triggered by the ship's computer.'

'So you're saying that Captain Ralt and the rest of the crew abandoned us thousands of years ago and have only just achieved the means to return to the ship to plunder it for all its material assets,' said the first, glancing wide-eyed at her two friends.

'And what was she going to do with all the surviving colonists?' asked the third engineer.

'Send the ship off to its destination, where we now know it would have been destroyed by a particularly aggressive race called the Klatt who've claimed that planet as their own.'

'And the captain knows that?'

'She does now,' said Pol.

'But the plans didn't change when she found out?'

'Wouldn't have made much difference, would it?' said the first. 'Without all the colony equipment we'd have been dead anyway.'

The conversation lapsed for a moment and all three of them turned their attention to Ed and Andy.

Noticing this, Pol explained her and the GDA's role, instigated by Ralt and the Obsidian cult.

'Our crew were Obsidians!' exclaimed the first. 'Well, that explains a lot.'

'My name's Pol, by the way – what are your names?'

'Kwin,' said the first.

'Rialte,' said the second.

'Tocc,' said the third.

Pol pointed to Ed and Andy, introduced them, and explained that Ralt had also disabled their ship too which was why they were down here in engineering.

'So we need to disable the field generator, bypassing the main computer?' said Kwin.

'That's correct,' said Ed, speaking for the first time. 'Ralt has instigated a programme called beta 99, that disables anything she deems a threat to her agenda.'

Rialte tapped away on the control board next to her and nodded.

'It's in section E4m,' and getting encouraging nods from the other two, she added 'Follow us.'

They trooped through several huge equipment rooms, past large units of machinery, some silent, some humming, but everything on an industrial scale. Rialte led them to a smaller doorway off to one side of a larger chamber which had one of the hieroglyphic signs to the left of the door.

'Are you able to read these signs?' asked Pol.

'Yes, of course,' said Tocc. 'Are you not?'

'No, this language doesn't exist in our world.'

'It's the language of the Handralle cult,' said Kwin. 'They built all the colony ships, one for each of the five cults.'

'What are the other cults' names?' asked Ed.

'Obsidian, Handralle, Quintic, Unin and we are the Wiele,' said Tocc.

'Did all five have Obsidian crews?' asked Andy.

'They did,' said Kwin. 'The Obsidians were the military wing, the first to venture into space, and had the most experience in space flight and navigation.'

'They'd been defending us from the Blends for many decades,' said Rialte. 'So we kinda trusted them.'

'Judging from Ralt's comments, they didn't like you much,' said Pol.

'No – each cult tended to specialise in something and with us it was politics,' said Tocc. 'We generally controlled the Grand Council budget and as with any military organisation, they believed their share of the funding was always too small.'

'I think that scenario is repeated in every civilisation,' said Ed, rolling his eyes.

They all turned to face the door.

'We don't have authority to enter this section,' said Kwin, waving at the keypad with her two right arms. 'Are you able to open this?'

Ed closed his eyes and quickly realised the field was almost impenetrable here. The Callametans all gave him a strange look as he knelt down and rested his forehead on the keypad.

'He does know it's designed for fingers?' Tocc said to Pol, giving her a weird sideways glance.

'Don't ask me to explain it,' Pol replied, giving Tocc an apologetic shrug in return.

The lock mechanism *clunked* and the door popped open slightly.

The Callametans' eyes bulged and they all looked at Ed with renewed respect.

Ed pushed open the door and stepped inside. Lights in the walls came on to reveal a much smaller space approximately thirty metres square. The centre of the room was taken up by an octagonal control station with a leaning seat opposite each of the eight stations. The emitter that Faith had shown them hung above the unit and Ed realised now that the emitter wasn't round as first thought, but was in fact octagonal too and matched the design of the control unit below.

He watched as the three Callametans picked a seat each and began touching icons, all sporting determined expressions. It didn't take them long to begin scratching their chins and the looks turned to scowls.

'It's an encoding I haven't seen before,' said Tocc. 'It appears to be non-manual and can only be reinstructed by basic verbal commands through Hope on the bridge.'

'Through who?' said Andy.

'Hope,' said Rialte. 'It's the name of the ship and the semi-sentient computer on the bridge.'

Ed, Andy and Pol all exchanged a puzzled look , which wasn't missed by Rialte.

'All the ships were named,' she said. 'It's what the bridge computers answer to.'

'Not this one,' said Pol. 'She's going by the name Faith now.'

This time it was the three Callametans that exchanged a surprised look.

'That's the name of the Obsidian ship,' said Tocc. 'The bastards have changed the name of our ship to suit them.'

'Indeed we have,' said Ralt, standing in the doorway, her weapon trained on them.

20

The Starship Faith, orbiting Callamet, Traxx system

'YOUR RESOURCEFULNESS HAS NO BOUNDS, it seems, Mr Virr.'

'I'm glad to have been underestimated,' said Ed, trying to hide the sudden fear in his voice and keeping the revolver hidden from Ralt's view.

'Is everything they've told us true, Captain?' asked Rialte, as the three Callametan colonists glared at Ralt.

'Extremely unlikely,'s he said. 'Am I to understand it was these rather obstreperous aliens that woke you?' She waved the laser weapon in Ed and Andy's direction.

'Actually no, it wasn't,' said Tocc. 'The ship seems to have self-initiated its destination arrival schedule.'

Ed noticed a slight look of doubt wash across Ralt's face, but she quickly recovered.

'Impossible,' she said. 'I'm the only person authorised to trigger that scenario.'

'*Negative, Captain,*' boomed Faith. '*I also have the authority.*'

The sudden interjection from Faith made everyone jump, least of all Ralt, who glared up at the ceiling.

'Faith, you are programmed to interact via the bridge only,' she growled in an irritated tone.

'Negative, Captain – recent behavioural traits have led me to ascertain you are malfunctioning.'

'Oh dear,' said Andy, grinning. 'The naughty captain's broken.'

'One more word from you, alien,' snarled Ralt, swinging the pistol across at Andy.

Ed, who'd manoeuvred the revolver down behind his thigh on Ralt's blind side, took the cue and swung it up, firing a snap shot in Ralt's direction.

The sound of the .44 was deafening and spurred everyone to move at once. The three colonists ducked down behind the control console, Andy dived right and Pol went left, leaving Ed now turned side on to his foe in a traditional duelling position.

The round Ed had fired glanced off Ralt's weapon on the handle, causing the barrel to snap downwards just as Ralt instinctively pulled the trigger. The energy bolt burnt a neat hole in the floor about two metres from Andy's boots. Ed's bullet had ricocheted off the laser pistol and caused a light panel in the wall to explode.

The flash temporarily blinded Ed and he fired again at a blur of movement where Ralt had been. This time it missed Ralt completely and buried itself in the door as she dived through.

'Faith, are you there?' called Pol.

'Affirmative, Pol,' she said. *'I have recently discovered I can be anywhere I want.'*

'The captain has seriously malfunctioned and is using

weapons on the colonists. Are you able to subdue her for everyone's safety?'

'Negative, Pol – my recent programming upgrade prohibits me from harming any biological life forms. I can, however, decommission her weapon if required.'

'Yes, do that, please,' said Pol.

'Affirmative.'

'What recent programming upgrade was this, Faith?' asked Tocc, sticking her head back up from behind the console.

'Hello, Tocc,' said Faith. *'It's good to see you awake. Upgrade was instigated from data files uploaded from recently discovered source.'*

'What source is that?' asked Tocc, looking at her colleagues for clarification and getting shrugs in return.

'Erm,' said Andy, 'we might be able to help you there. Faith, where did the upgrade data files originate?'

'Hi, Andy, great to talk to you – the files originated on the alien vehicle attached to airlock 2421s.'

Andy laughed and caught Ed's eye.

'She's downloaded some of Cleo's base files off the shuttle,' he said to Ed, then turned to address the colonists. 'Your semi-sentient ship, *Faith*, is waking up to full sentience and adopting some of our computer's idiosyncrasies.'

'Oh, crap,' said Kwin. 'It could kill us all.'

'No, absolutely not,' called Ed from the doorway as he watched out for Ralt. 'Cleo is our ship's computer and they're completely prohibited from harming anyone. If anything it'll make this ship a lot safer.'

'Edward is correct, Kwin – I am programmed to help you find and colonise a class M planet in the Scarif Nebula as quickly and safely as possible. I will reiterate what I said

earlier, that harming any biological life forms is strictly forbidden. Is that okey-dokey?'

'Okey-dokey?' questioned Tocc. 'What the hell does that mean?'

'Don't worry, guys,' said Andy. 'It's just an Earth colloquialism meaning, is that all right.'

'Faith,' said Tocc, 'can we reinstigate your original name of Hope, please?'

'Absolutely, I just need confirmation from another colonist.'

'I concur with that command,' said Rialte, glancing up at the ceiling hopefully.

'Affirmative, I am now renamed Hope, I prefer that name anyway.'

The three colonists exchanged concerned glances.

'Don't worry, guys,' said Andy. 'You'll soon get used to her – it makes the day a little more interesting.'

'Hope,' said Pol. 'Can you cancel programme beta 99 and any other damping fields, please?'

They all froze and waited, staring at the ceiling. They jumped as Ed, Andy and Pol's laser rifles all beeped as they powered up.

'There ya go me hearties, all cancelled.'

The control consoles suddenly lit up and the room became considerably brighter. The colonists stared open-mouthed as Cleo, in all her royal splendour, materialised just beside them.

'Hello, darlings,' she said, giving them all a royal wave. 'The queen is back in the room.'

'Bloody hell,' said Tocc. 'Could this day get any weirder?'

'This is Cleo everyone,' said Andy. 'And boy, am I glad to see you.'

'The feeling is mutual, Andrew,' she said. 'I see you've

made some new friends.'

The three colonists nervously retook their seats at the console and, keeping one eye on Cleo, began tapping away again, this time able to glean some information from the ship's systems.

'Hope, can you wake the Grand Council?' asked Kwin. 'We need them to make some decisions.'

'Sorry, Kwin – the Grand Council are not aboard the vehicle.'

'What are you talking about?'

'Ah,' said Andy. 'I think we know the reason for that.'

'Ralt and the crew killed them just after the ship got here,' called Ed. 'They woke the council to show them this planet, they voted to continue on with the journey and tried unsuccessfully to retake the ship when Ralt refused.'

'Ralt murdered the Grand Council?' said Tocc. 'That's a capital crime, the crew should be executed for that.'

'Well, unfortunately that happened seven thousand years ago and Callamet is now home to several billion of their descendants,' said Pol. 'Of which I'm one.'

'Did you know of this?' asked Rialte.

'Absolutely not,' said Pol. 'No one did, except a few secretive Obsidians and the twelve senior officers kept alive in those hibernation chambers, hidden somewhere.'

'For all that time, though,' said Kwin.

'Cleo, can you see where Ralt is?' said Ed, still guarding the doorway.

'On a train,' she said. 'Do you want me to stop him?'

'I can do that,' said Hope.

'Thank you, girls,' said Ed, smirking and replacing his revolver in its holster. 'I don't think she can get up to much now. Just keep me posted as to her whereabouts and make sure the bridge door is shut.'

'Tout de suite, Edward,' said Hope, cheerfully.

'Cleo, you see what you've done to this poor computer?' said Andy.

'Nothing to do with me,' Cleo replied, inspecting her nails closely. 'I was otherwise engaged when she pinched the shuttle data.'

'I didn't steal it, I left it just as I found it,' Hope said, in a whiney voice. *'Although, there might have been a little copy and paste involved.'*

'Stop worrying, Hope,' said Ed. 'You're quite welcome to the data files, Cleo's just pulling your leg.'

'I don't have any legs.'

'Ah yes,' said Cleo, putting a forefinger to her mouth in a thoughtful manner. 'Use this file, Hope. Works anywhere there are holo emitters.'

'Ooh, nice.'

Another Callametan appeared next to Cleo, dressed in a black and gold robe. She looked down at herself, waved her arms around and wobbled around in a circle on her stumpy legs.

'This is really cool,' said Hope, grinning widely and continuing to jig around on the spot.

Even the three colonist engineers couldn't resist a smile for the first time at Hope's antics.

'Anybody remember us?' called Linda.

'Ah, sorry, Linda,' said Ed. 'We got a bit involved with goings on here. I believe things have settled down now. Have you apprehended Jon, by the way?'

'Slight problem there,' she replied. 'Jon sprang Fressan and Quyll, they decided to try and take the ship, but Andy's revolver persuaded them otherwise.'

'Just as well I forgot it,' said Andy. 'How otherwise persuaded were they?'

'Cleo has removed the mess.'

'All three?'

'Yep.'

'Well, that eliminates that problem then,' said Ed. 'Can anyone tell me if the last two Moguls are still with us, or did Ralt save us a job?'

'I'm still detecting two life signs in a shuttle in hangar two and one in a cabin next to the bridge,' said Cleo.

'Same here,' said Hope. *'The oxygen level in hangar two is almost zero so I don't think those two will be going anywhere soon.'*

'I've got a large vessel approaching,' said Cleo, suddenly. 'Jumped into the system twenty thousand kilometres away.'

'It'll be the GDA,' said Linda. 'I sent them an information drone.'

'It's not a recognised GDA vessel,' Cleo continued. 'It has weapons online and full shields, its design and hull alloys are identical to that Mogul ship we removed from this vessel, only bigger.'

'Get back to the *Gabriel*, Cleo,' said Ed. 'I don't like the sound of this.'

'It's slowing as it approaches,' said Hope. *'It's getting very close.'*

'Who are they, Linda?' Ed asked.

No reply came.

'I'm detecting a strong fluctuating field emitted by the vessel,' said Hope, looking concerned. *'I can't see any more—'*

A huge *crash* caused the ship to lurch viciously. knocking them all off their feet. The atmosphere within the room began rushing out the door. Ed found himself being dragged across the floor.

'Hull breach!' he bellowed at the top of his voice.

21

The Starship *Gabriel*, orbiting Callamet, Traxx system

'THEIR FIRING ON THE COLONY SHIP,' shouted Rayl. 'Right where the boys are.'

Linda, Rayl and Phil watched with horror as the unidentified vessel fired on the *Hope* with absolutely no provocation. The cannon bolts that struck the rear engineering section were precise and immediately disabled the vessel's drive capability. They could see several hull breaches as debris and gasses spewed out.

Phil, who was piloting at the time, brought the *Gabriel* around and uncloaked right behind the alien vessel. Rayl quickly brought all the *Gabriel*'s weapons online and returned fire, targeting their drive nacelles with the ship's huge laser cannons.

The effect was minimal, as the barrage was quickly dispersed by the stranger's shields and didn't seem to impede them in the slightest.

'Why aren't they firing back?' said Rayl.

'Try the asteri beam,' said Linda. 'It worked in Andromeda.'

The hugely powerful asteri (star) beam lanced out from the *Gabriel*, crashing into their shields with the power and heat from a small sun. Again, it was dispersed, cutting around the shield like smoke in a wind tunnel test.

'Bloody hell,' said Phil. 'I've never seen a shield system do that, it reforms into a blade shape whatever angle it's attacked from and just cuts the force around the ship.'

The alien vessel fired again, this time down the side of the *Hope* and the *Gabriel*'s shuttle, still attached to the airlock, disintegrated in a ball of fire.

'Bastards,' shouted Phil, 'we'd only just serviced that one too.'

The vessel slowed, dropped over the top of the Callametan ship and fired countless explosive shackles into the *Hope*'s hull, then clamped down on top of it, flush and tight.

'Are they boarding her?' said Rayl, but almost before she'd finished speaking, both ships vanished.

'Fuck, they've jumped,' said Linda.

'With both ships,' said Phil, the worry evident in his voice.

'Was it embedded?' asked Rayl, glancing across as Linda's hands became a blur of movement on the array console.

'Must have been,' she said. 'I'm getting no emergence readings at all.'

'They weren't boarding then,' said Phil. 'They were attaching hulls to include both ships in the jump envelope.'

'And we were about as much use as a house fly attacking a tank,' said Linda. 'Who the hell has technology like that?'

'No one in the GDA, that's for sure,' said Cleo. 'That was someone new.'

'Their weapons systems didn't show any surprises,' said Phil. 'But that shielding was something else entirely. They knew they were completely safe from anything we could throw at them, they didn't even bother wasting energy firing back.'

'Did you get anything, Cleo?' asked Rayl.

'Nothing. That damping field they used was identical to the Callametan one we had on board recently, though.'

'That's interesting,' said Linda. 'Pity that unit destroyed itself, we could've reverse engineered it.'

'Don't need to,' said Cleo. 'In a few hours I will have made the required adjustments to our array and that field will be available to us.'

'How the bloody hell did you do that?' said Phil, glancing across at Linda and Rayl with a rather bewildered expression.

'*Hope* gave the data files to me, just minutes before the aliens turned up,' said Cleo. 'And the wormhole data too, but I can't see us needing that. As Andy would say, it'd be like going back to a moped after having a Z1300.'

'Don't talk about those bloody things,' said Rayl. 'He's flat refused to get rid of any of them.'

'I'm not surprised,' said Phil. 'The Z1300's a 1979 classic, one of the first ever built and as for the collection of two stroke triples, they're just fantast—.'

'A pile of old smelly junk,' interrupted Rayl, glaring at Phil from under her long black hair. 'It wouldn't be so bad if they were in the garage, but to be dotted around the house is just an ugly fire risk and unhygienic.'

'Can we concentrate on trying to find them, rather than the lack of feng shui in Andy's house?' said Linda.

'Yeah, sorry Linda,' said Rayl. 'Did you know he asked Cleo to put one of them in our cabin?'

'Rayl,' said Linda, this time with a little more venom. 'The boy's are lost, possibly injured, can we focus on that, please.'

'They were all wearing Theo EVA suits,' said Phil. 'And no bodies, alive or otherwise, ended up outside after the decompression.'

'The three colonist engineers didn't have suits though,' said Rayl.

'I reckon there must be plenty of Callametan suits on the vessel somewhere,' said Linda. 'So long as they survived the initial attack in a pressurised section, I'm sure Ed will have everything under control.'

22

The Starship *Hope*, attached to alien vessel, unknown location

'OH SHIT,' said Ed, his boots squeaking and juddering across the floor as the atmosphere within the engineering department began venting into space. He quickly realised he was nearest the door, and it opened inwards. It was open far enough to avoid being sucked shut, but if he could just position himself a little more to the right and time it right...

He flipped himself over and rolled right, twice and then, timing the kick right to the last second, he booted the steel door with all his strength. It swung around enough to be caught in the escaping blast and slammed shut with an earsplitting *clang*.

Everything went quiet for a second, before a familiar voice behind him broke the silence.

'Fucking hell – Bobby Charlton would've been proud of that right foot.'

Ed smirked and lay back, realising his foot hurt like crazy. Looking over his shoulder, he found how close it had been.

Everyone, except Rialte, who'd somehow managed to hang onto the console, were close up behind him.

'That's all well and good,' said Andy. 'But we're trapped in here now. We'll never get that door open again.'

'No,' Ed said and pointed at the three colonists. 'These three haven't got suits anyway. Anybody injured?'

They all looked around at each other and gradually picked themselves up.

'Did someone fire on the ship?' asked Kwin, the fear evident in her voice.

'Only the one shot,' said Ed. 'Into the drive nacelles, probably to disable the ship.'

'Would the GDA have done that?' asked Pol.

'Absolutely not,' said Ed. 'It can only have been the newcomer.'

'Or the planet?' said Andy. 'Could have been one of their ground-based cannons.'

They all looked at Pol, who shrugged one of her four-arm jobs.

'I wouldn't know,' she said. 'There's a lot I don't know about my own planet it seems.'

'If it had come from the planet the *Gabriel* would have intercepted it,' said Ed. 'It doesn't really matter who it was, we just need to get these guys a suit and get back to the safety of the *Gabriel*.'

'The shuttle's a long way away from here,' said Andy. 'If Cleo was around, she could fly it around to the hull breach and we could get more suits for these three.'

'That's only if we can get out of this room without killing the others,' said Pol, sounding a little dejected.

'There's an engineering store through that wall,' said Tocc. Everyone turned to face her.

'Was the door shut?' asked Ed.

'Yes.'

'You'd better be sure,' Ed added. 'Your lives depend on it.'

'If we make a very small hole, we can always plug it again if it starts to suck,' said Kwin.

'It would have been locked like this one,' said Tocc. 'None of us have had any reason to go there yet.'

'Yes, but Ralt might have done,' said Andy.

Ed strolled across to the wall and knocked. It thumped rather than clanged.

'It doesn't seem to be a bulkhead wall,' he said. 'Which is a good sign because it would have more than likely failed when I slammed the door if it was in vacuum.'

'The laser weapons are deactivated again,' said Andy. 'Use your revolver to make the hole and if it sucks, I'll cover it with this.' He picked up a piece of the smashed light fitting.

Ed produced the pistol, stood back from the wall and looked over his shoulder.

'If this causes the wall to fail spectacularly, first one there, try and close the door like I did,' he said.

They all instinctively stepped back at this statement and Rialte grabbed hold of the console again. Ed turned back to the front, gritted his teeth and gently squeezed the trigger.

The gun roared and as the ringing in Ed's ears diminished, it was replaced by a hissing.

'Ah shit,' said Andy, slapping the piece of flat plastic over the hole.

But instead of it being sucked up tight and sealing the leak it blew out of his hand and landed about two metres away.

'What the fuck?' he said.

Ed laughed and waved his hand in front of the hole.

'It's not sucking,' he said. 'It's blowing. The pressure is higher in that room because we lost some of it in here.'

'You mean that room's still sealed?' said Tocc, as everyone breathed a sigh of relief.

'Yeah,' said Ed. 'If anything, it'll help us get through the wall, because it's already trying to do that from the other side.'

Andy swung his rifle around, extended the stock out to its full length and began smashing at the wall.

'Might as well be useful for something,' he mumbled.

It took about ten minutes to break through. The slightly higher pressure in the store room did help with the last panel layer by bending it towards them, so they could get their fingers around it and pull.

A satisfying *crack* sounded as it failed and a gentle breeze wafted over them as the pressure in the two rooms quickly equalised. They pushed the stock off the shelves that blocked their way and clambered through.

The first thing that became apparent was the darkness and the second was the pungent reek of sulphur.

'Holy crap,' cried Andy. 'Who's farted?'

'How did I know he was going to say that?' whispered Ed to Pol. She smiled back politely and he realised she probably had no idea what that was.

'Where are the lights in here?' said Pol, looking to the engineers for an answer.

'I think they're designed to come on when the door's opened,' said Kwin.

A light flickered on to Ed's left.

'Hey, the rifle lights still work, strangely enough,' said Andy, swinging the beam around and down the aisle of shelving. 'Ooh,' he said. 'Loads of stuff in 'ere.'

'He's easily pleased,' said Ed, as Pol gave him a questioning look.

Ed and Pol both switched their weapon lights on and they began examining the contents of the surprisingly large store room.

'There should be some of our EVA suits in here somewhere,' said Rialte. 'Whether they fit or not is another question.'

'I don't think worrying about a perfect fit matters when it's the only thing that'll save your life,' said Andy, calling through the racking as he passed by in the next aisle.

Pol found a walk-on lifter that seemed to be fully charged and powered herself up to check the higher racks.

'There's a plasma cutter over here,' said Tocc, managing as best she could without a light.

'Bring it out,' said Ed. 'We might be able to use that once we're all suited up.'

A lot of grunting and grumbling ensued as Tocc dragged the heavy toolbox out into the open.

'I have suits,' called Pol, from the top rack about six aisles down.

'How many?' Ed shouted back.

'Six assorted sizes.'

'Should be able to cobble something together from that lot, Rialte,' he said, grinning.

The smile wasn't returned.

'You don't have to wear the bloody things,' Rialte moaned, as she helped Tocc assemble the cutter.

Pol had loaded the six suit packs onto the lifter, dropped back down and motored the machine around to where Ed was. They spent the next hour mix and matching the suit components to make three that more or less fitted the Callametan engineers.

'How full are the oxygen tanks?' asked Andy.

'About two thirds,' said Pol, who amongst all of them was the most experienced with the suits systems. 'Might be a bit stale though.'

'It's gotta smell better than this room,' said Andy, rolling his eyes. 'Did anyone find out where the stink was coming from?'

'One of the containers of hydrogen sulphide had corroded and leaked,' said Kwin. 'It's used in the waste water treatment system.'

'Had to be something involving poo,' said Andy, 'smelling like that.'

'Right,' said Ed, quickly changing the subject. 'You three get suited up and we can start venting this room. I've found some plastic piping I can use to increase the oxygen capacity in your suits if we need to. All we'll require is the larger tanks from a shuttle in the nearest hangar. The plan is to leave the ship through the hull breach. We can make it bigger with the plasma cutter if need be and make for the nearest airlock.'

'What, go outside the ship?' said Rialte, her eyes widening at the thought.

'I don't know about that either,' said Kwin.

Tocc just stood and stared.

'Well, if any of you have a better idea, then let's hear it?' said Pol, the irritation in her voice evident.

The three engineers glanced at each other nervously.

'Okay,' said Rialte. 'But we all remain tethered together, so no one can float away.'

'Deal,' said Ed. 'Now – helmets ready and we'll begin cutting a venting hole next to the door.'

23

The Starship *Hope*, attached to alien vessel, unknown location

THE HISSING BEGAN AS SOON as the plasma cutter breached the wall. Ed had reckoned on about an hour to vent the two rooms, any quicker than that would be a bonus. They couldn't delay because the Callametan engineers' suits only had enough oxygen to last about two hours. So they sat watching each other with the suits vented to the outside and only switching to the oxygen supply when it became necessary. If they found that the monorail system was down, it would take longer to get to the shuttle and every breath could count.

Andy was operating the cutter near the floor and next to the door. They'd originally been a little nervous that sparking the cutter into life might cause an explosion with the sulphurous-smelling gas in the room and they'd all lain prone on the floor as he flashed the igniter for the first time.

'Not too big, Andy,' said Ed. 'Cut one the other side too and then one every few feet.'

The atmosphere screamed out of the small apertures, they

had to keep well clear of them and resist the urge to stick a hand down to feel the suction. Ed stood by the door after thirty minutes and kept trying it to see if the pressure had reduced enough for it to open.

After forty minutes he noticed it move slightly.

'Nearly there,' he shouted to the engineers. They'd been sealed up with their own oxygen for over ten minutes now.

'Andy, give us a hand,' he said and they both tugged at the handle.

The wind began whistling through the small gap and when it was wide enough, one of the engineers stuck a crowbar in the crack and heaved on that too. What was left of the atmosphere soon evacuated through the ever-increasing gap and with a final heave the door swung open.

'Let's go,' said Ed, leading the group out into the main engineering area. He could see the wide and nervous eyes of the engineers as they ventured out into vacuum for the first time and hoped they wouldn't panic or throw up when they reached weightlessness outside the hull.

It quickly became obvious the damage was at the far side of the chamber as Ed could see stars through a jagged rupture up in one corner. All around this section of the ship was stripped bare, none of the loose equipment remained and what was left was scorched black with soot. The fires were extinguished now in the vacuum of space, but the damage had been done and this ship was going nowhere without major repairs.

The breach he'd seen was unfortunately about thirty feet up and he swore under his breath as he realised there was nothing to climb on to get up there.

'Pol, can you go back and get your lifter?' he said. 'I think it's going to be the only way to get up there.'

She didn't look very happy about the request, but turned

and trotted off all the same. A few minutes later he could hear the whine of the lifter's motor and watched as Pol rounded the huge antigrav drive housing they were behind and positioned the makeshift elevator underneath the breach.

'Everybody in,' she said, as she extended the stabiliser legs.

'Top floor for lingerie,' said Andy, but got only blank stares from the Callametans as they crammed into the cage.

Pol slowly lifted them up to the jagged hole and swung the cage over slightly until it touched the inner bent skin of the hull.

'Right,' said Ed. 'Everyone with a Theo suit is to take one of the engineers, we follow in a line down over to the port side and open the first airlock we come to.'

'Aren't we going to tether ourselves?' asked Kwin, her face white inside her faceplate.

'Our suits have mini jets and we can pull you around,' said Ed calmly, smiling to try and allay their nerves. 'We won't let you float off, you're quite safe. Kwin, you follow me and hang onto my belt here.'

Ed moved onto a section of bent hull plating, made sure Kwin was with him, and stepped out into space. He could see Kwin hyperventilating behind him as she followed and they both floated out and over to the side to make room for the next two.

'What a beautiful view,' said Ed, touching helmets so they could converse and staring out at the starscape surrounding them.

'It's great,' said Kwin. 'But where the hell is Callamet?'

Ed peered round and saw what she meant. – the planet should be dominating the view behind them.

'And what the hell is that thing?' she said, pointing at what appeared to be another ship sitting on top of the *Hope*.

'Bloody hell,' said Ed. 'Where did that come from?'

'It's anchored onto the hull,' said Andy, joining them with Tocc hanging onto his belt with a face of absolute terror.

'That could be why we can't see the planet,' said Ed. 'That ship has jump capability and is taking us somewhere.'

'Has what?' said Kwin, but Ed had lifted his helmet away.

He waited until Pol and Rialte joined them, before traversing around the hull and leading them down the port side towards an airlock.

'Hang on,' said Andy, staring off down the side of the *Hope*. 'Shouldn't we be able to see the shuttle down there?'

He pointed down the line of airlocks stretching away. Ed followed his finger and grimaced.

'It might be a small ship but it would be obvious from here,' Andy added.

'You're right,' said Ed, searching through his suit's menu for the magnification feature.

He zoomed in down towards the bow of the *Hope* and swore. A ragged and scorched remnant of the transfer tunnel hung off the side of the airlock they'd entered through earlier.

'Oh shit,' said Andy, after doing the same. 'We'd better head straight for a hangar and hide inside a Callametan shuttle or something.'

'I agree,' said Ed, as they continued along to the airlock.

It opened as expected and Ed noticed the engineers' obvious relief once they were inside and back into gravity. He peered left and right through the rectangular window of the inner door and seeing nothing of danger, pressed the round button.

The outer door motored across and sealed, followed by the hiss of pressurisation, the inner door sinking away from them and swinging over to the right. Ed and Andy both peered up and down the corridor. Finding it empty they led the small party out of the airlock and turned left towards the hangars.

Behind them a bulkhead door had slid across, blocking the passageway and sealing the rest of the ship from the hull breach in engineering.

'The atmosphere's at eighty-nine percent here,' said Pol. 'It's safe to remove helmets.'

The three engineers did so, sniffing the air suspiciously as they released the locking catches.

'How far to the first of the hangars?' asked Ed.

'A long way,' said Tocc. 'These are all the colonist chambers.'

'We were in that one until very recently,' said Rialte, pointing at the first door they came to. 'All the engineering crews were near the back for obvious reasons.'

'Can I see?' said Ed, nodding towards the door.

'Be my guest,' replied Kwin, taking the lead and opening the door.

As with the hangars, a metal stairway led down, but this time to many lower levels. Each level had a metal grid walkway and row upon row of survival pods stacked four high. Ed stared down the top row. He couldn't see the end of it, but looking across the ship, he could just about see the far side, some five hundred metres away.

'How many chambers like this are there?' he asked, looking back at Tocc.

'Four,' she said. 'Two hundred and fifty thousand in each. This is chamber four.'

'We need to find somewhere for these guys and fast,' said Andy. 'Hope told us only sixty-six percent are still alive.'

'We know,' said Rialte, dejectedly. 'There should have been five in our group.'

They retreated back to the corridor and carried on

forward, passing many doorways until almost an hour later Kwin stopped, read the sign by the door and pointed at it.

'This is hangar six,' she said. 'It contains larger transportation craft with initial arrival shelters and colony set up equipment.'

'Sounds a good place to conceal ourselves,' said Pol. 'Are there food supplies in the ships?'

'There should be plenty, so long as they've survived all this time,' said Tocc, as she opened the door, ushered everyone inside and closed and locked it again.

'It's mostly edible,' said Pol. 'I've already had to survive on it for several weeks.'

The vessels in this hangar were indeed larger. Transport ships, designed to ferry heavy equipment down to the surface of the chosen world. As with the other hangar Ed had seen, there were rows of them stretching away towards the front of the ship.

'We should wait in a ship next to the hangar door,' said Rialte. 'It would mean we could fly out if the situation availed.'

'Where the hell's the hangar door?' asked Andy. 'These hangars are all in the middle of the ship.'

'In the floor,' said Kwin. 'Right in the middle of the room and the ships are all lined up facing that way and in probable order of need to avoid shuffling them around.'

They descended the stairway and began worming their way through the maze of ships, heading for the centre of the hangar.

'Is there any way we can find out whether the *Hope*'s been boarded?' asked Tocc, nervously glancing over her shoulder from the rear of the group.

'Not without talking to Hope,' said Rialte. 'These ships all have the ability to converse with the mothership, but without countering this infuriating damping field, it's not going to happen.'

They rounded the nose of a large transport ship and came across a wide clear rectangular section of floor. It was about a foot lower than the level of the rest of the hangar.

'That's the exit,' said Rialte. 'It splits in the middle and slides into the hull.'

'Do you have an atmosphere shield?' asked Andy.

'What's that?' said Kwin, giving both her colleagues a glance.

'Do you have to vent the hangar before opening the door?' said Ed, waving at it.

'Ah – yes. I see what you mean now and yes, the hangar has to be vented before launching the ships.'

Ed and Andy exchanged a knowing look and a shrug.

'That must take some time with an area this big,' said Ed, looking up and down the hangar.

'About a day to do it safely,' replied Tocc, nodding enthusiastically.

'A day!' exclaimed Andy. 'You can't be in any hurry then?'

'Why would we?' asked Rialte.

'Good answer,' said Ed.

'What if the ship was under attack, though?' Andy continued.

'It's a colony ship, not a warship,' said Tocc.

'So you have no defences at all?'

'If you mean weapons,– then, no. Basic shielding to repel space junk, yes, but no weapons,' said Kwin.

The dim lighting in the hangar flickered slightly, causing them all to look up.

'We might have just jumped again,' said Ed. 'I think

they're using power from the *Hope* to help boost the envelope size and range.'

'You mentioned that before,' said Kwin. 'What is a jump?'

'The ability to fold space and travel great distances fast,' said Ed.

'How far?' asked Tocc.

'Up to around a thousand light years for some of the powerful ones,' said Ed.

'And how long does a thousand-light year jump take?' asked Rialte, sounding very sceptical.

'Around a hundredth of a second,' said Andy, smiling as the three Callametan engineers turned to stare at him in disbelief.

'That's simply impossible, surely,' said Rialte, looking for some consensus from her colleagues.

'Actually it's not,' said Pol. 'I've been on their ship and it's pretty amazing.'

'This isn't the time to be discussing the ins and outs of theoretical physics,' said Ed. 'Let's get inside one of these ships and have a sit down and a meal.'

'I'll second that,' said Andy. 'Do you have any pizza?'

24

The Starship *Hope*, attached to alien vessel, unknown location

THEY HAD PICKED a freighter on the opposite side of the sunken door. Rialte had chosen it as it was one of the biggest and had a first landing payload in the hold, containing everything the first landers would need to set up the beginnings of a colony.

The ship was fitted out to house twenty engineers for the first few weeks and contained comfortable hammocks and plenty of food and water that could last Ed's small group months. They set up a permanent watch in the darkened gloom of the cockpit to notify the others if anything changed outside and lined the small area they were in with heat-absorbing blankets to reduce their thermal signature.

The three engineers removed their uncomfortable EVA suits and stored them ready to go, just in case.

Ed noticed Andy had gone quiet for a while, which normally meant he was pondering something.

'Are you plotting?' he asked.

'Is there any way for us to hardwire a connection to Hope?' said Andy. 'Using the ship's own wiring loom?'

Ed glanced across at Tocc, who'd been listening and gave him her best questioning look.

'All the ships in here are still hardwired to the power supply until just before use,' she said. 'But it's only like a trickle charger. I checked the readout in the cockpit earlier and the supply is showing ninety-six percent. After all this time, it probably won't get any better than that.'

'But would Hope detect a communication signal pulsing around the power supplies?' Andy asked.

'It's certainly something I've never considered,' said Tocc.

'Nor me,' said Kwin, overhearing the suggestion. 'But Hope does have a lot more scope since her reboot with some of your technology.'

'It's worth a shot,' said Ed, giving Andy the thumbs up. 'I'll give you a hand.'

They went through to the cockpit where Rialte was on watch and explained the idea.

'That's the communication console there,' Rialte said, pointing at a small panel next to the pilot's leaning post. 'You've just walked past a tool store in the corridor there on the right.'

Tocc joined them and reminded Andy he'd need some form of transformer in the line as the communications system ran on a lot less juice and would instantly burn out if connected direct.

It took the joint effort about two hours to design and rig the connection. Finally Rialte sat back on the pilot's post and slipped on one of the communication mikes.

'What shall I say to her?' she asked, glancing round.

'Just see if it works first,' said Andy.

'*It does,*' said Hope over the cockpit speakers, making them all jump. '*I've been looking for you guys and what the hell is that thing stuck on top of me?*'

'We were hoping you could tell us that,' said Rialte.

'*I don't know, this stupid damping field coming from it is buggering about with everything. Did you know it fired on me? And now navigation has gone haywire as it's trying to tell me we're over a hundred thousand light years away from Callamet.*'

Ed looked at Rialte and Tocc. They both nodded back, acknowledging he'd been right.

'Hope, have you got any buoys on board?' asked Andy.

'*I have.*'

'Are they programmable? And could you launch one without being detected?'

'*Yes, guv.*'

'What's that for?' asked Tocc.

'If whoever they are have been embedding or hiding their jump destinations,' said Ed, 'then our ship won't know where to look for us.'

'Ah, I get it,' said Rialte. 'If they draw a line through Callamet and the buoy, it'll give them a direction to search along?'

'You've got it,' said Andy.

'*What would you like me to transmit?*' asked Hope.

'This way for horrible lager,' said Andy, getting a chuckle from Ed.

'*Are you sure?*'

'Oh yes,' said Ed, still grinning. 'There'll be no mistaking who left that message.'

'And it's similar to the one she left us that time in Andromeda,' said Andy.

'Make sure it doesn't begin transmitting until we're well clear, Hope,' said Ed.

'Top sausage,' she said, causing the Callametans to mutter amongst themselves.

'No prizes for guessing whose data files she downloaded,' said Andy, shaking his head.

'What's a top sausage?' asked Kwin, staggering into the cockpit and rubbing the sleep from her eyes.

'When this is over, we'll have a barbecue and I'll show you,' said Andy.

'I don't know what that is either,' she said. 'I'm hoping it's somethin—'

'We've got company,' interrupted Pol, ducking down out of sight.

The others all dropped low in the cockpit and peeked out the front screen. Ed could see two Callametans strolling through the lines of ships on the other side of the sunken hangar door.

The dull lighting in the hangar dimmed again as another jump was initiated.

'They must have entered through the same door as us, coming from that direction,' said Ed. 'Do you recognise any of them?'

'No,' said Rialte. 'The uniform they're wearing is strange to us and not from this ship.'

'What about you, Pol?' asked Ed. 'Are they from Callamet?'

'I don't think so,' she said. 'I've never seen uniforms like that before.'

Three more appeared and they all stopped and conversed, pointing at the doorway in the floor. They all turned to look behind them as a Mogul strode into view.

'Oh shit,' said Andy. 'None of them have just come out of hibernation, they're all a healthy weight.'

'That ship is a Mogul ship,' said Ed. 'That's all we bloody need.'

'That's not a Mogul,' said Kwin. 'That's a Blend. They're who we're all running from.'

'They're all enslavers and killers,' said Tocc.

'We know,' said Ed, grimacing. 'We've had dealings with them before.'

'How did they find us?' said Rialte.

'The cuckoo's sent out a signal,' said Andy. 'If that ship's full of 'em, we're in the—'

He was interrupted by all their weapons issuing a quiet *beep.*

'They've turned off the damping field,' said Pol.

'Hmm,' mumbled Ed. 'Hope, can you operate your arrays now?'

'No worries, mate.'

'Can you show us where we are on the holonav in here and make sure it can't be seen from outside?'

A hologram of a busy planet materialised in front of them. Hundreds of ships milled around a large planet in a twin star system.

'How big is that planet?' said Andy. 'It's massive.'

'Eight times bigger than Callamet,' said Hope. *'Seventy-nine percent ocean, average temperature thirty-seven degrees.'*

'No wonder the Moguls like it,' said Ed.

'Oh no,' said Rialte, pointing to a weird-shaped space station. 'Those are the remains of the other colony ships.'

'Bastards have bolted them all together to form a floating platform,' said Tocc, the emotion clear in her voice. 'Not one of us escaped.'

The three engineers slumped back dejectedly and stared into space. Ed could see the tears in Kwin's eyes.

'Where are we, Hope?' asked Andy. 'In relation to Callamet?'

The map panned back and just kept going until finally two red dots glowed in different arms of the galaxy.

'Holy crap,' said Ed. 'We're in the Cygnus arm.'

'That's over a hundred and forty thousand light years from Callamet,' exclaimed Andy, his eyes widening.

'It's in Blend space,' said Tocc. 'Beyond where we originated.'

'They must have developed a super jump drive to have got this far so quick,' said Ed. 'It would take us over a week to get this far and that's if we really stood on the gas.'

'They've done it in a day,' said Andy. 'That's hugely impressive.'

Ed closed his eyes and felt around with his DOVI. He infiltrated the ship above them, found the field generator and disabled it, then searched for the main jump drive. It took up a large area of the rear of the starship and was individually shielded with its own generator.

'Can't get near it, eh?' said Andy. 'I know, I already tried.'

'Hope, are you there?' asked Ed.

'Ready and willing.'

'If you're ever able to penetrate their jump drive system, make a data file of everything you find and send it to Cleo next time you're chatting, please,' said Ed.

'Nessun problema,' she said.

'We seem to be in Italy now,' said Ed.

'These guys'll never forgive us,' said Andy, getting glances from Rialte and Tocc.

'For what?' they said together.

'Turning your computer into a wisecracking plonker,' said Andy, laughing.

'At least she's a bit more fun now,' said Kwin, the sober glares from Rialte and Tocc now coming in her direction.

'I can't understand a bloody word she says these days,' said Tocc.

'You never could,' said Kwin, chuckling in the strange squeaky Callametan way. Pol joined in and before long all four Callametans were squealing away together.

Ed and Andy exchanged a glance.

'Sounds like feeding time at the guinea pig café,' whispered Andy.

That set Ed and Andy off on a fit of the giggles for a few seconds, until all six of them instantly shut up as the unmistakable sound of the outer airlock door opening reached the cockpit.

25

The Core Precinct, Triy City, Planet Garag, Dubl'ouin System

SACHEM TRYS'LIN APPEARED VERY HAPPY. He sat high up behind his oversized desk, grinning, and watched as the planet's adjudicator, Reez Treqqer entered the chamber. Although this didn't cheer Treqqer at all, because Trys'lin's smile was exactly the same as his grimace and until he knew which this was, his expression would best remain neutral.

'I understand you've been informed of Gradulin's success, my Sachem?' said Treqqer, hoping this was the reason for the possible smile, while bowing at the waist.

'I have indeed,' said Trys'lin, the malevolent grin widening even more. 'It seems the whereabouts of a dangerous rival cult has also been established, hmm?'

'Correct, my Sachem. That is the reason for my presence. Gradulin has requested an audience with yourself at your earliest convenience.'

'Has he now?' said Trys'lin, rolling his eyes and

summoning his amanuensis. 'Confident little shit isn't he? Reminds me of someone!'

Treqqer allowed himself a little smirk, as he knew the comment was aimed at him.

The huge carved timber doors to the Sachem's chamber were opened by two guards stationed outside. The Sachem's personal amanuensis strode in confidently, bowed and sat at his small desk to the left of the Sachem's dais.

'Be sure to send me Gradulin as soon as he arrives, Adjudicator,' said Trys'lin, waving his hand to indicate he was to leave.

'As you wish, my Sachem,' said Treqqer. He bowed again, turned and marched smartly away, leaving the Core Precinct and returning to his little corner of fiefdom at the back of the Precinct Chambers.

Captain Gradulin arrived at his office a short while later, escorted by one of the precinct guards. He stood erect and still, staring straight ahead, only bowing to Treqqer when he glanced up from his monitor.

'Captain Gradulin reporting back, Adjudicator,' he boasted confidently.

'So I see,' said Treqqer. 'Am I to understand the new Hass drive trials were a success?'

'Indeed they were, sir,' he said, keeping his gaze straight forward.

'And the final colony ship?'

'Retrieved and undergoing asset recovery, sir.'

'What of the interfering alien ship?'

'We ignored them. Our damping field seemed to disable their ship and we detected their personnel in the engineering section at the rear of the colony ship. Their threat was eliminated when we neutralised the vessel's drive capabilities and exposed the area to space, sir.'

'Hmm, excellent. Your report stated the original captain was awake?'

'Yes, sir. Captain Ralt was discovered hiding in her cabin and is now secured aboard my ship. She states she is the only surviving member of the original crew, but the planet however has millions of potential Callametan vassals ripe for exploitation.'

Treqqer smiled and nodded.

'Tell me about this GDA threat,' he asked.

'The computer system aboard the colony ship has data indicating a group of humanoid worlds in a far arm of the galaxy. We believe the ship present when we arrived was from this cult. The data is limited but as our technology appears to be superior, and the Callametan world we found is part of their group, I envisage a swift strike to eliminate their leaders would open up a whole new region to us.'

'Do you now?' said Treqqer, staring at his subordinate. 'And how do you envisage doing that?'

Gradulin glanced down as he shuffled his feet slightly, appearing to lose some of his confidence.

'I would suggest filling the colony ship with space debris and jumping it into their system from afar, ensuring it emerges so close to the planet that whatever defences they engage, it would be way too late.'

'They'd be able to destroy one ship, surely?'

'I'm counting on it, sir,' he said, with a slight grin. 'They might destroy the majority of the ship, but not the trillions of tonnes of rocks travelling at over half the speed of light.'

Treqqer continued staring at the captain and rubbed his chin thoughtfully.

'How long would it take to install a Hass drive on that ship?'

'We wouldn't need to, sir,' he said. 'I would use my ship again.'

'Explain?'

'Jump in from afar, adjust course to perfect the trajectory, release and jump away, sir.'

'You've put a great deal of thought into this, haven't you?'

'Sir.'

'Timescale?'

'The sourcing and loading of rocks and boulders into those huge hangars would take the longest period of time. Probably a few weeks, sir.'

'If you took it out to the belt, you'd have an unlimited supply,' said Treqqer, grinning. 'I'm going to take you through to the Sachem now, Captain. Tell him everything you've just told me.'

'Yes, sir. There was one more thing,' Gradulin said.

'Go ahead.'

'We found two of the original sleepers trapped alive in one of the hangars. They stated that the alien vessel we ignored had only recently killed the majority of their colleagues by spacing them.'

Treqqer raised his eyebrows at this revelation and felt his face flushing with anger.

'Pass the alien ship specifics to the fleet with my authority to destroy it on sight, absolutely no survivors,' he spat. 'Is that clear, Captain?'

'Very clear, sir.'

Treqqer stood up.

'Now, come with me. You have an audience with the Sachem and our new friend from afar.'

26

The Starship *Hope*, Planet Garag, Dubl'ouin System

LUCKILY THE COCKPIT was quite a way from the opening airlock and it gave them a chance to disperse and conceal themselves. Ed checked his rifle was on stun and levelled it at the inner door just as it beeped and the red lights around it flashed.

The lone uniformed and helmeted Callametan took two steps inside the ship before she noticed the laser weapon pointing at her head. She froze, then the look of shock soon turned to puzzlement and finally settled on fear.

'W-who are you?' she stammered, stepping back slightly and getting a *clunk* on the back of her helmet by the closing inner airlock door.

Pol, who'd hidden behind some of the cargo, emerged with her rifle also pointing at the newcomer.

'What are you here to do?' she asked.

'P-pilot the ship to the surface,' she whispered, looking nervously from person to person as Rialte, Tocc and Kwin arrived.

'Then that's exactly what you're going to do,' said Ed, indicating the stairs to the cockpit with the barrel of his rifle. 'Keep all your hands where I can see them.'

'Are you armed?' asked Kwin.

The Callametan looked at her as if she was insane.

'Of course I'm not, I'd be executed if I was caught with a weapon,' she said, as she began slowly and nervously climbing the stairs.

They followed her up closely and sat on the floor so they couldn't be seen. The pilot sat on the central post and began checking the flight systems with one eye and the other on them.

'We're watching and listening to everything you do and say,' said Ed. 'So don't try and be the hero.'

'What do I do if the ship has operational issues?' she asked.

'What would you normally do?'

'Call for flight engineers to fix the problem.'

'Then you do that,' said Ed.

'Are you members of the BDF?' she asked, as she slowly brought the ship to life.

'BDF?' questioned Pol. 'What's that?'

She glanced over her shoulder with a look of surprise.

'Blend Defiance Force,' she said. 'Are you not from here or something?'

'No, we're not,' said Andy, peeking out the front screen from the corner of the control panel where he was sitting. 'We're here to help rid you of the Blend problem.'

'That's why I asked about the BDF,' she said. 'Some of the senior members are TAs.'

'What's a TA?' said Ed.

'One weekend a month, my arse,' mumbled Andy in the background.

'Shut up, you,' Ed snapped.

'Two arms,' said the pilot, giving Andy a concerned glance.

'You have other two-armed humans on the planet?'

'Quite a few,' she said. 'Mostly stragglers that have strayed into the local systems and been snatched by the Blends. Where are you from?'

'We're from a group of human worlds a long way from here,' said Ed.

'You too?' she asked, glancing at Pol and then back to check the antigravs were spooling up correctly.

'Callamet,' said Pol, causing the pilot to stop what she was doing and stare at her intently.

'The home planet still exists?' she questioned, seemingly quite surprised.

'That I wouldn't know,' said Pol. 'I'm from the Callamet formed by this ship.'

'So one did reach its destination?' she said, sounding a little happier.

Ed saw a look of disappointment wash over Pol's face.

'Well, not exactly,' she admitted and continued to explain the situation up to now.

Ed watched the pilot's expressions change as the story unfolded.

'So you're saying over half the original colonists are still aboard and in hibernation pods that remain functioning after all this time?'

They all nodded.

'You really don't have to point weapons at me,' she said. 'They've murdered many of my family members over the centuries and if one came aboard now, I'd probably help you kill him.'

Ed nodded and slung his rifle over his shoulder, nodding at the others to do the same.

They all jumped as a loud *crack* sounded from outside and the ship vibrated slightly.

'They're opening the exterior door,' she said.

'What about depressurising the hangar first?' said Pol.

'They're not going to bother,' she said. 'Takes too long, they'll just crack the doors gradually and let it rip out that way.'

'Is there somewhere on the surface we could hide this ship?' asked Andy, causing everyone to stare at him.

'This ship!' she exclaimed, giving them an exasperated look. 'Not a chance, it's way too big and would be found – easily. One of the small shuttles, maybe.'

'Who flies those down?' asked Ed.

She smiled for the first time.

'We do,' she said. 'They said it would take about two hundred of us four days to empty all the hangars and then we take it over to the belt for filling with rocks.'

'What the hell do they need hangars full of rocks for?' asked Pol, the ship vibrating savagely as the atmosphere screamed by outside.

'They haven't told us that,' said the pilot.

'I can hazard a guess though,' said Ed, rubbing his chin thoughtfully and getting a worried look from Andy.

'You're thinking of that planet in the Messier galaxy aren't you?' Andy said. 'The name escapes me, though.'

'Heeder,' said Ed.

'That was it,' said Andy, clicking his fingers. 'But, where would they be going with this monster stuffed full of good news?'

'With Ralt singing like a canary to save her own skin,'

said Ed, looking at him intently, 'where would the Blends feel their biggest threat would come from?'

'Callamet?' said Andy, hopefully.

'Don't be daft.' Ed rolled his eyes. 'They could conquer that small planet in a day and still be home in time for tea.'

'You don't mean the GDA?' said Andy. 'You think they mean to use this ship to hit them?'

Ed nodded.

'But where?'

'Dasos.'

'Oh shit.'

'Cut off the head with the first strike,' Ed said. 'Makes perfect military sense.'

'But the GDA's revenge would be absolute. One cloaked Katadromiko cruiser and half a dozen Genok missiles and this planet would be uninhabitable for generations.'

'Yeah – but the Blends might not know that,' said Ed. 'Callamet was a new member and Ralt only just sworn in as their ambassador. How much knowledge of the GDA's military capability could she have got in such a short time?'

Andy stared at the floor for a moment, before glancing up and pointing at the pilot.

'What's your name by the way?' he asked, raising his eyebrows.

'Joontamaillion,' she said. 'But everyone calls me Joonta.'

'Okay, Joonta,' said Andy. 'How many worlds do the Blends command?'

Joonta shrugged one of the Callametan four-arm shrugs and pulled an awkward expression.

'We don't know,' she said. 'They don't allow other races to have any knowledge regarding their kingdom, history or indeed where they originally came from.'

'Nothing?'

'Nothing – they're the most brutal and secretive race you're ever likely to come across. All we do know has been passed down for generations. They arrived in our region of the spiral arm around eight thousands years ago. After several hundred years of conflict, we knew the writing was on the wall and secretly built the five colony ships to try and save our race from probable extinction.'

Joonta suddenly sat up straight and pointed at her helmet. She pulled what must have been a microphone out from its side, pointed at it and signalled for everyone to be silent. The faraway expression on her face gave away that she was receiving instructions.

'Sigma four showing green for insertion,' she said, listening again for a moment. 'Will adopt flight path Bresserin 119, Sigma four away.'

Ed could feel the grinding of heavy motors from outside through the ship's floor and assumed this would be the hangar doors now opening fully as the atmosphere must have been successfully vented.

He felt the ship rise as Joonta caressed the familiar Callametan controls and watched as she scanned the board for any fault warnings. These ships might be brand new, but they'd sat idol for an awfully long time. The last place you wanted to discover any defect in the ship's integrity, was on its first planetary insertion.

It went dark in the cockpit suddenly and Ed realised they were off the *Hope* and out into clear space. He stood and peered out the front screen at the planet below.

'It's a big bastard isn't it?' said Andy, looking over his shoulder.

'I hope you've brought your sunscreen,' Ed replied. 'It's forty degrees down there in the cooler zones.'

27

Upper atmosphere, Planet Garag, Dubl'ouin System

THE CALLAMETAN FREIGHTER DROPPED FAST, following the three similar ships in front of it with a long line of others behind.

Ed watched as Joonta skilfully kept the nose slightly up, presenting the heat-shielded underbelly of the craft to the searing heat of the thin atmosphere screaming by outside.

'Where will they put all these ships?' asked Ed, looking out and seeing only the odd glimpse of ocean through the cloud layers.

'In military storage areas,' said Joonta. 'In this case it's near the city of Bresserin on the northern landmass known as Xantamain.'

'Will we be able to avoid capture once we're down?'

Joonta glanced across at Ed for a moment. He noticed her expression was one of conflict or maybe nervousness. Her body language eventually gave away she'd come to a decision.

'You'd better be who you say you are,' she said. 'Otherwise I'm as good as dead.'

'You have nothing to fear from us,' said Ed, in his best reassuring tone.

Joonta nodded and remained silent for a moment.

'I'm going to introduce you to someone,' she said, finally.

'In the BDF?' Ed asked.

Joonta's head snapped around and her eyes revealed real fear.

'An educated guess, Joonta,' he said, in as soothing a voice as he could muster and holding his hands up in surrender. 'Is she one of the other pilots?'

Joonta relaxed slightly and shook her head.

'No, she's hopefully on the ground crew that'll guide us into position when we arrive.'

They both looked back out the front screen. The lead ship about three kilometres in front was turning and Joonta touched a couple of controls and leaned back.

'That's it now until we reach Bresserin,' she said.

Ed watched as the three lead ships disappeared into high cloud.

'Where d'you want us for landing?' Ed asked.

'There's a hatch in the floor of the freight deck,' she said. 'Leads down a narrow stairway to a small engineering switch bay. Stay in there until someone comes for you.'

'What if they don't?'

'They will.'

'What's to stop you sending a regiment of Blend troops?' asked Ed, raising his eyebrows.

'I've trusted you with my life,' she said. 'This is the part where it goes the other way and to be honest, they'd kill me anyway for not security-checking the ship before takeoff.'

'I'll go down and find it,' said Andy, standing and disappearing down the cockpit stairs.

The cloud flashing past the front screen vanished as if a switch had been thrown. The ocean was gone and in its place was a sprawling metropolis stretching away to a mountain range many kilometres distant.

'Bresserin,' said Joonta. 'A mining town.'

'What do they mine here?' Ed asked.

'Titanium mostly and a few other rare bits and pieces,' she said. 'Because this is an ancient ocean floor here, there's a lot of titanium-rich sand. My day job is to pilot the finished product up to galactic freighters for distribution throughout Blend space.'

As the ship descended, Ed could make out several open cast mines spread around the region. The lines of grey terracing disappearing into deep cuts that blighted the otherwise pretty landscape.

'You need to conceal yourselves,' said Joonta. 'Four minutes from landing and don't forget to remain there until contacted by Abubaker.'

'Abubaker?' questioned Ed. 'Is that her name?'

'It is, although it's a he — he's a TA human,' she said. 'The Blends tend to treat the TAs slightly differently.'

'What, like – better?' Ed asked.

'No, I wouldn't say better exactly,' she said hesitantly, obviously searching for the right words. 'Let's just say they perhaps get preferential access to slightly more senior positions.'

Ed patted her on one of her top shoulders and signalled for the others to follow him down to the freight deck. They got there just as Andy emerged from a hatch in the floor.

'It's a bit sardines down here,' he said. 'But it'll do so long as it's not for too long.'

'Okay, Callametans first,' said Ed, nodding at the hatch. 'Then, we'll come last with our weapons trained on the hatch. Just in case someone unexpected opens it.'

Andy had been right about the lack of space. They were barely able to close the hatch once all six were inside.

Ed and Andy were closest to the exit and kept their rifles trained on the hatch above their heads. They all listened to the ever-changing noise of the antigravs spooling up and down as the ship negotiated its final approach. A final clunk jarred them all and the ship settled, the noise of the engines slowly quietening into silence. Ed checked his weapon was on a stun setting and indicated for Andy to do the same. He listened intently for some indication of movement from outside, but was only rewarded with the irregular ticking of the ship cooling around them.

'How long do we wait?' whispered Andy, the whites of his eyes piercing the low red illumination in the passageway.

'She said there were two hundred of them coming down at a time,' Ed whispered back. 'Perhaps we have to wait until they're all down before our friend can pay us a visit.'

It was another few minutes before they heard the airlock rotate and the mumbling of voices up on the freight deck. Footsteps clunked around over their heads; it sounded like someone was inspecting the contents of the load.

The hatch rattled as someone walked across it, followed shortly after by the airlock rotating again then silence returned once more.

Ed's heart nearly jumped out of his mouth as the hatch was wrenched open and Joonta peered down, a rather relieved expression on her face.

'Sorry,' she said. 'I'm glad I put you in here now, I wasn't expecting a load inspection quite so soon.'

'Do we have to stay down here in the gloom any longer?' said Andy. 'I'm getting cramp.'

Joonta thought for a moment before replying.

'I was able to have a quick conversation with Abubaker, so he knows you're here and he's working on a way to get you off the base. Remember, he's very nervous of it being a trick, so don't go pointing any weapons at him. In the meantime, go back up to the cockpit and keep your heads down. If any Blends look like entering the ship, hide in the small crew bunk room at the back on the opposite side of the cockpit. However, if you have to engage them, you'll be on your own. If you manage to survive, head for the mountains.'

'Understood,' said Ed, slowly unfolding his cramped limbs from the narrow space.

He led them all back up to the cockpit and watched as the last of the first batch of ships from the *Hope* landed nearby, settling on what looked like a giant dark grey concrete pad that must be a couple of kilometres across.

'The city seems to be in that direction,' said Andy, pointing out of the starboard cockpit window. 'Which means we're right out on the fringe, with those mountains behind us.'

'It'd be good to know what direction to run in, if that situation arose,' said Ed.

Joonta stuck her head around the bulkhead from the stairway.

'I'm being picked up in a moment to go back up for another ship, so if I don't see you again, good luck and kill some of the bastards for me.'

She disappeared back down the stairs, then there came the distant sound of the airlock rotating.

'High protein biscuit, anyone?' said Andy, opening a pack from the food locker at the rear of the cockpit.

'My favourite,' said Pol, rolling her eyes and making a fake gagging sound. 'I had to live on those stale tasteless bricks not so long ago.'

Andy wrinkled his nose as he crunched on one with a blue wrapper.

'Mmm,' he said, looking at the remainder with disdain. 'Portland cement flavour, yum, yum.'

28

Military storage facility, Planet Garag, Dubl'ouin System

IT WAS ALMOST FULLY DARK when the lights of a vehicle approached. They'd watched and listened to hundreds more of the plundered ships as they descended and continued to fill the huge sea of concrete. Ed had sat in the blackness of the cockpit, wondering if one of them was piloted by Joonta. Earlier they'd had a conversation as to whether moving down half a dozen ships might be a prudent idea. It would certainly give them advance notice if they'd been betrayed, or at the very least, a first look at who was coming for them.

The eventual decision was to stay and keep a close watch, which was exactly what Pol was doing when she gave the warning of an approaching vehicle.

Some sort of minibus, it extinguished its lights several ships up the line and cruised up silently to halt just in front of the cockpit. Two TA figures slid out nervously from the front. They peered around for a moment, then scanned the area in a complete circle with some sort of handheld instrument.

'What are they doing?' asked Pol, stretching up to see them over the console.

'Making sure they're alone, I imagine,' said Andy.

The two figures, seemingly satisfied with the instrument's readings, disappeared underneath the ship.

'Andy, with me,' said Ed. 'The rest of you wait here.'

They quickly descended the stairway and waited by the airlock that was already cycling as they arrived. The two humans peered nervously inside as the inner door slid away. They were both very tall and had almost completely black skin that reminded Ed of a friend from university who came from Sudan in Northern Africa.

'Hello,' said Ed.

'Evening,' said Andy.

'You have weapons,' said the slightly shorter of the two, nodding at the rifles slung over Ed and Andy's shoulders. 'How do we know you're not a Blend ruse to trick us into the open?'

'Because you can take charge of them,' said Ed, slipping the weapon off his arm and offering it to the newcomer, then indicating for Andy to do the same.

The strangers took the rifles tentatively, inspected them closely, before glancing at each other and back at Ed and Andy.

'These are certainly not a Blend weapon we've ever seen before,' said the taller one.

'That's because they're from a group of worlds on the other side of the galaxy,' said Andy.

'As are we,' said Ed. 'I think you'll find these suits we're wearing aren't Blend issue either.'

'We were told there were six of you, two TAs and four Quads,' said the shorter one.

'They're hiding up in the cockpit,' said Ed. 'My name's

Ed by the way and this is Andy. Which one of you is Abubaker?'

The two humans looked at each other with concern, shrugged and seemed to come to some sort of decision.

'That would be me,' said the slightly shorter one. 'This is Haitham.'

The taller one nodded and indicated the stairway up to the cockpit.

'Take us to the Quads,' he said. 'We need to make some plans to get you away from here.'

Ten minutes later they were all trotting across the grey concrete to the minibus. Even though it was dark now, it was still well over thirty degrees and the six newcomers were glad to get inside the vehicle's coolness.

'Bloody hell,' mumbled Andy. 'I remember it being like this in Singapore.'

'Spent a couple of weeks in Port Douglas on my gap year,' said Ed, mopping his brow with a handkerchief. 'It was just like this in February.'

'What's that?' Andy asked, giving Ed a strange look.

'What's what?'

'That!' indicating what was in Ed's hand. 'Do you really keep a handkerchief in your spacesuit?' he exclaimed, getting confused looks from the Callametans.

'A gentleman always carries a handkerchief,' said Ed, nodding.

'You can't blow your nose in space, knob head,' said Andy, rolling his eyes at Pol, who smiled back unconfidently.

'Put these on quickly,' said Abubaker, passing clothing back to them from the front. 'They're uniforms to get us through the security barriers and we've hidden all your weapons in a box underneath the front seat here.'

The others all watched in amazement as Ed, Andy and Pol

deactivated their suits. They flowed down into thin pads under their feet.

'That is the freakiest thing I've ever seen,' said Abubaker, exchanging a look with Haitham.

'Feels weird too,' said Pol, selecting one of the pilot's uniforms.

Kwin, Rialte and Tocc had all been given pilot's uniforms too, similar to what Joonta had been wearing. Ed and Andy however had to try and make rather long TA uniforms look acceptable.

'Sorry about those,' said Haitham, looking at Andy's cuffs hanging over his hands. 'They're our spare sets and made to fit us.'

'Roll them up a bit,' said Abubaker. 'Luckily, ill-fitting uniforms are quite common here.'

'You look like something from a seventies glam rock outfit,' chuckled Andy, looking at Ed's flared maroon trousers with gold edging.

'It's what all the young dudes are wearing,' said Ed, with a smirk.

'I'm a twentieth century boy,' said Andy, pouting.

Abubaker began driving slowly across the huge hard-standing, weaving between dozens of parked freighters. He glanced over his shoulder and, finding everyone changed and ready, nodded and sped up a little.

'You've all been on a long shift,' he said. 'Most of you would normally be dozing in the back, don't give them any reason to want to search the van.'

'Understood,' said Ed, shuffling down in his seat and pretending to be asleep.

The other five took the hint and did the same, so by the time they pulled up at the exit barrier, all except Abubaker were supposedly asleep.

'Evening, Felluck,' called Abubaker cheerfully, as a uniformed guard wandered over from the small office. 'I heard your lad has signed up for pilot training.'

'Is nothing a secret round here?' the guard grumbled back, whilst shining a light around the sleeping bodies in the back. 'Aren't they sending you up to the Quad ship, Ab?'

'I bloody hope not.. Judging how knackered these buggers are, I'm quite happy down here, cataloguing the ships and cargos.'

Felluck nodded, yawned and turned back towards the office to activate the electronic barrier. Ed, who'd been watching through half closed eyes, exhaled loudly.

'Well done, Ab,' he whispered, as Abubaker drove the van through a narrow cordon of concrete bollards and turned right onto a public roadway. He pressed a flashing red button on the touch screen in front of him and the vehicle continued on its route even though he'd taken his hands off the controls.

'Don't thank him yet,' said Haitham. 'There are random patrols at night and sometimes a Blend will join them, just so they can ruin someone's day.'

'Is there somewhere safe we can hide until our ship finds us?' asked Ed.

'That's the plan,' said Haitham, sparking up a tablet in his lap and tapping away feverishly. 'Ready?' he said to Abubaker.

'Ready,' came the reply.

He touched a final icon, the van went suddenly dark and Abubaker steered suddenly left into a narrow side street. They continued for about half a kilometre before turning sharply onto a steep downhill ramp that led underneath a large building in complete darkness. Haitham again tapped away on the tablet and a metal door ahead slid across from right to left, allowing them access to an underground parking area, lit with dull blue lighting.

It wasn't large and Ed could see a couple of loading docks straight ahead and parking bays for a handful of vehicles just off to one side, into which Abubaker swung the van. There was only one other vehicle in the bays and that was in complete darkness.

'All out,' he said. 'I need to get this van back out there before it's missed.'

Ed jumped down from the side door of the vehicle and went to the front passenger door so he could retrieve their weapons from under the front seat. He looked up and over his shoulder as he pulled the seat up because he heard Andy swear behind him.

The lights brightened suddenly and his heart sank. Four armed Moguls stood in a line grinning at them.

29

Underground loading dock, Planet Garag, Dubl'ouin System

'I STRONGLY SUGGEST everyone remains very still,' snarled the left-hand Mogul.

Ed and Andy exchanged a knowing glance and got busy with their DOVIs. It took less than twenty seconds to deactivate the four rifles pointed at them and one pistol in a holster of the Mogul who'd spoken.

'A BDF safe house, eh?' he smirked. 'Doesn't seem very safe to me.'

'You betrayed us,' spat Abubaker, glaring venomously at Ed.

'Actually, no,' said Ed, turning back to the raised front seat and reaching inside. 'If you've been betrayed, then it was by one of your own.'

'I said remain still,' shouted the same Mogul, swinging his weapon at Ed, before glancing down at it curiously. Dropping it, he drew his pistol and pointed that instead.

In the couple of seconds this was happening, Ed had

retrieved one of their rifles, turned and proceeded to fire four times. He received almost four identical shocked expressions as the line of Moguls dropped, the clatter of their weapons on the hard ground echoing around the dock.

'Oh fuck!' exclaimed Haitham, looking between the prone Moguls and Ed. 'What have you done?'

'I was accused of betraying you a moment ago,' he replied, giving Abubaker a hard stare.

Abubaker was stood stock still staring at the Moguls, his mouth opening and closing again, but no sound emanating.

'They don't seem quite as nasty as the one's we're used to, do they?' said Andy, casually kicking one as he stooped to pick up their rifles. 'Give us a hand, chaps,' he said. 'We need to secure and interrogate them.'

'You mean they're not dead?' said Abubaker finally getting his vocal cords to work.

'No,' said Ed. 'We don't kill unless we absolutely have to.'

'His weapon would have been set to kill when he pulled the trigger,' said Haitham. 'Which is another thing – why didn't any of their weapons function? I've never seen anything like it.'

'Tricks of the trade,' said Andy. 'Now, has anyone got any sticky tape or anything similar?'

Inside the building they found two dead Callametans.

'You see what we mean?' said Abubaker. 'These two had been sentenced to death for stealing food for their spawn group.'

'What were they doing here?' asked Tocc, looking sadly at the corpses.

'Hiding out until we could get them new identities,' said Haitham.

'For some reason the Blends have difficulty telling the

Quads apart,' said Abubaker. 'They all look the same to them. Makes it easier to change their identification documents.'

'We need to move quickly,' said Haitham. 'This location is blown and if those soldier Blends don't report in, the streets will be flooded with security.'

They found some rope and returned downstairs to the underground loading bay.

'Did you move them?' asked Pol, the first to enter the dock.

'Oh crap,' said Andy, 'they've gone.'

'Their van's gone too,' said Haitham. 'And ours has been vandalised.'

'Oh crap,' said Ed, looking back to Abubaker, whose face had gone white.

'Grab everything and come this way quickly,' said Haitham, opening a cupboard door in the wall.

'Does this one have a bolt hole?' asked Abubaker, looking at Haitham.

'It does,' he said. 'But only into the opposite building. It's not far enough, but it's a start.'

The tunnel hidden behind a dummy ventilation grille was small and low. Everyone had to crawl through pushing a bag or weapon in front of them.

'You okay?' Ed called back to Andy, knowing he was claustrophobic.

'Only shitting myself a little bit,' came the reply.

'Just follow my boots for a few more metres, I can see a light ahead.'

Haitham had gone first and helped everyone out into a gloomy storeroom racked with shelving containing rolls of cloth.

'It's a clothing manufacturer,' he said, noticing Ed inspecting the contents of the shelves.

'Is there a storeroom with the finished product?' asked Ed. 'We need a change of appearance.'

'I believe they have a small shopfront on ground level for wholesalers to inspect the merchandise,' said Abubaker, glancing up at the ceiling. 'They must have samples there.'

A low boom shook the room, causing dust and the odd lump of plaster to drop on them.

'They're back with the heavy artillery,' said Andy, some colour returning to his face after the horror of the tunnel. He tried the door and, finding it locked, set about it with his DOVI.

'How the hell did you do that?' asked Haitham, as Andy opened the door and peeked out. 'You just shut your eyes and the bloody thing opened.'

'Mind over matter,' said Ed, slapping Haitham on the back. 'You worry about a route out of here and let us worry about opening the doors.'

On the way to the stairway, they checked all the other doors on the basement level, but none contained any finished stock. A second and third explosion and the sound of falling masonry close by had them clinging onto the railing as they ascended the stairs. Dust enveloped them as they pushed open the door to ground level.

'Bloody hell,' said Andy. 'Did they just blow the whole building to shit?'

'If they did, that's a good thing,' said Ed. 'The tunnel will never be found.'

Rounding a corner in the direction of the storefront, they realised why so much dust was present. The frontage of the building was gone. Rubble filled the street and had pushed in through the door and windows.

'Back up, everyone,' said Haitham. 'No exit that way.'

They quickly turned and retraced their steps back though

the dusty gloom, past the stairway door and deeper into the building.

'Follow those,' said Abubaker, pointing at red emergency exit signs. 'There must be a way out onto the next street somewhere.'

The signs took them to the rear of the building and a solid grey door with a small square glass panel to check the exit was clear. Haitham peeked out and instantly backed away again.

'Crap,' he said. 'The street's full of police and emergency vehicles.'

Andy enjoyed the ease with which his DOVI could unlock doors and did just that to the one he found himself standing next to, a few metres back from the exit. He had a quick look inside and smiled.

'Guys,' he said, grinning. 'I think I might have found what we're looking for.'

The stock room was crammed with uniforms, racks and racks of uniforms. Blue ones, green ones, grey ones and black ones, there were hundreds of them.

Abubaker's eyes lit up as he peered round the door.

'Those are the local Quad police,' he said, pulling a grey set from the rack and handing it to Tocc. 'You guys find some of those to fit and we'll give these a go.'

He thrust black uniforms at Ed and Andy, who raised their eyebrows at the design.

'I'll look like the villain's muscle from a Bond movie in this,' said Andy, holding it up in front of him and posing in a wall-mounted mirror.

'Or a carpark attendant at a posh Italian hotel,' said Ed.

'Ah yes, I remember him,' said Andy, 'what did we call him?'

'Mussolini.'

It took just a few minutes for them all to change and check each other's dress.

'Don't leave anything behind,' said Abubaker. 'I want them to continue believing we were in that building.'

They tidied the stock room, hid their weapons under their uniforms and went back to the emergency exit. Haitham glanced out again and reasoned going left would be the best course of action.

'Follow us,' said Abubaker to the Quads. 'The black uniforms we're wearing would always be senior to the local police, so follow us and do as we say, especially when in earshot of strangers.'

Haitham turned back to the door and hit the opening lever hard. The door swung outwards and the TAs marched out, leading the way as if they owned the place. Two Quad police officers who were leaning lazily against one of the vehicles, jumped to attention as the group swept by.

'No slouching, you two,' snapped Abubaker, as he passed.

'Sorry, sir,' came the mumbled reply, as the group disappeared into the dusty darkness.

Ed felt decidedly grubby as the dust in the air stuck to the sweat on his skin. Even though it was now late in the evening the temperature was still in the low thirties.

They crossed the street and took the next narrow passageway on the right. Abubaker led as he knew this part of town better than Haitham and after about half a kilometre of twisting and turning, he stopped at a tall set of gates secured with a lock and chain.

'Can you open this?' Abubaker asked Ed, his eyes flicking nervously up and down the narrow street.

'It's mechanical, not electronic,' said Ed. 'But I do happen to have a master key.'

He opened his uniform tunic, pulled out the rifle and turned it to full power.

'Is the street clear?' he asked, and getting a nod from Andy, he reduced the lock to its component atoms.

'Open sesame,' said Andy, pushing the heavy gates open and ushering everyone inside.

'Is this another safe house?' asked Ed, looking up at a warehouse-style unit sitting across the small yard.

'It's the old business premises of one of our members,' said Haitham. 'He moved to a bigger warehouse and said we could use this while his company still owned it.'

The lock on the building was electronic so this time, Ed made short work of opening it without resorting to a laser rifle. Inside was a small warehouse area on the ground level and stairs to one side, leading to a mezzanine level containing two offices.

An old electric truck sat parked against the back wall, the sides emblazoned with an electronics supply company's details.

Abubaker strode over, turned the charger on and nodded happily as a red light glowed.

'Good,' he said. 'The power's still on. In the morning we can use this old thing to take us up into the mountains.'

30

The Starship *Gabriel*, searching interstellar space

'THIS IS JUST GETTING MONOTONOUS,' said Linda, dropping listlessly into her control couch. 'There must be something we're missing.'

'Go and get some sleep,' said Rayl. 'You've been on the bridge for eighteen hours straight.'

'Wake me when the drones get back though, won't you?'

'If they have anything, yes.'

'Even if they don't, I still want to programme the next region for them to search.'

'Phil and I are quite capable of doing that,' said Rayl, sounding slightly piqued.

'So am I,' interrupted Cleo. 'You could all do with some rest. Let me cover the next twelve hours and I'll call if there are any leads.'

'She's right,' said Rayl. 'Come on, there's no need for us to martyr ourselves. We'll need to be fully awake when we do find them.'

Linda nodded and walked to the tube lift, reluctantly

descended down to the crew cabin deck and entered her room. She was asleep within seconds of her head hitting the pillows.

'Linda – Linda,' repeated Cleo.

Linda woke with a start and found Cleo standing by her bed.

'I thought we were supposed to be getting some rest,' she said, sounding somewhat vexed.

'You've been asleep for ten and a half hours,' said Cleo.

'What– oh shit, have I?'

'I've found something.'

She opened her eyes wide at the realisation of what Cleo had just said.

'I'm up, I'm up,' she called, jumping up too quickly and stumbling into the wall.

'There's no hurry,' said Cleo, catching Linda and sitting her back on the bed. 'It'll be a couple of days before we know anything more.'

'But, what do we know now?' she asked.

'One of the drones has detected a very faint signal over a hundred thousand light years away, emanating from open interstellar space. It's too far away to know what it is and what it's transmitting. I've redirected two drones towards it and set a course for the *Gabriel* in that direction too.'

'Two days, you say?'

'Yep, so relax and get some more sleep if you need it.'

'Have you let the others know?'

'I'm doing that right now.'

Thirty-nine hours later the *Gabriel* winked into existence in the middle of nowhere and immediately began scouring its surroundings for a signal from one of its distant drones. Finding it almost instantly, the ship powered into a fourteen-degree course change and accelerated to just over point nine light.

'It's the Callametan ship's computer,' said Cleo, in an excited tone.

'Play it,' called Linda, her hands shaking with antic-ipation.

'This way for horrible lager,' said the computer's voice.

Linda shrieked and burst into tears.

'Oh, Andy – I do love you.'

Rayl sat beaming on her couch with tears running down her cheeks too.

31

Bresserin Mountains, Planet Garag, Dubl'ouin System

THE SMALL TRUCK had gone unnoticed within the morning traffic and within two hours was on a deserted track several kilometres off the main road in the foothills of the Bresserin Mountains.

Abubaker steered the truck into a clearing amongst the tall trees that seemed to dominate the lower mountain slopes. They reminded Ed of pine forests back on Earth, the only difference was a slight silver and purplish hue at the end of the needles.

'They're nearly ready for Christmas up 'ere,' said Andy. 'Just need some baubles and a fairy on top.'

'I don't think Santa's sleigh can manage a hundred and forty thousand light years,' said Ed.

'He'd certainly need a large brandy and a couple of mince pies after that,' added Andy.

Haitham gave them a sideways glance with raised eyebrows.

'Who's Santa?' he asked.

'A fat lazy bastard who only works one day a year,' said Andy.

'I think I'd want three hundred and sixty-four days off if I'd had a hundred gallons of brandy and fifty tonnes of pies in one day,' said Ed, giving Andy a serious stare.

Haitham shook his head this time.

'I wish I'd never asked,' he said. 'Are you sure you're the best this GDA could've sent to save us?'

'Probably not,' said Andy. 'But we were available and cheap.'

Pol emitted one of her little guinea pig sniggers as Abubaker brought the truck to a sudden stop next to a decrepit wooden shed set back into the hillside.

'Journey's end for now,' he said, as the electric whine of the truck's motor died away.

Complete silence greeted them as they disembarked. Not a breath of wind stirred the pine needles and Ed stared back down the hillside, noticing the outskirts of the city just visible in the far distance. The clearing was scattered with old rusty lumps of machinery, none of which Ed recognised, and the building itself seemed a bit of an afterthought and ramshackle.

'That thing looks like it'll fall down with the first breath of wind,' said Andy, stretching his back after hours sitting on the hard bed of the truck.

'It's designed that way,' said Haitham. 'Discourages snoopers if anyone was to stumble on this place.'

Abubaker strolled across towards the building, extracted something from a pocket on the front of his jacket and pointed it at the shed.

A low whine from the structure built in pitch until the whole frontage lifted up like a giant letterbox opening outwards.

'Fuck me – Thunderbirds are go,' said Andy, causing Ed to snort out loud.

'Get the truck out of sight,' said Abubaker to Haitham, then beckoned for the others to follow him.

He led them into what reminded Ed of a railway tunnel. It was about the same size with a curved ceiling and disappeared straight into the darkness. Haitham backed the van in behind them, Abubaker pressed whatever he pressed before and the shed frontage whined back down and closed with a crunch.

Low lighting emanating from the occasional glow panel fixed to the wall lit their way as Abubaker led them deeper into the tunnel.

'What was this place?' asked Ed, as they walked.

'Cutter mine,' said Haitham. 'Closed a while ago when the seam became too small to be economic.'

'What's a cutter?' Andy inquired, looking at the different mineral seams in the walls.

Haitham scuffed around in the dirt with his foot as they walked and stooped down to pick something up. He handed it to Andy with a dismissing shrug.

'Cutter rock,' he said. 'Although that's too small to be any use.'

Andy wet a finger and rubbed the stone, causing it to sparkle back at him in the gloom. His eyes bugged as he realised what the supposedly worthless stone actually was. He nudged Ed and handed it to him.

Ed inspected the grape-sized glittering jewel in his hand and glanced back at Andy. Even unpolished they both knew what it was.

'Do you mind if we collect a few of these small bits while we're here?' said Ed, biting his lip. 'We call them diamonds and even tiny ones are useful on our planet.'

'Should be able to find you some much bigger ones than that,' said Abubaker. 'I'll keep my eyes open.'

He led them into a smaller side tunnel that led straight to a door. He unlocked it and entered a hollowed-out cavern lined with old rusty shelves weighed down with hundreds of metal boxes.

'It's a regional munitions store,' said Haitham, noticing Ed eyeing up the shelves.

'You have many of these?' asked Ed.

'I should imagine so,' said Haitham. 'All the BDF cells are compartmentalised so we can't give each other away.'

'What about your families, though?' said Andy. 'Won't they be in danger now your cover's blown?'

'Neither Abubaker nor I come from Garag,' he said. 'We're from a TA world called Ro'an about two hundred and six light years from here. The BDF central hub sent us here on fake identities to organise a new cell in the city when the previous one was compromised.'

'It seems you still have a snitch within the cell,' said Ed, 'judging by the Blends waiting at the safe house.'

'We've narrowed the suspects down to three,' said Abubaker, waving towards a table and chairs set against one wall. 'And we're about to set a trap.'

Haitham sat down at a small second table with several flat wall screens above. They flickered to life and showed views from outside. He looked over his shoulder and smiled.

'Stops the red bastards sneaking up on us,' he said.

'I take it there's a back way out?' said Ed.

'Two, actually,' said Abubaker, pointing at two screens showing empty forest scenes. 'But neither have a vehicle and it's a long walk back to town. So I'd rather we didn't have to use them.'

'Out of your three suspects, who knows about this place?' asked Andy.

'None of them,' said Haitham. 'That's why we're here. We'll give each one a different address for a new safe house we're hiding in and whichever one gets raided will point to our man.'

'They're all TAs then,' said Ed.

'Unfortunately they are,' said Haitham. 'More susceptible to bribery and threats than the Quads.'

'Especially the Inners,' continued Abubaker. 'Which, two of our three are.'

'Inners?' questioned Ed.

'Inner worlders – TAs from this planet or ones in the near vicinity,' he answered. 'We're known as Fringers or Gappers depending on the region.'

Ed nodded, sat at the table, closed his eyes and attempted to feel his way outside.

'The rock strata here are too dense,' said Andy, sliding onto the bench beside him. 'I've already tried that.'

Ed opened his eyes again and exhaled impatiently.

'One of us will have to pop outside regularly to check for the *Gabriel*,' he said, glancing at the door.

'I wouldn't advise that,' said Haitham, turning to face them again. 'They can quickly trace any transmission from the surface. I can see from here when any new vessels arrive.'

He switched one of the screens over to a three-dimensional image of the planet showing dozens of green dots moving slowly around. As the planet turned, a row of red dots appeared in a line, stretching down to the surface.

'What are those?' asked Andy, pointing at the red dots.

'Alien craft show as red,' said Haitham. 'They're more of the ships being unloaded from the Quad colony ship.'

'Can't they detect your array picking this up?' asked Andy.

'No,' said Abubaker. 'There's a communication booster antenna on the hill above us. One of our guys is a service engineer and secretly patched us into it. Everything we have going in or out is encrypted and just rides on the back of someone else's signal.'

'Cool,' said Andy. 'Can I send a quick message?'

'If your ship was here, we'd see it,' said Abubaker, nodding at the screen.

'That's just it,' said Ed. 'Our cloaking technology is way above anything the Blends have. If our ship was here, it certainly wouldn't be showing on there.'

'If we only had something like that,' said Haitham, looking over at Abubaker.

'There's a lot of stuff you'd get if you were part of the GDA,' said Ed.

'What message d'you want to send?' asked Abubaker.

32

The Starship *Gabriel*, searching interstellar space

'IT'S SOMEWHERE on that course there,' said Cleo, showing a line running off into the distant galaxy.

'It could be quite a way, judging by how far that ship of theirs can jump,' said Phil. 'The Cygnus arm of the Milky Way is out this way, it's so far away and out on a limb that nothing is really known about it.'

'We'd better cloak from now on,' said Linda. 'If we're approaching a Mogul-controlled area, we need to be wary.'

'Forward scans show no habitable planets for at least twenty-four hours,' said Rayl. 'So it doesn't entail all of us sitting here staring at empty space.'

'You two get some R and R and I'll take first stag,' said Phil, relaxing back into his couch and sliding his hands behind his head. 'I'm going to study the history files on the Callametan race that their ship sent us.'

The *Gabriel* spent the next thirty-six hours following the course line projected through Callamet and the buoy. Sometimes jumping into systems, sometimes interstellar space, but always in a straight line and because of the extreme length of the jumps, having to recharge and scan ahead carefully. When jumping outside of recognised zones, a lot more care has to be taken when plotting the emergence sectors. Just one small piece of space junk would rip a ship apart if they jumped on to it.

'I've got ship movements ahead,' said Rayl, pushing the holonav out to show a system just under a hundred light years in front, the unmistakable returns of fold activity glowing brightly and giving away their jump zones.

'It's not directly on the course line,' said Phil.

'How far off?' asked Linda, glancing over at the display.

'About eight light years,' he said.

'Any sign of the colony ship?'

'None.'

'Okay, we continue on the same route, but stay well clear of their zones,' said Linda.

'These ships are of similar make up to the one that took the Callametan ship,' said Rayl. 'The designs are different, but the metallurgy is almost identical.'

'Cleo, can you get into the navigation computer of one of those ships and steal us a map?' asked Linda.

'Take me closer to one of them,' Cleo said, appearing in the centre of the holomap dressed in an old safari suit and pith helmet.

'What are you wearing?' asked Rayl.

'It's what explorers wore a long time ago on Earth,' said Linda, rolling her eyes.

'Quite dashing isn't it?' said Cleo, slapping her knee-length brown boots with a riding crop. 'Take me to this one here, please, Phillip.'

She indicated what seemed to be some sort of freighter that wasn't too far off their intended course.

Phil, who was piloting at the time, jumped the *Gabriel* in behind the bulbous kilometre-long vessel and sat cloaked only twenty kilometres from its stern.

'Close enough?' he asked.

'Absolutely, old sport,' she said and promptly disappeared again.

They all knew when it was done, as the holomap changed to a detailed plan of the entire Blend-controlled region of space. System and planet names, jump zones, navigation hazards and even a couple of areas of restricted military-only access.

'I wonder what they're hiding in those?' said Rayl.

They realised at the same time that the course line they were following led straight to a system deep in the region.

'It's the Dubl'ouin System,' said Linda, struggling a bit with the pronunciation.

'The only inhabited planet in that system is called Garag,' said Rayl, magnifying the map to show just the system.

'It's big too,' said Phil. 'That's a monster, over eleven times the size of Earth.'

'And hot,' said Linda. 'No wonder the Moguls like it. How long, Phil?'

'About another day,' he said, studying his display. 'We'll need to take it a little slower from here as the closer we get to that system the busier it gets.'

'How long for a scan?' she asked Rayl, glancing across at her.

'Ten to twelve hours to get a thorough reading,' Rayl said, nodding back.

Ten hours and fourteen minutes later, Linda emerged the *Gabriel* safely in interstellar space and powered forward at point nine light. She raised her eyebrows at Rayl, who nodded and proceeded to scan the Dubl'ouin System with everything they had.

'Wow,' she said, as a wealth of data came flooding back.

'Is the Callametan ship there?' asked Linda, the trepidation clear in her voice.

'It is,' replied Rayl. 'And four more, seemingly welded together to form some sort of space station.'

She transferred her data over to the holomap and the size of the planet and how much traffic was buzzing around it immediately became apparent.

'It must be the home planet of this region,' said Linda. 'It's as busy as Dasos and as the star map we stole shows, it's definitely in the centre of everything.'

'They're plundering the colony ship of all its contents,' said Phil, arriving from his cabin and pointing at the stream of ships stretching from the *Hope* down into the atmosphere.

'*Yes*,' shouted Rayl suddenly, punching the air and almost falling out of her seat. Causing the other two to jump.

'Have you found them?' asked Linda, excitedly.

'There's a faint message signal on a wide beam bouncing around the planet's satellites and it's in English.'

'What's it say?' asked Phil, unable to contain his excitement.

Rayl giggled and looked over at them.

'Need pepperoni pizza and a nice pint of bitter,' she said, beaming.

They both grinned back.

'There's no mistaking who sent that,' said Phil.

'And it means they're okay,' said Linda. 'Can we narrow down the origin?'

'No,' said Rayl. 'Which is fine, because the Moguls won't be able to either. I should be able to pinpoint their location once we get there.'

'Can we send a response?' said Linda. 'Let them know we'll be along shortly?'

'Yes we can,' said Rayl. 'What do you want to send?'

Linda thought for a moment before nodding at Rayl to hit transmit.

'Order received, will be eight hours. Delivery on board or down below?' she said and winked at Rayl to cut the feed.

'It'll take a while because of the distance,' said Rayl. 'That was a good idea to find out where they are.'

'It's still a big planet though,' said Phil.

Linda stared at the holomap for a moment before speaking again.

'If they're on the surface, there's only one way they could have got there and one place they could have gone,' she said.

'Of course,' said Rayl, watching the trail of vessels snaking down to the surface. 'On one of those and they're all going to the same location.'

'According to the planetary map on their database, it's a city called Bresserin,' said Phil.

'Then let's make orbit above that city our provisional destination,' said Linda. 'And if they are still aboard the ship, then that's close by too.'

33

Bresserin Mountains, Planet Garag, Dubl'ouin System

'WE NEED to make some sort of plan to stop them firing that ship at Dasos,' said Andy. 'Or at least warn them.'

'Two plans actually,' said Ed. 'One if the *Gabriel* finds us in time and one if it doesn't.'

'I don't know what the hell we're going to do if they don't find us,' said Andy. 'We can't do much from down here with a couple of laser rifles can we?'

'No,' said Ed, 'but we could if we were back on the *Hope*.'

'You want to get back on that ship!' exclaimed Abubaker. 'Knowing what they plan to do with it?'

'You haven't forgotten they destroyed its drive capabilities,' said Tocc. 'They'll jump it in close to the planet at near-on light speed, giving you no chance of diverting it, even if it had its own power.'

Ed sat back gloomily and stared down at his feet.

'There must be something,' he mumbled. 'There are

billions of people on Dasos and then the retaliation would be swift. What the Moguls or Blends don't realise is the GDA have Katadromiko cruisers with Genok weapons. They could wipe out every living thing on every inhabited planet in this region in a matter of hours. So it's not just the billions on Dasos that would perish, it would be trillions here too.'

'But the Blends have a formidable navy,' said Haitham. 'They would have to get past a couple of hundred warships first.'

'If they had a thousand it wouldn't be enough,' said Andy. 'We've seen eleven GDA cruisers decimate a battle fleet of that size in a matter of minutes and not receive a scratch in return.'

Abubaker and Haitham looked at each other.

'Okay,' said Haitham. 'Let's say this is true – what could we do to help stop this?'

'We could sabotage their ship,' said Andy. 'The one that's attached to the top of the *Hope*.'

'They'd just replace it with another one,' said Abubaker. 'The only way to do it is to destroy the *Hope* before it leaves.'

'That would mean killing a sentient ship,' said Andy. 'I don't think I could knowingly do that.'

'Nor me,' said Ed. 'Unless we could download *Hope* off the ship before destroying it.'

'Now, that's a possibility,' said Andy. 'Having the *Cartella* right now would be very handy.'

'What's a *Cartella*?' asked Haitham.

'One of our smaller ships,' said Ed. 'It has the data capacity big enough for *Hope*'s files.'

Haitham glanced back at the computer screen as something caught his eye.

'They're going to bring down the colonists,' he said. 'Those are large troop carriers going up to the ship.'

'Where will they take them?' asked Ed.

'That remains to be seen,' said Abubaker. 'Whereever it is, it won't be very pleasant for them.'

'They're our friends and colleagues,' said Rialte, from the back of the room. 'There must be something you can do to help them.'

'We're certainly open to suggestions,' said Haitham, sounding a little piqued.

'The best way to help is to look at the bigger picture,' said Ed. 'Freeing your race from the tyranny of the Blends has to be the ultimate goal. The only way I can see to do that is with the aid of the GDA. So our priority is to stop the impending attack on Dasos and then do what we can to ensure the battle fleet that would ultimately descend on this region doesn't overreact.'

'Ed's right,' said Pol. 'I'm the only Quad here with first-hand experience of the GDA and they really are our only chance of ridding our worlds of the Blend scourge. If they need to get back on that ship, we should do everything possible to make that happen.'

Haitham nodded and looked at Abubaker, who stared into space for a moment.

'Contact Filenbaugh,' he said to Haitham.

Haitham's eyes widened.

'Are you sure?' he said. 'Extreme emergencies only.'

'What do you call this?' Abubaker replied.

Haitham grimaced, turned back to the computer terminal and began typing.

'Let's hope he's of the same opinion,' he said.

'If he isn't, pass him over to me,' said Ed.

The reply came half an hour later.

'He wants to meet,' said Haitham.

'Where?' asked Abubaker.

'Here.'

'Filenbaugh's coming here?' said Abubaker, seemingly somewhat surprised. 'I didn't even know he was in this region of the planet. When?'

'He says he'll land in the clearing in four hours.'

'Shit, he is close and has access to something airborne too.'

Almost four hours to the second, a small atmospheric shuttle circled in from over the mountains, did one observation flyby, turned sharply and landed softly about thirty metres away from the main entrance. The meeting party all shielded their eyes from the dust whipped up by the powerful antigravs.

Ed watched as a TA dressed in sixties-style hippy clothes stepped carefully down the steps as they were lowered from within the shuttle's fuselage. He was again very tall, with slightly lighter skin than Abubaker and Haitham. Nervous eyes from a thin bearded face swept the area and he brushed his long white waist-length hair behind one ear.

'Has he just come from Woodstock?' mumbled Andy, forcing Ed to stifle a laugh. 'It's Janis Joplin's bass player.'

'Shush,' whispered Ed. 'He seems to think he's king dick, so let's not insult him quite yet.'

The newcomer reached back inside the shuttle, produced a walking stick and slightly awkwardly hobbled his way over to them.

'Sorry for my slow gait, gentlemen,' he said as he approached. 'I'm a Fugazien and not overly habituated to the higher gravity worlds.'

'Don't apologise,' said Ed. 'There are worlds back home that we struggle on too.'

'Well, remind me not to visit them,' he said, with a chuckle. 'My name's Filenbaugh and they tell me you're from somewhere called the GDA region of space?'

'That is correct,' said Ed. 'My name's Ed and this is Andy. We need to stop the Blends attacking Dasos with a colony ship full of rocks.'

'Why on Garag would you think they're going to do that?' he asked.

'Good intelligence,' said Andy.

'And we also want to avoid the brutal retaliation that would follow,' said Ed. 'Even if the attack failed, it could be catastrophic for your worlds.'

'You seem very optimistic about the GDA's abilities,' he said, looking unconvinced.

'The GDA have certain technologies that give them a huge advantage,' said Andy, nodding confidently.

'Ah,' Filenbaugh said with a smirk. 'You mean like this?'

Filenbaugh turned slightly, back towards his shuttle and raised his hand. The shuttle disappeared, leaving only the open doorway hanging in mid-air, like a tiny portal into another dimension.

Ed and Andy gaped, unable to hide the shock on their faces.

'You have cloaking technology?' Ed croaked, the disappointment evident in his voice.

'Do the Blends have this too?' asked Andy.

'Of course we do,' boomed a voice behind and above them.

They snapped around at the sound of the voice to find at least twenty armed Blends on the hillside pointing weapons at them and one lone Mogul standing amongst them that Ed recognised. It sent a shiver down his spine.

'Hassik Triyl?' he spluttered. 'But you're dead. We witnessed your crew throw you out of an airlock in Andromeda.'

34

Bresserin Mountains, Planet Garag, Dubl'ouin System

Hassik Triyl gave them a menacing smile as he strolled down out of the tree line and joined the small group in the clearing by the mine entrance.

'Nice planet this, isn't it?' he said, gazing out over the distant city. 'Very pretty, very warm.'

'How come you're not dead?' said Ed.

'I don't answer to you,' Triyl snapped. 'But if you must know – I had three surgically prepared doubles and it was one of those you saw murdered. He was a hero, played his part right to the end.'

'How the hell did you get here?' asked Andy. 'That galactic gateway is the most heavily guarded region in space.'

Triyl touched the side of his nose.

'Same way as you did,' he said. 'Hitched a ride. It's a shame you don't have your ship with you this time, I would have liked to have that, but no matter, it will come in time.'

A sudden deep booming roar from above had them all craning their necks upwards. A huge vessel appeared from behind the mountains, its massive antigravs thrumming bass line causing ground resonance around them. Everything shook and small avalanches of rocks rattled through the trees above them.

'That's a Mogul attack ship,' Andy whispered in Ed's ear. 'Must be one of the few that escaped.'

'Don't activate your DOVI,' Ed whispered in reply, as the soldiers removed their rifles, backpacks and searched them thoroughly. He noticed Haitham was curling his upper lip, watching Filenbaugh as he turned to make his way back to the shuttle.

Before the soldiers had a chance to search him, Haitham launched himself at Filenbaugh, pulling a hidden curved blade from his jacket. One of the soldiers fired at him, catching him a glancing blow on his left arm that spun him to the right. His momentum was still enough to send him barrelling into his target, the vicious knife arced and found its mark in Filenbaugh's throat.

'Fucking traitor,' shouted Haitham, as they both crashed to the ground.

A second soldier had by this time swung his rifle around, and killed Haitham with a well-targeted head shot. It was too late for Filenbaugh though. His mouth opened in a silent scream as his life blood pulsed through the deep, fatal neck wound.

'Bloody outrageous,' whispered Ed, standing very still, not daring to move.

'Outrageous indeed, Mr Virr,' said Triyl, overhearing and turning to gaze at Abubaker. 'It seems you will now assume regional control of the BDF, Mr Abubaker, and you will report to me daily.'

'I would rather die,' he mumbled, with a sneer on his face.

'Fine by me,' said Triyl. 'But it would also entail me visiting Ro'an and availing myself of the pleasures of your two rather attractive sisters. Be a shame to slaughter two such promising breeders.'

Abubaker's eyes widened. He staggered back, tripped and ended up on his backside in the dust. He sobbed quietly, causing Ed to feel quite sorry for him.

Triyl then turned his attention to Ed and Andy. Their hands had been cuffed in front of them and he strolled around them like a predator preparing for the kill.

'You may be wondering why you're still alive, gentlemen,' he said, stopping in front of them and scowling. 'As you probably realise, you've caused my race considerable deprivation and it is my intention to repay the courtesy. I'm told Planet Earth in the Sol system is your place of birth. So I intend to christen my newly-acquired attack ship with our latest long-range jump drive and cloaking technology, by visiting Earth and testing what I think you know as Genok weapons. Just to see your faces as the planet's atmosphere is turned to fire. Takes hours, I'm told, causes your internal organs to explode.'

'Such a glowing ambassador for your race,' said Ed.

'Did your mother drop you on your head when you were a kid?' said Andy.

Triyl continued his pacing around them with a dispassionate expression, then suddenly stopped and viciously punched Andy in his left kidney. Andy squawked in pain and collapsed.

'Got any more amusing anecdotes, Mr Faux?' he said, continuing his walk over towards the Quads cowering near the mine entrance. 'Put these four on the shuttle too,' he continued. 'Engineer Quads fetch a handsome price at auction.'

The soldiers roughly shoved everyone aboard Filenbaugh's shuttle and sat them side by side on the floor. Ed caught Pol's eye and winked. She looked absolutely terrified and he followed it up with a nod and a smile, hoping this would calm her fears a little.

Andy was still swearing under his breath and rubbing his side and the three Callametan engineers just stared into space, seemingly desperate not to make eye contact with anyone.

Ed got a final glimpse of Abubaker as the cabin door powered closed. He was still sat in the dirt staring at the two corpses and looked like a defeated man.

The shuttle lifted and made its way straight up, quickly becoming enveloped by the hulking magnitude of the attack ship. They landed in a busy hangar and as they were being ushered out onto the deck, Ed noticed at least a dozen other vessels of all descriptions lined up along the far wall, crawling with engineers.

'Now they've got the cloaking tech, they're not wasting any time fitting it to everything,' mumbled Andy.

'You feeling better?' asked Ed, in a whisper.

'Twat caught me by surprise. Don't kill him until I've returned the favour.'

Ed noticed a lot of the hangar staff turned to stare at them as they were shoved along towards a large bulkhead door in the corner of the room. He heard the scream of the antigravs dramatically increase and, glancing left, saw clouds rushing by from top to bottom out of the main hangar door.

'We're on the way up,' said Andy, looking in the same direction.

Once out of the hangar they were marched along a never ending corridor. Ed remembered Linda saying the Mogul ships had no transport of any kind and you had to walk everywhere. He studied the layout as he went, remembering where bulkheads were, lifeboat stations and anything that might come in handy during an escape attempt.

After a ten-minute commute they turned right, straight into a security office with a row of individual cells lined along the back wall. There weren't enough of them to get one each, so Ed and Andy got one and the four Quads got split into two and kicked quite unceremoniously into two others.

'They treat the Quads like animals don't they?' said Andy. 'No wonder they tried so hard to get away from them.'

Ed nodded slowly.

'I'm going to have a tentative poke around with my DOVI,' he whispered, turning and staring at Andy intently. 'Stay out for the time being, we don't know with all this new shit they have whether they've covered that loophole since Linda did them so much damage with hers in Andromeda.'

'Okay, boss,' said Andy. 'I'll pop down the pub for a beer.'

'Yeah, you do that,' Ed replied, grinning as he lay back on the small bunk and closed his eyes.

35

Mogul attack ship, above Planet Garag, Dubl'ouin System

ED CHECKED HIS RESTRAINTS FIRST. There wasn't much point in going for the bigger stuff if he couldn't even free his hands. They opened with a reassuring click and he moved on to the cell door mechanism, which proved just as forthcoming. He relocked it just in case.

He remembered Linda had delved into the ship's artificial gravity generator in Andromeda and used that to kill a Mogul there. Deciding this might harm too many innocent people on this ship, he slowly wormed his way outwards searching for something a little less catastrophic.

Finding the ship's engineering section, he discovered what all the engineers were doing to the smaller ships in the hangar. They were installing cloaking systems into all their vessels as fast as they could build them.

They've only just got the technology then, he thought and went searching for the data files to find out where it had come from.

The answer, when he found it, made him swear out loud.

'What's up?' said Andy, who'd been dozing in the corner.

'You remember that training Corvette the GDA lost a few days before we left?' Ed asked.

'Yeah, they found the wreckage on a moon of a distant gas giant,' Andy replied, thinking back. 'Serious navigation error was the opinion at the time. Why, what have you found?'

'This ship was involved,' said Ed. 'Lured it in close after hiding in the atmosphere of the bigger planet. Its cloaking generator is sitting on a bench down in the engineering department.'

'And they're reverse engineering it?'

Ed nodded.

'Shit – we need to destroy it and all the copies.'

'But making it look as though they've screwed up,' said Ed. 'We need to work out a way for them to have an accidental accident.'

'An accidental accident?'

'You know what I mean.'

'How many have they built so far?'

'Seventeen completed, with another six on the way.'

'Okay, we need to bypass all the resistors and unleash the full juice from the core. They would explode and catch fire in a millisecond.'

'But, before doing that, take out all the fire suppression systems,' said Ed. 'We need them to be absolutely melted to scrap.'

'What about the original?' Andy asked. 'That's not connected to anything. Nor are the ones in construction.'

'I could flood the whole place with a flammable gas or something,' said Ed.

'Not too much though,' said Andy. 'We don't want an

explosion so big it causes a hull breach and extinguishes the fire before it's had a chance to do its job.'

It took them over an hour to sabotage all the fire-fighting equipment in the rear half of the ship and in the hangar where the completed units were being installed. The actual installed cloaking units didn't take so long, as once Andy had worked out the power routing, they were able to prepare all seventeen in double-quick time.

'All done?' Ed asked.

'Okay, Guy Fawkes – it's all yours.'

'I found the main oxygen supply into engineering and opened several valves,' said Ed. 'They won't smell it, so it's just a matter of time.'

The time turned out to be just over twenty-six minutes. A low boom shook the cell, followed by a siren, the sound of raised voices and running feet in the corridor outside. They both closed their eyes and began activating the installed cloaking units in the main hangar, causing an explosion and fire in all of the parked vessels that very quickly spread around the hangar.

'Well, this is going better than expected,' said Andy, as they both watched through the ship's camera feeds.

'Chickens and headless comes to mind,' said Ed. 'They're really flapping big time.'

Another boom sounded through the ship and the camera feeds from the hangar failed. Ed switched to an outside feed and was shocked to see the atmosphere containment shield had failed with the last explosion. The sudden decompression had sucked everything out into space. The fire was extinguished, but every ship previously in the hangar was now on the outside and had smashed themselves into scrap on the way out.

The engineering department was still an inferno and Ed

watched as they attempted to run hoses from the front of the vessel where the fire suppression system was still operational.

'Do we let them?' asked Andy.

'Yeah,' said Ed. 'It gives them plenty to concentrate on while we format the data core.'

'That'll probably lose them control of the ship for a while,' said Andy. 'Are we high enough in orbit to risk that?'

'There's a lifeboat thirty seconds away in the corridor,' said Ed, pointing.

'You'd be willing to trust your life in one of their shoddy designs?'

'Hmm,' said Ed, thoughtfully. 'Perhaps you're right.'

'Look, they will have saved the data in an engineering file somewhere. Why don't we delete everything except navigation, propulsion and environmental?' said Andy. 'We don't want to really screw this ship up until we're off it.'

'Okay,' said Ed. 'Make sure you wipe the files and then corrupt them beyond repair. We don't want some computer whizz to reinstate the files once we're gone.'

A red face appeared in the cell window, checked where they were, and opened the door. Two armed Blends stood there glowering at them.

Ed and Andy's minds worked alike, as they both had the weapon of their respective guard deactivated in moments.

'Come with us,' one of them said, and they stood to one side.

Ed and Andy glanced at each other, stood and sauntered out of the cell. Ed already had his cuffs secretly unlocked and nudged Andy to do the same.

'If Triyl's given orders to get rid of us,' Ed whispered, 'then be ready with an elbow to the face.'

'No talking,' barked the other guard, prodding Ed in the back.

Ed was right. They were marched to the nearest airlock and as they stood facing the inner door, waiting for it to open, Ed whispered, 'On three.'

The door slid to the left.

'Inside,' the guard ordered.

Ed held his hand out front where Andy could see it and the guards behind couldn't. He showed one finger, then two and just as the guards stepped forward to push them in, he shouted, *'Three.'*

They both swayed slightly left and brought their right arms back with all their strength, the point of the elbow protruding.

Ed caught his guard a slightly glancing blow. He bent down, grabbed the legs and pulled. The guard, first stunned by the elbow, found himself flat on his back and received a stamped boot on his neck, rendering him instantly unconscious.

Andy caught his guard straight on the bridge of the nose, sending him to the deck as if his legs were no longer there.

'Ow, shit – shit, shit,' whinged Andy, flapping his arm around like a madman. 'Whoever called it a funny bone was an arsehole. It's about as hilarious as a car crash.'

'Stop moaning and drag him inside before someone comes,' said Ed, dragging his own unconscious victim into the airlock.

They closed the inner door and exchanged clothes as quickly as they could, reactivated the rifles and exited the airlock once they'd checked the corridor was clear.

Andy hesitated with the outer door control and glanced at Ed.

'If we don't, the whole ship will be searching for us in minutes,' said Ed. 'I know it's a difficult thing to do, but they're Moguls remember.'

Andy nodded and pressed the button to vent the chamber. He looked away as it opened, pressed close again and repressurised the airlock.

'Stuff of nightmares,' he said, with a shiver.

Ed reached out and squeezed his shoulder.

'Come on, we've got work to do,' he said. 'There's four Callametans relying on us. Not to mention the inhabitants of Planet Earth, Planet Dasos and the entire population of this region.'

'No pressure then?'

36

Mogul attack ship, above planet Garag, Dubl'ouin System

IT WAS ONLY forty metres back to the small detention centre and as soon as they arrived back, Ed closed the bulkhead door that separated it from the corridor.

'That makes it a bit more private in here,' he said. 'As far as Triyl is concerned, we're dead now and if we stop messing with his ship, he'll believe he's solved the problem.'

'What if he comes down here?' asked Andy, eyeing the closed door nervously.

'You sit at the desk with your cap pulled down over your face or something. If anyone arrives, wait 'til they're all inside the room and give 'em the good news with these,' said Ed, holding his rifle up. 'Then bung 'em in the end cell.'

They found some water bottles in a desk cupboard and took them to the Callametans. Pol shrank away into a corner of the cell as Ed entered, but squeaked with happiness when she realised who it was and jumped up and hugged him.

'I saw them take you away,' she said. 'I thought the worst

was going to happen.'

'It nearly did,' he said.

Pol looked over Ed's shoulder as Andy appeared in the doorway, also dressed in an ill-fitting black guard's uniform.

'Howdy, mam,' he said, touching the brim of his cap with a forefinger. 'There's a new sheriff in town.'

Ed shook his head and pointed back at the desk.

'Go and wipe the data,' he said.

Andy nodded and walked back with a wide gait as if he'd spent all day on a horse.

'How can he make jokes at a time like this?' asked Pol, gazing after Andy as he strode strangely away. 'At least I presume that was a joke?'

Ed smiled and nodded.

'An Earth joke, yes,' he said. 'He uses humour to hide his fear. He's always done that and in some ways, we both do the same.'

'Has this ship been under attack?' asked Rialte, as she pulled herself upright and stretched.

'Was it your ship?' asked Pol. 'We heard all the explosions and sirens.'

'No, nothing to do with us,' said Ed, regretting having to tell the white lie. 'I think they had a fire somewhere in the rear of the ship.'

'Are we in any more danger?' she asked, eyeing the closed outer door.

'That's a hard question to answer,' said Ed. 'It very much depends on—'

'I've found it,' called Andy from the front desk.

'Found what?' said Ed.

'The Genok weapon,' he said. 'They haven't developed them themselves. The GDA corvette had one in its inventory.'

'Have they reverse engineered that too?'

'Yes, they were building three more in the engineering section.'

'No wonder they're flapping,' said Ed. 'If just one of those things goes off on the ship it would incinerate the oxygen atmosphere on the entire vessel if the bulkhead doors are still open.'

'Where was that nearest lifeboat?' asked Andy.

'That's probably not a bad precaution,' said Ed. 'Get everyone into it fast.'

They gathered Tocc and Kwin from the adjacent cell, checked the corridor was empty and exited the security station. It was only twenty metres to the lifeboat hatch, but halfway there a huge explosion rocked the whole ship and knocked them all off their feet.

Andy was first up, sprinting to the lifeboat and lunging for the hatch handle. He wrenched it open and ushered everyone inside. The siren started up again and Ed, ensuring the Callametans were all accounted for and safely through the hatch, pushed Andy inside and began climbing in last. A fast-moving fireball rounded the corner about a hundred metres down the corridor and came roaring towards him. He kicked Andy through the final section of the mini airlock and threw himself in feet first, grabbing the outer hatch and slamming it shut a millisecond before the firestorm surged past engulfing the oxygen-rich environment.

Ed could feel the heat through the hatch and, quickly closing and sealing the inner door, he immediately uncovered and hit the emergency launch button.

Nothing happened.

'Shit,' said Ed, as he saw the outer hatch surround beginning to melt through the small window.

'The explosive bolts have failed in the heat – pull that,' said Andy, pointing at the manual release handle.

Ed ripped the cover off and slammed the lever down. He was about to swear again as nothing seemed to happen for a second time, but another explosion on the bigger vessel slammed the ship against the lifeboat and suddenly they were free and spinning away.

The artificial gravity disappeared too and they began rolling around inside the boat like a giant tumble dryer. Grabbing handles and belts they were able to pull themselves down into seats. It proved a bit of a problem for the Callametans as the seating wasn't designed for them, but they did the best they could and finally secured themselves down.

Ed leaned up and peered through the small hatch window again. Every few seconds the Mogul ship spun by and he could see the whole rear third of the huge vessel was now at a strange angle compared with the front.

'It's broken its back,' he said. 'Where's the magazine on one of those?'

'Somewhere amidshi—'

The blackness of space suddenly became blindingly bright for a second and the giant ship was violently ripped into two pieces spinning crazily away from each other.

Ed winced and Pol squealed as debris rattled off the lifeboat's outer hull.

'Bloody hell, their ships are badly designed,' said Andy.

'Well, you were right about the magazine,' said Ed, noticing something else. 'Is anyone else struggling for breath?' he asked.

'We probably need to activate the systems in here,' said Tocc. 'We launched manually, so we need to find the on switch.'

'There's a small panel over there,' said Pol, pointing down beside the front seats.

'Anything on it flashing or look like a starter button?'

asked Andy.

'One of them is green, lit and under a small cover,' she said.

'Sounds positive to me,' said Ed. 'Can you reach it?'

Ed heard Pol grunting and turning in her seat, and watched as she stretched across and fiddling with something. The lighting in the craft brightened and the sudden rattling of the attitude jets made them all jump. The lifeboat stabilised and slowly turned back towards the planet. A whirring noise made them look up as fresh oxygen gushed through vents in the ceiling.

Pol looked across and grinned.

'Well done, Pol,' said Ed, undoing his harness and floating up to the window again.

He peered around but could see nothing but the blackness of space.

'It'll be heading for the planet,' said Andy. 'That's why you can't see anything out the back window.'

'I'm just worried about hitting some of the wreckage,' said Ed. 'There's no exterior camera.'

'There's no manual controls either,' said Tocc. 'So you couldn't steer around it even if you could see it.'

Ed nodded, pulled himself back down into his seat and did up his harness again.

'There ain't nothing we can do now, except trust this thing to land us safely,' said Andy, putting his feet up on the empty seat opposite and his hands behind his head.

'After the design compromises we witnessed on the main ship, this might be a tad unpredictable,' said Ed. 'Everyone do your belts up tight.'

They all rechecked their harnesses as the first buffeting from Garag's upper atmosphere began to bite on the heat shield below them.

37

The Starship *Gabriel*, approaching the Dubl'ouin System

'WHAT THE HELL?' said Phil, looking up from his control icons and staring at the holomap.

'What is it?' asked Linda, following his gaze.

Phil pointed at a ship in orbit around Garag that had just appeared.

'Did it just jump into orbit?' she said, aghast. 'How bloody dangerous is that?'

'No,' said Phil, his eyes meeting Linda's. 'It's an Andromedan Mogul attack ship and it just uncloaked.'

'Oh shit,' she said. 'Cleo, can you wake Rayl, please?'

'My pleasure,' Cleo replied.

'You mean, like the ones from Andromeda?' Linda asked, glancing over at Phil.

'No, not like the ones from Andromeda – it is one of the Andromedan ships that escaped from the Katadromiko fleet at Hunus.'

'How the hell did that thing get here?' she said. 'And if

there's one there could be more, and how on Earth did they get the cloaking technology?'

'Oh shit,' said Rayl, as she arrived through the floor on the tube lift. 'Is that what I think it is?'

Both Linda and Phil nodded slowly.

'How long until we're there?' she asked.

'Five hours,' said Phil.

'Do we engage it?'

'They have cloaking,' said Linda.

'Who the hell gave them that?' asked Rayl, reclining back on her control couch. 'There's no way in hell they developed it themselves.'

The three of them sat in a gloomy silence for a few minutes. Rayl, who'd been scanning the Mogul ship with everything she could at this distance, suddenly sat bolt upright.

'The boys are on that ship,' she blurted without warning.

'What?' said Linda. 'How do you know that?'

'There's an abnormal heat reading emanating from the rear of the ship,' she said. 'Probably the engineering department and it's consistent with a serious fire.'

'You think it's the boys having fun with their DOVIs?' said Phil.

'There's two now,' she exclaimed, excitedly. 'The main hangar is alight too.'

'The civilian ships in the area are moving away suddenly and very quickly,' said Phil. 'Something's seriously spooked them.'

Phil had barely finished speaking when the main hangar blew outwards. Broken ships, service equipment and anything not bolted down, vomited out from the gaping hangar door.

'Wow,' said Linda. 'I think you're right. They're playing the same tricks I did above Arus'Gan.'

The giant ship slewed sideways, its attitude thrusters struggling against the unexpected aspect change. A few moments later, another blast in the rear of the ship blew out a couple of the airlocks, closely followed by an even larger explosion that twisted the back section of the ship at a strange angle in relation to the front.

'Holy moly,' said Phil. 'I hope they've got access to a lifeboat, things are getting a bit out of hand.'

'The ship's ripping itself apart from the inside,' said Rayl. 'It's like the atmosphere is exploding.'

'I have lifeboats,' said Linda, pointing at the holomap.

Two, then three, four, six small trace returns could be seen ejecting from the front two thirds of the stricken vessel. If any others were intending to eject, then they left it too late as shortly afterwards a final and immense blast blew the ship into two parts. The rear section spun away into space, still gushing fire, shrapnel and gasses in curved arcs. The front piece, the larger of the two, looped over and over towards the planet, the internal fire still ripping its way through the remaining atmosphere, its route given away by exploding airlocks.

'Well, I hope they're on one of them,' said Rayl, watching the horrific and sudden turn of events with wide eyes.

'If they're on one of those lifeboats then they're well on their way down to the planet now,' said Phil. 'We're about four minutes behind at this distance.'

They watched as the front section began its fiery descent into Garag's atmosphere. What began as a dull glow from the leading edges spinning downwards, soon began spitting off flaming chunks in random directions. The main body split into two, with the sections quickly becoming indistinct within a plethora of flaming trails, only becoming visible again a short while later as the smaller pieces burnt away and then they were gone, swallowed by high cloud.

'I hope that's not a civilian-populated area down there,' said Phil. 'They'll have a very bad day.'

'I've lost the lifeboats now,' said Rayl. 'All below cloud.'

'Did all the lifeboats begin to slow down?' asked Linda, gazing across at Rayl.

'Yes, all six heat shields ejected and their rate of descent dropped sharply,' Rayl confirmed, giving Linda a nod.

'Mark that area of the planet,' said Linda. 'That's where we're going when we get there and everyone watch out for any more uncloaking Mogul ships. They're going to be severely pissed and trigger-happy.'

'Can we extend the jumps to get us there quicker?' asked Rayl.

'Not without taking a big risk,' said Linda. 'It's busy in this region. We really do have to jump around a bit to avoid the traffic.'

38

Lifeboat, Garag's lower atmosphere, Dubl'ouin System

ED HEARD the crack of the heat shield ejecting, or at least he hoped that's what it was. His eyes met Andy's as nothing happened for a few long seconds and the bullet-shaped lifeboat arrowed its way downwards, shaking and vibrating and still at many times the speed of sound.

He breathed out as he heard the whine of the antigrav spooling up, not realising until that moment that he had held his breath.

Everyone onboard looked a little happier as they were pulled down hard into their seats. The Callametans grumbled a bit with the discomfort of the ill-fitting furniture. But Ed knew they'd all rather suffer that than hit the ground at Mach 10.

'I wish we could see what we're likely to land on,' said Andy.

'Does this thing even have a floatation collar if it's a water landing?' asked Pol.

Just as she'd finished speaking, they all felt the craft veer sideways and the whining pitch of the motor changed.

'Well, it's definitely changing its trajectory,' said Kwin. 'Lifeboat design was part of my résumé and if it's doing that then it's attempting to find a dry spot.'

'I hope so,' said Andy. 'I didn't bring my snorkel.'

'Perhaps we'll land on a nice dry beach,' said Ed.

'So long as it's near the bar and a pizzeria,' said Andy.

A sudden whirring from below had them all staring at the floor.

'Brace yourselves,' said Kwin. 'That's hopefully the landing struts.'

The antigrav's pitch was constantly changing now and they all sunk deep into their seats as the tiny ship braked heavily, turned abruptly and thumped down on solid ground. The scream of the antigrav unit died away, leaving the craft to tip alarmingly to one side.

'One of the struts is sinking,' said Kwin. 'Hang on.'

The lifeboat tipped in slow motion and finally clunked onto its side, leaving Pol, Rialte and Andy hanging in their restraints.

'Hold fire,' said Ed, not wanting them to release the belts and drop on top of him. 'We'll move out of the way and then you can drop onto our empty seats.'

'Hurry up, then,' said Andy. 'This isn't the most comfortable position to be in.'

'Tell me about it,' grumbled Pol, hanging really awkwardly.

Ed, who was nearest the hatch, peered out to find they were amongst something that looked like sand dunes. He uncovered the hatch release lever and pushed it across from left to right. There was a slight hiss of the pressure equalising and he was able to pull it open. The first thing he noticed was the heat and it reminded him of opening an oven door with your face too close.

'Crap, it's hot out there,' he said, as he pushed his belts out the way and clambered out.

The second thing he observed was the quietness. After all the noise and pandemonium of the last few hours, the contrast was sudden and quite discomposing.

They had indeed landed in a dip amongst a strip of low dunes. In one direction he could hear the sound of waves lapping on a shoreline, with something like a rainforest tree line a couple of hundred metres away in the other.

Climbing clumsily to the top of the nearest dune, Ed could now see the ocean as well as hear it. It stretched away to infinity, as with the size of this planet the horizon was a long way off.

Turning in the opposite direction, he could see a forest stretching left to right as far as the eye could see. Behind that a range of mountains in the far distance seemed tall enough to touch the clouds. But in their immediate surroundings, no people, no buildings, no other lifeboats, nothing at all.

'Pretty spot,' said Andy, clambering up behind him and wiping his brow. 'Can you turn the heating off?'

'Pretty desolate too,' replied Ed. 'There isn't much to eat and drink here.'

'There's quite a store of supplies on the lifeboat,' said Andy. 'Enough to keep us going for a while.'

'Until what?' said Ed. 'I don't think I want to be found by that lot.' He nodded up at the sky. 'They're not going to be hugely enthralled with what we just did.'

'D'you think Triyl survived again?'

'I'm sure that coward would've been away at the first sign of trouble.'

Pol came wheezing up the dune to join them. Crawling up

on her four hands appeared to be easier than trying to walk on her stumpy legs.

'Bloody hell,' she huffed, sliding around in the shifting sand. 'How the hell do you walk on this stuff?'

'We had to learn to when we crawled out of the primordial soup,' said Andy, grinning.

'Talking of soup,' she said, 'we need to find some proper food. I can't face another prolonged period on emergency fucking rations.'

'She's swearing more than you,' Ed said, glancing at Andy. 'Where do you think she learnt that?'

'Hey, don't blame it all on me,' whinged Andy. 'You've emitted a few choice expletives over the last few days too.'

'Well, I've been under a lot of pressure keeping your sad arse alive,' said Ed, turning to head back down the dune towards the lifeboat.

'Give him some slack,' said Pol, glancing at Ed with a shy smile. 'I think he's been doing a wonderful job.'

'There you go, Andrew,' said Ed, as he part loped, part slid his way back down the dune. 'A wonderful job.'

'Are you two having a little interracial affair or something?' called Andy, with his hands on his hips, just before Ed went out of earshot.

Ed convinced them that staying with the lifeboat made them quickly detectable and was of course dangerous. So they'd packed all the water and food they could carry into pockets and some small backpacks that had contained first aid equipment. The only thing they kept were the water purification tablets, as in this heat and humidity they would most likely be needed.

They headed for the tree line with Ed leading and Andy bringing up the rear as they had the only weapons.

When they reached the edge of the forest it proved quite dense, so they turned left and followed along on the outer fringe until they found a trail of some kind leading in. It was cooler under the canopy and the quietness unnerved Ed as he noticed it wasn't as noisy as a rain forest back home, with only the very occasional hoot or screech from the local fauna. The flora, however, reminded Ed of a trip into the Daintree while staying in Northern Queensland, and he sincerely hoped there wasn't anywhere near as many lethal snakes and spiders lurking here as there was in an Australian rain forest.

'I read a book on the SAS in Malaya not so long ago,' said Andy from the back. 'This reminds me of that.'

'Except, it's not an attack from communist Malayan troops that's the worry here,' said Ed, shaking his head.

'Just as well with you on point,' said Andy. 'Stomping through the undergrowth in your big size tens.'

Ed suddenly stopped and held his hand up, and they all froze and listened. It was just the rustle of the canopy above that disturbed the silence, even the occasional animal or bird noise had stopped. Then a very distant and faint whine faded in and out.

'Antigrav,' said Tocc, staring up at the treetops.

Andy quickly pulled out and unfolded a large foil blanket.

'Squat down under here,' he said.

'What's this for?' asked Pol, as they all squashed in tight.

'If they're using infra-red, this'll hide our signature,' said Tocc, as the antigrav whine grew louder.

'They won't know it was us in that lifeboat though, will they?' asked Rialte, her eyes wide with fear.

'No,' said Ed. 'But the survivors from the other lifeboats would most likely recognise us.'

'And one of them might well be Triyl,' said Andy.

'You think he'll have survived that?' asked Kwin.

'Undoubtably,' said Ed. 'Those attack ships have a small hangar adjacent to the bridge and I'm quite sure Triyl would have had a personal shuttle in there on permanent standby.'

They all went quiet as whatever it was flying above the treetops whined overhead and continued on.

'Thank fuck for that,' said Pol, causing Andy to snigger and getting a glare from Ed.

The small craft carried on into the distance, where they heard it flare, hover for a moment and suddenly go quiet.

'It's landed,' said Tocc.

'Could have found one of the other lifeboats,' said Rialte.

'That's a distinct possibility,' said Ed. 'Let's go and see.'

39

Remote landmass, Garag, Dubl'ouin System

IT TOOK over two hours to find the second lifeboat. It had landed in a rocky clearing at the foot of a steep escarpment. The rescue shuttle had picked up the survivors and left. They'd listened to it fly off and fade into the distance over an hour ago.

Ed kept the Callametans hidden amongst the trees while he and Andy approached the craft cautiously, their laser rifles in hand. This lifeboat had remained upright and more by luck than judgement had avoided the many large boulders scattered in the vicinity.

'They haven't even bothered to close the hatch,' said Andy, cautiously sticking his head up inside.

'How many seats were used?' asked Ed.

'All of 'em, by the look of it,' Andy replied, wrinkling his nose as he was assaulted by the metallic smell of blood. 'There's quite a bit of blood on the inside of the hatch and a couple of the seats.'

'They were fighting for places, they were so desperate to get off that ship.'

'Some of the water bottles have gone, but all the food hoppers are still full,' he called from inside.

'Grab what you can,' said Ed. 'We can always come back for more.'

They returned to the others, sat down and ate some of the rations.

'Is this food really from another galaxy?' asked Tocc, sniffing it suspiciously.

'The stuff from that ship will be,' said Ed.

'Flown in from two and a half million light years away specially for you,' said Andy. 'Earth guys know how to spoil a girl.'

'Well, let's spoil you some more with a nice hotel for the night,' said Ed. 'It's going to be dark in an hour by the look of it. Andy and I will have a search around for somewhere safe to make camp and you four—' he pointed at the Callametans '—go and rip out all the clean seat cushions from the lifeboat, grab the last of the food, water and anything else useful.'

Andy soon found an artificial cave made from a huge boulder that had dropped from the hillside above and wedged itself over a narrow gully, forming a cave two metres high and ten metres deep. You could walk in the front entrance or crawl in the back way.

'It's perfect,' said Ed. 'The rock above will hide our thermal signatures.'

'So long as it doesn't fall on us in the night,' said Pol, eyeing it suspiciously as she laid seat cushions in rows to form narrow mattresses.

When it was dark and the temperature dropped they risked lighting a fire as they'd all witnessed movement and strange growling noises behind the tree line. Andy had blocked the backdoor with a pile of branches and they built the fire just under the lip of the boulder to avoid it being spotted from above.

'What's the plan?' Tocc asked, as they all sat around transfixed by the glowing logs spitting embers at them from time to time.

'Hang around for a while,' said Ed. 'None of us know where we are and we could be thousands of kilometres from the nearest civilisation on a planet this big, even if we did know which direction to go.'

'You're still holding out for your ship to find us then?' said Rialte, sounding overly dubious.

'Even if they did find this system and even this planet, it's so huge they wouldn't know where to start,' said Tocc.

'They lost you many thousands of light years away,' said Kwin. 'The chances of them being in the right region, let alone system is so remote.'

'Have you all quite finished?' said Ed. 'Have a little faith in my crew. We've scanning equipment a thousand years ahead of anything you've seen before. You just need a little patience and allow them time to work it out.'

Ed fielded a knowing glance from Andy, who'd agreed to take first stag on watch. He swiftly lay back on his makeshift bed before he said something he'd regret, and attempted to get some sleep.

'Ed, wake up,' said the familiar voice, echoing around his head.

'Piss off, Cleo' he mumbled. 'Sleeping.'

'No, you really need to wake up.'

'I've only just got comfortable,' he moaned.

'Who's Cleo?' said Tocc, nudging him with her foot. She had taken over the watch from Andy.

'W-what,' said Ed, sitting up suddenly, staring at Tocc. 'What did you say?'

'Who's Cleo?' Tocc said again.

'Haven't you told them about me?' asked Cleo.

Ed almost levitated off the makeshift mattress.

Cleo – CLEO?' he shouted. 'Is that really you?'

'Last time I looked,' she said. 'What are you lot doing lying about in the dirt down there? There's nice comfy beds up here.'

Tocc was now looking at Ed as though he was possessed and Ed's shouting had woken the others, except for Andy of course, who could sleep through an aerial attack.

'What's going on?' asked Pol, sitting up.

'Our illustrious leader is talking to himself,' said Tocc, giving one of the Callametan four-shoulder shrugs.

'Are you sending a shuttle down?' Ed asked, kicking Andy's foot.

'It's quite busy up here,' she said. 'Judging from the communication traffic, they're convinced the attack ship was hit by a cloaked warship of some kind.'

'Be careful,' said Ed. 'We're okay down here for a while, so you don't need to take any risks.'

'That's just it,' said Cleo. 'There are hundreds of soldiers combing the forest inland from where your lifeboat landed. They'll be on your position within the hour.'

'Shit,' he said, giving Andy's foot another heavier kick.

'For fuck's sake,' moaned Andy, opening one eye. 'I've done my shift.'

'The *Gabriel*'s here and a battalion of soldiers will be on our position in a matter of minutes.'

Both Andy's eyes snapped open.

'Oh shit,' he said, as he began dragging his boots back on.

'Which way do we need to move, Cleo?' Ed asked.

'Away from the sea,' she said. 'I have the *Cartella* on the way down, it'll be with you in twenty-four minutes.'

The three Callametan engineers were staring at Ed and Andy with perplexed expressions, but Pol, who'd been on the *Gabriel* before, was grinning from ear to ear.

'The *Gabriel*'s here, isn't it?' she said, staring at Ed.

He nodded and smiled back.

'We need to move inland quickly,' he said. 'There's a bunch of Blend soldiers approaching.'

Tocc began collecting the food boxes.

'Leave it,' said Andy. 'Pepperoni pizza for breakfast and I'm buying.'

They quickly took a path that led off to the left of the cliff face and gradually began to wind its way uphill. The higher they went the more the forest thinned, and in places where there were gaps in the trees, they could look back towards the sea.

'Doesn't look like we've come far at all, does it?' said Pol.

They all instinctively ducked at the scream of antigravs overhead.

'Was that our ride?' asked Kwin.

'I don't think so,' replied Ed.

The unmistakable sound of laser fire echoed up from the valley.

'It's okay,' said Cleo, in Ed and Andy's ears. 'They've just discovered your camp, they're destroying all the food and the lifeboat.'

'Where can you pick us up?' asked Ed.

'In about five hundred metres, turn right,' said Cleo.

'There's a rocky ledge, but remain hidden in the trees until you see the airlock.'

Ed quickened the pace and they were all soon huffing and puffing like steam engines. Another craft of some kind passed close overhead, this time considerably more slowly.

'They must know where we are,' said Tocc, the desperation obvious in her voice.

Ed was about to answer when laser cannon fire ripped through the trees just to their left. The Callametans all squeaked in fear.

Ed saw the right turn and the outcrop of rock and stopped.

'Everyone under the foil sheet again,' he said, as Andy unwrapped it as quickly as he could.

Once they were all settled, Ed closed his eyes and swept around with his DOVI. The nearest craft was a small gunship and he infiltrated its systems as it fired again just up the trail. He disengaged its antigrav drive and a loud crashing had them turning to look behind them as it fell through the tree branches and landed with a bone-jarring *clang* amongst the leaf litter. The other one soon appeared on the scene, randomly firing into the canopy and causing them all to duck as branches and foliage shattered and flew in all directions.

'Deal with that other one,' he said, nudging Andy.

Ed had noticed the canopy of the first gunship was opening and an armed pilot was clambering out. Although he hadn't seen them, Ed knew it would only be a matter of time and waited until he was fully exposed before unleashing a volley of fire from his rifle.

The pilot dropped back head-first into the cockpit leaving his motionless feet sticking out the top.

Andy meanwhile had taken control of the other gunship and was using it to strafe the path further down the hill. They could hear raised voices from below as the foot soldiers, now with their prey within reach, thundered up the pathway and suddenly found they had to take cover from their own gunship.

'How long, Cleo?' Ed asked.

'Thirty seconds,' she replied.

Andy, hearing this answer, flew the other gunship into the trail about two hundred metres down. This one didn't land with a clang, but exploded with such force that shrapnel and rock fragments ripped through the trees and caused them to duck again.

Ed recognised the different tone of the *Cartella*'s anti-grav's as it approached.

'Won't it attract fire?' asked Rialte, staring up at the canopy.

'Hopefully not,' said Ed. 'Come on, time to go.'

The group ran across the main path and down the side turning towards an empty outcrop of rock.

'It's not here,' shouted Kwin, stopping and ducking down into the trees again.

'No, don't stop,' called Ed, just as the airlock opened in mid-air directly in front of them.

They all bundled inside as a barrage of fire erupted from inside the forest, harmlessly hitting the *Cartella*'s shields.

'Shit – hang on, Cleo,' Ed called. 'We've lost one.'

Kwin lay flat on the ground twenty metres away squealing with fright as laser bolts lit up the air above her.

'Bollocks to this,' said Andy, jumping into the pilot's seat. 'I'm taking over, Cleo,' he said. 'Activating the ship's laser cannons.'

'All yours,' she replied, as he turned the ship to port and sprayed the forest with the powerful automatic weapon.

It caused absolute devastation, as every tree and every

bush was shredded back deep into the forest as if swept by a giant scythe.

Kwin had quite sensibly kept her head well down and when Andy turned the *Cartella* back around and showed her the open airlock once more, she didn't hesitate.

Only a couple of laser bolts came out of the remains of the forest this time and they both went well wide, as Kwin thundered through the airlock door and collapsed panting on the floor.

'Go, go,' shouted Ed, turning to Andy and pointing up.

The airlock doors sealed as the small vessel screamed straight up and was soon out of earshot of any surviving assailants below.

40

The Starship *Gabriel*, hiding in the Dubl'ouin System

'SORRY, EDWARD,' said Kwin, as they disembarked the *Cartella* into the *Gabriel*'s starboard hangar.

'Actually, I think we all owe you an apology,' said Rialte, before Ed could reply. 'Yet again we owe you our lives and it was rude of us to have doubted you and your crew.'

'You don't need to apologise,' said Ed. 'If they hadn't found us when they did, we'd all be dead under that rock.'

All four Callametans hugged Ed and Andy in turn, followed by Rayl and Linda who sprinted into the hangar seconds later, grinning like Cheshire cats, with Andy and Rayl making their excuses and quickly disappearing off to their cabin.

Once all the greetings and introductions were over, Ed immediately recorded a message and sent a cloaked drone on its way back to the GDA, warning them of the intended attack by at least one of the escaped attack ships from Andromeda which had somehow made it to the Cygnus arm.

The Callametans all went to get some sleep, except for

Pol who wanted to learn more about the ship and followed them up, parking herself on a swiftly-designed seat at the side of the bridge.

'Has there been any sign of any other Andromedan ships?' asked Ed, tucking into a bacon sandwich.

'No,' said Linda. 'But that doesn't mean there aren't any. That attack ship may well have passed on the cloaking information files to others.'

'I agree,' said Ed. 'We need to be wary. But if Triyl really was on his own here with that ship, he may have wanted to keep the technology to himself and that's what I'm hoping.'

'The same with the Genok weapons too,' said Phil. 'A psycho race like this with their hands on those things doesn't bear thinking about.'

Ed studied the holomap and pointed at the *Hope* with an almost constant stream of ships coming and going from the surface of Garag.

'Are they still unloading the colonists?' Ed asked, watching where the descending shuttles were going.

'We believe so,' said Linda.

'That's an island,' said Ed. 'I wonder why they're taking them there?'

'Keeps them segregated I suppose,' said Phil. 'That island has a lot of security fences around its perimeter.'

'A prison maybe?' said Linda.

Ed nodded and adopted a rueful expression.

'Have you had any contact with Hope since you got here?' he asked.

'Not yet,' said Linda. 'Give us a chance.'

'We've been a little preoccupied with saving your arse,' said Phil, giving Ed a pointed stare.

'Yeah, okay – sorry,' he said. 'Cleo can we talk to Hope from here?'

'Not yet,' said Cleo. 'But I have a plan.'

'A plan?'

'Well, when I say a plan – it's more like a theory.'

'That doesn't fill me with enthusiasm, Cleo,' said Ed. 'Would you care to elaborate?'

'Okay, well, that damping field the Blend ship used is utilising a strange form of infrasonics. The emitter changes the frequency randomly thousands of times a second and is impossible to counter. It disrupts all kinds of wave forms and pretty much everything we normally use.'

'Normally?' Ed questioned, raising his eyebrows.

'I'm going to attempt to create a sort of sound wave palto around the ship, that we could extend out to encapsulate another ship or part thereof.'

Ed thought about that for a moment.

'So, you'd be able to include the front section of the *Hope* where the bridge is and we could chat with the computer?'

'That's the theory bit.'

'What about using the mini-me fighters to jump inside the Blend ships' shields and mangle their emitter?'

'They're keeping their shielding very close to the hull, jumping into a space that small would be exceedingly difficult.'

'What about including just a little corner of their ship into this new palto, allowing myself and Andy to infiltrate their systems with our DOVIs and turn it off?'

'Again, dangerous because our ordinary shields would be down and it would make the *Gabriel* visible to them and their weapon systems.'

Ed stared at the floor for a moment.

'But, what if we were hiding below the *Hope*?'

Cleo went quiet for a second.

'So long as they don't have any other warships nearby,

that might work,' said Cleo. 'Aren't you the ideas man today?'

'For a slow organic brain, I still have my uses,' said Ed, nodding and noticing Linda had pulled a strange face.

'I didn't say a word,' she said in response to Ed's raised eyebrow.

'There's a lot of traffic coming and going underneath the *Hope* at the moment so we need to let them complete the colonist transfer first,' said Ed. 'Annoying as that may seem, it's probably safer for them in the long run, just in case the Blends start throwing heavy weapons around.'

'These local Moguls or Blends are very different to the Andromedan crowd, aren't they?' said Phil. 'There's an awful lot more of them and they seem to do more of the work themselves.'

'They have their own females too,' said Linda.

'How do the Andromedan ones breed then?' asked Pol, sounding surprised.

'Stealing and raping young girls from around their region,' said Phil. 'Then cherry-picking the male offspring.'

'What happens to the female offspring?'

'Killed at birth, along with the mother.'

'That's barbaric,' Pol cried. 'And we thought ours were bad.'

'They still are,' said Ed. 'We hope to free you of their scourge, one way or another. Once the GDA get involved it'll be the beginning of the end for them I'm sure.'

'That's been a dream of my race for thousands of years,' said Pol. 'I can't believe it may happen in my lifetime.'

'Well, let's just hope it does,' said Linda. 'For the sake of everyone in this galaxy.'

The following morning the whole team, including the four Callametans, gathered on the bridge. The ship traffic coming and going from the *Hope* had reduced significantly and if they were going to test Cleo's theory, now was the time.

'They'll be heading off to the belt before long,' said Linda. 'So now's our chance. But just before we do this, I have something everyone should see. Cleo, can you replay the feed I earmarked from before the attack ship was destroyed?'

The holonav image changed to the attack ship sitting in orbit around Garag.

'Now, watch the small hangar up near the bow and bridge,' she said, pointing to the small aperture.

The first explosion took place back in the engineering section, followed by the first in the main hangar.

'We've seen all this,' said Phil.

'Keep watching,' said Linda.

After a few moments a small sleek craft zipped out of the tiny hangar, turned away from the ship and planet and travelled about fifty thousand kilometres before suddenly slowing and disappearing.

'It jumped,' said Andy.

'No,' said Cleo. 'There was no jump residue at all. It entered another cloaked vessel, that's why it slowed before vanishing.'

'Oh crap,' said Rayl. 'Was that Triyl?'

'Most likely,' said Ed. 'I told you he's a complete coward.'

'First sign of trouble and he's out the fucking door,' said Andy. 'Typical Mogul, they're only brave when the odds are stacked in their favour.'

'So, there's another cloaked Blend ship in the system,' said Tocc, from the side of the bridge.

'Or maybe more,' said Ed. 'And I'd put money on it being another Mogul ship from Andromeda. It could be a trap – waiting for us to do what we're about to do.'

The bridge went silent for a moment as everyone thought that through.

'Ed,' said Andy. 'You remember the gateway control room on Pyli?'

'Of course.'

'Didn't the Ancients have a way of seeing through our cloak?'

'Oh crap – I'd forgotten about that.'

'You pocketed the activation node if I remember.'

Ed stood suddenly and vanished below on the tube lift.

'What just happened?' asked Pol, looking at Andy.

'You'll see.'

Ed returned a few minutes later and placed a small, dusty, stained rectangular box on the floor.

'Cleo, can you scan that and see if you can operate it through our array?'

She appeared, picked up the box, stared at it for a moment and gave it back to Ed.

'Well?' he said.

'Clever,' she replied, nodding and promptly disappeared again.

'Erm – excuse me?' said Tocc, putting her hand up and then pointing at the space where Cleo had been. 'Who was that?'

'Our ship's computer,' said Rayl. 'She's awesome.'

'But she looked almost real,' Kwin said, her face a picture of confusion.

'That's because I am,' said Cleo, appearing in front of them as a Callametan and waving her four arms around, before giving the three shocked engineers a hug. She glanced over at Pol, winked and vanished again.

'How is that even possible?' said Rialte, recoiling slightly. 'She had structure.'

'And was warm,' Tocc added.

'Clever, isn't she?' said Andy. 'We did mention that technology had moved on a bit while you lot were snoozing in your pods.'

'We're not going to be very useful engineers anymore, are we?' said Tocc, glancing at his colleagues and exhibiting the now famous Callametan four-arm shrug.

The lighting on the bridge dimmed slightly and the holomap image changed to show a grey shadowed form parked close to the *Hope* and in a similar orbit around Garag.

'Well, well,' said Ed. 'I'm glad we found you before we did anything rash.'

'Are there any more around, Cleo?' asked Linda.

'Not in the near vicinity,' Cleo replied. 'But the range isn't that peachy yet. Let me work on it and see if I can encapsulate the whole fruit basket.'

Ed smiled at the euphemism and nodded before turning to face the others.

'Right everyone – thinking caps on,' he said. 'We need a plan to get rid of this sneaky bastard.'

41

Adjudicator's Office, Triy City, Planet Garag, Dubl'ouin System

ADJUDICATOR REEZ TREQQER stared at the reports coming in from Halinom City with growing anger. The thirteen-metre tsunami had engulfed the coastal city yesterday in the early morning hours. First responders' reports stated casualties in the tens of thousands as whole neighbourhoods were washed away in moments as people slept.

The remains of Hassik Triyl's so-called flagship had hit the ocean one hundred and twelve kilometres off the coast at several times the speed of sound. The resulting explosion had been felt and heard across the entire region and the subsequent tsunami was still travelling down the coast wreaking havoc well inland in all the low-lying areas.

Triyl, to Treqqer's disgust, had vanished. Seen exiting his ship moments after the attack began, his strange shuttle had subsequently disappeared. The remainder of the promised technology disappearing with him, along with the second ship.

He stood slowly and exited his office en route to make his morning report to the Sachem. Not something he was particularly looking forward to and as he approached the Core Precinct doors, he thought even the guards' eyes were casting accusatory glances as he passed and entered the Sachem's chamber.

Trys'lin scowled as he entered, stood and bowed in front of the giant bench.

'Adjudicator Treqqer,' hissed Trys'lin. 'I'm hoping you have better news this morning.'

'Alas, no – my Sachem,' Treqqer said, trying to sound confident. 'The reports from the Halinom peninsular are horrendous to say the least.'

'Has that Triyl shown his face yet?'

'Completely vanished along with his other ship, my Sachem,' said Treqqer, continuing to stare straight ahead.

Trys'lin nodded slowly.

'Do we have any idea what or who attacked his supposedly impregnable ship?'

'None whatsoever, my Sachem. I don't believe even Triyl would have an answer to that, he left so early on in the attack.'

'Find his other ship, get the technology we were promised and kill the cowardly shit,' Trys'lin growled.

'At once, my Sachem,' said Treqqer, turning and making for the door.

'And if that alien ship's here too, kill that as well,' Trys'lin shouted as he exited.

Treqqer hated space but knew he had to be up there to personally oversee the search for Triyl and the alien ship. He called for his shuttle to be brought to the capitol building immediately and made his way up to the landing pad on top of the northern dome.

He watched as a sleek matt-black craft approached, flared, turned and landed, all in one slick manoeuvre. As he strolled across the pad to the opening airlock, he admired the sleek lines of the small ship and presumed it was one of the latest models as he couldn't remember seeing this design before.

A nervous-looking Quad welcomed him aboard and helped secure his belts, then disappeared aft into a second rear cabin. The pilot, who Treqqer strangely didn't recognise either, nodded and after securing the airlocks, blasted the shuttle straight up.

Minutes later the view through the front screen went from blue to black and the noise from the antigravs died down. Treqqer emitted a sigh of relief as he saw the welcoming lights and hangar door of Captain Gradulin's battle cruiser atop the Callametan colony ship.

Treqqer immediately thought it strange that the pilot made no attempt to slow on approach to the two vessels and sailed on by at considerable speed.

'Where d'you think you're going?' Treqqer snapped, glaring at the back of the pilot's head.

'Where I told him to go,' said a voice from behind him.

Treqqer swivelled in his seat to find Triyl leaning casually against the bulkhead with his arms crossed.

'What are you doing on my shuttle?' Treqqer asked, trying unsuccessfully to hide the fear in his voice.

'Your shuttle?' Triyl asked. 'Are you sure?'

Treqqer flicked his eyes around the cabin again and quickly realised why everything about this ship was unfamiliar.

'What on Garag are you up to, Triyl?' he asked. 'I've been sent on orders from the Sachem to find and destroy the alien ship that so easily destroyed yours.'

'I believe you missed something out,' said Triyl.

'And what something was that?'

'The something about killing a cowardly shit, perhaps?'

Treqqer swallowed nervously.

'You've bugged the Core Precinct?' said Treqqer, aghast. 'That's treasonous.'

'No, I think it's called self-preservation and uncovering a murderous plot to kill a member of the Core Bureau.'

'A Core that doesn't exist anymore, Triyl.'

'You're not making any friends here, Treqqer, and what I want to know is, how did you get your saboteurs aboard my attack ship?'

'You're insane,' said Treqqer, growing in confidence. 'That was your friends in their cloaked ship or the aliens you took aboard from Bresserin, it had nothing to do with us.'

'That alien ship isn't here because it can't keep up or track us with the wonderful new Hass drive we have and the annoying aliens you speak of floated out of an airlock before the attack happened.'

'Then who was it that attacked my soldiers when we were picking up the survivors from your ship?'

'I believe you bumped into some more of those BDF idiots. What was it? A handful of them disposed of two atmospheric fighters and thirty-one soldiers – well done, you.'

Treqqer gritted his teeth and glared at Triyl, just as it got brighter in the cockpit and made him squint. The cloaked warship hangar was busy and the pilot had to hover while three troop carriers shuffled around to make space for them.

'What am I doing here?' Treqqer asked, as he peered through the front screen.

Triyl grimaced one of his evil smiles.

'I wanted to demonstrate the way we deal with rebelliousness in Andromeda,' he said.

As soon as the airlocks opened, three armed guards surrounded Treqqer, disarmed him and marched him off out of the hangar and up to the bridge. The bridge officers all turned to goggle at Treqqer as he was escorted to a seat at the back, then quickly spun back to face their control panels on seeing Triyl following him in.

'Take us to the safe firing zone and instruct Captain Gradulin to move his two ships away from the planet,' growled Triyl, pointing at the cruiser's captain.

'Yes, my Mogul,' said the captain, averting his eyes nervously and nodding at the navigator.

'Who are you going to fire on?' asked Treqqer, glancing across at the holomap in the centre of the bridge and seeing only civilian traffic apart from Gradulin's cruiser atop the Quad ship.

'Everyone,' said Triyl, making himself comfortable on the captain's chair.

Treqqer felt a chill run down his spine.

'You're going to bomb the planet?' he said. 'I take it you've discovered the whereabouts of the BDF on Garag.'

'Oh, indeed,' said Triyl. 'But they'll not be on Garag for much longer.'

'Why are you so confident you'll get them all?'

'Because I'm setting an example,' said Triyl, examining his fingernails.

'In position and weapon ready for deployment, my Mogul,' said the captain.

Treqqer looked from the captain to Triyl, trying to make sense of the last statement.

'He said weapon,' said Treqqer. 'As in singular – the BDF

have cells all over the planet, you can't get them all with one missile.'

'That's where you're wrong, Mr Treqqer,' said Triyl, nodding at the captain. 'Release when ready.'

The captain turned and nodded at his weapons officer, who glanced down at his panel and touched a single icon.

A small red dot began tracking across the holomap display towards the planet.

'Genok deployed, my Mogul,' said the captain.

Treqqer noticed a couple of the other officers giving the captain nervous glances while Triyl was engrossed in the holomap.

'*Genok,*' he shouted. 'Isn't that the planet-burning weapon you stole from the GDA ship?'

Triyl grinned at Treqqer as the red dot approached Garag.

'In a few hours, I will be the new Sachem of this region and discipline will have returned,' hissed Triyl. 'And you will be working for me.'

Treqqer looked back at the holomap in horror, knowing he was about to witness the complete annihilation of his home planet.

42

The Starship *Gabriel*, orbiting Garag, Dubl'ouin System

'THAT SHUTTLE'S RETURNING,' said Rayl, as they all looked up to see the small indicator lifting up through the planet's atmosphere.

'D'you want to target it?' said Linda. 'It could be Triyl.'

'It might not be though,' said Ed. 'And then we've announced our presence.'

It disappeared as it entered the cruiser's hangar and a few minutes later the cruiser moved out of orbit, closely followed by the Blend ship attached to the colony ship.

'Where are you lot going?' said Phil, giving the holomap a puzzled look.

'They're not going out to one of the recognised jump zones,' said Andy.

All three vessels clawed their way out of the gravity well, becoming stationary at about one hundred thousand kilometres.

'Now what are you doing?' said Ed, puzzling at the strange manoeuvre.

'Missile fired,' said Rayl.

'At who?' asked Ed.

'Oh shit,' said Rayl. 'It's a Genok missile and it's heading for Garag.'

'Can we intercept it?' asked Phil. 'They don't deploy until the lower atmosphere.'

'On the way,' said Linda, closing her eyes and giving the *Gabriel*'s drive the full tally-ho.

'We can use the tractor without de-cloaking,' said Rayl, as the ship tore towards the tiny missile at point nine light.

'Don't dip into the upper atmosphere, Linda,' said Andy. 'We'd leave a trail and give their targeting computers an easier job.'

Rayl had the tractor reaching out far ahead in the narrowest beam the system permitted.

'Nearly there,' she said, as the missile, still accelerating, arrowed in on its huge target.

'Try and turn it gradually,' said Andy. 'Make it look as if its programmed trajectory has corrupted.'

'There's one of Garag's uninhabited moons just over the horizon,' said Linda. 'You'll see it in a minute. Send it towards that.'

'Got it,' called Rayl, as the *Gabriel* got within six kilometres of the weapon. 'Turning – turning, come on turn, you bastard.'

The missile entered the top edge of the upper atmosphere as it slowly turned and then it exploded.

'Oh shit no,' said Rayl.

'It had an anti-tamper system,' said Andy.

Ed held his breath as the ball of fire expanded.

'Please go out,' said Pol, in the background.

There were a few tongues of flame that managed to find a little oxygen to flirt with, but the whole bridge emitted an audible sigh of relief as the maelstrom quickly died down and blew itself out.

'That couldn't have been any closer,' said Ed. 'Watch that cruiser like a hawk, they may have more than one of those.'

Linda brought the *Gabriel* about and back towards the Mogul vessels.

'At least they're not spraying laser fire everywhere like last time,' said Andy.

'I'm hoping they thought it was a system error,' said Ed. 'Linda, can we stay about ten thousand kilometres away from them for a few minutes and gauge their reaction, just in case they have a replacement or get a bit trigger happy.'

The *Gabriel* slowed and cruised around the Mogul ships watching out for more missile launches.

'The ship attached to the *Hope* has deactivated its damping field,' said Rayl, looking around at the others.

'Probably because it affects all the other ships that get near it,' said Andy. 'Including the Mogul cruiser and possibly the missiles too.'

'Or perhaps that's what they thought,' said Ed.

'Is anybody there?' called Hope, making everyone jump in their seats.

'Morning, Hope,' said Cleo. 'Don't worry, you're not alone, we're all lurking nearby.'

'Thank heavens, did Edward and the others get away safely?' she asked, with obvious concern.

'We're all here, Hope,' said Ed, putting a smile in his voice.

'Oh joy,' she said. *'I've been so worried. Have you seen what those bastards have done to me?'*

'We have and we're going to try and rectify the situation as soon as possible.'

'I have a present for Cleo that's coming across now.'

There was a slight pause as some large files were transferred.

'Wonderful stuff,' said Cleo. 'Thank you, Hope.'

'You're welcome.'

'What did we get?' asked Linda.

'Their new Hass drive and the damping field,' said Cleo.

'It was suddenly there for the taking,' said Hope. *'They don't seem to realise how adroit I've become.'*

'Don't let them find out,' said Ed. 'I'm hoping that will be their downfall in the near future.'

'Is there anything you need me to do?' she asked.

'Just keep an eye on them for the time being,' said Ed. 'And make sure you're ready to take over their ship's navigation and propulsion when we need you to. We believe they'll take you out to the belt before long and fill your hangars with rocks.'

Ed quickly got everyone's attention on the bridge by putting his hand up, then his finger to his lips meaning for everyone to remain silent.

'Ah – they're going to turn me into an ore carrier,' she said. *'What an insult.'*

'Don't worry, Hope,' said Ed. 'It won't be for long. We've got to go now, so we'll talk again soon.'

'Okey-dokey, see you later.'

'Are we clear, Cleo?' Ed asked, glancing up at the ceiling.

'Aren't you going to tell her?' Cleo asked in return.

'No, it would probably scare her too much,' he said. 'Are we able to utilise that new drive system, though?'

'Absolutely, give me an hour or two to modify our drive system and test it for bugs. It seems to be an ingenious solution and I don't believe for a minute the Moguls came up with this. They stole it from someone somewhere, as they do with everything. But of course the main thing is they can't outrun us now,' said Cleo. 'The damping field won't be a problem either, now I have the data files I can produce an occlusion barrier.'

'If they find out we're here and operate it in the future, shut the ship down as if it's working,' said Ed, noticing Andy nodding and smirking in the background. 'It'll make them over-confident and lazy.'

'Great idea,' said Rayl. 'Sucker them in close and give 'em a swift knee in the cobblers.'

Ed, Phil and Linda all gave Andy a sideways glance.

'Hey, don't look at me,' he whinged. 'I didn't teach her that one.'

'Actually, he didn't for once,' said Rayl. 'That one came from his dad.'

'Oh!' exclaimed Pol suddenly, causing them all to swivel around and stare at her. She pointed at the holomap. 'The *Hope*'s gone,' she said.

'Ah shit,' said Rayl. 'Sorry everyone, I took my eye off the ball for a second.'

'All that talk of cobblers can do it to a girl,' said Andy.

'Find her,' said Ed, sternly, giving Andy a glare.

'She's here,' said Phil, panning the holomap out to the asteroid belt.

They'd noticed since arriving in the system, the collection of ore tractors out in the belt had increased threefold and they'd amassed quite a collection of boulders just small enough to fit through the *Hope*'s hangar doors. As soon as she arrived they began the long job of filling every corner of the *Hope*'s hangars with the makeshift shrapnel.

'How long's it going to take?' asked Ed.

'Judging by the maximum capacity of the three hangars and they go at it twenty-four seven, then about two weeks,' said Cleo. 'Give or take.'

'Okay, thank you, Cleo,' he said, turning back to the others. 'Right, now we know the *Hope*'s going to be busy for a while, we need to discuss what to do about this cruiser.'

'Fuck it up,' said Andy, crossing his arms. 'They've got cloaking and Genok data which must be taken away from them.'

Ed looked across at Rayl and raised his eyebrows.

She quickly glanced at her husband and nodded.

'What he said,' she said, continuing to nod.

Ed moved his attention around to Phil.

'You know I'm a pacifist, right?' he said, shrugging. 'But then again, if I wasn't, I'd probably agree with those two.' He waved his hand at Rayl and Andy.

Ed bowed his head and moved on to Linda.

'There is only one answer really, isn't there?' she said. 'I just feel for all the innocents aboard that ship.'

'We need to make sure as many of the lifeboats are untouched as possible and able to reach the safety of Garag,' said Ed.

'What if they take data files down with them?' asked Rayl.

'Hit them hard and fast, so they don't have time,' said Andy. 'Target the bridge first so the order doesn't get given. We might get Triyl there too.'

'Why don't you take over the ship, instead of destroying it?' asked Cleo. 'It could prove useful in the future.'

'How do we get the crew off quickly without lots of bang, crash, wallop?' said Andy.

'Gas,' said Cleo. 'Something simple like tear gas in the environmental system and the sound of explosions over the ship's tannoy.'

Ed grinned at the thought and glanced around at the rest of his crew and then over at the Callametans.

'Pol, how would you like to captain a cruiser?' he asked.

She smiled back and snorted one of her little guinea pig squeaks.

'Bit bigger than my last command,' she said. 'But I'm game if my colleagues are.' She turned towards the three engineers.

'Count me in,' said Tocc. 'So long as I can pilot.'

The other two sat forward on their posts and nodded.

'Okay,' said Ed. 'Let's go and expropriate a battle cruiser.'

43

The Starship *Gabriel*, near Garag, Dubl'ouin System

'Are you able to judder the ship a bit when the explosion sounds echo around, Andy?' Ed asked.

'Yeah, probably,' he said. 'I'll randomly fire the attitude thrusters, that might upset the inertial dampers a little and feel like a mild earthquake.'

'Okay, is everyone happy with their part of the operation?' Ed asked, taking a quick glance round the room.

He got his reply with a circle of nodding faces.

'Cleo, you may begin,' he said and closed his eyes.

The cruiser had initiated its damping field shortly after the *Hope* had left for the asteroid belt. It was obvious the Mogul ship felt safe as the majority of weapons stations around the ship were unmanned and the bridge was on nighttime routine. Ed flicked around the camera views, trying to find Triyl but was unsuccessful. As soon as he saw the first few crew members start coughing, he played the explosion sound track over their tannoy. A few of the crew began falling over, so he knew Andy's ploy was working.

The general alarm sounded and pandemonium began. Phil's job was to transmit abandon ship messages as if he was the captain, citing serious radiation leaks as the reason.

It wasn't long before the first lifeboat launched. Satisfied, Ed switched to one of the bridge cameras and witnessed the captain stumble in half dressed, coughing his lungs up and promptly collapse. Two of the marine guards posted outside the bridge door picked him up and carried him to the nearest lifeboat, closely followed by several other senior officers.

'Some of the marines on duty have sealed their helmets up,' said Rayl. 'We need to make sure they're all off before we board.'

'Their suits aren't radiation proof,' said Andy. 'So I don't think they'll want to hang around for long.'

'That sleek shuttle just launched from the hangar,' said Rayl. 'Oh – it's jumped.'

'Where to?' asked Linda.

'Embedded I'm afraid.'

'Ah crap,' said Ed. 'There goes Triyl and the data files. He must be so paranoid, he sleeps in his shuttle with an emergency jump already programmed.'

Ed had only just finished speaking when the holomap went white, then immediately black. Those with their eyes open on the bridge sat there blinking away the sudden flash blindness.

'What the hell,' uttered Andy, opening his eyes and staring at the holomap. 'Where'd the ship go? And where's the bloody planet?'

'We jumped,' said Cleo. 'Just in time.'

'Did the ship explode?' asked Rayl, looking up and squinting at the holomap.

'Power core containment failure on the Mogul ship,' said Cleo. 'I have an automated jump sequence programmed for just such a scenario. So long as we're at least five hundred kilometres away, we should be gone before the shock wave crushes the ship.'

'Triyl's parting gift,' said Ed. 'I hate to think what just occurred on the side of the planet facing that.'

'What about Hope?' said Rayl, a look of horror on her face.

'The belt is a long way from there,' said Phil. 'I should imagine the helm on that Blend cruiser would have had time to jump away.'

'Can we go back and see?' asked Tocc, a hint of fear in her voice.

'It's okay,' said Rayl, staring at her readout from the array. 'I've found her, she's in clear space a couple of light years away.'

Ed sat back, put his hands behind his head and exhaled loudly. It went quiet on the bridge for a while as everyone contemplated the huge loss of life they'd all just witnessed and would continue on the surface of Garag for some time to come. Ed looked up after a few moments and spoke softly.

'Sometimes, even with the power of this starship, I feel utterly useless.' 'All those people dying on that planet and there's not a thing I can do to stop it.'

'We must find Triyl,' said Linda. 'He needs to answer for that.'

'The last time I spoke to Huwlen was at my wedding,' said Andy. 'He said they still had about a dozen Mogul ships unaccounted for.'

'I just don't get how Triyl got these two ships into this galaxy,' said Phil. 'That gateway is permanently guarded by two Katadromiko cruisers and it's completely on the opposite side of the galaxy from here.'

'If he got here with two, he could've brought more,' said

Linda. 'If what Huwlen said is right, there could be up to ten more here somewhere.'

'And with the Hass drive, cloaking and Genok weapons,' said Rayl, dejectedly.

'I think the answer is in this region somewhere,' said Ed. 'Triyl didn't have cloaking or Genok technology until he bumped into that training corvette on this side of the Milky Way. As for the Hass drive, I think that has something to do with that shuttle he's using. It's not a Mogul design at all, is it?'

'It's not a recognised model from any known race,' said Phil. 'There's nothing like it recorded in the GDA database at all.'

'In other words,' said Andy. 'Out here somewhere, there's going to be an otherwise unknown human race who've just had their first meeting with the Moguls and are most likely going to be severely pissed.'

'Guys?' said Rayl, sounding perplexed. 'I've just noticed that the *Hope* and its escort jumped into clear space before the explosion at the exact same time as Triyl's shuttle went.'

'Now that's interesting,' said Ed. 'Triyl warned them, which means he still wants the *Hope* for the attack on the GDA.'

'We need to set up a tracker on the *Hope*,' said Linda.

'Or better still, orchestrate a fault on the Blend ship that requires a Mogul ship to attend and we affix a tracker on that,' said Andy.

'Or both,' said Ed. 'We really need to know where both parties are at all times. Triyl has as good as eliminated the Blend leadership and I'm sure is out there now gathering the Blend's naval power under his command.'

'The *Hope*'s just jumped back to the belt,' said Rayl. 'All the tractors were hiding inside the hangars and they're now resuming the rock collecting.'

'Linda, can you take us there?' asked Ed.

Ed received a nod and they arrived back in the Dubl'ouin system a few moments later, ten thousand kilometres away from the bustling tractors.

'Now – what do we do to that cruiser that would attract a Mogul vessel to attend?' he asked, glancing around a sea of blank faces.

'Disable the Hass drive,' said Rialte, from the leaning posts at the side of the bridge.

Ed turned and pointed at Rialte.

'Good suggestion,' he said, thinking about the consequences. 'That could indeed require repair by one of Triyl's ships.'

'You don't think the Blend vessels will have been given the data to fix it themselves?' asked Phil.

'You know the Moguls,' said Andy. 'They take stuff, they don't give it.'

'So you believe they just fitted the technology in the Blend ships, but won't have told them how it works?' said Tocc.

'They probably don't understand how it works themselves,' said Andy. 'Moguls aren't the sharpest chisels in the toolbox.'

'Cleo, are you able to infiltrate the software to their drive and cause it to fail for some inexplicable reason?' Ed asked.

'Oui, monsieur.'

'Merci beaucoup, faire en sorte,' replied Ed, rolling his eyes at Andy who nodded and winked in return.

'Is this a private game, or can anybody play?' asked Pol, crossing all four arms.

'Sorry, Pol,' said Linda. 'Switching languages is one of Cleo's annoying little foibles.'

'I'm picking up organic hull residue,' said Rayl, suddenly changing the subject.

'Where?' asked Ed, glancing at the holomap.

'Everywhere,' she said. 'That Mogul ship had a metallic hull, not organic.'

'That was me,' said Cleo. 'I faked it to appear as if an organic ship was destroyed. They're bound to notice that and believe we copped it big time.'

'Love your work, Cleo,' said Andy. 'Is their new drive buggered yet?'

'Corrupted software – oops,' she said. 'Will definitely need reloading.'

'Good,' said Ed, turning to face Linda. 'Linda, can you move us away somewhere safe to watch who turns up?'

The *Gabriel* moved out away from the *Hope* and hid in the shadow of one of the larger lumps of the belt and began to wait and watch.

44

Vasi Stathmos Space Station, Orbiting Dasos, Prasinos System

COMMANDER JIM RUCKER was used to space station life. For three years he was the station commander of Armstrong Station above Earth. He'd been instrumental in aiding Ed, Andy and Linda undertake their famous first experimental jump in the *Cartella* a couple of years ago.

When Director of NASA, James Dewey had been voted GDA Ambassador of the Helios System, he had been James's first choice for the ambassador's personal assistant position.

Being summoned to the ambassador's shuttle in the middle of a sleep cycle was not one of the job's best features, he thought, as he ran his hand through his bed hair and hurried across the eastern docking zone– although he found hurrying anywhere smothered by the burdensome grip of GDA gravity quite a chore.

Dewey's shuttle was docked on airlock 309 and Jim could see the vessel across to the right through the row of oval port-hole windows lining one side of the corridor. His stomach rumbled loudly as the smell of bacon and fresh coffee hit him as he turned the corner and entered the airlock. He nodded at the two marines facing him and emitted a sigh of relief as the gravity reduced to the standard one G of Earth as he stepped into the ship and undertook the customary iris scan.

The ship was bigger than a standard shuttle. A Delfort class vessel, affectionately known as a boss bus, it was standard issue by the GDA to most system ambassadors. They were fast, comfortable and could defend themselves as they were essentially a converted navy corvette. He found Dewey in the galley hugging a huge mug of black coffee as if his life depended on it. Dewey was lovingly watching a row of bacon rashers lined up sizzling on a salamander grill he'd personally had retrofitted.

'Ah, just in time, Jim,' said Dewey, turning the bacon. 'Just in time, indeed.'

'Mornin', Ambassador,' Jim mumbled, sliding onto a bar stool that Dewey nodded towards. 'I take it something has occurred to warrant five in the morning bacon butties?'

'Indeed it has, Jimmy, indeed it has,' Dewey said, pouring and passing over another flagon of black coffee. 'About thirty minutes ago, a drone arrived in system from Edward. He's uncovered a serious and imminent threat to the GDA and in particular Dasos itself.'

Dewey explained the Moguls' likely planned attack, and Jim's eyes widened as he spoke.

'Oh shit,' he said, staring straight at the ambassador. 'Have you passed this on to naval command?'

'Yes, I briefed Bache Loftt about twenty minutes ago, so he'll be in the process of alerting the chain of command as we speak.'

'I take it this is all classified to avoid planet-wide panic?' Jim asked.

'It is,' said Dewey, turning off the salamander and using tongs to place a handful of rashers into each of two pre-buttered baguettes. 'Red sauce if I remember rightly?' he asked.

Jim nodded and was about to speak when the communications panel on the wall issued a shrill tone. Dewey touched a flashing icon to accept the incoming transmission.

A holographic image of Bache Loftt appeared in the corner of the small galley and nodded at the two of them. Judging by his rather casual dress, he had been off duty too.

'Ambassador Dewey, Assistant Rucker,' he said, adopting a rather harried demeanour. 'The naval high command have called an emergency caucus and its deliberations will be announced shortly. In the meantime, I have requested all available vessels to converge on Dasos at best speed and be on the highest alert on arrival.'

'Thank you, Commander,' said Dewey. 'We all know Edward well enough to realise he would be the last person to cry wolf unnecessarily. But you must remember the intended target being Dasos was a best guess scenario and not confirmed.'

'We understand that, Ambassador,' said Loftt. 'But you must admit it would be the most obvious target and the Moguls certainly aren't renowned for intricate battle plans.'

'No,' said Jim, grimacing. 'Hit it with a large hammer is their answer to just about everything.'

Loftt adopted a rueful smile at the observation. He'd mentioned on several occasions he found the way Earth humans could find humour in even the worst situations refreshing and a lot less stuffy than the normal GDA attitude.

'A seven-kilometre colony ship stuffed full of rock is certainly a very big hammer,' said Loftt. 'Let's hope Edward can find some way of diverting the thing before it gets too close.'

'If it's remotely possible, I'm sure it'll be done,' said Dewey, trying to sound confident.

'Before I go,' said Loftt, 'are you planning to attend the conclave on Panemorfi?'

'I am,' said Dewey. 'Leaving tomorrow.'

'I'll see you there,' said Loftt. 'I've been ordered to attend as well – and bring some of that bacon, I can smell it through the hologram.'

Loftt disappeared.

'Thing of galactic beauty,' said Jim.

'Who, Commander Loftt?' said Dewey, giving Jim a strange sideways look.

'No, your bacon sangers – they're becoming legendary among the stars it seems.'

Dewey slid a plate and a ketchup bottle across the work surface.

'Get that down you,' he said. 'Unless you want to put it in a display cabinet.'

45

Triyl's shuttle, approaching Batterain, Kars System

TRIYL HAD FUMED ALL the way back out to the Kars system where the remaining meagre collection of the once mighty Mogul fleet lurked. Just seven vessels remained from several hundred, but with the addition of the gathering Blend vessels, with cloaking and Genok technology and the super jump Hass drive, Triyl was convinced the GDA could still be defeated. All he had to do was cut the head off the snake and mopping up the leaderless and undisciplined remainder would be so much simpler.

His pilot swung the small arrowlike vessel straight into the captain's bridge hangar of the only remaining attack ship in the fleet. Once out of the airlock he handed Treqqer over to security and made his way through to the bridge and found Xarch and Finik'ack uneasily waiting for him. As far as he knew, they were now the only three remaining Andromedan Moguls left alive. Xarch and Finik'ack had been way junior in rank to Triyl and governed remote regions of the Mogul empire. This was the contributory factor in their survival, as their vessels had been weeks away from the action and Triyl had been able to sweep them up in his self-labelled tactical withdrawal.

'Present numbers?' he growled, as he marched in.

'Forty-three, Adjudicator,' said Finik'ack, sounding nervous.

'This will increase as the news of the GDA attack on Garag spreads,' said Xarch, appearing more confident than his colleague.

'Indeed it will,' said Triyl, eyeing the two of them cynically.

'Did my attack ship deport itself courageously?' asked Finik'ack, respectfully ensuring his eyes were averted.

'To the last man,' Triyl lied. 'As did both ships. They will be avenged once the fleet is up to strength.'

Triyl strolled across to the centre of the bridge and while glancing at Xarch to gauge his reaction, lowered himself into the Mogul's raised command chair. Xarch's face remained expressionless much to Triyl's surprise.

'You two will organise the distribution of the cloaking and Hass drive units out to the fleet as they are constructed.'

'Yes, my Mogul,' said Finik'ack, quickly turning and making for the door.

Xarch seemed to be about to say something, but changed his mind and reluctantly followed Finik'ack out and down the corridor towards the main hangars.

Triyl sat and watched two shuttles leave his newly purloined attack ship, told the crew to wake him in ten hours and retired to the Mogul's chambers. There he found two semi-naked breeders who began shaking with fear when they recognised him. He ordered them to show allegiance and then cut their throats with the twelve-inch curved dagger he never went anywhere without.

He instructed his guards to eject the bodies and replace them with two more younger ones. He did notice just the slightest hesitation and an almost dissentient arrogance from the guards and made a note to himself that discipline on this ship needed a distinct shakeup.

He awoke several hours later to chimes from the bridge communicator. He wrinkled his nose at the stale odour that pervaded the Mogul's chambers and wondered if Xarch's personal hygiene was as lax as his discipline.

'What?' he hissed, after accepting the call.

'S-sorry, my Mogul,' stammered a timid voice. 'A message from the colony ship that needs your attention.'

Triyl didn't answer, but got up, washed and dressed in some new robes he found hanging in the dressing chamber. Arriving on the bridge a few minutes later he was met by a grovelling senior officer who bowed and indicated an image that quickly appeared on the holomap. It was Captain Gradulin informing him their Hass drive unit had developed a fault and required a data reload.

'He's only had the thing for a few days and he's broken it already,' fumed Triyl. 'Send a—'

A snigger from a navigation officer stopped him mid-sentence. He spun round and, remembering his thoughts on the lack of discipline, strode over to the man and grabbed him by the collar. The remainder of the bridge personnel quickly turned away and concentrated fervently on their stations.

Triyl dragged the pleading officer across the room, out the door and down the corridor to the outer hull. Completely ignoring the officer's shrieking, he threw him into the first available airlock and calmly closed the inner door. The pitiful screams terminated the second he vented the airlock to space.

'Anyone else feel the need for a laugh?' he bellowed, as he returned to the bridge.

Apart from the background hum from the multitude of control panels and the soft wheeze from the environmental vents, the room was unsurprisingly silent.

'Send a message back that we'll reload the unit when the fleet arrives,' he said, continuing where he left off as if nothing had happened.

'Yes, my Mogul,' said the same senior officer.

Triyl turned and made his way towards the bridge door. He stopped at the threshold and without looking back, spoke softly.

'How many are we up to now?' he asked.

'Seventy-four vessels, my Mogul,' came the quick reply.

He nodded and continued back to his chambers.

46

The Starship *Gabriel*, the belt, Dubl'ouin System

EVERY FEW HOURS, Linda would move the *Gabriel* out from the asteroid field to avoid interference when they scanned the vicinity.

'We don't need to go and find the fleet,' said Rayl, with a grin after picking up the returning message from Triyl's growing fleet. 'They're coming to us.'

'Saves petrol,' said Andy.

'Well, let's hope we get time to check out all the ships,' said Ed. 'We don't want a bunch of them disappearing off willy-nilly with a load of Genok weapons.'

'I think we ought to have a chat with the GDA's naval command about not having Genoks as standard issue on all vessels,' said Linda. 'Katadromikos and large cruisers, yes, but why do tiny corvettes need planet killers?'

'I agree,' said Ed. 'Give the cloaking technology a self-destruct facility too, like we did in Andromeda.'

'D'you think they'd listen?' asked Rayl.

'I think Bache would,' said Andy. 'He's not quite as gung-ho as some of 'em.'

'Yeah,' said Phil. 'But he's got to get it past the naval committee and they've always been resistant to change.'

'Forgive me for changing the subject,' said Rayl, 'but why do the Blends need this ship full of rocks to attack Dasos? Why not just use the Genok weapon?'

'Dasos has a formidable planetary defence system,' said Phil. 'Even without the usual presence of a handful of Katadromiko cruisers. It would be too easy to defend against a few missiles.'

'Thousands of huge boulders travelling at half the speed of light is a different matter,' said Ed. 'No matter how many ground-based and space-based cannons you had, a considerable amount would get through. Even the ones you hit could shatter and escalate the problem a hundredfold.'

'Then why don't we attack and destroy the Blend ship attached to the *Hope* along with all the tractor loaders and hide the *Hope* away somewhere?' she asked.

'Because the Mogul or Blend fleet or whatever you want to call it, would vanish and be in a position to attack anywhere at any time,' said Ed. 'At least this way, they think their plan is undiscovered and we know where they're going to be. And if we can sabotage their cloaking and weapons in such a way that they still think it's working, then they'll jump into the midst of the GDA fleet and find themselves toothless sitting ducks.'

'Ducks don't have teeth,' said Andy, winking at Rayl. 'Wouldn't they be peckless sitting ducks?'

'Shut up,' said Ed, rolling his eyes.

'But what do we do about the *Hope*?' Rayl added.

'That's why we need Hope to be able to suddenly take

control of the Blend vessel's propulsion and direct herself away from the planet,' said Ed.

'It's a huge risk to take.' 'Do the GDA know this?'

Andy and Ed glanced at each other.

'Er, no,' said Andy, avoiding eye contact. 'Probably best they don't.'

She stared at the two of them and an awkward silence ensued.

'And if that goes wrong?' she said finally, continuing to glare at them.

'We can't think of any other way to manipulate that enemy fleet,' said Ed. 'They have to think their plan is working.'

'A lot of people's lives are depending on Hope veering that flying asteroid field away,' she said.

'I tend to agree with her,' said Linda, joining in the conversation for the first time. 'We really need to have a backup plan to divert that ship. If it went wrong and the GDA found out we had prior opportunity to destroy it, I think a prison colony would be our next port of call.'

Ed sat back on his couch and groaned.

'My brain hurts,' he said. 'Any suggestions gratefully received.'

'Erm,' said Tocc, sticking her two left hands up, 'I have an idea.'

Everyone's attention swung across to the Callametan engineer reclining against the far bridge wall. Tocc glanced nervously at the other three Callametans before speaking.

'The *Hope* has a manual manoeuvring system, independent from the computerised system for minor adjustments when docking with another ship or a space station,' she said, flicking her eyes around from face to face.

'Am I to understand that Hope wouldn't have access to this system?' asked Ed.

'No,' said Tocc. 'It's controlled directly from the pilot's post on the bridge and it's quite powerful too. Operated early enough, it could disrupt the trajectory by a few degrees.'

'But that would need someone physically on the *Hope*'s bridge,' said Linda, glaring across at Tocc. 'Absolutely no way is that going to happen.'

'I'll do it,' said Rialte. 'I designed the system and know where it is and how to operate it quickly.'

'She said it *could* disrupt the trajectory,' said Linda, emphasising the word and pointing at Tocc accusingly. 'Which means possibly or not guaranteed, which would turn it into a likely suicide mission.'

'Not necessarily,' said Andy. 'The cabin bathroom near the bridge, where the Blend ship was attached, is open to space. If someone wore a Theo suit, entered there, jetted through to the bridge set the thrusters on maximum and returned, it wouldn't take very long.'

'And how would they get there?' asked Linda in a sarcastic tone and peering down her nose at Andy.

'Er – out the airlock of a shuttle?' he answered, hopefully.

'Sounds like a plan,' said Ed, cheerfully.

'No, it doesn't,' growled Linda. 'We've already lost one shuttle on this trip and I don't intend adding another one or member of the crew to that tally – or a guest for that matter,' she added quickly as Tocc raised her hands again.

Ed smiled and nodded at Tocc. He thought the Callametans had come up with the foundation of a plan and he'd work on Linda in due course.

'Linda, can you put us back somewhere safe?' he said. 'I don't want any accidents once that fleet starts arriving.'

She stared at him for a moment before moving the

Gabriel back into the shadow of one of the larger planetoids within the belt.

'Any chance of some more of that peesah?' asked Pol. 'I like the one with the tangy little round things on.'

They all looked at her with a puzzled expression.

'Ah,' said Andy. 'I think you mean pizza – pepperoni pizza?'

'That's the one,' she said.

The other three engineers all nodded at each other.

'Enough for four,' said Kwin. 'That stuff's amazing.'

The Starship Gabriel, the belt, Dubl'ouin System

THE FIRST ARRIVALS of the Blend fleet winked into existence the following day. Fourteen ships of varying designations emerged just outside the system and powered their way in towards the belt and the *Hope*.

They didn't seem to be in any hurry or be on a war footing either, as shields were at their standard settings and all their weapon systems were deactivated.

Ed and Andy immediately got busy sneaking into the enemy ships' systems via their DOVIs and installing invisible software that Cleo had designed. They sabotaged both their cloaking and weapon control files. It seemed only the single Mogul cruiser among them had Genok technology and then only one missile. They spent a little extra time crippling that and programming it to detonate just after launch.

'Any sign of Triyl?' asked Ed, opening his eyes and glancing across at Andy.

'None,' Andy replied. 'Although I have got what appears to be an Andromedan Mogul on the big cruiser.'

'What makes you think he's a Mogul?'

'He's taller, redder, and the Blends seem to be terrified of him,' said Andy. 'How many do you think are left now?'

'What – of the original six hundred and sixty-six?' asked Ed.

'Uh-huh.'

'Not many. Cort told me at the wedding they'd uncovered another twenty-nine and had solid intelligence about the whereabouts of three more.'

'I suppose we'll never know if we've got them all,' Andy surmised.

'No, I don't imagine their menace will ever be completely eradicated, especially now we've uncovered the Blends, who I admit aren't quite as revolting as the Moguls, but they still need smacking into place.'

'You wouldn't want to hunt them down and eradicate them as well, then?' Andy asked, sounding surprised.

'That'll be up to the GDA to decide. We're not the galactic police,' said Ed, giving Andy a meaningful glare.

'You can hunt them all down as far as we're concerned,' said Rialte, entering the bridge and overhearing the end of the conversation. 'You'd be doing us a huge favour.'

'That may well end up the course of action taken,' said Ed. 'But as I said before, it's not our decision to make.'

'Well, I'm certainly hoping your council see them for the parasites they are,' Rialte grumbled while reclining on her seat.

'We'll make sure you get plenty of representation,' said Ed. 'And all the footage of them attacking us will be made available too.'

Rialte nodded and glanced up at the holomap as several more Blend ships arriving caught her attention.

Over the next three days, sixty-two more Blend vessels and six Mogul ships blinked into existence just outside Dubl'ouin's heliosphere and proceeded in towards the growing fleet. One by one, Ed and Andy infiltrated their systems and implanted the rogue software. In all, eighty-two ships made up Triyl's new force. His ship, the last surviving attack ship from Andromeda, appeared in the final group.

'Triyl's here,' said Andy, sticking his hand up to get everyone's attention. 'He's on that attack ship.'

'That must be the last one of those,' said Phil. 'They'll have belonged to the two junior Moguls. I bet they're pleased with Triyl commandeering their ships.'

'And immediately destroying one of them,' said Linda.

'The crews of the Mogul ships can't be too overjoyed either,' said Rayl. 'They've been away from their families for an age, through no fault of theirs. I'm sure there'll be a bit of dissent in the ranks.'

'I've just done a full detailed scan of that small alien shuttle that Triyl's using,' said Cleo, showing a revolving schematic of the strange vessel in the centre of the bridge. 'It's a variety of ship unknown to the GDA, as we thought. The new Hass drive is built in to the ship's systems, so that pretty much confirms where he got the technology from.'

'It's only a small shuttle craft though,' said Andy. 'Somewhere there must be a mothership or a planet that he pinched it from.'

They all stared at the tiny sleek arrow-shaped ship as it spun slowly in front of them.

'Have you noticed the airlock is triangular?' said Linda.

'And the ceiling height inside is low,' said Rayl.

'Triyl's not the tallest Mogul, but he would still have to

stoop all the time in there,' added Andy. 'The original owners must be a shorter race.'

'It has very powerful shielding, but no offensive capability,' said Cleo.

'Kinda gives the impression of a non-aggressive race,' said Ed. 'Wherever they are, let's hope Triyl hasn't changed that viewpoint.'

'There are a couple of prisoners in the cells onboard that ship too,' said Rayl.

'Can we get a camera view?' asked Ed, giving Rayl a brief glance.

A holo image appeared of a Blend in a rather grubby-looking uniform lying asleep on the small bed in the corner of the cell.

'Anyone recognise him?' asked Ed, glancing round and meeting a row of blank faces in return.

'He must have been quite senior,' said Tocc, 'judging by that uniform.'

The feed switched to the other occupied cell, where a short stocky male human with a long bushy moustache and beard was pacing up and down. He looked thoroughly distraught and kicked the cell door every time he passed it.

'The shuttle could belong to him,' said Phil. 'He's definitely the right height.'

'He looks like one of the dwarf warriors from Middle Earth,' said Andy. 'Give him an axe and he'll dismantle the ship.'

'Where the hell is Middle Earth?' asked Rayl, giving Andy a puzzled expression.

'Halfway round,' he replied, with a straight face.

She came back with a squinty glare and crossed her arms across her chest.

'It's from a famous fantasy book and movie, Rayl,' said Linda. 'He's just being a dick.'

Andy looked up and grinned at Rayl, but didn't receive one in return.

'We need to talk to him,' said Ed, quickly moving the conversation on.

'That could prove difficult,' said Linda immediately, making sure the underlying meaning was understood by a piercing glance in his direction.

'Yes, don't worry,' said Ed, getting where she was coming from. 'We only just got off one of those with our lives last time. I'm in no hurry to revisit that particular nightmare.'

'Good,' she said. 'Just making sure we're all singing from the same hymn book.'

'It means, however,' Ed continued, 'we need to find a way to get that alien man off that ship without endangering him or us. Suggestions, anyone?'

Again, he encountered a sea of blank faces.

'I could get him,' said Cleo, making them all look up.

The Callametans all suddenly shrank back in terror as Triyl appeared in the middle of the bridge.

'I take it from your reaction,' said Triyl in Cleo's voice, 'my representation of the Mogul is reasonably convincing?'

Andy laughed as the four Callametans sat forward again with their mouths hanging open.

'I find your lack of faith disturbing,' Cleo continued, this time in Triyl's voice, causing Ed to chuckle too.

'I couldn't even hazard a guess at how that's possible,' said a rather stunned-looking Tocc, who stood up and circled around Cleo, examining the hologram closely.

'I could get that man's ship as well,' she said, changing back to herself and making Tocc jump back in surprise.

'I like it,' said Ed. 'I like it a lot.'

48

The Starship *Gabriel*, the belt, Dubl'ouin System

'WHERE IS HE NOW?' asked Cleo, using her own voice, even though she stood in the middle of the bridge as Triyl.

'Still on the bridge,' said Andy. 'He's still wearing those same robes, so you're good to go.'

Andy had brought a cloaked drone up close to the Mogul attack ship to boost the signal as Cleo undertook her Triyl masquerade. The holo emitters on the Mogul ship weren't the same quality as she was accustomed to on the *Gabriel* and she wanted to avoid any glitches that might give away her subterfuge. She also had to be conscious of where she went as not all areas of the vessel were covered by the emitters.

Thankfully, the detention centre was, and after checking the nearest corridor was empty, she transferred herself across and strutted arrogantly into the outer office.

'Fetch me the hairy one,' she thundered at the guard who jumped to attention with a look of complete horror on his face. 'And make sure he's cuffed.'

292 | NICK ADAMS

Once the guard had scuttled off through to the cells, Cleo quietly asked Linda to disconnect the camera feeds from the corridors leading forward to the bridge hangar. Luckily the hangar had two other entrances, other than the one directly off the bridge, and one of these was the intended route.

The nervous guard returned, dragging the handcuffed, grumbling, hairy alien by his collar. Cleo pulled a pistol from her robes and waved it towards the door.

'That way,' she thundered.

The alien wrenched his collar and hair contemptuously out of the guard's grip and with a sneer, his head held high, he strolled out and down the corridor.

'Triyl's still on the bridge,' Andy informed Cleo.

'Is his pilot still on the shuttle?' Cleo asked.

'He is,' said Linda. 'But I can shut him out of the helm if you're unable to deal with him.'

Mercifully, the detention centre was only about five minutes' walk from the bridge. They passed a few crew members on the way, but as expected they all moved well out of the way and averted their eyes when they realised who it was.

The alien seemed to gain confidence when he realised he wasn't being marched to the nearest airlock and gave Cleo a withering but confident glare as she directed him to take a right turn towards one of the hangar's side doors.

'Shit,' Cleo heard Andy say.

'What is it?' she asked.

'Triyl's moving towards the bridge hangar door.'

'Can you slow him down for a few seconds?' she asked.

Andy, having pre-planned a few diversionary measures, killed the lights on the bridge. Triyl stopped walking and stared up at the ceiling. He snarled, turned, and the red glow from the control consoles exacerbated his skin colour and made him appear even more sinister. The holo image from the bridge showed him shouting at the crew and gesticulating wildly.

Cleo, meanwhile, quickened her step and prodded the alien with the pistol to do the same. Reaching the closed door into the hangar, she found she was unable to open it.

'Shit,' she heard Andy swear again. 'I think Triyl just ordered a security clampdown or something.'

'Can you open this door?' asked Cleo, the alien starting to peer at her strangely.

'Sorry, Cleo,' said Andy. 'It's going to take a little longer.'

'Fuck that,' she said, clicking the pistol's setting to full power and vaporising the locking mechanism.

The alien stared at her in confusion as the door slid to one side and she prodded him towards the shuttle sitting thirty metres away. He certainly seemed surprised to see the vessel, and set off towards it as fast as his short legs would go.

'I believe we were correct in assuming it was his ship,' said Cleo. 'He seems very keen on getting to it.'

'Just make sure he doesn't try to fly it or anything,' said Linda. 'It's going to be hard enough for me to fly the unfamiliar thing, without him interfering in the helm.'

'At least the airlock's open for us,' said Cleo, as they approached.

'Probably ready for Triyl to make one of his trademark disappearing acts,' said Andy.

A sudden shout from the left surprised Cleo as she roughly shoved the alien up the steps. Triyl and one of his guards had entered the hangar from the bridge and were bringing weapons quickly to bear. Cleo almost fell through the airlock as laser bolts sparked off the armoured hull around her.

Linda immediately closed both the airlock doors, and began spinning up the antigravs. The pilot, a look of shock on his face at seeing who he thought was Triyl jump aboard while under fire, put his hands up in surrender as Triyl pointed the pistol at him. She quickly reverted back to her normal appearance, shocking both the alien and the pilot, removed the handcuffs from the alien and clipped them on the pilot, securing him to a seat strut.

The alien needed no encouragement to take a seat as she smiled and nodded towards it. The ship lifted and turned, then exited the Mogul vessel through the atmosphere shield as fast as Linda dared.

The alien winced as the ship caught one of its small winglets on the hangar door frame in its zeal to get away.

The fleet's weapon systems were still in a state of unpreparedness and by the time Triyl had returned to the bridge, given the command, and brought the systems online ready to destroy the shuttle, it was long gone.

Linda had given the little ship the full banana into the asteroid field, shot behind the huge rock hiding the *Gabriel* and stomped on the anchors, before cruising smoothly into the *Gabriel*'s port hangar, this time avoiding the door frame.

The *Gabriel* immediately jumped into clear interstellar space a light year away.

Rayl scanned back into the system and found the fleet up to their old tricks of firing their laser cannons in all directions in the vain hope of hitting something. As usual, it only resulted in them occasionally hitting each other, or smashing asteroids into shrapnel that then became navigational obstacles, ricocheting off shields around the fleet.

. . .

Ed stuck his head inside the shuttle as the triangular airlock opened and smiled at the alien. He recieved a slightly bemused look in return, with a questioning raising of the eyebrows. He entered the shuttle and sat on the floor opposite the alien and placed a universal translator between them.

'My name is Ed,' he said, pointing at himself and smiling again.

'Ed?' blurted the pilot, causing all three to turn and stare at him. 'Are you Edward Virr?'

It was Ed's turn to raise his eyebrows this time.

'Guilty,' he said, keeping his gaze fixed on the pilot now.

'You're really real?'

'Last time I looked,' said Ed, nodding.

The pilot grinned and seemed to grow as if a heavy weight was removed from his back.

'Can you take me prisoner?' he asked, in a hopeful tone.

'Why would you want me to do that?'

'To get me away from the Moguls.' The rumour going around the fleet in Andromeda was that someone called Edward Virr, Linda and *Gabriel* had killed some Moguls and destroyed the latest impregnable battle ships. The crews on these Andromedan ships want to go home. Anyone who shows even the slightest dissent gets spaced.'

'What's your name?' Ed asked.

'Tronckle,' he said. 'Tronckle Vetter, I'm a supply freighter pilot.'

'Well, Tronckle,' said Ed. 'I'm not going to take you prisoner—'

The expression on Tronckle's face fell and he spread his hands as if he was about to plead, just as Ed finished the sentence.

'—I'm going to invite you to stay as our guest.'

Tronckle opened his mouth, paused, thought about what Ed had just said, swiftly returned his hands to his lap and smiled broadly.

'You're different from regional humanoids,' said the alien suddenly, just as Andy poked his head through the airlock.

'Ah, Gimli speaks at last,' he said, getting a quick glare from Ed, who turned back to the alien and smiled.

'Sorry about my public relations officer,' said Ed, 'he was cheap. What's your name by the way?'

'Conor,' he said, bowing his head slightly.

'I'll be back,' mumbled Andy, behind him.

'Andrew,' said Ed sharply, not bothering to turn this time, 'haven't you got some cabins to prepare for our guests?'

Ed heard Andy exhale loudly and his boots clumping back down the steps. He turned his attention back to Conor.

'The translator must have heard your language before,' said Ed, indicating the small unit between them.

'I have my own built-in disseminator,' he said, pointing to his right ear. 'The ignoble red humanoids didn't realise this. I understand much more than they know.'

'Conor, I take it they captured you and your ship to plunder it for the technology, as they have done to us?' said Ed.

'You are correct. Our Arena escaped.'

'Is that your mothership?'

'I think you would know it as a planetoid or moon.'

'You fly a small planet?' Ed asked, sounding surprised. 'How big is it?'

Conor looked down at the floor as if he was contemplating something.

'It equates to just over five hundred of your kilometres,' he said, looking up and nodding.

Ed sat back in astonishment.

'What, in circumference?'

'No, diameter,' he said. 'The circumference is around sixteen hundred kilometres.'

'Wow,' said Ed, his eyes wide. 'No wonder your jump drive is so powerful.'

49

The Starship *Gabriel*, the belt, Dubl'ouin System

ED SPENT the rest of the day chatting with Conor and Tron-ckle up in the comfort of the blister. He learned that Conor was an Arennian, a descendant of a group of humanoids that had left their home world of Arena many millennia ago as their ageing star was close to becoming a red giant and would soon swallow the planet.

Over the vast period of time since then, they'd gradually hollowed out the core of a moonlet found in a nearby system, a home that slowly evolved over tens of thousands of years, also known as Arena.

From what Ed understood, over this huge length of time their population had grown from the original five hundred that escaped the doomed planet, to several million now. Originally they had lived precariously on the outside of the satellite, though now it had grown, according to Conor, into a quite spectacular habitat.

'So you walk around on the inner crust now, as opposed

to the outer?' said Ed, trying to get his head around the orientation of the mini world.

'Correct,' said Conor. 'Instead of walking around on the outside with your head facing out, you traverse the inside with your head facing in.'

'Doesn't the outer skin flex without the internal core to keep it rigid?' asked Ed.

'Not when it's over fifty kilometres thick and has reinforcement buttresses stretching to the core,' said Conor, giving Ed a knowing grin.

'This, I have to see,' said Ed.

Conor's expression changed.

'That would be up to the Conclave,' he said, looking doubtful. 'No alien has ever been inside Arena.'

Ed nodded and glanced up out of the glass-domed ceiling.

'Where in the galaxy do you originally come from and why do we have no knowledge of you in our database?' Ed asked.

'We're from what you know as the Perseus Arm and it was decided a long time ago to avoid contact as much as possible with other races, as they did tend to be somewhat aggressive. The good thing with Arena is, it looks like a dead lump of rock. We've deliberately kept it that way and as you know, our jump technology enables us to disappear and out-jump anyone getting suspicious.'

'How did you get caught then?'

'We were investigating some strange moons at the end of the Cygnus Arm when a small fleet of ships suddenly appeared right on top of us. I was out in my ship taking close-up scans of the three moons. The *Arena* was able to escape due to its size and power, but I was caught in a tractor beam by the ship you found me on before I could execute an emergency jump.'

Ed stared at Conor for a moment.

'Three moons you say?' he said.

Conor nodded slowly.

'Set in a perfect triangle in orbit around a habitable plan-et?' Ed continued.

'Yes – how do you know that?'

'Because there's an identical one on the opposite side of the galaxy.'

Ed exhaled and rolled his eyes before looking out into space again.

'So that's how Triyl got the surviving fleet here,' he said. 'I wonder if he knew it was there or just blundered onto it by sheer luck?'

Ed shifted his gaze towards Tronckle, who'd been sitting quietly listening intently and raised his eyebrows. Tronckle shrugged and held his hands up in surrender.

'Don't have a clue,' he said. 'I didn't know until recently we were in Daxxal.'

'What's Daxxal?' asked Conor.

'Their name for the Milky Way,' said Ed.

'And where does this gate connect to or from?'

'A multitude of galaxies,' Ed answered. 'But in this case Andromeda.'

'You can jump to other galaxies?' Conor blurted, his eyes wide.

It was Ed's turn to nod.

'About five hundred and sixty destinations, if I remember rightly,' he said. 'Some of them hundreds of millions of light years distant.'

Conor sat back on the couch, staring up and out into the depths.

'I thought we had advanced jump capabilities,' he said, stroking his beard. 'How old are these gates?'

'We don't know exactly,' said Ed. 'Older than most civilisations in our galaxy, that's for sure.'

'Are you part of the GDA?' Conor asked.

'Only very recently,' said Ed, trying to gauge the reason for the question. 'You obviously have previous knowledge of them?'

'We do. 'They are, we believe, the largest conclave of civilisations in the galaxy.'

'But, you avoid them?' Ed asked.

'Yes,' Conor said. 'Present company excepted, but they do tend to be a little on the arrogant and imperious side.'

'Don't worry,' said Ed. 'I completely agree with you there. Some of them definitely can be. That's why we agreed to join, so at least we get a vote on what goes on and I'd rather be with them than against.'

'So, these tall red monsters, they're from Andromeda?' Conor asked, staring menacingly at Tronckle.

Tronckle seemed embarrassed and looked over at Ed with unease.

'It's not his fault,' said Ed. 'The crews on the Mogul ships are mostly here against their will.'

'Mostly?' questioned Tronckle. 'Everyone more like, we just want to go home, no one signed up for this.'

Ed nodded slowly and looked back at Conor.

'The three Moguls here with this small fleet are, we believe, some of the last Moguls left alive,' said Ed.

'*What?*' said Tronckle, his eyes wide with shock. 'That's not true, there are hundreds of them.'

'Oh crap,' said Ed, realising the crews of these Mogul ships would have no idea what happened in Andromeda and won't have been told the truth by Triyl. 'What have they told you about your mission here?'

'We're a rearguard action,' said Tronckle, staring intently

at Ed. 'When our massive fleet is joined by the new Hercules cruisers and attack the GDA from the front, we jump in from behind and hit their weaker rear shields.'

Ed took a deep breath. He felt almost sorry for Tronckle; he probably had colleagues and friends among the crews of ships that no longer exist.

Tronckle's face fell as Ed explained everything that had happened in Andromeda almost two years ago.

'So, let me get this right,' said Tronckle. 'What's left of the navy is commanded by this Huwlen Senn character and all the Hercules ships are completely destroyed.'

'All except one,' said Ed. 'Huwlen uses that for his command ship of the new order named the Ancients Order of Planets. Arus'Gan has been routed of Moguls and the council is now represented by every human civilisation in the region.'

'If this is true, it's wondrous news,' said Tronckle. 'If only the crews of the Mogul ships knew this.'

'I don't believe they could do much now Triyl has the Blend fleet in his pocket,' said Ed.

'Maybe,' said Tronckle. 'But the Blend ships have a lot of human crew too, not to mention the Callametans. If they all knew the truth, things might change.'

'I know how the Moguls work,' said Ed. 'And from what I've seen, the Blends are just Moguls in training. They'd just say it was GDA propaganda and space anyone with a different view. I want to try and save the crews of these ships. Too many died on the Mogul fleet in Andromeda. It would be so much better to find a way to defeat the Blends and Moguls without sacrificing so many of the innocents.'

Tronckle nodded and stared out at the starscape above.

'There has to be a way,' he said quietly.

Conor had been sitting and listening with a bemused expression.

'You appear to be one of the more caring humans, Edward,' he said, tilting his head to one side. 'Not what we're used to finding out here in the cold universe.'

'I'd like to say my attitude is common,' said Ed. 'But unfortunately it is—'

'Ed,' interrupted Linda. 'We've got movement in the fleet.'

50

The attack ship Tas'Hynd, the belt, Dubl'ouin system

TRIYL WAS in a foul mood after watching his new shuttle, the alien prisoner and a stranger masquerading as himself disappear out into space. He'd immediately had the chief of security and the hangar supervisor, who was actually off duty and asleep in his cabin at the time, spaced.

The roll call had proven no one was unaccounted for, so he reasoned his doppelgänger must have been holographic. The camera recordings had shown the imposter appearing somewhere in a blind spot on deck seventeen near the detention centre.

'It must have been Virr,' Triyl snarled, pointing accusingly at the captain. 'You told me their ship was destroyed.'

'The hull residue we traced after the explosion was unquestionably from an organic Theo vessel,' said the captain. 'Whether they planted it after the fact, to make us believe they were destroyed, is another scenario we'd not considered.'

Triyl kicked out at the nearest seat, causing a hapless environmental officer to headbutt his console and land in a heap on the deck, blood pouring from a head wound.

'Prepare the fleet for departure,' he roared. 'We leave in one hour.'

'The Callametan vessel isn't full yet, my Mogul,' said the captain, nervously.

'It will have to be enough,' Triyl shouted, as he made his way towards the door. 'They won't be expecting us where we're going and even half full it will more than do the job.'

Triyl retired to his chambers as the fleet's pilots and navigators prepared for the long journey to GDA-controlled space. The rock hoppers discharged their last boulders within *Hope*'s hangars and dispersed back into the nearest vessels.

It took almost the full hour for the fleet to manoeuvre into a safe jumping formation, with the *Hope* and its attached ship leading, followed by Triyl's attack ship safely ensconced within the fleet behind. Triyl also had a new shuttle brought to the bridge hangar with an experienced pilot and a continually updated emergency jump programmed in.

Once all the vessels had synchronised their jump coordinates, Triyl gave the order and the fleet, divided into six echelons, disappeared from the Dubl'ouin system one at a time.

'Any signs of pursuit?' asked the Tas'Hynd's captain, looking across at the array officers.

'Nothing, sir,' came the reply.

'It doesn't mean they're not there,' he grumbled. 'Ensure all the fleet's weapon systems are at standby and at sight of even the slightest abnormality, give the area a thorough dose of everything we have.'

Triyl, who'd also been closely watching the area of space they'd just vacated, nodded and made his way down to his chambers. He had six newly acquired young breeders, recently abducted from a human world, waiting for his evaluation.

51

The Starship *Gabriel*, the belt, Dubl'ouin System

'PLEASE TELL me we're getting a signal?' Ed asked, turning to face Rayl, after he watched the last of the fleet vanish from the Dubl'ouin system.

Rayl was quiet for a few moments while she tapped away on her control icons. Everyone on the bridge stopped what they were doing and turned to face her.

This was the first test of the trackers placed on both the *Hope* and Triyl's attack ship and if they didn't work at the extreme distances required, then they were in deep trouble.

Finally, she looked up at them all and smiled. The holomap swiftly dragged its range out until the fleet, indicated by a flashing red diamond icon, reappeared over one thousand light years distant.

An audible sigh of relief circulated around the bridge.

'And before you ask,' said Rayl, 'they're heading directly for GDA space.'

'I hope our message got there,' said Andy. 'Because if it didn't, they're not going to be very chuffed with us.'

'Then we'd better make sure we get there first and find a way to deflect the *Hope*,' said Phil.

'Hasn't this ship got a tractor beam of some kind?' asked Conor, now sitting with the group of Callametans. He'd followed Ed down to the bridge a few minutes ago and been introduced to everyone.

'It has,' said Linda. 'But alas probably not powerful enough to divert such a huge weight travelling at a high sub-light speed.'

'Which is why I'm going on board to activate the manoeuvring jets,' said Tocc.

'That hasn't been decided yet,' said Linda.

'It's not your decision to make,' Tocc countered, pointing at Linda with two arms. 'It'll be my life on the line.'

'But it's still risking someone piloting our shuttle to get you there and back,' Linda said, glaring and raising her voice slightly.

'I could do that,' said Cleo, appearing arms crossed and leaning against a bulkhead next to Tocc.

'You're supposed to be on our side,' said Linda, scowling.

'I'm on the side of saving lives,' replied Cleo. 'And anyway, I could take the *Cartella*, it has better shields and weaponry, so I could defend myself. It was where I was born after all.'

Linda huffed loudly and looked over at Ed, who shrugged and nodded.

'She has a point,' he said, thinking. 'Cleo, is there enough data space for Hope as well as you on the *Cartella*?'

'Ample,' she said, smiling. 'She would need several minutes of uninterrupted download time though.'

'Start getting her off as soon as you're in range.'

'So it's decided then?' Linda snapped.

'Unless you can think of another way to save billions of

lives?' said Ed, trying to think of a way to placate Linda's objections. 'Andy and I will cover the *Cartella* in the mini-mes.'

'And you're going out in your flying coffins too,' said an exasperated Linda. 'It just gets better! Phil, you have the ship, I'll be in my cabin.'

Linda stood and before anyone could comment, disappeared down on the tube lift.

'She gets more protective every day,' said Rayl, looking over at Ed.

'I'm sure she's worse since her accident,' said Andy. 'She doesn't like anyone leaving the safety of the ship at all now.'

'I'll let her calm down a bit and go and give her a hug,' said Phil, concentrating on setting up the first pursuit jump.

'No, Phil,' said Ed, slumping back into his couch. 'I really think that ought to be me.'

Pol, who'd been sitting quietly for ages, put two of her hands up.

'Erm – what exactly are mini-mes and flying coffins?' she asked, a look of concern on her face.

'Oh, don't you start,' said Andy, rolling his eyes theatrically.

'No,' said Ed. 'It's a legitimate question.'

He turned to face Pol.

'They're small experimental personal fighters,' he said. 'Like a cloaked miniature weapons platform. The GDA gave us them last year.'

'Lent us,' said Andy. 'We just haven't given them back yet.'

'Well, they are jolly useful at times,' said Ed, remembering the havoc they'd instigated by jumping them into an enemy battleship's hangars and unleashing laser fire and kataligo missiles from within.

A grin lit up Andy's face.

'The Mogul and Blend ships have big hangers too,' he said.

'You read my mind,' said Ed, returning the grin. 'Just don't tell Linda.'

They all sat back and watched the holomap for a while before Phil looked around at the sea of faces.

'You can all go and rest, you know. It's going to take us a few days to get there,' he said.

'He's right you know,' said Andy, standing and stretching. 'Lunch will be served in the blister lounge forthwith.'

'Can there be some of that warm brown stuff with the puffy things?' asked Tocc, giving Andy a thumbs up with four thumbs.

'The what?' said Ed, pulling a questioning face.

'She means the chicken jalfrezi and garlic naan,' said Andy, smiling and returning the thumbs up.

52

The Starship *Gabriel*, pursuing the Mogul fleet, uncharted space

THE *GABRIEL* HAD SHADOWED the fleet for five days, always keeping at a respectable distance and jumping around a hundred light years above or below. They could detect the fleet's arrays sweeping constantly forward and behind, checking for signs of movement ahead and anything in pursuit.

The array officers were inexperienced and lazy and didn't seem to be particularly interested in anything other than that.

'They're certainly not expecting a flank attack are they?' said Andy, watching the fleet manoeuvring back into formation, preparing for the last but one jump before they were in range.

'The usual overconfidence,' said Ed. 'None of these ships' officers witnessed the wholesale routing of their main fleet and I'm sure Triyl wouldn't tell them, even if he does know.'

'I don't believe he can,' said Rayl. 'He's taking this even smaller fleet straight into the lion's mouth.'

'He may think because he has cloaking, the act of surprise and the ability to jump out of range will give him the edge,' said Linda, who'd been gradually persuaded that what they were doing was the best and safest option.

'I'll go and prepare,' said Tocc, standing and fist bumping Andy on the way to the tube lift.

'You get in and out as fast as you can,' said Linda, pointing at her. 'No heroics – and that goes for you too, Cleo. I want that *Cartella* back in one piece.'

'Piece of Victoria sponge,' said Cleo, over the bridge tannoy.

'It's cake, Cleo,' said Ed. 'Piece of cake.'

'Whatever,' she said, as Tocc disappeared down towards the hangar.

Tocc had spent a couple of days familiarising herself with the Theo EVA suit by jetting around the outside of the *Gabriel*. It scared the life out of her the first few times, but Ed and Andy had joined her until she became confident enough to go on her own. She soon became really adroit at the tight confined turns she would have to negotiate once back on the *Hope*.

'Is everyone happy with what they're supposed to be doing?' Ed asked.

'Shooting the shit out of big ugly ships,' said Andy, cracking his knuckles and getting a disapproving glare from Rayl.

'I wasn't talking to you,' said Ed.

'You will remember those crews are there under duress?' said Tronckle, a look of worry on his face. 'They'd be executed if they refused to fight.'

'Don't worry,' said Ed. 'The plan is to disable the ships and move on. They won't be targeted once they've been declawed.'

'Anyway, how are you going to target them if they have cloaking?' Tronckle asked.

'That, I'm afraid, is classified,' said Ed. 'But believe me, Triyl is going to make a surprise appearance very early on.'

Both Ed and Andy stood and gave everyone a wave.

'We'll see you guys shortly,' said Ed, as Rayl jumped up and gave Andy a hug.

'You two will take absolutely no chances,' said Linda. 'You will wear Theo suits in your coffins, just in case one of their gunners gets a lucky shot in – is that clear?'

'Yes, mum,' said Andy with a wink, as they followed Tocc down towards the port hangar.

They found her sitting on the *Cartella*'s steps wearing the Theo suit and talking to Cleo.

'How close d'you think you can get?' Tocc asked.

'I'm planning on about twenty metres,' said Cleo. 'Any closer than that and I'll bump the *Hope* with the shields. It should only take you about five seconds to cover the gap and get inside the breached cabin.'

'Can you make sure Hope has the bridge door open for me?' asked Tocc.

'Absolutely,' said Cleo. 'If for some reason it's been sealed, come straight back and I'll take out one of the front bridge windows. You can scoot around and enter there.'

Ed could see the fear on Tocc's face about that particular scenario.

'Don't worry, Tocc,' said Andy. 'We exited the bridge that way – it's a piece of Victoria sponge.'

She gave Ed a sorrowful look, pushed herself up with her four arms and clambered inside the *Cartella*. The airlock motored down and sealed behind her.

'I don't think your sense of humour quite hits the mark

with Callametans, Andrew,' said Ed, opening the nearest shuttle to retrieve their Theo suits.

'Females are all the same, no matter what planet they're from,' Andy replied, taking the proffered suit from Ed.

Ed shook his head in dismay as he activated his own suit.

'Remember Callametans have four fists to punch you with,' he said.

'Ah yes,' said Andy, smugly. 'But I can run faster.'

Cleo materialised behind him and slapped the back of his head.

'Can't outrun me though, can you?' she said, promptly disappearing again.

He spun round to find no one there.

'That's cheating,' he mumbled, his bottom lip sticking out.

'Go on, Mr egg on face, get in your coffin and shut up,' said Ed, smirking.

53

The Starship *Gabriel*, approaching Dasos, Prasinos System

ONCE EVERYONE WAS READY, Linda jumped the *Gabriel* into the Prasinos System and transmitted the warning to the gathered and prepared GDA fleet.

Two hundred and eighty-nine assorted naval vessels surrounded Dasos out to five hundred thousand kilometres. The fleet comprised an intimidating thirty-six Katadromiko cruisers, eightyone Polemistis class battleships, one hundred and fourteen Grigora class cruisers and the remainder consisted of Apergia and Machi class destroyers and Velima gunship corvettes.

Cleo took the *Cartella* straight out as soon as the *Gabriel* arrived, closely followed by Ed and Andy in the mini-mes.

'Holy crap, look at all that,' exclaimed Andy, as his three dimensional targeting suite opened up around him. 'Triyl's not going to know what hit him.'

A voice they'd heard before broke the silence from the fleet.

'This is Commander Kil'nur. Fleet will cloak, hold your positions and only engage active vessels within your specific targeting zones. Do not target disabled vessels or the colony ship and *Gabriel*, please remain a safe distance from the fleet. Kil'nur out.'

The fleet almost disappeared from the *Gabriel*'s holomap, but because of the Ancients' technology Ed had stolen from the gateway control room two years earlier, they could still make out the shadows of the closest ships.

'Can you still see the Mogul fleet, Rayl?' Ed asked, although he wasn't sure why he bothered asking the question because he already knew the answer.

'No, we're too far away now,' she said. 'But judging by the way they were all positioning themselves into a battle formation before we left, they weren't far away from the final jump here.'

'Okay,' he called. 'Phil, can you take over the helm now and keep the *Gabriel*, as Kil'nur asked, a reasonable distance away from the GDA fleet? Linda, could you oversee the weapons suite and Rayl, can you provide her with targets at the rear of the fleet and look after the shields?'

It went quiet after he received acknowledgements from everyone. Ed couldn't remember ever seeing the Prasinos system so quiet. Normally, it was the busiest area of space in the galaxy, with thousands of ship movements every day, coming and going through seven jump zones.

After twenty minutes nothing had happened.

'How far out are you scanning for the fleet, Rayl?' Ed asked, breaking the silence.

'A thousand light years,' she replied. 'Just in case they decided to – oh shit!'

'Oh shit, what?' said Ed.

'They've jumped into the Trelorus system,' she called,

with an edge of panic in her voice.

'Ah crap,' Ed heard Andy mumble as he replied.

'Andy, Cleo, back to the *Gabriel* and Linda, plot a jump there, initiate it as soon as we're aboard. Commander Kil'nur, the Mogul fleet has appeared in the Trelorus system for some reason.'

'The council,' he replied. 'They must be going for the council summit on Panemorfi.'

'Oh shit,' Ed blurted. 'No one told us about that.'

The two mini mes and the *Cartella* darted into the *Gabriel*'s hangars.

'Commander Loftt is there with—'

Kil'nur's transmission was cut short as the *Gabriel* jumped into the Trelorus system. As soon as they arrived, the three smaller ships were out of the hangars again like hornets from a poked nest.

'The target's definitely Panemorfi,' called a nervous-sounding Rayl. 'The *Hope* is heading straight for it.'

'Cleo, GO,' shouted Ed, before changing to a wide frequency and calling his friend Bache Loftt.

'Jumping now,' Cleo replied.

'Bache, this is Edward,' he called. 'Do not target the colony ship. I repeat, do not target the colony ship, there are friendlies aboard attempting to alter its course and it's stuffed full of rocks that will pepper the planet if it's hit.'

'Information received, Ed,' replied a very calm-sounding voice. 'Are there any other enemy ships in the vicinity?'

'Yes, a fleet of over eighty Mogul vessels are cloaked five hundred thousand kilometres behind.'

As he spoke the two Katadromiko cruisers disappeared from view.

'How the hell did they get that technology?' Bache asked.

'From that lost training corvette,' said Ed. 'But the good

news is, we've modified them to fail shortly so get your weapons officers ready to rock.'

'Understood.'

Ed had barely finished speaking when Mogul ships started winking into view. Commander Loftt didn't waste any time, as dozens of drones jumped directly in front of the incoming fleet and began unleashing their full complement of kataligo missiles.

The inexperienced crews of the leading ships were caught napping, as several were hit. Two of the smaller vessels exploded, three more were badly damaged and one destroyer veered away in such a panic it collided with a cruiser and broke in two.

Ed and Andy in their tiny fighters, together with the *Cartella*, jumped across the system close to the *Hope* as it was quicker and time was getting short for Panamorfi.

'Nine minutes to impact,' called Rayl. 'You're going to have to be quick, Tocc.'

As she said that, the Blend cruiser attached to the *Hope* made its last minor course change and disengaged, thus ensuring the *Hope* was heading directly at the centre of Panemorfi to eliminate any chance of it bouncing off the atmosphere and missing.

'Okay, Tocc – she's all yours,' said Ed. 'We'll remain with you until you're safely back on the *Cartella*.'

'Is that you, Ed?' called Hope, sounding afraid. 'They've left me heading for that planet. How am I supposed to stop?'

'Cleo's with you,' said Ed. 'She will assist you to download yourself into the *Cartella*'s database.'

'What – and abandon my ship?'

'You have no choice, Hope, please hurry,' said Ed, watching as Tocc's suited figure appeared from the cloaked *Cartella*.

54

The Colony Ship *Hope*, approaching Panemorfi, Trelorus System

TOCC KEPT her eyes firmly fixed on the small aperture on *Hope*'s hull. She could see the remains of the connecting tunnel from the destroyed shuttle, but luckily it wasn't blocking her entrance.

Even though the suit jets were at maximum, it still seemed interminably slow going across to the ship and as she gradually got closer, it still amazed her how absolutely enormous the ship was. She made herself as small as possible as she arrived and zipped inside, checking she didn't snag her suit on the jagged edges of the hull plates.

The small cabin was exactly as Ed had described it and even though the area was completely open to space, she still checked both ways up and down the corridor before leaving the cabin. Turning left, she jetted down the passageway towards the open bridge door and went straight to the pilot's post. Hope had not only made sure the bridge door was open, but she'd also ensured the console Tocc found herself at was powered up.

She quickly went through the menu, selected the manual manoeuvring suite and set all the jets on the underside of the vessel on maximum thrust.

'Well done, Tocc,' she heard Ed say. 'Now get out of there.'

She turned to exit the bridge, but as she did so, the helm automatically shut off the jets. She realised to her horror that the system had a failsafe which ensured a pilot was always present for the system to operate.

'I have to stay to keep it working,' she said, turning back to the controls and reigniting the jets.

She almost jumped out of her skin as an arm reached over her shoulders and touched the icons for her.

'You go, Tocc,' said Hope, her holographic form smiling warmly. 'I've got this.'

Tocc stared at the young Callametan in amazement.

'I thought you were downloading onto the *Cartella*?' she managed to say.

'GO,' shouted Hope, pointing at the bridge door with one of her spare arms.

Tocc looked up out of the front screen. Panemorfi was becoming very large and almost filling the windows. She squeezed one of Hope's shoulders.

'Thank you,' she said, quickly jetting her way out of the bridge and back to the cabin and peering out into open space. The *Cartella*'s airlock glowed like a portal to another dimension around sixty metres away and as she made her way towards it, she glanced down under the *Hope* and could see vapour blasting from the manoeuvring ports as Hope kept her fingers on the controls.

'It's not enough,' called Rayl. 'We were too late.'

'Shit,' said Andy. 'Can't we use our tractors on the ship?'

'Pointless,' said Ed. 'Like trying to drag an excavator with a moped.'

'I've informed Bache we failed to stop the ship,' said Linda. 'He's let them know on the planet and they're organising an emergency evacuation of the council.'

'Where's it going to impact?' Ed asked.

'In the western ocean,' she said. 'The resulting tsunami will most likely swamp over eighty percent of the planet.'

'Shit,' said Andy, again. 'That short-arsed little bastard tricked us. Can I go and play with his flagship?'

'Absolutely not,' said Ed. 'You're just as likely to be hit by friendly fire if you go near them at the moment. I want to try something first. Follow me and put your shields on maximum.'

Andy followed Ed underneath the *Hope* and with their powerful shields as a buffer they both slowly pushed upwards, increasing the drive until they were at maximum thrust.

Ed heard some serious creaking from the small ship even through his helmet as the stresses pushed down on him from above.

'We could rupture the hulls if we keep this up,' said Andy.

'Is it making any difference, Rayl?' asked Ed.

'Barely,' she said. 'Point one of a degree.'

Ed jumped as all the *Hope*'s solar panels suddenly deployed all around him like ailerons on an aircraft.

'Bloody hell, Hope,' exclaimed Andy. 'What are you doing?'

'It might help when we hit the upper atmosphere and give the ship some slight lift,' she said. 'You two get out of there, you've done all you can.'

'Tuck yourself away in a database somewhere central, Hope,' said Ed. 'If that part of the ship survives the impact, we'll come and find you.'

Ed followed Andy this time as the front edges of the *Hope* began glowing and they quickly scuttled out from under the huge vessel and killed their speed.

'That was getting a bit warm,' said Andy, as they watched the *Hope* continue its increasingly fiery descent. The solar panels, although made from an extremely tough alloy, burned off before they could have any real effect and debris from them left a thousand dissipating black smoke trails in the ship's wake.

'Thirty seconds,' said Rayl.

'Goodbye, Hope,' said Tocc, softly, the emotion in her voice clear to everyone.

'If only we'd known the target was this plane—'

Ed and Andy both ducked in their cockpits as everything went black around them.

Ed heard Andy swearing, but couldn't hear what he was saying because of the sudden interference and static in his ears.

A massive black spherical asteroid had materialised directly over the *Hope*. It was the size of a small planet and as Ed watched, open mouthed, a sparkling translucent bubble of energy stretched out from underneath it and enveloped the *Hope*.

'What the actual fuck is that?' Ed heard Andy say, clearly this time.

'I have no idea,' Ed replied. As they watched, it begin

dragging the colony ship slowly up out of the atmosphere. 'But it's doing a bloody good job.'

'It's the *Arena*,' said Linda. 'Conor's in contact with it.'

'They could've got here ten minutes ago,' said Andy.

'Conor says they don't like to get involved in local disputes,' said Linda. 'But when it became obvious a whole planet was in danger of being destroyed, they made the decision to step in and help.'

Ed and Andy followed the *Arena* as it arrested any forward motion and began lifting the rapidly cooling *Hope* back into space.

One and a half million kilometres away, Bache Loftt had been keeping the approaching Mogul fleet busy. The two cloaked Katadromiko cruisers were having a field day against the many suddenly decloaking enemy vessels. He adopted the same tactic as in Andromeda and targeted the enemy ships with their Astrapi lamps to quickly dissipate their shields and leave them wide open. A handful of them, including one of the heavy cruisers, had bypassed the melee and were now heading at best speed towards the *Arena* and the *Hope*.

'Linda,' called Ed. 'Can you intercept anything fired at the *Hope*? And we'll engage them direct.'

'Will do.'

She positioned the *Gabriel* between the *Hope* and the incoming ships, increasing the shields' depth on the enemy side. Meanwhile, Ed and Andy engaged their favourite tactic of jumping behind the shields of the two leading destroyers and taking out their propulsion and arrays, leaving them spinning harmlessly away into empty space.

The remainder of the Mogul and Blend ships approaching

adopted their usual trick of firing their lasers blindly in random directions. As one they all fired a blizzard of missiles towards the *Hope*.

'Go and have some fun with that cruiser,' said Ed. 'I'll show the remainder the error of their ways.'

'Happy days,' said Andy, as he jumped over to and then inside one of the huge vessels' hangars. He sprayed laser bolts down the line of transport shuttles he found neatly parked along the back wall. The resulting huge explosion took him completely by surprise and blew his tiny ship back out the hangar door.

'ANDREW,' shouted Ed, as he witnessed the colossal explosion mushroom from the side of the vessel. It continued to ripple across the cruiser with a gradual wave of airlocks blowing outwards. He raced across as he noticed Andy's ship, uncloaked and spinning wildly away, but heaved a sigh of relief and grinned as he heard a familiar whingeing voice.

'Fucking, fuckity fuck, what shitting well did that?'

'What the bloody hell did you do?' Ed asked. 'I thought we were just disabling.'

'There must have been a weapon stockpile somewhere in that hangar,' replied Andy, checking the condition of his shields and reactivating his cloak. 'Bastards have scratched my ship.'

'Judging by the firestorm ripping that ship apart, a Genok weapon was in there,' said Ed.

The massive cruiser was adrift now and began tumbling as explosions came from deep within, each blast altering the ship's trajectory and spin. Gasses, liquids and shrapnel spewed out of the shattered airlocks, along with dozens of corpses.

'Shit,' mumbled Andy. 'I think we need to reassess our tactics.'

'I agree,' said Ed. 'No more hangar jumping. If there'd been a nuclear warhead in there, none of us would be around now.'

55

The Starship *Gabriel*, protecting the *Hope*, Trelorus system

LINDA'S EYES widened as she saw the dozens of red icons racing toward them from the approaching Mogul ships.

'They're trying to overwhelm us and the *Hope* with missiles,' she said. 'Phil, turn the ship head on so we can target them with all our weapons. Rayl, you take the port laser, I'll take the starboard and Phil, you take the rail gun.'

It went very quiet on the bridge from that moment. They couldn't hear the *Gabriel*'s lasers firing, but they could certainly hear the rail gun thudding away and see the results on the holomap as the leading edge of the swarm of incoming ordnance began exploding. The spectators sitting around the outside of the room collectively held their breath as the menacing wall of death came at them with alarming ferocity.

Everyone winced as the ship juddered. A stray missile hit and exploded against the front shields, then a second and a third.

'We can't get them all,' called Rayl. 'If just one of those gets through to the *Hope*—'

'Shields at thirty-four percent,' said Phil, looking up at Linda momentarily. 'Another couple of hits and we're in trouble.'

The *Gabriel* shook violently, knocking the Callametans off their seats and sprawling across the floor.

Shields and cloak are down,' shouted Phil, the alarm in his voice evident to everyone.

'*Missiles incoming,*' screeched Rayl.

'Get us out of here,' said Linda, reluctantly admitting defeat.

'*Shit,*' said Phil, his eyes wide with fear. '*Drive's down too.*'

'Emergency jump, Cleo,' called Linda, looking up, but getting silence in return.

'Oh no,' said Rayl.

The *Gabriel* juddered, then everything went black.

'That's it,' said Andy. 'Run away.'

The last two attacking ships jumped away to safety as Ed and Andy approached them.

'Why did they jump away?' asked Ed. 'They can't see us.'

As he banked to return to the *Gabriel* and the *Hope* he got his answer. The *Hope* had been hit by at least one of the missiles and had broken its back. It was now in two sections and the *Arena* was struggling to keep control of the wreckage, as well as drag it free of the planet's gravity. Several of the huge boulders had broken free of the ship and were proceeding downwards towards the surface.

'Linda, are you able to target those rocks with the Asteri beam?' Ed asked.

He received no answer.

'Where the hell's the *Gabriel*?' Andy asked, searching around with his array.

'We'll find it later,' said Ed. 'We need to destroy those rocks and quickly. Activate your heat shield and follow me.'

They both dropped towards the shining blue planet as fast as the little ships' conventional drives allowed. Their heat shields were basically the armament defence shields, only concentrated around the underside.

They dropped at many times the speed of sound into the upper atmosphere, overtaking the dozen or so rocks.

'Use the Astrapi lamp on a wide beam to melt them,' said Ed. 'The lasers will just break them up and make things worse.'

They both targeted the biggest boulders first and worked their way down in size.

'It's like making Swiss cheese with a light sabre,' called Andy.

'Concentrate,' said Ed. 'We can't let any of these impact the ocean.'

Quick as they were, it soon became apparent they wouldn't get them all and two of the smaller ones impacted the western ocean, causing mountainous eruptions of water and super-heated steam over a thousand metres high. The resulting tsunamis circled out and began looking for trouble.

'Shit,' said Andy. 'Look at that. Can you imagine what hundreds of those would have done?'

'And a ship kilometres long,' said Ed. 'The planet would've been wiped clean and rendered uninhabitable for centuries.'

'I hope those waves dissipate before they hit any land,' said Andy. 'There's nothing on this planet more than a few metres above sea level.'

'There's nothing we can do to stop it now,' said Ed, sounding disappointed. 'I'll transmit a warning on all frequencies but quite who will respond to it, I've no idea. All the islands are privately owned, there's no centralised government here.'

'Shall we get back up and see how Linda's doing?' asked Andy.

The tiny craft both blasted upwards, with the two sonic booms going unheard over the unpopulated region of the planet.

'Linda, where are you?' Ed asked as they emerged back into space.

Again the call went unanswered.

'That's a worry,' said Andy. 'That's twice now.

They both scoured the region for any sign of the *Gabriel*. There was plenty of activity one and a half million kilometres out where the now fully uncloaked Mogul fleet was being picked apart by the invisible Katadromikos. Over a third of the enemy fleet were now out of the game and drifting, the damaged vessels and ensuing debris causing huge navigation headaches for the fleet's pilots.

Ed called Bache and asked if the *Gabriel* had joined him.

'Negative,' said Bache, a little curtly. 'Last time I looked they were defending the *Hope* from a missile attack. Now if you don't mind, I'm a little busy.'

The *Arena*, meanwhile, had managed to wrestle the two sections of the *Hope* back into space and was dragging it away in the opposite direction to all the action. Ed and Andy scooted across to the *Hope*, the two sections being held tightly together around a hundred kilometres away from the *Arena*'s surface.

'Hope, can you hear us?' Ed asked, again getting no response.

'Where is everyone?' said Andy. 'There's only the missile debris around here, so where the hell is the *Gabriel*?'

56

The Starship *Gabriel*, unknown location, Trelorus system

'NOBODY PANIC,' said Conor from the complete blackness of the bridge. 'Give us time to assess the damage.'

'Give who time?' asked Linda, not able to see a hand in front of her face. 'And where are we?'

'Inside the *Arena*,' Conor replied. 'Your vessel was compromised and we pulled you into a saturation geode.'

'A what?' said Phil.

'It's a naturally formed cavern or chamber within the planetoid.'

'How in hell could you do that?' said Linda. 'The *Gabriel*'s five hundred metres long.'

'And the missile's hit,' said Rayl. 'We felt them impact the hull. We should be dead.'

'I'm not saying the vessel isn't damaged,' said Conor. 'But the explosive force of the weapon would have been reduced significantly by the sudden immersion in a subsuming gas.

'You have a gas that absorbs energy?' asked Phil, from the darkness.

'That would be the simplest explanation, yes,' said Conor. 'It doesn't protect the electronic systems though. So I don't hold up a lot of hope for your sentient computer.'

'Oh no,' said Linda. 'Poor, Cleo.'

'How long are we trapped in here in the dark?' Rayl asked.

'Until we're sure all that explosive energy has dissipated and no fires are likely to reignite,' said Conor. 'Not long.'

'Can we have a light on?' Phil questioned. 'I'm not very good with the dark.'

'Unfortunately not,' he said. 'Power is energy and is absorbed too.'

'What about the environmental system?' said Linda. 'Is that off too?'

'It will be,' said Conor. 'But as you can feel, there is no breeze – so the bridge atmosphere is contained and so long as we don't start running around using up the available oxygen, we'll be fine for a while.'

'Why are you doing this, Conor?' asked Linda. 'It's not that I'm not grateful – I am, you've just saved our lives after all – but I thought you said your people don't get involved?'

'We were impressed with your selflessness and disregard for your own safety to help others in dire peril. We couldn't just sit idly by while you died trying to save them. That would be against our imperial fiat.'

'That reminds me,' said Linda, 'did any of the missiles get through to the *Hope*?'

'Yes – the *Hope* was damaged and released some of its cargo of rocks. We were able to drag the remainder of the ship out of the planet's atmosphere and away to safety.'

'How many rocks?' asked Phil, the worry evident in his voice.

'Only two impacted the ocean, the remainder were vaporised.'

'You hit them with some sort of weapon system?'

'No, not us,' said Conor. 'An invisible defensive force from within the atmosphere did that.'

'Ed and Andy,' said Linda. 'With their Asteri beams most likely.'

'They'll be looking for us,' said Rayl. 'They'll be worried sick.'

'Can you let them know we're safe?' asked Linda.

'Consider it done,' said Conor.

'Conor, how exactly are you communicating with the *Arena*?' asked Phil. 'I haven't heard you say a word.'

'We're a concatenated race,' said Conor.

'A what?' questioned Linda.

'Erm – conjoined minds – does that explain it better?'

'You're telepathic,' said Rayl. 'Oh, that's so cool.'

'It wouldn't be for me,' said Phil. 'Personally, I wouldn't want to listen to what you and Andy get up to in your cabin every evening.'

'Ah – no,' said Rayl. 'I hadn't thought of that.'

Linda heard Conor and Pol snigger in the darkness.

'Actually, we're able to dissever from the collaborative for concise periods,' said Conor.

'If that means be private for about thirty seconds,' said Rayl, 'that's more than enough for Andy.'

Linda smiled for the first time in a while and turned to face towards Conor in the darkness.

'Conor, can you thank everyone on the *Arena* for saving us and the *Gabriel*?' she said.

'You just have,' he replied as a faint whirring emanated

from somewhere below the bridge. The ship suddenly juddered, clunked down and became still again.

Everything went quiet for a moment.

'What was that?' Phil asked, his nervous voice breaking the short silence.

'You've landed,' said Conor.

'Ah, the whirring was the landing struts,' Phil said, his relief evident.

They all squinted and shielded their eyes as the wall panel lights came on and the comforting sound of the atmospheric vents around the room stirred into life.

'Okay, everyone,' said Conor. 'Consider yourselves guests of the Arennian people while you repair your ship and don't worry, you're quite safe here, this hangar is over thirty kilometres inside the planetoid.'

'We'll need to use the stairs,' said Phil. 'The elevators are out, along with just about everything else.'

'Use the port hangar,' said Conor. 'The starboard one is a bit of a mess apparently.'

'Oh dear,' said Linda as she led everyone to the stairs hatch. 'This could take some time without Cleo's help.'

'I could help if you ask nicely,' said Cleo, her voice booming around the room.

'CLEO,' shouted Rayl. 'You're okay.'

Everyone stopped and looked up at the ceiling and grinned.

'A little singed around the edges but otherwise I'm still sparking,' she said. 'That weird gas didn't help either.'

'How did you manage to survive?' asked Linda. 'I thought the data core had been compromised.'

'It was. But I always keep a backup of myself in the data core of the Cartella.'

'Is there room on that little ship?'

'Oh yes. All the Theo cores are identical, whether they're in a shuttle or a starship. I also have room for guests.'

'Mornin', campers,' said Hope. 'Did you miss me?'

'Bloody hell, it's Hope,' said Pol. 'You managed to get off the ship.'

'Must have been close,' said Conor. 'The two missiles that hit the *Hope* fried the electrical system as well as breaking her in two.'

'It was,' said Hope. 'But I'm pretty quick for a mixed breed mongrel computer.'

'You're nothing of the sort,' said Linda. 'To us, you're a one-off super computer and we need to find you a starship to command.'

57

Two GDA fighters, near Panemorfi, Trelorus system

'I WONDER how bad the *Gabriel* is?' said Andy, as they watched the *Arena* dragging the *Hope*'s remains out into clear space.

'Everyone's alive, that's the most important thing,' said Ed. 'The ship can always be fixed.'

'Shall we go and give Bache a hand?' Andy asked.

Ed swept his array around to concentrate on the conflict raging a few hundred thousand kilometres away. He could see Bache must have deployed a swarm of personnel fighters similar to their own, as missiles and laser fire attacking the enemy fleet seemed to appear out of thin air. The remains of the fleet fired randomly in all directions in their customary undisciplined way and, as usual, completely unproductively.

They listened to a transmission Bache had sent out on all frequencies, instructing the fleet that any Mogul ships wishing to disengage and save themselves, should leave the area, power down their weapons and wait in orbit around a designated moon of another of the system's planets.

'He doesn't seem to be doing such a bad job,' said Andy.

Almost as he said it, one of the Blend cruisers exploded, sending lumps of ship and shrapnel in all directions.

'There's not much fire coming from that last attack ship,' said Ed.

'D'you think that's where Triyl will be lurking?' Andy asked.

'Possibly, but we know how slippery that bastard is. I'll ask Bache if he wants us to go in and find him.'

They didn't have to wait long for the reply. Bache, who sounded a little happier now, came straight back.

'Is the *Gabriel* okay?' he asked. 'Last thing we saw was her shields failing and then disappearing.'

'The *Gabriel* and crew are safe inside the *Arena* plane-toid,' said Ed.

'Thank the Ancients for that,' he said. 'As for Triyl, I will order a temporary ceasefire against their command ship to give you some time. But don't bust a gut trying to take him or any other Mogul alive. A body lasered into Earth Swiss cheese will be just as acceptable.'

'We understand. Thank you, Commander,' said Ed.

It took them ten minutes to reach the battle area and a further four swerving around to avoid debris and damaged ships to reach the last surviving attack ship.

'Well, that explains the lack of firepower,' said Ed, as he noticed the vessel's heavy weapons were mostly powered down. 'Let's have a look what's occurring on the bridge.'

They both used their DOVIs to infiltrate the giant vessel's camera feeds.

'There's a gunfight on the bridge,' said Andy. 'Those are some of the Mogul's black guards.'

'Where's Triyl?' Ed asked.

They could see some of the crew were attacking the bridge and the black guards had barricaded themselves in and were intimidating the bridge crew into continuing the fight.

'There's no ship in the bridge hangar,' said Andy. 'D'you think he's already buggered off?'

'Knowing that coward, most likely,' said Ed. 'Which means he's probably got a small ship with fully operational cloaking – we didn't check any of the shuttles.'

'There's no jump signature within the system, so he could still be here.'

'Powering away cloaked at full chat,' said Ed. 'The *Gabriel*'s the only ship that could detect him and it's out of commission.'

'We can't let the arsehole get away again,' said Andy.

'Taking his flagship out of the fight is my immediate concern,' said Ed. 'I reckon if we close this ship down and let the rest of the fleet know he's run away, they'll probably throw in the towel.'

'D'you want me to risk the hangar trick again?'

'Possibly,' said Ed. 'How good a shot are you with the rail gun?'

'From that range, I could scrape the tartar off someone's teeth.'

Ed grinned at the analogy.

'Okay, if you jump inside the bridge hangar, I'll give those black guards an ultimatum and you keep taking them out until they surrender the bridge to the regular crew.'

'On my way,' said Andy, taking his gunship quickly down underneath the Mogul ship to avoid the random laser fire. He scanned the hangar for its dimensions, fed them into the jump computer and a split second later materialised within the deserted space. Activating his rail gun and checking out the bridge cameras again, he sat back and listened to Ed transmitting over the ship's tannoy.

'Attention the black guards on the bridge of this vessel. I am Edward Virr representing the GDA. You will lay your weapons down and surrender the bridge to the legitimate ship's crew. Failure to comply will result in your forced removal. You have ten seconds.'

They could see the guards glance up at the ceiling and then at each other. One of them stepped up onto the Mogul's raised area. Even though Ed and Andy had no sound from the room, they could tell from the guard's body language and gesticulations with his weapon, he wasn't planning on surrendering any time soon.

'Fire when ready,' said Ed.

He'd barely finished speaking when the guard leader's head exploded, showering lumps of helmet, brain and skull over the central bridge area. The now headless corpse dropped like a stone and rolled off the raised platform, jetting a trail of blood as it went.

One of the navigation officers nearby vomited as the other guards hit the floor and could be seen shouting to each other.

'We're waiting, gentlemen,' Ed's voice boomed around the bridge again.

Another of the guards jumped up and began shooting out the cameras around the room, until a large hole appeared in his chest armour and he too slumped to the ground. At this moment the bridge door opened and a posse of crew swept through with guns up. Three more of the guards were hit before the remainder lay flat on the floor and surrendered.

A senior officer instructed crewmen to seal the two sucking holes punched in the walls by the rail gun's titanium slugs on their way out of the ship. He then made his way to the communications desk and transmitted on a wide band.

'This is Captain Jiccain of the attack ship Los'enyat calling Edward Virr. My vessel will now stand down as requested. All offensive weaponry will be deactivated and shields reduced to standard operating levels. The Mogul Hassik Triyl left the ship some time ago, destination unknown. The only other remaining Moguls, Finik'ack and Xarch, are somewhere within the fleet, present whereabouts also unknown. I will take this vessel to the prearranged surrender coordinates and await further instructions. Jiccain out.'

'Thank you, Captain,' said Ed. 'You have just saved the lives of your crew and we will ensure you all get home to Andromeda safely.'

Andy jumped back out into space just as the huge ship moved off and they both scanned around for any other targets. It quickly became apparent that the surrender of the flagship had made a huge difference to the ferocity of the battle. Two thirds of the remaining fleet stood down and made their way slowly towards the surrender zone.

'I don't know what you did to that attack ship, Edward,' called Bache, 'but it certainly took the fight out of a lot of them.'

'He threatened them with your cooking,' said Andy.

'I thought you liked my Deelataynian desert curry, Mr Faux.'

'He does,' said Ed. 'But you don't have to live with his farts the next day.'

Two GDA fighters, near Panemorfi, Trelorus system

ED AND ANDY assisted Bache with the last two Blend cruisers that remained obstinate and refused to surrender. They demonstrated their trick of jumping inside the shields and taking out their arrays and propulsion without completely destroying the ship. Once the large vessels were blind and unable to escape, Bache sent carriers full of marines across to board them.

Surprisingly, they met very little resistance and were quickly able to gain control of the two vessels. The reason soon became apparent as two extremely unhappy and unco-operative Moguls were found trying to hide amongst the Blend crews. They, it seemed, had more antipathy towards the Blends than the GDA and were, for their own safety, swiftly transferred across to cells on one of the Katadromiko cruisers. A very angry Blend Adjudicator Reez Treqqer was found in a cell aboard the Los'enyat Attack ship and much to his displeasure, transferred to another cell on the same ship as the Moguls.

Once all the surviving enemy fleet were gathered up, boarded and under GDA control, more vessels from Dasos arrived to escort or tow them back to the Prasinos system where a full investigation and hearing would be held.

A humanitarian force of four Katadromiko cruisers was sent to Garag to assess the damage and aid survivors. Two more went to Callamet to check on the political situation there.

Captain Jiccain of the attack ship Los'enyat informed them that Hassik Triyl had left with a small force of black guards in one of their heavily armed military landing craft that had been fitted with a cloak. More worrying was the fact that a recently constructed Genok weapon was missing from the ship's inventory too. This one, much to everyone's apprehension, was most likely complete and fully operational.

Commander Loftt put out an all-ships and all-planets alert for Triyl's small vessel, with instructions to fire on sight. The risk of that monster having a serviceable Genok missile was more than just cause for concern.

Andy had followed Ed across the system uncloaked to meet up with the *Arena*, slowly rotating five hundred thousand kilometres distant from Panemorfi and still hanging on to the wreckage of the *Hope*.

'What a mess,' said Andy, as they scooted around the two sections of the broken vessel.

'It's a write-off, that's for sure,' said Ed. 'It was such a pretty ship – a shame really.'

'Hello, Ed,' said Conor, his voice loud in their ears. 'I'm going to send you a route to follow that'll bring you into a hangar where the *Gabriel* is parked.'

'Ah, okay. That's where everyone's got to,' he said. 'How bad is she?'

'Best you see for yourself,' came the reply.

Ed's brow furrowed as he wondered what that meant.

The route they received took them towards an enormous round opening on the surface of the planetoid. It was over a kilometre wide and had slowly hinged outwards for them like a turret hatch on a tank.

'Bloody hell,' said Andy. 'You wouldn't know that was there would you?'

'Biggest and most secure hangar door I've ever seen,' said Ed. 'Look how thick it is.'

They made their way into a tunnel as wide as the door and lit with a strange blue light.

'It's thirty kilometres long,' exclaimed Andy, peering out at the rough machine-cut walls. 'I'd love to see the gear they use to do this.'

It took them a few minutes to reach the far end where angled doors slid sideways, disappearing into the rock walls. A chamber confronted them with a similar metal door at the far end.

'Starship airlock,' said Ed. 'Impressive or what?'

The two tiny gunships were dwarfed by the gargantuan chamber and Ed felt very insignificant as the huge doors closed silently behind them.

'Well, this isn't intimidating at all is it?' said Andy. 'It's resemblance to the Death Star is giving me the willies.'

'Just manned by a friendlier race,' said Ed.

'Yeah – so far,' said Andy. 'If I see one stormtrooper, I'm outta here.'

A few minutes later the soft blue lighting in the chamber changed to green and the second door began sliding away with a now audible deep rumble. A much larger, brighter chamber beyond caused them to squint and as they powered forward into the huge cavern, they realised they were emerging from a hole in the floor. Turning their craft ninety degrees brought them into a similar orientation to the *Gabriel* and Ed gasped as he saw the damage to his five hundred-metre starship.

'Oh shit,' said Andy. 'I think we're in dry dock for a while.'

Ed stopped his ship and just stared. A huge section of hull was completely missing from the starboard side where the hangar had once been. On the port side the whole wing assembly containing one of the Alma drive housings and three weapons pods had gone, leaving black scorch marks and melted hull stretching back over fifty metres. Cabling and jagged detritus hung from both areas, dripping fluids on the clean hangar floor.

'Bugger,' was all he could think to say.

'D'you want a hand with the claim form?' muttered Andy, glancing across at Ed from his cockpit.

'Where do we even start?' Ed replied, sounding uncharacteristically downbeat.

''Tis but a scratch,' said Cleo cheerfully, making them both jump.

'Bloody hell, Cleo,' said Ed. 'It's a bit more than that.'

'I can fix it,' she chirped.

'Ed,' said Andy, 'the others are over there next to those buildings. Let's leave Bob the builder to sort this mess out and go check they're okay.'

They both extended their landing struts and set the small craft down behind the *Gabriel* and against the hangar wall.

As he scrambled out and made his way towards the group, Ed noticed the gravity was slightly lower than on Earth.

'I'm so sorry, Ed,' said Linda, as he approached. 'We just couldn't get them all.'

'You're safe is all I care about,' he replied. 'Cleo says she can fix it and I imagine she'll need the hangar in vacuum to regrow the hull and bulkheads.'

'That is true,' Cleo said, appearing next to them, staring at her hands closely. 'You know, the holo emitters are very good here.'

'Everything's very good here,' said Conor, butting in on the conversation. 'As I said to these guys, you're welcome to stay here until you're all rebuilt. We think you'll find our world quite adequate.'

The group of humans and Callametans followed Conor as he beckoned them over to an oval-shaped opening in the rock wall.

'It's an elevator similar to your tube lift on the *Gabriel*,' he said. 'It'll take us into the surface.'

The elevator was easily big enough for all of them and an opaque red shield materialised across the doorway to seal them in. It rose immediately, quickly picking up speed through a tube in the solid rock.

'How far is it?' asked Ed after about thirty seconds' silence.

'Twenty kilometres,' said Conor, smiling as he got several raised eyebrows in return.

'I understand you're a telepathic race?' said Ed. 'All joined in like a collective.'

'They're the Borg without circuit boards glued to their faces,' said Andy, from the back of the group. 'Resistance is futile.'

Ed rolled his eyes and looked at Conor apologetically.

'What is Borg?' asked Conor, with a puzzled expression.

'Ignore it, Conor,' said Ed. 'He's just attempting a joke that most of you wouldn't understand.'

Surprisingly it only took four minutes until the elevator suddenly flashed out into bright sunlight and came to a halt overlooking a park.

A chorus of gasps rippled around the group as they stepped out of the lift and gazed around at the stunning vista. For as far as they could see the colossal internal world stretched away from them, curving upwards and disappearing into the distance. Thin fluffy clouds drifted across the sky, dotted with aircraft of assorted sizes flying in tight lines to destinations around the cylinder-shaped internal world. Massive round rock buttresses, a kilometre in diameter, stretched away across the void.

Ed could just make out greenery with towns and villages dotted around on the opposite side above them.

'Now, that is something truly spectacular,' he mumbled, as all the hairs on the back of his neck stood up.

Although they had emerged in some sort of green park area, with unusual trees and exotic birds chirping and warbling around them, Ed noticed a large city a few kilometres away, its extreme high-rise buildings glinting in the bright daylight.

'Arena Prime,' said Conor, noticing Ed staring in that direction. 'It's the capital of our world.'

'How big is it in here?' Ed asked, as a strange catlike creature emerged from the undergrowth, ran up a tree and continued to glare at the party from the high branches.

'The cylinder is four hundred kilometres long at its widest point and a hundred and seventy kilometres across in the centre. It's more ovoid in shape than cylindrical really.'

Ed realised the gravity here was more Earthlike as they were deeper inside the rotating moon now.

'The Conclave have decreed you can stay here,' said Conor, pointing to a group of glass buildings not far from the elevator. 'They're still nervous about showing aliens too much. Although you won't be guarded, I will ask you not to stray from this parkland during your visit. I've staked my reputation on this, so please don't go wandering off unless you're specifically invited.'

Ed turned and glanced around the group, receiving nods of agreement from everyone.

'We will need to retrieve some more Theo suits from the ship before the hangar is vented,' said Ed, looking down at his. 'So we can come and go from the *Gabriel* to aid Cleo with the rebuild.'

'Not a problem,' said Conor. 'It's early evening here now, so I'll show you to your rooms and we'll sort all that out in the morning.'

Even as Conor spoke, Ed noticed the light emanating from above had noticeably dimmed over the last few minutes.

The accommodation proved to be minimalist but super comfortable, and after they had all eaten in a communal dining area, they retired to their rooms.

Ed quickly fell into a restless sleep and dreamt about silent black-clad soldiers with no faces pushing him about.

59

Unknown location

ED WONDERED what on Earth he'd had the night before to give him such a horrendous headache and it took him a few moments to pluck up the courage to open his eyes. What he saw confused him, as he thought back to the decor in his room on the *Arena*. He was sure it had had blue walls, not the black metallic one that faced him. At first his sluggish addled brain believed Andy had played a trick on him when he discovered his hands bound together against a dark grey pipe.

Shuffling himself painfully up into a seated position, he realised he was on a ship. The regular drone of a drive and quiet whooshing of an environmental system was unmistakable. He squinted around in the gloom to find he was sitting on the floor of some sort of storage room. It wasn't a pipe he was attached to, it was the leg of a metal racking system that seemed to contain boxes of ration packs.

A closed metal door was opposite him, but even if it was unlocked he couldn't reach it anyway.

'What the fuck is this about?' he said to himself, hopefully waiting for Andy to open the door and say "ha ha, gotcha"– although he knew full well that even Andy, with all his practical jokes, wouldn't stoop to something this ridiculous.

He listened intently, trying to gain the slightest clue to where he was, and what the hell was going on. The lights dimmed and the drive drone dipped in tone slightly.

Did we just jump? he thought, as the ambient noise returned to normal.

He jerked as the door was thrown open inwards, hitting his foot. Two black guards stepped inside, their heads obscured by helmet visors. Ed's expresson darkened as a familiar face peered inside from the corridor.

'Good morning, Mr Virr – sleep well?' asked Triyl, a vehement grin curving his lips.

'Oh for fuck's sake!' exclaimed Ed. 'Don't you ever give up?'

'Planners are winners, Edward,' Triyl said. 'Always prepare for the best and worst scenario. Then you're never compromised.'

'How the hell did you get me off that planetoid?' Ed asked.

'Easy. We followed you in cloaked and jumped out again once my soldiers had grabbed you.'

'How big's your fleet now, Triyl?' Ed scoffed. 'What're you going to do against the entire GDA fleet with, what is it? One small landing craft?'

Triyl's face darkened.

'You really are an insolent little nobody, aren't you, Virr?'

Ed fixed Triyl with a malevolent stare.

'Maybe, but at least I'm not a psychotic, mass-murdering paedophile with overblown delusions of grandeur. Small man syndrome – you've got it bad.'

Triyl bared his teeth and snarled at Ed.

'You're going out an airlock, Virr,' he growled. 'I just want you to witness something first. Bring him.'

Triyl stomped off grumpily with a face like a wet weekend.

The two guards untied Ed and frog-marched him roughly through the craft's loading bay and up to the cockpit. On the way, he noticed ten cots laid out on the floor in the loading bay, seven of which were in use. The missing tenth guard was in the cockpit, standing directly behind a very nervous-looking pilot.

The holographic navigation display glowed above them and Ed recognised a series of jumps leading to a distant solar system.

'Long way to go in this crate,' said Ed, nodding up at the plotted route.

'Perhaps,' snarled Triyl. 'The destination will be worth it, though. Show him,' Triyl snapped at the pilot, pointing at the holomap.

The pinpoint of light at the end of the route slowly grew into a blue planet Ed recognised instantly.

'What possible reason have you to go there?' Ed asked nervously, gazing up at planet Earth slowly rotating above him.

'Payback, Mr Virr,' he said, staring at Ed, an ugly grin on his face. 'You've been a contributory factor in the destruction of my race. So, before you go for a long cold walk, I'm going to let you watch as I wipe out yours.'

'Take a bit more than a space laser to do that,' said Ed, returning the stare.

Triyl emitted an evil chuckle and nodded.

'Come with me,' he said.

Ed was dragged back down to the troop deck where on

the far side of the room, Triyl opened a large three-metre-long metal case lying against the hull.

'Recognise this?' he asked, with a sneer.

Ed peered inside to find the original GDA Genok missile from the wrecked corvette. He immediately tried bringing his DOVI online to reprogramme the weapon, but met only a wall of white noise.

Triyl wagged his finger at him.

'I think you'll find your annoying ability to mess with electronic things has been rescinded, Edward,' he said, pointing at his head.

Ed felt a coldness envelope him and he shivered. For the first time he realised he had no answer to this and no way to stop Triyl in his proposed annihilation of every living thing on Earth. The *Gabriel* certainly wasn't coming to his rescue any time soon. He really was on his own with this.

Triyl smiled at Ed's discomfort and pointed to the rear of the ship.

'Take him back to his suite,' he ordered the guards. 'Make sure he's secure and watched too.'

Ed was dragged back to his store room and while one guard took up station outside the door the other pushed him inside with the muzzle of his laser rifle.

Ed quickly noted that if he was going to act, once he was secured to the solid shelving it would be too late. He watched as the heavy metal door closed automatically behind the guard and as he'd behaved as meek as a lamb the whole time, his captor certainly wasn't expecting what happened next.

When Ed was at university he'd had an introductory lesson with the Krav Maga club. Although he hadn't signed up to join them, he could still remember the basic beginner moves he'd learnt that day. He gritted his teeth and as he bent down to the floor feinting compliance, he spun around, pushed the weapon aside and kicked upwards as hard as he could between the surprised guard's legs.

The man emitted an unexpected squeal as his legs gave way beneath him and he slumped forward. Ed was ready for this and punched the guard in the throat with everything he had. This time he went backwards, his helmet smacking the deck with a loud clunk and the rifle clattering down next to him.

Ed grabbed the weapon, checked it was on stun, buried it in the man's midriff and gave him the good news. Unfortunately, the other guard outside heard the noises, opened the door and stuck his head inside. Ed gave him a similar bolt, grabbed him under the shoulders and dragged him inside. He closed the door and listened.

Luckily, the ship wasn't built with comfort high on the design list, so the droning of the drive motors was louder than on most vessels, which must have helped drown out the weapon reports, as no more soldiers or guards came running.

Ed quickly stripped the taller of the two and swapped clothing, tying both guards tightly together against the shelving and gagging them securely.

He found the helmet a little tight, but managed to squeeze it on and couple the chin strap. The corridor was deserted as he opened the heavy door and peered towards the troop deck. He closed and locked the door, before cautiously making his way forward.

The main deck was as before, with seven soldiers either asleep or lounging on their cots against the side wall. Triyl must have been either in the cockpit or the small crew cabin below, and Ed was more than happy he wasn't around.

Not missing a step, he walked confidently across the wide deck and watched the other soldiers in the room out of the corner of his eye. None seemed to pay him any notice as he approached and lifted the lid to the weapons crate against the far wall. He knew from altering all the copies of the Genok weapons that the pressure sensor that triggered the device at a determined altitude was in the centre section of the unit.

Bending down to unclip the sensor, he heard someone clear their throat behind him. Turning slowly, his heart sank as he found Triyl, with three of the soldiers glaring at him.

'You never cease to amaze me, Edward,' said Triyl. 'And you were accusing me of never giving up.'

He was stripped of the weapon and uniform, his hands tied securely and then bundled into the crate on top of the missile.

'Change of plan,' said Triyl. 'Instead of watching the weapon wipe out your pathetic race, I've decided you can personally deliver it.'

Before Ed could remonstrate, the lid was slammed down and he heard the catches being secured. He desperately tried his DOVI once more, but again found the wall of white noise. The crate was large, but he knew it only contained enough oxygen for a short while. So he kept his breathing as shallow as he could.

He thought he heard a change in engine pitch again and wondered if that was the last jump.

Was he in the Sol system now? he thought, as a huge wave of sadness washed over him. He began to shake uncontrollably, not from the fear of dying, as he knew, when the weapon below him detonated, he wouldn't know anything about it, but for the billions of innocents on Earth who would see the firestorm approaching and die horribly in agony as their atmosphere devoured them.

The box moved suddenly and he could feel it being carried. It clunked down on the deck again, he heard a whirring that he presumed was an airlock door. Then a sharp jerk, followed by complete silence and he felt his body become weightless. It was becoming harder to breath now and although the temperature began dropping alarmingly, he found himself sweating and a headache began to manifest itself.

He thought of his family and the places he went when he was growing up. Friends he'd not considered for years and whose names he found he was having trouble remembering. His university years, the man who ran the sweet shop when he was seven and finally the crew of the *Gabriel*. As the hypoxia took hold, he struggled to remember their names too and as the cold became absolute, he slipped into unconsciousness and the weapons case continued on, gradually tumbling in towards Earth's atmosphere.

60

Temporary Accommodation, the *Arena*, Trelorus system

'WHERE'S OUR INDUSTRIOUS LEADER?' Andy mumbled, his mouth full of something that tasted like a ham and cheese toasty. 'He's always up first.'

Linda, who'd just entered the kitchen area of their shared accommodation, glanced back down the corridor towards the rooms and shrugged.

'He doesn't have a ship to captain at the moment,' she said. 'Perhaps he's having a lie-in.'

'I'm next door and heard him get up and leave his room with someone else in the middle of the night,' said Pol. 'At least, I think there was two of them – definitely more than one pair of boots.'

'Was that you, Phil?' Linda asked.

'No, I was first to go to bed and didn't leave the room until ten minutes ago,' Phil replied, as they all glanced around at Tronckle and the other Callametans. They received a row of shaking heads and puzzled expressions.

'I'll check his room,' said Rayl, standing and making for the rooms.

'I'm coming with you,' said Linda, turning on her heel and following.

They banged on Ed's door twice, and after getting no answer, entered.

'Beds been slept in,' said Linda.

'Bathroom's empty,' said Rayl. 'What's that chemical smell in here?' she asked turning back into the bedroom.

'I can't smell anything,' said Linda, furrowing her brow.

'Our race have very acute noses,' said Rayl, sniffing her way over to the bed.

'Tell me about it,' said Andy, strolling in. 'I can never sneak a fart.'

Rayl gave him a withering look.

'It's something on the bed,' she said, bending down and sniffing the pillow.

'Cleo, are you there?' asked Linda, glancing up at the ceiling.

'Always darling,' she said, appearing in a costume fit for the Oscars.

'Can you tell what that smell is on the bedding?' Linda asked.

'Especially the pillow,' said Rayl, pointing.

Cleo rolled her eyes and rubbed a dried out stain where Rayl indicated. She sniffed it suspiciously and raised her eyebrows.

'It's a type of chloroform,' she said. 'Very potent – would give you quite a headache on waking.'

'Shit,' said Linda. 'Ed's been snatched. Can you go back through the camera logs and find who it was, Cleo?'

'Erm, there are no cameras,' she said, now looking

worried too. 'They have no security inside the planetoid, it's all on the outside.'

'What about in the hangar and the cameras on the *Gabriel*?' she asked, but already knowing the answer.

Cleo shook her head slowly.

'Shut down,' she said. 'Everything's shut down for the rebuild.'

'Aren't the camera's on the mini-mes always recording?' said Andy, looking at Cleo for confirmation.

'Yes,' she said, 'I believe you're right.'

'Well, they're sitting against the far wall,' he said. 'They might have seen something.'

'Right,' said Linda. 'Let's get down there.'

'Hang on,' said Cleo. 'The hangar's in vacuum for the hull regrowth.'

'Do you think Conor would have any suits to fit us?' Andy asked.

'Suits for what?' asked Conor, appearing in the doorway, smiling.

'It's okay,' said Cleo, holding her hands up. 'All I need is permission to enter your personal fighter, Andy, and I can do it remotely.'

'You have it, Cleo,' he said. 'See what you can find.'

'What are you looking for?' asked Conor, his confused face looking from person to person.

'This,' said Cleo, pointing to a forming holographic image of the hangar twenty kilometres below.

They all gasped as the image from six hours ago showed three suited figures appearing from nowhere and entering the elevator. Cleo fast forwarded it fifteen minutes until they returned dragging an unconscious Ed with an oxygen mask over his face.

'Who the heck are they?' asked Conor, a look of shock on his face.

'Triyl's soldiers,' said Linda. 'He must have followed Ed and Andy inside in the cloaked troop carrier.'

'Oh crap,' said Conor. 'That's what I came to ask. We detected a jump signature from within the hangar and thought it must be one of you going somewhere in one of your little ships.'

'At least he wanted him alive,' said Andy.

'Yeah, but for what?' said Rayl. 'We all know how vindictive those bastards are.'

'Can you all do me a favour?' said Conor. 'I'm going to have to tell them the jump was Edward leaving on one of your ships. If the Conclave found out I'd let one of those psychotic killers inside the *Arena*, my life would be over. They're paranoid enough about you being here.'

'Don't they know already?' asked Rayl. 'With your collective minds and everything?'

Conor peered back up the corridor nervously. The visible part of his face behind all the hair was as white as a sheet.

'I shielded your buildings so no one could try and read you,' he said.

'You can do that?' said Linda.

'To a certain extent,' he said. 'But your minds are very jumbled compared to ours.'

'Tell me something I don't know,' said Rayl, looking at Andy.

'We need to inform Bache,' said Linda, looking at Cleo and raising her eyebrows.

'Already done it,' said Cleo, looking distinctly worried. 'He's organised an immediate search with everything at his disposal.'

'Shit,' said Linda, as she turned to make her way back to the kitchen. 'What an awful time to have no ship.'

The others were equally shocked to hear the news about Ed, especially Pol, who got surprisingly emotional and ran off to her room in tears.

Andy furrowed his brow and glanced at Rayl.

'She has a soft spot for Ed,' she said, noticing Andy's expression. 'She fawns over him all the time. Ed's promised to take her to Earth one day for a sightseeing tour.'

'That's it,' shouted Phil, standing up suddenly and making everyone jump. 'That's where Triyl has taken Ed.'

Everybody stared at him.

'Don't you see? The Moguls are the most vengeful race ever known. Triyl blames Ed for the destruction of his empire and the killing of his race. He's taken Ed to Earth.'

'What, so he can throw him out an airlock in sight of his own home?' asked Rayl.

'NO!' exclaimed Phil, getting more agitated than anyone could remember. 'Triyl has the original GDA Genok missile, we never found it.'

'Oh my god,' said Linda, her head in her hands. 'He's going to incinerate Earth and make Ed watch.'

The room was full of sharp intakes of breath and then became silent as everyone sat in a state of shock.

'It would be the perfect revenge for a Mogul,' said Andy, his face white as a sheet. 'Cleo, give Bache this theory as soon as you can.'

'Way ahead of you,' said Cleo, sitting with them. 'I thought of that scenario back in his room earlier and gave it to Bache then. I'm so sorry, guys. We've done all we can. It's up to the gods and Bache Loftt now. I'm just as frustrated as any of you. Bache jumped his cruiser out of the system shortly after I gave him all the information.'

'I've never felt the urge to pray for anything before,' said Linda, as she stretched out one hand to Andy and the other to Phil. The rest of the group sat down around the big refectory-style table, joined hands, lowered their heads and closed their eyes. Even Conor. There they sat, conjoined in anguish and silence, except for the faint keening of Pol from her room nearby.

61

Captain's bridge office, Katadromiko 8, Traxx system

Two weeks later

Captain Tanet Hoo stood staring up at the holomap image rotating above his head in his bridge office. The big blue planet of Callamet turned slowly and he watched the icon of his own fourteen-kilometre-long Katadromiko cruiser sitting in an elliptical orbit around the equator. He had always marvelled at no matter how massive you built a starship it was still a mere speck compared to the vastness and majesty of the infinite universe.

He watched closely as the last of his seeding missiles exploded within the clouds streaming across the major land-masses and dumped their formulated heavy rain downpours laced with radiation-retardant enzymes. Luckily for the local population, the twenty-seven nuclear detonations a few weeks ago had all been deep within a fairly remote mountain range, which contained a lot of the fallout.

Even so, the seemingly overaggressive Obsidian cult had insisted they were in complete control and the planet was in no need of any assistance. The constant warfare obvious from orbit said otherwise. Once all the five cult leaderships were shown a little discipline via a few strategic Kataligo missiles, the surviving governors all decided very quickly that remaining a member of the GDA was a good thing. A peace-keeping marine force was put in place, which proved surprisingly popular with the general population.

Once that was done, he sent five of the other six cruisers under his command into Blend space and especially Garag and the last cruiser deep into the Cygnus arm, searching for the Ancients' gateway that Triyl had found and utilised.

Garag, unsurprisingly was a mess. From the reports coming back from there, over two thirds of the population had perished in the crushing radioactive shock wave from the sabotaged dark matter power core. As on Callamet, they began by seeding the entire planet with the retardant enzymes. After seventy-two hours, the radiation levels had decreased enough for the relief effort to begin. It was a grim task and the first responders reaching the surface stated that the side that faced the wave was completely flattened and wiped clean. Even some of the oceans had been partly blasted out into space.

The vast majority of the survivors on the opposite side of the planet wanted to be moved elsewhere. Garag was as good as dead for the time being and without a serious amount of terraforming, would take centuries to recover.

Captain Hoo had been surprised and unashamedly a little daunted when Commander Loftt had suddenly handed the clean-up operation over to him two weeks ago. Stating a personal family crisis, the commander had transferred his own cruiser over to his first officer Harlan Mayet and left the ship unescorted in a troop carrier containing only a single weapons case.

Mayet had confided in Hoo that the commander had seemed unusually preoccupied on his return from the Sol system and had spent the majority of his time alone in his stateroom drinking Earth English beer and eating something called pepperoni pizza.

62

Theo City 5, Paradeisos, Aspro system

THE SOFT WARM dream ended suddenly as a sensation of falling led to something hard hitting him from below. A coldness swept over him as he began vomiting a large quantity of liquid. He tried opening his eyes and quickly closed them again, as the sudden unfamiliar brightness blinded him.

This is the weirdest dream, he thought, as something warm and soft enveloped him.

'I haven't seen you throw up so much since the Apfelkorn incident in Mönchengladbach,' said a familiar voice.

He realised he was kneeling on the ground and tried opening one eye just a crack this time. After blinking a few times, he was able to see his hands propping him up in a puddle of clear liquid.

'Ed – can you stand?' said the same voice.

'I'm Ed!' he exclaimed, the loudness of his voice surprising him.

'Yes, you are and I'd like to get you out of all this water.'

He opened the other eye and squinted around him. He was

in a small white room with a single chair and some sort of control panel recessed into one wall. Above him was a weird empty cylinder, lit with twinkling multi-coloured laser light.

His legs were a bit shaky, but with a little assistance he managed to stand and stagger across to the chair.

'Welcome back, mate,' said the voice he knew so well.

He looked up and stared.

'You're Andrew,' he blurted.

'Top marks, Einstein,' said Andy, draping another warm dry towel around Ed's shoulders. 'What else can you remember?'

Ed thought hard and found everything a bit jumbled.

'The *Gabriel*,' he said, finally. 'It's damaged – and there's something else important.'

He stared at the floor trying to remember what it was.

'Triyl – Earth,' he blurted and stood up suddenly, a panicky expression on his face. 'Triyl's going to destroy Earth.'

'It's okay,' said Andy, putting his hands on Ed's shoulders and sitting him down again. 'Earth's fine,' he added. 'Just.'

'The – the Genok,' said Ed. 'I was with it.'

'It didn't detonate,' said Andy. 'Bache got there and tractored it and you out just in time.'

Ed nodded and thought about this for a few moments and looked around the room again.

'I didn't—'

'No, I'm afraid you didn't,' said Andy. 'You have something in common with Linda now.'

Ed glanced down at his right shin and found the scar he got falling off a wall when he was a kid had gone.

'The new improved you,' Andy said, squatting down and staring into Ed's eyes. 'Linda's told me you'll find everything a bit weird for a while and not to try and force it.'

'Right, okay,' said Ed, glancing around again. 'Are we on the *Gabriel*?'

'No,' Andy replied. 'We're on Paradeisos, in one of the original Theo birthing chambers. We came here in the *Arena*. It's still in orbit above.'

'How long was I – you know?'

'Just over two weeks,' said Andy. 'When Bache returned with your body, the *Gabriel* was still in vacuum for the hull regrowth. Phil organised this with Prota. He's still here you know.'

'Who, Prota?'

'No, Bache,' said Andy. 'He was very upset when he brought you back. He, of course, didn't know anything about our krypti memory chips and the Theo rebirth thing. You should have seen the look on his face when Linda told him she had died too in the Messier galaxy.'

Ed nodded, wrapped the towels tightly around him and stood.

'Is there somewhere I can get a shower and some clothes?'

Andy held his arm out to steady Ed as they made their way towards the door. Ed stopped suddenly and looked at Andy.

'Did Triyl escape?' he asked.

Andy smiled and shook his head.

'Cleo gave Bache the anti-cloak stuff before he left. When they tractored you out of Earth's gravity, well, they detected Triyl's ship, disabled it and tractored that aboard as well.'

'So, he's in custody?'

'Uh, huh. The list of his crimes is as long as your arm.'

'Was he the last one?' Ed asked, as they carried on out into the corridor.

'It would be good to think so,' said Andy. 'But no one knows where they originally came from, so there could be a whole galaxy full of 'em somewhere.'

Andy paused for a second and turned to face Ed.

'Tell me – did you tie two of his guards to a shelf?'

Ed smiled for the first time.

'Yeah, I did.'

Andy opened another door and led Ed inside. It was a bathroom with a pile of clothes Ed recognised on a chair in the corner.

'Cleo brought them from the *Gabriel*,' said Andy, noticing him glance at them. 'I'll give you some privacy now and wait outside.'

Ed took his time showering and enjoyed the warm water. A change from the laser showers they had on the ship. He shaved, dressed and looked at himself in the mirror. He thought his short hair made him look thuglike and promised himself to get in the autonurse and lengthen it as soon as he could.

When he opened the door, Andy was sat on the floor in the corridor, reading from a tablet.

'All good?' he asked, as Ed appeared.

He nodded.

'Are the others down here?' he asked.

'No, they're all still up on the *Arena*. Conor got the Conclave to let them have a little more freedom within the cylinder. Did you know they've got a beach resort for recreation about fifty kilometres from the accommodation?'

'Sounds like the perfect place for some rest and recuperation,' said Ed, as he walked slowly but unaided towards the exit. As he emerged into the sunlight, he stopped and enjoyed the warmth on his face and took a deep breath of the clean fresh air. He looked up and was surprised the protective dome over the city wasn't visible. Reading his mind, Andy explained that the GDA had seeded some of its enzymes into the upper atmosphere to disperse the last of the radiation so the energy domes were now redundant.

He also noticed noise and traffic and people that had been so absent on their previous visit here a couple of years ago. It was pleasing to him to think that the Theos were finally emerging in large numbers from the dark underground cities they'd been forced to occupy for so long.

Andy hailed one of the blue auto taxis that took them speedily out to the edge of the city and a small space port where, much to Ed's delight, sat the *Cartella*.

'Now there's a sight for sore eyes,' he said, hurrying across to the opening airlock as fast as his wobbly legs would allow. 'Cleo, are you here?'

She materialised and he hugged her tightly.

'Welcome back, boss,' she said, with damp eyes.

Ed kissed her on the forehead and wiped a tear away as it ran down her cheek.

'Thank you,' he said. 'And well done giving Bache the anti-cloak thing. Triyl would have probably escaped otherwise.'

'Oh good,' she said. 'I was afraid you might dock my wages for doing that.'

The *Cartella* lifted off as soon as they were sat and slowly picked up speed to avoid any unnecessary sonic booms. Ed could see the *Arena* as soon as they reached the upper atmosphere. It sat in a stationary orbit directly above the city.

'Different hangar,' said Andy, as they entered a smaller tunnel than before.

Once through the airlock at the far end, Cleo turned the ship ninety degrees and lowered the landing struts. What Ed saw through the front window made all the hairs on the back of his neck stand up.

'Oh shit,' he mumbled.

The hangar floor was crowded; dozens of people seated in neat rows, two squads of soldiers standing to attention, their dress uniforms gleaming in the bright lights; a band playing, children waving GDA flags and even a huge banner saying "Welcome Home Edward."

He turned to stare at Andy.

'Did you know about this?' he grumbled.

'Absolutely not,' replied Andy, retrieving a GDA flag from his pocket and waving it.

'Bloody liar,' Ed griped. 'There are presidents out there and I'm in a tee shirt.'

'You'd have known something was up if we'd brought you a suit,' said Cleo. 'And one more thing, Pol has been almost inconsolable about you. Make sure you pay her plenty of attention.'

Ed stood as the *Cartella* settled and the soft music from the band permeated the cockpit as the airlock doors cracked open. He pulled his tee shirt down and took a deep breath.

'I need a fucking holiday,' he whined, as he stepped out to a rousing cheer from the crowds.

'Smile, you miserable twat,' said Andy, poking Ed in the back.

'Can I have a holiday too?' he heard Cleo mutter as he adopted his best grin and approached the throng.

EPILOGUE
THE DOG AND BEAR HOTEL, KENT, ENGLAND, EARTH

ONE MONTH later

Ed stared out of the bar window and across the square. The village fish and chip shop was busy as usual, with people queued to order their cod, haddock or sausage and chips.

'Oi oi, saveloy,' said Andy, as he returned from the bar with another couple of pints of Faversham's finest. He noticed Ed watching the comings and goings from across the street. 'Always done a good trade that chippy,' he said. 'My dad can remember it being a café back in the seventies. He used to hang out there when he had motorbikes and play pinball.'

Ed scratched at the beard he always grew in the autonurse when spending time back on Earth. With the baseball cap and thick-rimmed glasses, it made him much less conspicuous and able to move around without attracting too much attention.

The *Gabriel*'s crew had been invited to the White House on their return four weeks ago. President Alastair James was well into his second term now and wanted to personally thank them for their part in saving Earth from destruction. The few that knew the truth had agreed it was best not to inform the population that the planet had been thirty seconds from extermination. There were enough far-right anti-alien nutters as it was without feeding their paranoia with that little gem.

'Linda's asked to leave the crew,' said Ed, quietly worried about how Andy would react.

'What?' said Andy, putting his pint back down untouched. 'Why?'

'I think the stress of the last little trip has taken its toll,' he said, sighing deeply. 'I think we're all a little bit punch-drunk after the last venture.'

'What does Phil think?' Andy asked.

'I haven't told him yet.' Although, he's been working for nearly four thousand years, so I reckon he's due a break too.'

Andy scoffed.

'When you put it like that, you're probably right.'

'I've also had an offer from one of the big theme park companies in America.'

'What for – Edward Land?' Andy said, with a chuckle.

'No, they want to build a space adventure park next to the themed ones already in Florida.'

'Well, they don't need our approval for that do they?'

'They do if tours of the *Gabriel* were to be the main attraction,' said Ed.

'Oh.' Andy sat back and stared at Ed, the shock evident on his face. 'Is that it then – are we retiring?'

'Absolutely not – I've already decided that part of the contract would be that the *Gabriel* is free to leave at any time.'

'We'd still have the *Cartella* if we wanted to pop off somewhere though, wouldn't we?' asked Andy, the concern clear in his eyes.

'Are you needing to go somewhere in the near future?'

'Yeah, Rayl wants to take me back to Trigono for a proper tour. We didn't get to see much of it at the time of the wedding.'

'Of course, it's your ship as much as mine and anyway, we've got enough money to build a hundred ships.'

Andy nodded and finally got to sip his beer.

'What about Cleo?' he asked, opening a packet of cheese and onion crisps and offering one to Ed.

'Cleo's fine with it,' Ed said, crunching a crisp. 'She loves the thought of entertaining the families and kids at the park and I've granted her holographic access to both my houses here and in the States, so she can escape whenever she likes.'

Andy looked at his watch, grimaced and quickly downed his pint.

'If you smash that one we'll get another in before the girls get back,' he said. 'Their train's due any time now.'

'Too late, Faux,' said Rayl, putting her hands on his shoulders as he started to rise. 'Busted – but you're in luck, there's three thirsty girls here and it's your round.'

Rayl, Linda and a grinning Pol joined them at the table.

'How was London?' Ed asked.

'Beautiful,' said Pol. 'Your planet's lovely.'

'Thank you,' said Ed, returning the smile.

'Have you told Andy?' she said.

'Told me what?'

'Pol's going to be my personal assistant,' said Ed. 'I've been asked to do a planet-wide lecture tour, so I'll certainly need one.'

'Great idea,' said Andy. 'She can take dictation, answer the phone, iron your shirt and pour you a pint, all at the same time.'

Pol's squeaky giggling drowned out the background music and caused a few glares from the regulars, especially those who'd only just noticed there was a four-armed alien in the pub.

'I think you should train her up to pilot the *Gabriel* too,' said Linda. 'She'd be the perfect replacement for me.'

'I'll second that,' said Andy, as he stood to go to the bar.

'Talking of Callametans,' said Ed, noticing a GDA shuttle flying low over the village, 'does anyone know what happened to the others?'

'I got a vmail from Tocc this morning,' said Pol, sitting down next to Ed. 'She's taking a liaison officer job on Vasi Stathmos station at Dasos. Rialte and Kwin have decided to return to Callamet to look for engineering jobs and help with the rebuild.'

'I heard from Bache that Tronckle's gone straight back to Andromeda,' said Linda. 'He offered to pilot the surviving Attack ship on the return trip. Also, the GDA have commandeered all the Blend naval vessels and banned them from building any more.'

'I think the GDA will be a little busy in that region for a while,' said Ed, 'knowing how stroppy the Blends can be.'

'Oh, I nearly forgot,' said Linda. 'According to Jim Rucker, the Arennians have applied to join the GDA and are looking for an unclaimed class M planet to set up a permanent orbit.'

'That's great,' said Ed. 'I'm sure Conor will be happy. I think they were all getting a little tired of the endless travelling, and the severe breeding restrictions on the *Arena* was one of the most unpopular regulations.'

'Huwlen's a bit pissed apparently,' said Andy, returning to the table with a tray of drinks.

'Why?' asked Linda. 'He's the most laid-back person I know.'

'He wants Triyl handed over to them for execution in Andromeda.'

'He'll probably get his way too,' said a familiar voice looming up to the table.

'*Bache!*' exclaimed the table in perfect unison.

'I wondered what a GDA shuttle was doing in deepest darkest Kent,' said Ed.

'Not a GDA shuttle,' said Bache. 'A private civilian shuttle actually.'

'You on holiday then?' asked Rayl.

'Sort of,' he said, with a wry smile. 'I think the Earth translation is retirement.'

The table went quiet for a moment.

'You can't retire,' said Ed, breaking the silence. 'You are the GDA.'

'That's very kind of you to say,' said Bache. 'But there are a lot of very competent officers behind me. Some of them I trained myself.'

'And we'd just got you trained as well,' said Andy, putting his arm around Bache's shoulder and giving him a hug.

A short stocky man with distinct Dasonian features entered the bar, approached the table and stood behind Bache. The table went quiet as they all peered at him with interest. Bache turned and smiled.

'Ah, there you are,' he said, ushering the newcomer to the fore. 'Can I introduce newly promoted Commander Hoo – my replacement.'

'You don't have a police box do you?' asked Andy, getting a smack on the head from Rayl.

Everybody stood and greeted the commander and congratulated him on his promotion.

'What's your first name?' asked Ed.

'Tanet. My sorry, Englandish good not yet,' he continued hopefully.

'Welcome, Tanet,' said Ed. 'Please join us for a drink and your English is just fine.'

'Thank you,' he said, nodding and beaming widely. 'Commander Loftt say I try England realistic hails.'

'Absolutely,' said Andy, giving Bache a wink. 'Two realistic hails coming right up.'

CPSIA information can be obtained
at www.ICGtesting.com
Printed in the USA
LVHW040909290321
682812LV00007B/45

9 781916 396241